BITTER HARVEST

A Selection of Recent Titles by Jeannie Johnson

FORGOTTEN FACES
JUST BEFORE DAWN
LIKE AN EVENING GONE
A PENNY FOR TOMORROW
THE REST OF OUR LIVES

BITTER HARVEST *
LOVING ENEMIES *
SECRET SINS *
WHERE THE WILD THYME BLOWS *

* available from Severn House

BITTER HARVEST

Jeannie Johnson

This first world edition published 2008
in Great Britain and the USA by
SEVERN HOUSE PUBLISHERS LTD of
9–15 High Street, Sutton, Surrey, England, SM1 1DF.

British Library Cataloguing in Publication Data

Johnson, Jeannie
  Bitter harvest
  1. Children of suicide victims - Fiction 2. Fathers and
  daughters - Fiction 3. Douro (Portugal) - Fiction
  4. Domestic fiction
  I. Title
  823.9'2[F]

  ISBN-13: 978-0-7278-6643-1   (cased)
  ISBN-13: 978-1-84751-068-6   (trade paper)

All Severn House titles are printed on acid-free paper.

Typeset by Palimpsest Book Production Ltd.,
Grangemouth, Stirlingshire, Scotland.
Printed and bound in Great Britain by
MPG Books Ltd., Bodmin, Cornwall.

One

William Shellard raised his glass. 'To my brother, Walter. And Ellen, his lovely bride. To the bride and groom!'

Four hundred guests rose to their feet and responded. 'To the bride and groom!'

The mirrors in the banqueting suite of the Royal Hotel reflected the gathering of well-heeled men and women. Silk dresses made a hushing sound as the ladies sat back down, gathering their skirts beneath them. Once they were seated, a hum of conversation resumed against a background of tinkling glassware.

Walter Shellard inclined his head towards his younger brother in a barely perceptible manner; a mark of approval. His smile was unusually wide. William gave him a brief nod in response, noting that his brother's smile was of the kind he used on having made yet another enormous amount of money. In a way, he had.

His bride Ellen was all pink cheeks and sparkling eyes. William raised his glass to her and smiled. She smiled back. In fact he was sure she hadn't stopped smiling all day.

She's happy and amazingly innocent, thought William and wondered how long it would last.

The assemblage was a who's who of the British Isles elite; there were bankers from London, landowners from Lincolnshire, shipping magnates from Liverpool and titled lairds from Scotland. All had gathered to celebrate the wedding of Walter Shellard of the famed Shellard Wine and Port Company, and Ellen Parker, daughter of an equally wealthy man. She was also his second wife.

The wedding guests chatted, laughed, made subtle comments and some not so subtle, remarking on the enormous success of the old and much respected company. Walter, they all agreed, had injected the firm with a dynamic modernism. Unlike some companies that had failed to adapt to the new world following the Armistice in 1918, Shellards – more specifically Walter – had grasped new opportunities with open arms. The new bride had bagged herself a winner!

Ellen Parker, who had now become Ellen Shellard, glowed with happiness. She was twenty-eight years old and considered herself lucky. The battles of the Somme and Ypres and all those others of the Great War had taken the flower of British manhood. Marriageable women far outnumbered marriageable men, though it was not out of a sense of time running out that she'd married a man almost twice her age. Walter was successful, wealthy and still a fine-looking man. Theirs had been a whirl-wind romance and although she would have delayed marrying, her parents urged her to accept when he offered.

'Better than being an old maid,' her mother had said through rigidly smiling lips. 'And there are going to be plenty of them, my darling.'

Ellen had taken the hint and so far there were no regrets.

This was a grand day, as grand as their surroundings. The Royal Hotel was a splendid building that boasted playing host to heads of state and kings of England. Wood panelling and brass banisters graced its thickly carpeted stairs. Gilt-edged mirrors lent light to its sumptuous, red-carpeted staterooms. This room, named the Rose of Denmark after Queen Alexandra, consort of King Edward VII, was by far the most luxurious.

Ellen Parker had been swept off her feet by Walter Shellard. She didn't mind admitting it.

'I couldn't resist,' she'd exclaimed to anyone who'd pointed out that he was approaching fifty.

There was general agreement that she'd made a good match. She was from a wealthy family with a bottling plant and banking interests, and Walter Shellard was one of the wealthiest wine producers in the city of Bristol, if not the whole of the British Isles. On top of that he'd bought into shipping and transport interests. Despite the age difference, it was a good match. The courtship had been short; four months from start to finish.

'I love you,' said a radiant and romantically inclined Ellen and kissed her husband on the lips.

A muted cheer ran among the guests. Walter Shellard touched his wife's cheek. 'You're very pink, my love.'

'It's the champagne,' she murmured, and tried not to feel disappointed that he hadn't reciprocated and told her that he loved her. But in time he would, she told herself and for the moment believed it.

The band they'd hired for the occasion began to play Ellen's choice, 'Let me Call You Sweetheart'.

The guests began to clap. All eyes were turned towards the top table where the bride had half risen and the bridegroom had not.

'Walter. They're waiting for us to dance,' said Ellen, imploring him with her eyes to get up and do what was required of him.

She tried not to get upset at the sight of that strained, impatient look she was only just beginning to get used to. Strangely enough, she couldn't remember him ever looking like that in their courtship. It's the strain of the wedding, she told herself. There'd been so much to organize, and then there were the rehearsals. At her mother's insistence she'd had six bridesmaids. They were all dressed in deep turquoise and wore little caps of crocheted silk and carried bunches of violets. She herself wore a straight dress of shantung silk with an overdress of Nottingham lace. Her veil fell flat and long from a circlet of white roses interspersed with lilies of the valley. Here and there was the odd violet to match those her bridesmaids were carrying.

Walter hated dancing, but counselled himself that this would be the first and the last time he would have to put himself out. On this occasion they were the centre of attention so dereliction of duty would be inexcusable. But he didn't like *having* to do things he disliked. It felt as though he were being ordered, and Walter George Sebastian Shellard did not take orders; he only gave them.

He smiled at her as he began to rise. 'Best not keep them waiting,' he said, taking hold of her hand.

They waltzed to the music, circling the floor three or four times before others joined them.

Comments about how handsome they looked together abounded. One or two dancing matrons wiped a stray tear from a misted eye.

'*So romantic.*'

'*Made for each other.*'

Her eyes were still sparkling and her cheeks were pastel

pink when Ellen Shellard made her way to the powder room, beset on all sides by yet more congratulations.

'Welcome to the Shellard family.'

The husky voice belonged to Diana, William's wife. She was waving her champagne glass around like a flag. Her face was far more flushed than Ellen's and she owed her sparkling eyes to champagne rather than excitement.

Ellen thanked her and they shook hands. So formal, thought Ellen, but that was the way it was. No one in the family demonstrated any great degree of affection. Ellen had told herself it was because no one knew her that well yet.

'It's early days,' retorted Ellen, disarmed by Diana's sickly sweet smile and wondering what thoughts lay behind it.

'Of course,' said Diana, her smile turning from sweet to salacious. 'And there's tonight of course when all will be revealed.' Her thickly made-up lashes fluttered into a wink that was as salacious as her smile.

Ellen felt her cheeks burning. 'Well . . . yes . . .'

Diana flashed her ever-so-white teeth, took her cigarette from her mouth and leaned close so that her full red lips brushed Ellen's ear. 'And that will be only his body, darling. This family is riddled with secrets.'

'One of them drinks too much,' said Ellen, throwing Diana an accusing look.

Ellen had always prided herself on being able to get on with anybody, but she wasn't quite sure of Diana, her brother-in-law's wife. She could never tell when she was telling the truth and when she was lying. On top of that it wasn't the first time she'd seen her drunk. Her Methodist father had instilled in Ellen his own dislike for drink, and although they both sipped on special occasions, such as her wedding, Ellen found people who drank too much quite objectionable.

Diana didn't appear to notice her comment. Her gaze had already moved on, her hazel eyes fixed on the two brothers. Ellen followed her gaze.

William Shellard was eyeing his drink, swirling the amber liquid around his glass. Walter was talking avidly, his drink gripped in his right hand, his words falling into the ears of Seth Armitage who was standing between the two brothers.

'Look at them,' said Diana, a hint of a smile twitching her

crimson mouth. 'My dear husband's afraid of his brother. Did you know that?'

Ellen was taken off guard. This was not the sort of blatant truth she expected to hear on her wedding day. She dithered. 'Well, I don't really . . .'

'It's quite true,' Diana interjected. 'William's a darling; good at what he does within Shellard Wines – though not ruthless like his brother.'

Diana's velvet-brown eyes narrowed as she scrutinized her brother-in-law. 'What Walter wants, Walter gets, and woe betide anyone who gets in his way.'

'You make him sound unscrupulous.'

Diana turned to her. Her eyes glittered with a look Ellen could not quite fathom. Her mouth and her jaw tightened before she spoke.

'If you think you married Prince Charming, darling, you really are a sleeping beauty. I suggest you wake up before a hundred days are up, let alone a hundred years.'

Although Walter Shellard continued to talk business with Seth Armitage, his financial director, his eyes missed nothing. He'd known Ellen for barely four months, yet already he could read her expression; knew when she was happy, sad or plain disconcerted as she seemed now. The reason was standing right next to her.

'William,' he said, interrupting old Seth's run of words. 'Your wife is upsetting my bride. Deal with her.'

One glance and William was shamed. Diana held a cigarette holder in one hand and a glass in the other. She was swaying in a strange, abstract way as though listening to a slow serenade no one else could hear.

'Christ!'

A sense of déjà vu and blood-red anger surged through William Shellard's brain. He slammed his drink down on a passing tray held high by a waiter and strode across the banqueting hall. His mouth was set in a grim line. His dark eyes turned from steel grey to slate. Bloody Diana! Today of all days!

Throwing an apologetic smile at his sister-in-law, he grabbed his wife's arm. 'Come along, darling. I think it's time you went home.'

Diana looked surprised to see him, almost as though she couldn't quite remember him being invited. Realization eventually cleared something foggy from lustrous eyes, eyes that belied Mediterranean parentage, though the majority of Diana's family hailed from Shropshire.

'Darling Willy. It's you! Are you taking me home to beddy byes?'

William looked furious. Again he apologized to Ellen before turning his attention back to his wife. 'You're going home, Diana. And don't call me Willy,' he growled through gritted teeth.

'I don't want to go home. I'm thirsty.'

William grappled the champagne glass from her unwilling fingers. 'Yes, my darling. You are.'

Nodding a last acknowledgement to Ellen, William guided his errant wife out of the banqueting hall. The reception area was cooler than the room he'd left behind. The grand entrance doors were opened and shut by a grey-haired concierge wearing a black top hat and a pinstriped tailcoat. As William approached, he lifted his hat and opened the door.

'Get my wife a cab, my good man,' ordered William.

He barely noticed the man's nod of approbation or the flash of contempt in his eyes.

'There's one already here, sir,' said the man.

Just as the concierge had guessed, William had wanted to leave Diana with him, closing the door on her yet again. Time and time again he'd asked himself why he'd married her. The answer was always the same; she owned a vague resemblance to someone he'd once loved, someone who'd been cruelly taken from him.

Once the cab door was safely closed and the driver given instructions plus a crisp pound note to see her safely in the hands of their servants, William retraced his steps.

He saw that his brother and Seth Armitage were still talking, but he had no inclination to rejoin them. Walter, his brother, was the true heir to the Shellard business if aptitude alone were anything to go by. He was just the spare, a secondary son to be held in reserve in case of accident; a bit like a lifeboat.

He danced with one of the bridesmaids, aimlessly guiding her around the dance floor. His thoughts were back when

Walter had told him he was marrying Ellen. He ground his teeth as he relived the emotion and heard his own words echoing in his head.

'You're deserting Leonora? Surely you owe her more than that, Walter. The woman's lived with you for years.'

Walter had been unmoved. 'I know Leonora better than you do. Everything will be all right. I shall offer her everything I can; a nice little place in Lisbon; an income; and once the honeymoon is over, so to speak, I can call in and see her from time to time.'

'Not everything. You're not offering her what she really deserves,' William had snapped, his fists clenched as though he were ready to smash his brother's face to pulp. But he wasn't ready to do that and anyway, Walter had the knack of taking the wind from his sails.

His brother had smiled disarmingly. 'Come on, William. I can't marry her. What would W.W. Shellard and Company Limited have gained from marrying her? Nothing. Think what Ellen's bringing to this marriage.'

'A business,' William had growled.

Walter had shaken his head and used that all-knowing, all-conquering smile. Sometimes William felt as though he were once again standing before his father; the two of them were so alike, giant egos that smothered everything in their path. It was becoming increasingly obvious that Walter intended bypassing his father's achievements, growing what had started as a humble wine shop into a worldwide empire.

'Ouch! We're doing a waltz, not a foxtrot.'

The hurt voice of his dancing partner brought him back to the present.

'Sorry,' said William. 'Do excuse me. I think I need a drink.'

He left the bespectacled bridesmaid rubbing her toes and returned to his drink, tipping champagne into his throat. He looked at the drained glass, just a film of clear liquid coating its bottom. Perhaps if he stopped drinking, Diana might do so. The idea had his merits. In effect he'd be supporting his wife. He wondered if Diana would see it that way.

He sighed. It was all a pipe dream. Diana did as she pleased. He grimaced at what was left of the champagne. 'Bloody bubbly,' he muttered and turned to a passing waiter. 'Fetch me a whisky, please.'

'Certainly, sir.'

As he awaited his drink, William watched his brother and his new sister-in-law waltzing around the dance floor. His expression was grim on account of his thoughts.

'A penny for them,' said someone at his elbow.

He looked down into the face of Seth Armitage. He had been their father's compatriot, helpful in making the company what it was today and was an extremely useful financial director.

William set his sights back on his brother. 'She's pretty,' he said.

'Pretty rich,' said Seth, his face masked with cigar smoke. 'That was your brother's main criteria for marrying her.'

William gave a cursory nod. His eyes stayed fixed on the happy couple.

Seth Armitage watched him with one cocked eyebrow. William was the more likeable of the two Shellard sons, but Walter was the one likely to go places. Seth had hitched his wagon to Walter's coat tails and hoped to gain from his action. If pressed, he couldn't say that he liked Walter, more so that he respected him. Walter sometimes shocked him, sometimes surprised him, and sometimes he heartily disliked him. Yes, William was easier to read and therefore easier to deal with.

'You're thinking of the Portuguese girl,' said Seth.

'He should have married her,' growled William, barely able to control his anger at the thought of what his brother had done.

The waiter came back with his drink.

Seth raised one snowy-white eyebrow and eyed William with a single narrowed eye. 'And that was all she had. Ellen came with a bottling plant. Old man Parker's got no sons and Walter will be calling the shots. Ellen Parker was too good an opportunity to be missed.'

'And my brother never misses a good opportunity,' said William, the whisky tasting like ash on his tongue. Never mind. He threw back his head and downed what remained in one gulp. Tasting bitterness on his tongue, his hard stare returned to Walter and his new bride. What would Leonora do now? he wondered. Walter had said that she would be taken care of, but William thought he knew Leonora better than that. Memories of her dark eyes and beautiful face sometimes haunted his daytime moments as well as his dreams. He'd fallen in love with her at first sight, but Walter, his elder brother, had seen her too. As usual, it was Walter who had won and he, William, had ended up with second best. With Diana.

And now . . . ?

Once their father was dead and buried, what had happened was inevitable. Although the business was, on paper, divided between them, it was Walter, the ruthless one, who'd taken the reins. It wasn't supposed to happen, but a board of directors who saw their wealth increasing were glad, even grateful, to make Walter Chairman and President of the company.

Unlike William or their father, Walter was not so much interested in the product they sold as in the expansion of the company into an empire. Very soon the company was to be renamed Shellard Enterprises. Their portfolio was growing, and it wasn't all down to port, wine or sherry.

Walter had leapt into the business straight from an army commission. From the start he'd run things as though he were going into battle. He had always wanted to be commander in chief of a huge battlefront, and that battlefront would be Shellard Enterprises.

William wondered why he was feeling so peeved about it all. Even as a child his brother had wanted everything that was William's. That covetousness had included women. Leonora had been the one he'd wanted most of all.

William had met her first and fallen deeply in love with her, not able to sleep at night for thinking about her and her lovely face hidden behind her white mantilla. Unfortunately he'd got drunk one night and related his feelings to his brother, going on and on about how beautiful she was. Walter had not been able to resist. He'd had to seek her out and had waited outside the church where she prayed.

As a child Walter had sometimes returned William's possessions, but not Leonora. Not until now.

Feeling disconsolate and light-headed, he took his leave of Seth Armitage and walked out of the hotel. Ribbons of peach sunset threw a pale light over College Green. The trees rustled in the breeze. He closed his eyes in order to blank out the trams going up Park Street and took a deep breath. He recalled what Walter had said to him just before his marriage.

'You can see her once she's resettled. Anyway, you must

come over to Porto. When was the last time you were at the Castile Villanova?'

William couldn't bear to answer.

Walter answered for him. 'Not since Leonora was installed there.'

He said installed as though she were a piece of machinery, something of use. William grimaced and wished he wasn't such a coward. Why couldn't he be more like his brother? Impossible! He could not.

'One of these days you'll meet your match,' he murmured. A sudden breeze tousled his hair and took his words. 'One of these days,' he repeated and hoped it would be so.

Two

Catherine's mother, Leonora Rodriguez, died on the day of the race between the *rabalos*, the cask-carrying boats of the great port wine lodges.

The day started well enough. Twelve years old and on the brink of adolescence, she greeted the new day, laughing as she ran up the twisting steps that led to the roof of the Castile Villanova, the grand house owned by her father, a wealthy wine merchant and vineyard owner.

Her hair was raven black, and her dark-grey eyes danced with delight. She had been blessed with her mother's good bone formation, arched eyebrows, and a wide mouth that seemed always to carry an enigmatic smile.

She could hear her nurse scolding her from the bottom of the ancient stone steps leading up to the roof, gasping for breath between each scold and each laboured step.

In all honesty, Catherine was getting too old for a nurse, too old for toys and games and the innocence of childhood. But Conceptua clung on with the tenacity of a woman who has no other objective in life but to see that this girl remained a child for ever. She was blinkered to the fact that Catherine was no longer the thin, gangly girl with a ravenous appetite and eyes that seemed too big for her face. Even the coltish legs were developing some shape and the first signs of breasts were pushing against her bodice.

Conceptua's fat hips waddled from side to side like panniers of round cheese as she struggled up the last steps. She was not built for chasing anyone and slowed as each step seemed to double in height. Three-quarters of the way from the top, she clung more firmly to the wrought-iron banister and caught her breath, her flat, square hand resting on her copious bosom. She carried Sophie, Catherine's doll, beneath her other arm. The doll had been one of Catherine's favourites when she was younger. Conceptua still carried her around, wanting her little girl to remain just that.

Catherine knew she'd be a few minutes catching her up, so took time surveying a view she never tired of. The slopes around the capital of the Portuguese vine-growing region, one of the locales that had given the country its name, sloped green and rich towards the River Douro.

The same breeze that blew silky dark tresses across her face also filled the sails of the *rabalos*, the wine trade river-boats, the marks of their respective wine lodges, emblazoned on their sails. Like fat birds they were wallowing, reined in until the shot sounded that would start the race.

'Your breakfast. You have not had your breakfast,' her nurse puffed as she finally made the roof, sitting on the top step, her big bottom filling the gap between two stone balustrades. Sophie lay at her side.

'Hmm,' murmured Catherine, totally engrossed in what was going on down at the river.

Her cheeks glowed pink in the early morning air. She took in the scene of a city lately roused from sleep. The warm sunshine was already kissing the twin domes of the cathedral and the roof of the Palacio da Bolsa, Porto's stock exchange. Her gaze stayed fixed on the boats as they awaited the gunshot signalling the start of the regatta, an integral part of the Sao Joao Festival held every year in June. Weighed down with casks from stem to stern, the *rabalos* lay low in the water. Their sails were gathered to one side so they would not fill with wind. At the start of the race the crew would let go and the sails would billow like sheets on a washing line.

Leaning forward, she clenched her fists in anticipation of the sound of the starting pistol.

Crack!

She jumped at the sound and gave a little gasp of surprise. It seemed louder and earlier than in past years and took her by surprise. Stiffening with excitement, she willed the boats to move. They didn't.

Frowning, she turned to remark on it to her nurse in time to see a flash of brown skirt as Conceptua disappeared back down the steps. She called out. 'Conceptua? Where are you going?'

She listened for a reply. Instead she heard wailing prayers being offered up to the Virgin Mary.

Silly woman, she thought, and gave it no serious mind. Conceptua was always muttering prayers and crossing herself against some real or imagined disaster. Perhaps the gunshot had frightened her. Catherine turned her face to the scene on the river, relishing the fact that she was here unfettered by Conceptua's fussing concern. She had a good view of the race, but not so good that it couldn't be improved that bit more.

Unsupervised by her overprotective nurse, she climbed on to the wall scraping the toes of her shoes on the rough stone. Only a wrought-iron rail protected her from the towering drop, but the climb was worth it. The view was tremendous, far superior to lower down.

Another gunshot, as muffled and distant as in previous years, surprised her as much as the first one had. The crowd roared. The boats edged forward. If she stood on tiptoe she could just about make out the words on the sails, the name of the port wine lodges: Taylor's, Graham's, Sandeman and Shellard. Catherine felt a great surge of pride. Walter Shellard owned vineyards in Spain as well as Portugal and also acted as a middleman for many of the great wine lodges besides selling his own vintages in England. He dealt in wine, port and the Shellard Bristol Sherry which he boasted was a better quality than that of the famous Harveys.

The boats disappeared behind the trees and buildings of the Ribiera, Porto's riverside. She would have liked to see the end of the race, but no one had offered to take her.

'Your father will take you when we are married,' her mother had told her.

The promise had been made a long time ago. Her mother had great faith in her father. Catherine, although only a child, had ceased to believe the promises she'd heard year after year. She had smiled and said she would be patient because her mother chose to continue believing them and it pleased her to think she did.

The distant river was now empty of boats: the crowd had moved on and her stomach rumbled. She was ready for her breakfast. Climbing down from the wall, she caught her skirt on an iron leaf protruding from the ornate trellis. There was a ripping sound and a shard of cotton lace from her petticoat trailed from beneath the hem of her dress. Nurse would not be amused and breakfast might be late in coming or, if she were in a particularly unforgiving mood, might not come at all.

Accompanied by another rumble from her empty stomach, the entire length of lace was ripped, wound into a bundle and hidden behind a bush.

She looked down the dark stairway and thought it strange that Conceptua had not reappeared. She didn't usually leave her alone for so long. An uneasy feeling fluttered in her stomach; it couldn't be put down entirely to hunger. She picked up Sophie from where Conceptua had left her. Holding the doll by one leg, she swung her to and fro as with dark, serious eyes, she looked down the stone steps.

The sound of running feet echoed off the tiled walls in the corridor below. A wail like the screech of a buzzard, though drawn out and more plaintive, made her turn cold. Someone was crying in the same way as her mother cried when her father had broken another promise. The wail rose again. Then there was silence, a dreadful cold silence like a church empty of people, colour and statuary.

Catherine placed one foot on to the top step and considered going back down but something held her back. The passage at the bottom seemed terribly dark, like a big black mouth set to devour her. Eventually Conceptua appeared, her lower face covered by an enormous handkerchief. She blew her nose, wiped at her eyes then blew her nose again. Her eyes were red-rimmed and her bottom lids drooped, exposing fleshy crescents.

Conceptua froze two steps from the top. She stared, blinked

and made a great effort to contain herself, holding herself stiff as if making a decision. After taking one more swipe at her nose she pushed her handkerchief up her sleeve.

'We're going out,' said Conceptua decisively, her plump face set like a waterless jelly. She held out her hand, the fingers curved and moving like a claw. 'Come along. Quickly!'

'I'm hungry,' whined Catherine, not wanting to go, wanting to stay and find out what was going on.

'We'll go and watch the *rabalos*. We'll buy bread. We'll buy fruit. We'll have a wonderful day. Sophie will enjoy it too.' She spoke in quick, sharp gasps, gripped Catherine's hand very tightly, and almost ran along the passage.

Though she had reservations that things weren't quite right, Catherine was jubilant. She'd always had to content herself watching the regatta from the roof, but now she was off to take a closer view. She pushed concern for her mother to the back of her mind, promising that she'd tell her all about it when she returned. Despite Conceptua's weight and inclination to breathlessness, they began to run.

Running didn't last long. Conceptua's physical condition got the better of her. She began puffing like a steam train as Catherine surged ahead of her, dragging her along the passage. For once the pious peasant woman didn't object. Her loose-fitting shoes – bought for comfort rather than speed – slapped on the hard stone floors as they ran.

Catherine made as if to turn for the main part of the house. She was bursting to tell someone – principally her mother or even her rarely faced father – that she was going out.

Conceptua pulled Catherine away from the passage leading to the main staircase. 'Not that way!' She took her instead through the cool passages and stairways used by the servants and tradesmen. This time it was Conceptua who led their head-long dash. To Catherine's innocent mind, it seemed as if the overweight nurse was trying to put as much distance between them and the main house as possible. Just in case we get found out, she thought, and someone tries to stop us.

She'd been told she had a quick mind and was instinctive, and that was why she couldn't quite trust what was happening. On the other hand she craved excitement; she mixed so little with the outside world and led a sheltered life within the Castile.

Outside the June sun was beginning to get hot. Northern Portugal was not as hot as the south, thanks mainly to the cool breezes coming down from the hills above the river.

The mood of the crowds along the River Douro was infectious. There was drinking, there was shouting, there was dancing and lots of eating. The bread and fruit were good, and the air was fresh and tainted with the aroma of toasted almonds, fresh ham and the heady smell of vintage port drawn straight from the barrel.

Overflowing with excitement, Catherine talked a lot, even with her mouth full. For once Conceptua said nothing about ill manners. She was strangely silent. Every so often she dabbed at her eyes with a huge lace-edged handkerchief. She sniffed incessantly, her nose turning redder and redder with each swipe of stiff lace.

'You need to wash that handkerchief in lemon juice,' said Catherine.

In response, Conceptua sucked in her lips and nodded.

The day was full of colour and gaiety. Catherine decided to make the most of it, observing and taking in everything in great detail so she could relate what she'd seen to her mother.

As the sun dipped down towards the Atlantic, Conceptua finally took her home. Catherine chatted all the way, her excitement bubbling over as she recalled each tiny titbit of the scene.

'I'll never forget today,' she blurted excitedly.

Conceptua's body stiffened, but her face drooped as though someone had stolen her bones. 'Me neither,' she muttered.

To Catherine's surprise, they re-entered Castile Villanova the way they had left. The coolness was welcome, but the house seemed oddly still, a place of shades and shadows after the glare of the late afternoon sun. Every so often its silence was interspersed by a sob or a sigh, running feet and shouted instructions.

Catherine's earlier disquiet returned the moment they left the sunshine and entered the shadows. A sudden chill ran down her spine. The air trembled. The walls glistened with moisture. Their footsteps echoed. She could almost believe that they were the only people in the house, except for the sobbing, the echoes of sadness radiating down from the house above them. She shivered and knew instinctively that everything had changed. She rarely left the house, and today had been such a great adventure, but for what reason, for what price? Her shrewd mind – inherited from her father, according to her mother – analysed the events of the last twenty-four hours, and her thoughts went straight to her mother. She had sounded so hopeful for the future, but last night she'd been crying. Suddenly, she wanted to be with her.

She lunged forward, meaning to escape Conceptua's hold. 'Mamma!'

'No!' Conceptua gripped her hand more tightly.

Catherine struggled. 'I must go to my mother. I have not seen her this morning. She needs me.'

'No,' Conceptua repeated. 'Wait.'

'Mamma!'

Her cry echoed off the cool walls and glazed tiles.

A footman appeared where the passage intersected with another. He stopped when he saw them and indicated he wished to speak to her nurse. Conceptua brought herself and Catherine to a halt. The adults acknowledged each other with a swift nod, their eyes meeting in a way that made Catherine feel slightly sick.

'Wait here,' warned Conceptua, letting go of her hand. 'And don't move. Promise?'

Although she was desperate to go to her mother, there was something about Conceptua's tone of voice that made Catherine obey. She had a strange sensation of having swallowed a bowl of wriggling worms as she watched Conceptua lean head to head with the footman. Cupping his hand around his mouth, he whispered something in her ear. She tried to gauge what was being said from their changing expressions. Not easy.

At last Conceptua nodded, muttered, 'Yes, yes, of course.'

Catherine sensed something bad had been whispered, something that concerned her. She searched for the cause on Conceptua's face. Her nurse was giving nothing away. There was an enforced blandness about it, as though the task set her was unpalatable but had to be done. All the same, the furtive shiftiness in her eyes was there to be read.

'We can't go into the house yet,' she said, grabbing Catherine's hand. With hurried steps, she dragged her back along the passage.

Again Catherine looked up at Conceptua's face and tried

to read her expression. Something was definitely going on that they didn't want her to know about. Adults only took on such furtive looks when something bad had happened.

Catherine suddenly felt as though she'd been dipped in ice. 'Where's my mother?'

Conceptua seemed to choke before managing to find her voice.

For a brief moment Catherine thought she was going to be told the truth but Conceptua was no different from the other adults. What Conceptua said next confirmed Catherine's suspicions.

'Have you ever seen the wine cellar?'

Angered by an obvious attempt to keep her occupied, Catherine frowned. 'You've got something to tell me but you won't. Why? What is going on?'

Conceptua winced before the force of the little girl's accusing glare and matter-of-fact tone. She tried blustering and adopting a merry expression, as though nothing was wrong; as if today was no different from any other.

'I think your father would approve of you looking around the wine cellar. It is how he makes his living. The wine is what buys you pretty dresses, your lovely pony and everything you have. It would be good for you to see it.'

Catherine sighed and resigned herself to the fact that for now she would go along with it if it would get her to her mother.

She reeled off what she knew anyway. 'Father has told me about the wine lodges and the casks. They're very big. Very big indeed.'

Taking advantage of the turn of conversation, Conceptua laughed nervously. 'Tell me how big they are. Think of the biggest thing in the house that you think resembles the casks, and tell me.'

Catherine was in no mood for platitudes. 'As big as your backside!'

Conceptua's jaw dropped.

Catherine tensed. At first, it seemed a rebuke was forthcoming, a swift slap for being cheeky.

Instead, she laughed, loudly and forcibly, as though she had to gather together all her laughter in one heap to be able to laugh at all. 'You are right. My backside is as big as a wine cask.'

Catherine eyed her sidelong. She had meant to be rude and still expected admonishment. None came and her feeling of impending disaster deepened.

Conceptua cleared her throat and looked thoughtful, her tiny mouth pursed, her black eyes flitting around as though searching for something.

'We could count the bottles. We could guess how many would fit in one of the casks.'

The task was mundane. Catherine was not easily fooled and normally would have said so. But today was different. The feeling of unease would not go away. With an air of resignation more suited to an adult than a twelve-year-old, she sighed heavily and gave in. 'Then show me the wine cellar.'

A draught of cold air smelling of stone dust and old oak belched out to meet them as the door was pulled open.

'It is very cool,' said Conceptua who for her part was glad of the coolness on her plump cheeks, and equally glad to be away from everything happening in the house. Today was a bad day. The worst day in all her service to this household.

'We sit,' she said, patting the space beside her.

Surrounded by the best of bottled vintages, Catherine joined her, sitting on a stone step, her hands clasped around her knees and Sophie dangling from her hands.

Conceptua prattled on about her own family and how things had been when she was a girl. Catherine wasn't really listening. Her thoughts were with her mother. She had a strange feeling about today, guilty at going off to watch the port wine boats. She hoped her mother was managing without her. She was such a fragile, beautiful creature, her skin as creamily smooth as a porcelain doll. Although Catherine didn't doubt that her mother loved her, she knew that Walter Shellard was the most important thing in her mother's life. Her world revolved around him. She'd dressed for him, kept house for him, waiting patiently until such time as he came to Portugal, sometimes only for days, sometimes for precious weeks.

Conceptua sat droning on about the wine in the bottles around them. Carried away with memories of the taste of ruby, tawny, white port, and the Amontillado specially transported from vineyards near Jerez in Spain, her face brightened as she went on to tell Catherine of the times she'd sipped the dregs left after dinner. 'But don't tell your mother that,' she said, then halted, her face reddening. 'Oh!' she said, her fleshy cheeks and chin creasing like squashed dough and her voice breaking with emotion. 'Oh!'

Suddenly she looked terrified – as though, like a wild rabbit, she'd strayed into a place very dangerous for her kind.

Catherine felt the hairs rise on her arm. Her blood turned cold. She sat very still, very silent, her round eyes studying Conceptua's plump face and knowing without any words being said that the badness she'd sensed was indeed to do with her mother. She could see the truth in Conceptua's eyes.

Catherine thought of the night before, her mother's tears, previous quarrels, her father's fleeting appearances, his trips to England and then, she thought of the loud gunshot before the one that had started the race this morning.

Cuddling the doll tight against her chest, she spoke the cruel thought that had lurked at the back of her mind. 'My mother's dead, isn't she?'

She heard Conceptua's sharp intake of breath. She'd often seen her nurse looking flustered, but never had she known her to look so shocked. Round-eyed and round-mouthed, her face was as stiff as a gargoyle.

Catherine looked down at the cold stone floor. Her beautiful mother, with her long black hair and her slinky dresses, had left drifts of perfume wherever she happened to be. When Catherine had wanted to find her in this house of many rooms, she had followed her nose, sniffing for the familiar flowery scent.

Conceptua began to cry. 'My poor Catherine, my poor child!'

Catherine held back her tears and stayed dry-eyed. Her pain turned inwards. It was sharp, like a shard of ice piercing her heart and creeping through her body.

'How did it happen?' she asked in a small voice.

Conceptua shook her head and continued to cry, though managed to throw in a few words between sobs and wails. 'No, you must not ask. I am not supposed to tell you.' Louder now, her voice turning shrill. 'Do not ask me.'

'Did she quarrel with my father?' The question was not out of place. She'd heard them quarrelling before, usually about marriage.

'Why don't you marry me and legitimize your child?'

Legitimize was a long word and had something to do with marriage, of that Catherine was sure. And she was the child.

'Your father is in England.' She paused and swiped at her nose before the tears resumed. 'He sent a telegram telling her . . .' The plump nurse dabbed at her eyes, her nose and her mouth. She was drowning in tears. 'Poor lady,' she kept saying over and over again. 'Poor lady.'

Catherine felt cold inside. Right behind it came a feeling of great courage. She did not *ever* want to snivel like Conceptua snivelled. Things happen and have to be dealt with. 'Conceptua, please stop crying. Whatever's happened has happened and can't be changed.'

Conceptua stopped for a brief moment, red-rimmed eyes wide with amazement. Words failed her. Perhaps in an effort to escape the fact that her charge was more grown-up than she was, Conceptua got up from her seat. The barrel rocked on its base as her big backside left it behind. The cellar door squealed on iron hinges as she opened it, looking out this way and that, asking a question of any servant who passed by.

Catherine stayed put. There was no comfort in cuddling her doll, no matter how close she held it. Her world and herself were like ice.

And it's your fault.

The fault lay with her father. That's why her mother was dead.

She rested her chin on Sophie's head, thought about the doll, then looked into its round, china face. Suddenly Sophie was the sole representation in this cellar of the man responsible for her mother's unhappiness. And just as suddenly she decided she hated the doll she'd once loved avidly.

With a strong backward flip of her hand, she threw the doll towards the wine racks. It disappeared among the dusty, dark bottles. She would never see that doll again. She was also sure she would not see her father – not for a very long time.

For now it seemed like a bright light had been extinguished from her world. And she could not cry. For some reason, she could not cry.

Three

The funeral was quickly arranged and discreet, the thin cortège standing in a churchyard on the outskirts of the city in a crumbling suburb of silent alleys and dusty streets where no one knew her name.

Leonora Rodriguez
1894–1924

No dearly beloved wife, no sadly missed mother. Her epitaph was brief and nondescript, almost like her life. She was unmarried, therefore her role as a mother should not and could not exist.

Only Catherine and a few servants attended the funeral. She looked around for her father. His daughter had still expected him to turn up, even if a bit later than everyone else. He was always absent, always late.

'He is still in England,' her nurse explained. 'He will probably send another telegram,' she hissed bitterly.

Catherine sensed by the way Conceptua gritted her teeth that she'd like to say a lot more but something held her back.

Catherine stared tearlessly as the earth rattled like hailstones, bouncing on the coffin lid and rolling along its sides. It was as though life had become unreal and she was watching herself standing there dressed in black, just the child of a woman who had loved and lost, had been used until her father had tired of her dark looks and absurd loyalty.

The childish exterior hid a festering anger but also a fear. Her bags were already packed. She was being sent away at a time when she badly wanted to throw her arms around someone who felt the loss as greatly as she did. Her father had not put in an appearance; neither had he sent for her.

'Not even a note,' she'd heard Conceptua whisper to Jocasta, the cook.

The two women shook their heads and made disapproving sounds with thin, pursed lips. The whispers and the pitying looks of servants were too much to bear, more so when she was told that her name would revert to that of her mother. She would be known as Catherine Rodriguez; no longer Catherine Shellard.

'Your mother was not married to your father,' sneered one of the younger housemaids with undisguised glee. 'She was a rich man's plaything. You will probably end up the same.'

Catherine slapped her face.

Everyone now gave her scant regard. It was as though she no longer existed. Her mother had been everything to her, and if she was so like her, then so be it. She *would* be like her; *exactly* like her!

Unbeknown to them all, she had heard the other whisper, the gossip that tingled like electricity throughout the household. She had crept back to her old room at the front of the house. Through the adjoining door, she'd peeped into her mother's room. One of the servants was in there kneeling on the floor before a huge leather chest. Bright shiny padlocks hung from the thick leather straps binding it.

'Look at madam's clothes,' she whispered to one of the housemaids. 'She's sent two chests of clothes ahead of her and one more coming with her on Tuesday.'

The two women gasped as they brought out a peacock-blue dress, hanging it before their eyes so they could scrutinize it more easily.

'It's beautiful.'

Catherine was on the point of shouting that they leave her mother's clothes alone, but held back. These clothes were neither the style nor the size her mother had worn. A different woman was taking her mother's place.

The servants continued to make the same admiring sounds before putting each item away into what had been her mother's wardrobes.

Suddenly, one of them asked, 'Is she bringing her wedding dress?'

The other housemaid shook her head. 'I wouldn't think so. They're already married.'

Maria made a disappointed moue with her thin pale lips. 'I suppose so. Shame, though. I would have liked to see it. I love weddings.'

That night Catherine cried. The fact was obvious. Her father didn't want her any more, and worse than that, it was his fault that her mother was dead. *His fault!*

Two days after the funeral, she was told she was leaving Castile Villanova. Conceptua made ready to accompany her to the home of Lopa Rodriguez, her mother's aunt. Catherine had never met the woman; neither had her mother ever mentioned her in much detail except to say that she lived in a *quinta* – a farmhouse high on the green slopes above the upper Douro.

'You'll love it there,' said Conceptua, her voice shaky and not sounding entirely convinced. 'You can pick almonds and lemons from the trees, run in the grass and paddle in the streams.'

'Can I take my pony?'

Conceptua's expression was pained and she avoided eye contact. 'No.'

'Is the house like Castile Villanova? Does it have lots of servants?'

Conceptua's eyelids fluttered over a furtive look. Catherine was an astute child and knew her nurse was loath to answer.

'It's a *quinta*; a farmhouse and not as big as this place. I don't know whether your aunt has servants.'

Catherine studied Conceptua's face as the nurse reached to fasten the brown velvet buttons of her coat and fixed her hat on her head just as she always had.

Catherine pushed her hands away. 'Then perhaps I should learn to look after myself.'

She saw Conceptua's discomfited expression, the way she only half turned her head so that Catherine couldn't see her whole face. In the space of a few days her life had changed for ever and so had she. Just a sideways look, a whispered comment, and she knew that things would not be good for her. Everything was changing.

Conceptua was bustling with a few small items left on the dressing table, sparkling glass bottles that her mother had given her. They'd once contained perfume. When her mother had used up the contents, she'd passed the bottles to her daughter. Catherine used to pretend to dab her ears with what was left of the scent, in effect the essence of her mother.

'Are you not coming with me?' she asked her nurse.

It seemed inconceivable that she could live without Conceptua washing her face, choosing her clothes and dressing her.

'Of course I am. We shall travel on the train together.'

For a brief moment Catherine felt a great sense of relief that some semblance of her life would be travelling with her. There was hope, she thought, but on re-examination she realized that wasn't exactly what Conceptua had said.

Conceptua was wrapping the last of the perfume bottles in tissue paper before packing them in a small wooden box inlaid with patterns in ivory.

There was a nervous shiftiness to Conceptua's face. Catherine knew immediately that there was something not being said. 'You're only coming with me on the train? You're not coming to live with me and my aunt?'

Conceptua was purposely evasive, her eyes fixed on the perfume bottles, wrapping them in yet more tissue paper. 'You'll enjoy the train.'

Catherine had never travelled on a train before and in normal circumstances, the prospect of a long journey away from familiar surroundings would have excited her. However, it seemed odd that they were not being taken all the way to her great-aunt's distant *quinta* by car. Conceptua would only be able to carry a small amount of luggage. Judging by the tough, brown cases, it looked as though Catherine would have to carry some too. She'd never had to do it before. There had always been servants, but today they were keeping out of her way, and those she did see either looked at her with pity or disdain.

A feeling of being discarded – like dead flowers or burned ashes – stayed with her. And it wasn't just the servants. Conceptua led her along the corridor past the servants' quarters towards the rear entrance, just as she had on the day of her mother's death.

Catherine, not a little frightened, managed to sound indignant. 'Why aren't we going out of the front door? My mother is dead and buried. What else are you trying to hide from me?'

'Wait,' said Conceptua, setting down the luggage as they reached the door leading into a courtyard where the cars and horses were kept.

The chauffeur, a swarthy man named Antoine, loped over in something between a run and a leap, his eyes constantly looking around him.

'Quickly,' he said as he grabbed the luggage.

'Why didn't you come round to the front door?' Catherine demanded, aching to understand why things had changed so much, frustrated and confused that no one answered her questions.

Antoine and Conceptua exchanged swift glances.

Out of necessity, Conceptua recovered quickly, pulling open the car door before even Antoine had chance to do it for them. 'Get into the car, Catherine. We have a train to catch.'

Sighing and feeling sorry for herself, Catherine clambered into the back seat of the car.

Antoine started the engine. Catherine's eyes watched his hand move on to the shiny handle of the gearstick, squeezing it before easing it forward. Always after, she would remember that moment, the squeezing and the pushing forward; it marked the moment of her severance from everything she'd held dear.

Her attention went from there to the walls of the house itself. Mean windows with wooden shutters looked out on to the rear courtyard. Forward of this were grander rooms and the inner courtyard where fountains played and an arched colonnade offered shade even at midday.

The smells of ripe fruits and trees heavy with leaves followed them all the way down the drive. Eventually those same trees framed the imposing frontage, the shadows they threw bluish black against the honeyed walls, the colourful tiles surrounding arched windows dating from Moorish times.

Not far from the main gate, she strained her neck to glimpse the last of the only home she'd ever known. The main body of the house was now hidden by foliage. All that remained on view were the clay roof tiles of the central pergola, gleaming like embers in the glare of the morning sun.

The day was warm and her coat too thick. Catherine dozed.

Thinking she was sound asleep, Conceptua, who had opted to sit in the front seat next to Antoine, sighed and slid her feet out of her stout lace-up shoes. She much preferred her old sloppy ones, but had considered them unsuitable for travelling. She was uncomfortable enough at the prospect of this journey without her feet being uncomfortable too.

Sighing deeply, she shook her head and rubbed at her red-rimmed eyes with finger and thumb. She hadn't had much sleep of late, and wouldn't until this was all over. Once it was she was off to look after her sick sister. She would not stay in service to the Shellards.

She sighed again.

Antoine glanced at her, his nose twitching with curiosity over a thick brush of grey moustache. 'Stop sighing. It's none of your business, woman.'

Almost as though in defiance, Conceptua sighed again. 'I can't help it, Antoine. I can't serve someone for all these years and then not be affected by the way they're treated. I wish we could have left by the front door. First she is a beloved daughter, next she is a bastard.'

'Who are we to criticize?' said Antoine with an indolent shrug. 'It was the master's wish that she leave as quietly as possible and without fuss. There's no room for a bastard child at the Castile Villanova now, not with the new wife moving in. He had no wish to have her coming out of the front door when his new bride was about to cross the threshold. Stands to reason the new wife knows nothing about the child or her mother.'

'As though the poor child does not exist and never existed. That is what is so bad.' Conceptua shook her head. 'Her mother gave her life to that man. She lived for him, poor creature. And died for him too,' she added, crossing her copious chest.

'This aunt she's going to, is she rich?' Antoine asked.

Conceptua shrugged. 'What does it matter? The child needs a home even if it is in the middle of nowhere. Her father no longer wants her.'

'This new wife will be angry if she finds out about the girl. What will Mr Shellard do then?'

Conceptua laughed bitterly, her eyes narrowing as she thought about all she'd seen over the years. She lowered her voice as though she were imparting an unknown confidence, though Antoine had been in service to Walter Shellard as long as she had and knew him as well as she did. 'Neither is it likely that she knows how many women have lived in Villanova before Leonora. Walter Shellard has acquired and discarded more women than he has shoes.'

'Such is the way of the English,' said Antoine gravely.

'Such is the way of men,' spat Conceptua.

Catherine stayed very still, her eyes closed but her ears burning and her heart beating fit to burst.

Four

Coming home was usually how Walter Shellard described his return to his house in Portugal. Today he was accompanied by his new wife.

Home was the Castile Villanova; an opulent mansion situated a few miles south of the city of Porto. Grand and built in a mix of styles, the house was bounded by opulent greenery. Oranges, lemons, figs and almond trees cast shadows over the rich earth. With each breath of wind petals and perfume mixed with the dusty richness of the adjacent vineyards. Castellated battlements topped with tiles, as red and rich as the earth, ran the whole length of the flat sun-baked roof. At sunset its creamy walls were turned salmon pink. Along its drive an avenue of cypress trees threw pointed shade.

Castile Villanova had retained its ancient atmosphere, its bright tiles, its flat roof and its sense of history. Lavish furnishings acquired from France, England and Italy adorned its many rooms. High, wide doorways opened on to a pillared colonnade around a courtyard. The courtyard was sprinkled with spray from half a dozen fountains – a Moorish fashion adopted centuries before.

Ellen burned with excitement and was almost moved to tears by the glory of this place. It was nothing like anything she had ever seen before. And this, she told herself over and over again, is to be my home; my Portuguese home, she corrected, though already she was beginning to favour this place over the house back in England. She knew also that Walter loved this place.

'It is the epicentre of my existence,' he'd said to her.

She'd thought he was exaggerating how wonderful it was and how he felt about it. She now knew he'd been speaking the absolute truth.

'Are you happy, my dear?' he asked as a matter of form more so than any real need to ask the question. He could see the delight on his sweet wife's face.

'The smell,' she exclaimed, taking deep breaths of air laden with the heady smell of herbs, vines and all things growing. 'Plants never smelled as rare as this back in England.'

'It's the sun,' he said, enjoying her childish delight. 'The sun warms everything; a little overnight dew, a sudden and very short shower, and the plants give off their scents.'

Her face was flushed when she turned to look at him. Her greyish-blue eyes shone with delight.

'I don't think I'll ever want to leave this place,' she said, sighing deeply.' She turned her eyes back to the castellated roof of the house. 'It's like a palace and so terribly romantic.'

'That's because it *was* a palace back in the days of battling Moors and Catholics. My family took it over a hundred years ago; added and improved to their taste, and made it their own. Thanks to Napoleon they made a fortune in port wine.'

'I know,' she said before he had chance to explain further. 'There was an embargo on French wine, so the English bought Portuguese – only it didn't travel well – so they fortified it. You've already told me that, Walter.'

He chuckled and shook his head, delighted because Ellen made him feel like a young man all over again. When they'd first met, he'd delighted in telling her about port wine and how his family had started in the business. It pleased him that she'd retained that information so ably. Even though he was getting close to the age when people started repeating themselves, Walter did not do that and did not expect to have to do that. As with business he stated facts that he expected to state only once. Age was something that happened to other people. He could never see it happening to him.

Ellen was wearing a powder-blue outfit. Her auburn hair was captured in a net of antique gold. Her skin was so white, so porcelain fine. He'd prefer her to keep it that way. Too much sun would tan her or, worse still, turn her skin pink. Yes, he decided. Too much sun was best avoided.

'You must remember to use your parasol when you go out,' he advised.

'Now, Walter,' she said, throwing him a look of outright rebuke. 'Do remember that I'm not a silly girl. I do declare, my darling, that you're acting the callow youth, almost as though you've never been married before.'

She shook her head, tutted and turned back to the view.

As she did so, the smile faded from his face. Referring to his first marriage had stirred up bitter memories. It was all very well informing her of how the family had started the business; how their first base had been a small wine shop in a street of the same name in Bristol. The Shellard family had been ambitious enough to purchase a warehouse where casks of wine and sherry could be stored in cool cellars off Trenchard Street and close to the quay. With the onset of the Napoleonic wars, they'd bought a ship and bought Portuguese wine – the famous port – running the chance of being intercepted by the enemy as they picked up the south westerlies – the trade winds – home.

In order to strengthen their holdings and their grip on the wine trade, marriages and alliances were made and with it had come a London warehouse, ships and vineyards. The Shellards firmly believed that two families engaged in the trade were better than one – especially when the two were combined.

Walter Shellard fixed his gaze on his new wife. Each time she turned away from the view to face him and make a comment, he was ready with a winning smile and a kind word. He loved her – in his own way. She fitted in so well with his plans – just like Diana.

William had been in the depths of despair when Walter had introduced him to Diana. Just as he'd planned, William had seen her resemblance to his lost love, Leonora, who by then was warming his brother's bed at Castile Villanova. In order to add a little spice to his game, Walter had pretended to be interested in Diana, but on this occasion had let his brother win the woman.

'The best man won,' said William, beaming on his wedding day.

'Of course,' said Walter, his eyes bright with triumph and

a cold, cruel smile on his lips. 'She's the daughter of Jesmond Denton. The best thing that could ever happen to W.W. Shellard and Company.'

Walter had slapped his brother on the arm. In anyone else William would have considered the action one of affection. Coming from Walter, along with the tart comment, it was like a hammer blow.

'What do you mean?' William had asked, his colour draining from his face.

Sleek and smart in a fine suit tailored by the best outfitters in Savile Row, Walter had leaned one arm on the mantelpiece. With his free hand he smoked his customary best Havana cigar.

'William, Jesmond Denton is a director of Denton and Gibson Bank. I've been talking refinancing for the last eighteen months.' His eyes had darkened with subversive glee. 'And now we're all signed up. Had to come on board now he's part of the family, didn't he?'

William had turned pale, his eyes staring. 'You bastard! You rotten, lousy . . .'

Walter gave no sign that he'd seen his brother's hands forming tight fists. He felt no fear, indeed he'd predicted what would happen next. William stormed off – as per usual.

'I trust this doesn't ruin things for you,' Walter had called out after him.

Walter did not give in to emotions of remorse and never, ever apologized for anything. To his mind William's marriage would do the company no end of good – and if it helped William get over Leonora then that was good too.

Walter was ambitious – more ambitious than his antecedents. Port and sherry were not enough. He wanted to expand; he wanted to produce good quality wines good enough to rival the French vineyards. Ellen's father would back him to the hilt, and his bottling interests wouldn't go amiss. She was of the right family.

Becoming a widower had given him a second chance. The opportunity had presented itself and he'd taken hold of it with both hands. But there'd been casualties he hadn't planned for.

He eyed the rosy, Portuguese evening and thought of Leonora. He did not consider himself a cruel man and neither did he think himself arrogant, selfish or unfeeling. But business was business. William had been devastated.

Walter did not let on to anyone how shaken he'd been on receiving the telegram with the news that Leonora had shot herself. In fact he did not disclose that any such thing had occurred. He'd told William that she'd decided to enter a convent, just as she'd wanted to do when she was younger. He wasn't sure whether William believed him. Neither did he tell him about Catherine. In time he might find out . . .

Leonora had always been highly strung. It was going to happen sooner or later.

He rested his head against the cool leather of the seat and let the last swaying of the car journey take him back in time.

Leonora had been seventeen when he'd met her. She'd been coming down the church steps, her blue dress like a piece of fallen sky.

But that was all in the past. Now there was Ellen. His wife was twenty-eight years old. Her figure was trim and she had money. She'd also been undeterred at the prospect of living abroad for a great deal of the time.

She suddenly looked over her shoulder at him. 'We're here,' she said, her voice hushed like a child on Christmas Eve.

Gravel scrunched beneath the tyres as the chauffeur brought their car to a halt. The servants had been warned what time to expect them. They came in single file out of the house and stood in a neat row waiting to be introduced to their new mistress.

The chauffeur went round to Walter's side of the car first and opened the door. Walter got out and went to open the door on his wife's side.

'My dear,' he said, taking hold of her gloved hand.

The servants smiled and curtsied to their master and his new wife. Ellen, her eyes sparkling, smiled back and wished them a good evening.

Walter eyed her with a mixture of amusement and pride. He treated his servants well enough as long as they did their job. He did not normally smile and greet them like long-lost relatives. Ellen was naïve and he liked that. In his opinion naïve women were submissive women, which suited him fine. He still had another woman in his life, but she knew how to be discreet. Sanchia was the least submissive woman he had had anything to do with, but luckily she was besotted with him.

Curious eyes followed their progress into the shade of the

front porch where brightly coloured climbing plants clambered over honey-coloured stonework.

Ellen gasped with delight. 'This is so extraordinary,' she exclaimed, her eyes widening as she took in the marble floors, the ornate fretwork running the length of an overhead balcony, the fact that plants were climbing into the main house from an inner courtyard. The fountains were especially fine. He loved watching them, mesmerized by the falling water. So was Ellen, he noticed, the silvery droplets reflected in her eyes.

'I'm glad you like it, my dear.'

Walter flashed her a wide smile before kissing her hand. Servants bustled past them. Their luggage was being unloaded with swift efficiency.

Her face flushed with excitement, Ellen whirled round on the spot, trying to take everything in at once. 'I'll never get over this place. I think it's the loveliest house I've ever seen.'

'The house probably feels the same about you,' Walter returned with a smile, letting her hands drift from his.

'This house has a mistress at long last,' said Ellen in response. 'The first for thirty years?'

'Indeed it has.' His smile hid the half-truth he'd employed. His first wife, Gertrude, had hated leaving England so had never set foot in Castile Villanova. That much was true. However, he had not mentioned Leonora; nor would he.

'I love this place too,' he added. 'More than anything else I own.'

She rushed to him, placing her hands on his shoulders and gazing up into his face. 'More than me?'

He clasped both of her hands in his. 'You're not a house. It's not the same thing.'

She accepted his explanation. The truth was he loved this house more than anything and that included her. But she was a woman and, he reasoned, would read into that comment a whole host of pleasantries to keep her satisfied.

Walter had what he wanted, with one or two notable exceptions.

'Have you noticed that this place has too many rooms for two people?'

He saw the colour rush to her cheeks. As she smiled, she bit her bottom lip in a hint of shyness.

'Is that why you were in such a rush to get married?' she asked.

'It's a well-known fact, princess, that when I make up my mind about something, I act quickly. That's why the business interests passed on to me by my father have doubled since my tenure.'

It was more or less the truth. The excuse to return to his business abroad made the swiftness of the marriage socially acceptable. He'd pushed the obvious consequences to the back of his mind, convinced that Leonora would fall in with his plans. There had been too many reasons for not marrying Leonora. There were too many reasons in favour of marrying Ellen, so he'd gone ahead and made her his wife.

Tomorrow night a great party had been organized to welcome him and his bride to Portugal. All his business associates – and his competitors – had been invited.

'But tonight's for us,' Ellen said to him, her complexion glowing in the soft light. 'Thank you, my darling.'

Walter was pleased with his choice of bride. Ellen promised him that whether his bed was in England, Portugal or Spain, she, as his wife, would also be there.

'To the only man in my life,' she said raising her glass in a toast.

He did the same, raising his glass to his lying lips. 'To the only woman in my life. Now and for ever.'

Ellen delighted him, but Walter Shellard was not a man to be swayed by beauty alone. At the centre of his universe were the Shellard estates, vintages and warehouses. No woman had ever supplanted that. No woman ever would.

An hour before midnight he excused himself to his study. 'You go on to bed,' he told her and kissed her on the forehead. 'I'll be along shortly.'

She kissed his forehead in return. 'Don't be long.'

Sweet, he thought, maintaining a fixed smile until she was gone.

Some minutes after she'd left him and made for their bedroom, his head of household – he couldn't really call him a butler, he was housekeeper as much as that – came along to see him.

Walter was stalking the room, smoking and frowning as

though the taste of the cigar clenched between his teeth was not quite to his liking.

José, a slim man with elegant features and striking eyes, padded towards him like a cat stalking a sparrow.

'José, how did it go?'

'It was a quiet funeral, sir.'

'How did my daughter take it?'

'Quietly.'

He grunted and averted his eyes, thinking that he might have treated Catherine differently if she'd been a boy. But even then, a son might have taken on his mother's weaknesses. Catherine looked like her mother, but might have inherited some of his own characteristics. He thought about that for a moment, slightly anxious as to the sort of woman she'd turn into.

The man recognized when he was being dismissed and left the room, the door whispering to a close behind him.

Walter sorted through his mail with practised arrogance. If it didn't look interesting or important, he didn't read it straightaway. He came upon the one from Lopa Rodriguez, Leonora's aunt. The handwriting was beautifully executed; amazing that such a rough-living woman should have such an elegant hand, he thought.

This was a letter he didn't wish to read. His daughter was being looked after. That was all he needed to know.

He took hold of the envelope with both hands, ripped it down the middle and threw the two halves into the wastepaper bin. That particular period of his life was over. There was a new lady now and, given time, a new family.

Five

Throughout the long journey, Catherine fought to keep her eyes open despite the jolting of the carriage. The view from the window was sometimes breathtaking, sometimes mundane. Her eyelids grew heavy and she slept.

The train followed the indented edge of the river until it arrived at Pinhao; a town set among vineyards flooding down from granite hills, the very heart of port wine country. By the time they'd reached their destination, her eyes were quite sore and she felt languorous and stiff due to her fitful sleeps. She felt numb about her surroundings, numb about what was happening to her.

When I am grown-up I will do as I please, she thought, and I will live in the Castile Villanova again. The thought of returning to the place she loved lifted her spirits.

But how will you do that?

She frowned at the unwelcome thought. 'Conceptua,' she said, tugging at the plump skirt. 'How much would it cost to buy the Castile Villanova?'

Conceptua's response was brief and indifferent. 'Don't talk nonsense, child.'

'I'm not a child,' said Catherine in a small, hard voice. 'I'm going to live there again – one day.'

It didn't matter that Conceptua didn't hear; that she was busy organizing their luggage. Catherine was speaking to herself. In the meantime she would have to live with this great-aunt.

She took deep breaths in order to reinvigorate her weariness. She wanted to be alert. She wanted to hate her mother's aunt, but she was also curious. This was new territory, a land she'd never seen before.

In the meantime she sought to occupy herself. She would not plunge into despair.

No! You will live, she told herself. First, you will learn.

The station building was covered in colourful tiles depicting the story of how port wine was produced. There were figures planting, watering and harvesting vines; figures driving carts; figures pounding the juicy grapes between huge wooden wheels.

Catherine took too long looking at them, poring over each pattern, putting off the moment when she would say goodbye to Conceptua and thus sever her ties with the past for ever.

Her heart ached and the emptiness in her stomach would not go away. She wondered if death itself was something like this. Perhaps her father wanted her to be dead, just as he had her mother. She'd convinced herself of the fact.

Conceptua kept giving her sidelong glances, her brow furrowed with concern. Catherine refused to meet her looks, angry that her nurse had a part to play in this even though the poor woman had no say in the matter. She was a servant and merely carrying out her employer's orders.

For her part, Conceptua was feeling low about letting her charge go. Appearing impatient and bad-tempered seemed the best way of dealing with her feelings. 'Come along, child,' she said brusquely. 'There's no point in dawdling.'

She narrowed her eyes, inwardly cursing that her sight was not as good as it should be. 'Someone should be here to collect you,' she snapped. Picking up the cases, they struggled out of the station; Catherine kicking the dust as she went, her last chance to convey her despair.

The yard in front of the railway station was dusty and simmered in the heat of the sun. Beyond the whitewashed houses the hills were a mix of green, blue and mauve.

There was only one car; a gentleman who had also been travelling on the train hailed the driver, who was obviously his chauffeur. A bevy of station staff and a valet struggling with his belongings followed behind.

Besides the car there were a number of horse-drawn vehicles, their drivers sporting flat caps over faces the colour of toasted walnuts.

Catherine's attention was drawn to a single dog cart pulled by a shiny chestnut with jingling bells hanging from its bridle. The driver, a boy no older than fifteen, looked back at her.

Conceptua set down the tan leather bags she carried, stretched, rubbed at the ache in the small of her back and kneaded her ample backside with her fists.

'You,' she called, suddenly spotting the boy who eyed her as if waiting to be spoken to. 'Lopa Rodriguez?'

He nodded casually. She got the impression he didn't care whether he spoke to her or not. 'Lopa Rodriguez sent me.'

The boy had a sardonic look, as though nothing the world could say or do to him would come as any great surprise.

'Then help us with this luggage,' snapped Conceptua. She was frowning at him in annoyance and her tiny mouth was pursed. Catherine knew that she'd snap plenty more if the boy didn't move quickly.

His hair fell over his face as he bent and effortlessly picked up the luggage. Catherine glimpsed a smile. An upstart. Too cheeky for his own good. That's what Conceptua would say if she'd seen it. For the first time in weeks, Catherine smiled, though chose to hide it. The feeling of being abandoned made her defensive. She wondered if she pointed out his rudeness, Conceptua might take her home. Home! The vision was clear in her mind; sun-kissed walls, their warmth at the end of the day, the fountains, the swallows nesting beneath the eaves. A single tear seeped from the corner of one eye, but she brushed it away.

'Conceptua!' she cried, determined to mention the boy's behaviour. She had no chance to say any more. He was brown, lithe and moved fast. Taking her by surprise he picked her up and placed her in the seat of the horse-drawn buggy.

Catherine was speechless. It was the closest contact she'd had with any human being since her mother had died. Conceptua never cuddled her, and the other servants wouldn't dare.

'Have you been paid?' Conceptua asked, delving with an air of hesitant reluctance into an old-fashioned pocket strung on a ribbon from her waist.

The boy stood with his hands on his hips, one knee bent. The smile still played around his lips. 'No.'

Conceptua looked outraged. 'You mean I am to pay you? What is wrong with the woman? This is her great-niece. Her own flesh and blood.'

His smile broadened. 'There is nothing wrong with Lopa Rodriguez. She just likes holding on to her money.' He held out his open palm.

Sighing, Conceptua counted out a few coins. 'There.'

Catherine watched, only barely holding back a whole earth-quake of feelings.

After paying the boy, Conceptua turned swiftly away, not saying goodbye, not meeting Catherine's frightened eyes.

For her part, Catherine felt as though she were on the edge of a precipice; the safe ground, the place she knew was behind her. An unknown chasm stretched before her, and it wasn't a case of jumping off. She was being pushed.

Catherine let out a sharp gasp. For the first time since her mother's death, for the first and only time in her life, her courage deserted her. 'No. Don't leave me.'

Conceptua waved but did not look back.

'I have to go,' she shouted over her shoulder. 'Be a good girl. I'm sure your aunt will love you very much.' Head bent and her backside fluid, she waddled back to the station with short, swift steps.

Catherine wasn't sure of any such thing. Her bottom lip trembled and she suddenly wanted to pee. She'd been sent away from everything and everyone she had ever known. Conceptua might not be the most beautiful or loving of women, but she'd been a fixed point in her life, part of a daily routine like breakfast, lunch and dinner. Now she was entering a different world far away from Porto and the luxurious surroundings of the Castile Villanova. Oh, how she wished she were back there.

Conceptua disappeared from view. Catherine stared at the curved and empty archway of the station entrance. She was now alone.

Her knuckles turned white as she gripped the bar running along the front of the seat. Her eyes remained fixed on the station. She would remember this day. She would remember this time and, at some point, she would return to the Castile Villanova.

Logic far beyond her years convinced her that her father would never allow her to return. But she wouldn't go back there on his terms. She would go back on her own. Regaining the place she loved would be up to her. Gritting her teeth, she stared straight ahead. The boy turned the horse away from the station and the town. Adults ran the world. The past was dead and no matter how hurt she felt she had to be brave and face whatever came next.

Thoughts of home filled her mind as she fixed her gaze somewhere between the horse's ears. Her father had married someone else.

Catherine was helpless to do anything about it, at least, not yet. The sun was bright. The road shone and the bells on the horse's harness glittered like stars and made her blink. She sat stiffly, weighed down by her thoughts. Tired from the journey and hot in the turquoise hat and coat, her head fell on to the boy's shoulder and she slept.

In her dreams she was home again and her parents were watching her play whilst they sipped rosé in the shade of a lemon tree.

A sharp dig in her ribs roused her from a warm, pink-faced sleep. She blinked as she looked into his face. In a single instant, and quite unconsciously, she stored his features in her memory. The colour of his eyes was like liquid chocolate. His nose was straight and his mouth was wide and he was smiling again. *Did he always smile?* Although at first his hair appeared dark, sunlight picked out streaks of fiery red.

'Come on. Wake up. My arm has gone numb.' Although he spoke brusquely, the smile remained.

Catherine blinked herself awake and straightened, rolling her head from side to side to alleviate the crick in her neck.

'Take off your coat. It is too thick for here,' he said. 'Do you think you are in England?'

Catherine looked around her. Despite being conversant in the language, she'd never been to England but couldn't imagine it looking like this.

The town was left far behind in the valley, yet she could still see it, a patchwork of tiled roofs between heaped green terraces and the sparkling river.

They'd climbed very high, the road dusty and winding between tiered terraces of vines sloping from the peak down to the valley floor. There was suddenly a huge noise, like thunder but louder and soon over.

'Don't worry,' said the boy, grinning into her worried face. 'It is just a blast.'

She didn't ask what he meant. Asking questions was a waste of time. No one ever answered her.

The boy misinterpreted her silence. He presumed she was too frightened to ask questions so went out of his way to explain.

'The rock is being blasted to make new terraces for new vines. They use dynamite,' he said and looked proud that he knew so much.

Catherine looked at the brown hands that so deftly handled the reins. Her gaze wandered up his arms and perceived the adolescent contours slowly growing into muscles.

'My name is Francisco,' he said, his voice crackling with the first signs of manhood. 'What's yours? It's best you tell me now. We are going to know each other a great deal. I do a lot of work for your aunt.'

She was taken aback. When was the last time anyone had

asked *her* a question? For a moment she considered being petulant, but something about his open smile made her change her mind.

'Catherine. Catherine Shellard – Rodriguez,' she corrected, vowing never to use the Shellard name again.

'Right,' he said, his chest expanding as he pulled the tired horse to a standstill, 'now we know each other's names, we can become friends and perhaps I can tell you with no fear of rebuke that you have a very red face. I think you should take your coat off.'

Catherine raised her fingers to her buttons, then stopped and stared at him blankly.

'What's the matter?'

'I've never unbuttoned my own coat before.'

Francisco's jaw dropped. He stared at her as though she were a creature from another world.

Catherine felt her face getting redder, not just from the heat, but because she was embarrassed.

Francisco's look was full of pity. 'Do you want me to unfasten them for you?'

As Catherine considered his offer the reality of her situation began to make itself clear. In the past she had relied on Conceptua to dress her. Now Conceptua was gone it didn't make sense to rely on anyone else to do things for her. She had to learn how to do things for herself if she was ever to achieve her dream.

'I don't need *anyone* to unfasten them. I will unfasten them myself.' She began doing so, sliding the velvet-covered buttons out from the holes.

'All right,' he said, pulled on the brake at a level spot on the uphill climb, and leapt on to the road. 'I won't be a minute.'

He ran off behind a pile of rocks that hid him from view. By the time he came back, her coat was off.

'Do you need to go?' he asked her.

Realizing what he meant, she stared at him. Was he really meaning that she had to relieve herself here? Behind a rock?

He seemed to catch the drift of her thoughts. 'There is no privy nor bathroom out here and we have a long way to go. Likely we will not reach our destination until sunset and it's a fair climb still. Do you want to go or not?'

The thought of waiting until sunset was out of the question.

The urgency of her need overrode modesty. He attempted to lift her down.

She hit his hands away. 'No, I want to get down by myself.'

Adjusting might not be easy, but Catherine was determined to do things without a servant to do it for her.

Hidden behind the rock, she found the buttons on her drawers and did what she had to do. After that, she cried, her arm bent against the rock, her head resting on her arm. By the time she emerged from behind the rock, she'd wiped the wetness from her face.

The boy was at the horse's head allowing it to tear at a patch of grass. He glanced up at her then lowered his eyes to what the horse was doing – as though it were more compelling. 'Do you also wish to climb up by yourself?' he asked her.

'Of course.'

Unencumbered by her coat and hat, she tucked up her skirt and counted to three in her mind. One good push and she was back on board.

The boy climbed up beside her. He didn't immediately urge the horse forward, but sat gazing around him, almost as though he were seeing this scene for the very first time.

He let out a deep sigh. 'You know, I am always glad when I get back up here away from the valley. It's cooler, greener and,' he said, pausing to take a deep breath, 'breathing is like drinking water from a mountain stream; cool, fresh and totally free of the dust and dirt of the city.'

Catherine took in the same scene he was seeing. The road curved up ahead of them where the branches of almond trees threw speckled shade on to the road. To their right fruit trees and vineyards fell to the valley and the river below.

The countryside was breathtaking, so wouldn't the house also be imposing? The image of Castile Villanova was clear and crisp in her mind; she could almost hear its tinkling fountains, smell the rich earth of its flower beds and hear her footsteps echoing amongst its ancient tapestries and marble floors. Nothing could be as wonderful as that particular house. All the same, she was mildly curious.

'Is my aunt's house very big?'

Francisco shrugged. 'Big enough.'

What did he mean by that? She wanted to ask him, but did not want to appear unduly frightened or stupid. She wanted to ask him about servants. Her mother had had servants. Did her great-aunt have servants?

She decided not to ask. In a way she'd allowed him to know too much about her. She didn't want to expose her fears in case he asked more about her mother, about her death. He might also have heard gossip and might mention the word 'bastard'. And this great-aunt that she would hate; perhaps if she displayed her hatred very much, she would be sent back to her father. As the horse trotted amiably onwards, she planned how she would behave.

Her reticence to declare more of herself to Francisco paid off. The boy – 'the boy' was how she would forever think of him – seemed refreshed by their stop. His tongue was especially refreshed. By the time they reached her great-aunt's house, she knew everything there was to know about Francisco Nicklau. His father owned one of the best vineyards in the region, one famous for declaring more good vintages than any other. He was the only son, had four sisters and his love for the Douro Valley glowed in his face.

'Your great-aunt has a farmhouse on our land. It too used to be a *quinta*, but was bought by my grandfather many years ago and rented to your aunt. Your aunt has no interest in wine. She makes a living in some other way.' He shrugged. 'I do not know. No one does, but she goes travelling a lot. Perhaps that is when she makes her money, though I wouldn't dare ask her. No one would dare.'

Catherine turned pale at the thought of this unseen dragon and made him laugh.

'She is not that bad,' he said, still amused by her expression. 'Not everyone thinks she is a giant ogre. I don't.'

Catherine's determination to be less than convivial was melting away. She wondered what sort of woman her great-aunt was that no one dared asked her a question, not because they wouldn't get an answer, but because they were terrified of her.

As the sun began to dip behind the highest granite hilltop, Catherine grew colder. She put her coat and hat back on, but no matter how tightly she buttoned it, she couldn't stop shivering. The thought of meeting her mother's aunt filled her with dread.

One more bend in the road, one more sway of the cart, and

she saw her new home. The farmhouse had a red tiled roof, was long and low and, because of the colour of the stone that formed its walls, seemed to be part of the landscape. The air around it smelled of things growing, breathing gently in the night air, spicing the darkness with sweetness.

Aunt Lopa heard the horse's neigh and the clop of hooves. The rough wooden door flew open and crashed against the wall. A blaze of light fell out from within, then was gone, blocked by a giant of a woman who took just three strides across the yard before swooping Catherine from the cart and into her arms.

'Child,' she cried.

Catherine found herself suffocating beneath a shower of kisses, tightly clasped to Aunt Lopa's wide but flat chest. Her feet were swept a foot from the ground.

'Did the boy look after you?' asked her mother's aunt in a loud, booming voice.

'Yes.'

Catherine kept her voice small. All thoughts of being difficult had totally dissolved into thin air. She tried to take in as much as she could about Aunt Lopa; she even dared look up into the square, bluff face. The brown eyes were hooded, her skin was ruddy and healthy, the complexion of someone used to an outdoor life. There was nothing about her looks to fear, but Francisco's comments had found fertile ground. Aunt Lopa was of ogre proportions, but had a kind face.

In a brief moment of panic, the thought of Francisco leaving was suddenly too much to bear.

She managed to turn her head away from Aunt Lopa's less than generous bosom in time to see the horse being turned away. 'Francisco?'

He stopped and turned. She savoured the last of his smile before he disappeared into the darkness.

An arm as heavy as a sack of corn was thrown across her back. 'You must be tired. Starving. Thirsty too. Come. Into the house.'

Her mother's aunt crooned an unrecognizable tune as they entered the airy room that served as eating, washing and living area in the house of Lopa Rodriguez, the most wonderful woman Catherine would ever meet in her life. But Catherine didn't know that yet.

The girl who had been used to a former palace now took in the details of a humble farmhouse. The walls were of rough plaster and appeared freshly painted. A series of cracks ran from floor to ceiling.

The furniture was basic and rustic, though of good quality. There was a pine table and five mismatched chairs, one of which was a rocking chair. A pile of what looked like knitting sat on the table in front of it. Two ornate armchairs with cabriole legs together with a three-legged stool jostled for space in front of a fireplace. The fireplace took up one corner, its flue cutting off the angle of the corner all the way to the roof. To the side of the fireplace was a pot hanging on a tripod, a spit for roasting meat and the metal door of the bread oven. Near the fireplace was a red curtain interwoven with bright yellows, oranges and greens.

'That's the door to my room,' said Aunt Lopa, drawing back the curtain to reveal a simple wooden bed, a woven rug and an ebony crucifix hanging on the wall.

'Your room's up there,' Aunt Lopa added, her big body having a rolling gait as she ambled over to where a wooden ladder disappeared through a hole in the ceiling.

Catherine's eyes grew large at the sight of the ladder. The whole farmhouse would have fitted into the stables at Castile Villanova. At her old home the smell of her mother's perfume, beeswax and flowers had predominated in the spacious rooms full of expensive furniture collected through the ages. Here the smell of fresh bread mingled with that of animal feed and one or two animals themselves. A black cat lay curled up on one of the handsome chairs. Its kittens lay mewling in the other.

'It'll be different to what you're used to,' said Aunt Lopa as though she'd read her mind. 'But get used to it you will.' Her bold expression softened along with her voice. 'But at least you're wanted here.' With a sniff that could have been a stifled sob, she ruffled Catherine's scalp with a meaty hand, before turning away. 'Supper first. Then bedding down.'

She was fed a hearty rabbit stew washed down with a glass of milk like none she had ever tasted.

'I keep my own goats,' said the big woman, having noted Catherine wolfing down the milk.

Aunt Lopa stood over her as she ate, her fists resting on

her ample hips. In looks at least she was nothing like Leonora, Catherine's mother. Her voice too was different, almost masculine in its strength.

'Drink. Grow big and strong. We'll not have you growing up like your mother. Stick of a girl. Weak,' she finally said, shaking her head as she turned away. 'Weak and silly. Damn that man. Damn all men. Glad I never got saddled with one.' She wiped the corner of her eye.

'Dust,' she said, noticing that Catherine had seen her do it. 'I've got dust in my eye.'

Catherine pretended to believe her and turned back to the food. It was all she'd had since leaving Porto, and even then she hadn't eaten much. In fact she'd hardly eaten anything since her mother's death. She managed to finish the whole dishful.

Aunt Lopa's face glowed with joy. 'Do you like the stew? Would you like more milk?'

Catherine nodded. Her great-aunt had an abrupt way of speaking that must frighten some people. Catherine saw through the bluff exterior, the broad body, the strong face crowned with a head of iron-grey hair streaked with pure white wings at the temples. She wore it in a long plait down her back that swung like a rope when she walked. Her skirt was woven out of the same stuff as the curtain. Her blouse was embroidered like that of a gypsy.

Aunt Lopa settled herself in the rocking chair. Once it was pulled away from the table, Catherine could see how splendid it was, far too splendid for the simple surroundings. It had carved lion heads on the arms with red tongues and green eyes.

'Eat,' Aunt Lopa ordered, and was satisfied that Catherine did the rustic fare justice, eating a second bowl of stew.

As she ate the nourishing and tasty food, Catherine took in both her great-aunt and her surroundings. Aunt Lopa was taller than most men, and her shoulders were wide enough to fill a doorway. She was angular, her hands were big and she took long strides when she walked. Her dress was plain and clean, gathered at the waist and stopped just short of her ankles. Her shoes were made of wood and had metal tips on the toes. In time Catherine would recognize these as clogs.

Once she'd got used to the animal smells, she detected the smell of fresh hay and the sweetness of grapes, almonds and apple logs. A cow lowed from a nearby bier. Catherine imagined a cock would crow and chickens would cackle in the morning.

Aunt Lopa stifled a huge yawn. 'Tomorrow, Francisco will show you around. You'll meet his family. Tonight you sleep in your bed up in the roof.' She pointed again to the narrow wooden ladder made of rough tree branches, the bark still peeling like short, grey ribbons. 'Francisco made your bed. I don't go up there. Would get stuck if I did.'

Catherine eyed the ladder and the opening through which it disappeared.

'It's your job to clean and look after the room yourself; to change the bedding. And put your own things away. No servants here. No mother to run around after you . . .'

It was the longest sentence Lopa had uttered. It was also the one that finally broke through Catherine's iron resolve.

'My mother's dead! My father killed her!'

Lopa raised her eyes. Her strong expression melted away and her face was almost beautiful. There were tears in her eyes. Her voice moderated. 'Catherine, forget I said that. I wasn't thinking. I'm used to being alone. I forget how I should speak. I'm nothing but an old fool.'

Catherine put down her spoon. She held her head to one side and turned cool, resolute eyes on to her great-aunt's ruddy face. 'He married someone else and sent me away. But I'll live there again one day, you just see if I don't.'

Aunt Lopa's stern expression relaxed into a sadness seemingly centred on her eyes.

She hesitated, as though considering carefully what she should say.

'I think you will,' she said softly. 'And with all my heart, I hope that you do. God bless you, child.'

Now it was Catherine who didn't know what to say. She recalled her plan to hate Aunt Lopa. Not once had she been hateful to this woman, and all that she'd received from her was kindness.

The pain of losing her mother was still with her. So was the pain of being expelled from her home. No, the farmhouse was nothing like Castile Villanova, but it had a warmth as tactile as her mother's loving arms. There were no servants, but on the journey here she had done some simple things for herself. Surely looking after her own room would be simple too. And it would be her private place, her own domain. 'I think I will quite enjoy making my own bed.'

Aunt Lopa looked at her with one eye closed as if she could weigh her worth better that way.

'Learning to shift for yourself will make you strong. Your mother was never strong. Beautiful, but not strong.' Her expression turned hard. 'Best to make your own way in the world and set yourself goals. Never count on a man to feather your bed. He'll let you down.' Her eyes seemed suddenly to darken as though a worrying thought had crossed her mind. 'With those eyes you'll need to be wary of men. I see passion in your eyes, just as I did in your mother's. But I also see self-awareness. Strikes me you'll always be the one driving the cart.'

Catherine thought she knew what she meant. 'You mean I'll always be in charge. Not like my mother. My father was in charge, wasn't he?'

Aunt Lopa swiped at a tear that threatened to run down her cheek. She nodded, overcome by what her great-niece had just said. 'I will try to make you happy here.'

Two hours later, after helping her great-aunt to clear away and unpacking her things, Catherine lay in her bed beneath a patchwork quilt, her head on cotton pillowcases that were prettily trimmed with crocheted lace. The bed was on a level with a window that jutted out through the eaves. She had the whole of the night sky to look and wonder at. The stars fell like a waterfall on to the blue and black of the trees, hills and acres of vineyards. Here and there a light blinked in the darkness. It was like sleeping outside, without walls.

Just as her eyes began to close, she heard a sound. Rising on one elbow she looked out on to the yard where it met the trees and the vegetation clustered around their roots.

She heard her great-aunt making a cooing sound and saw her taking big but cautious steps towards the bushes. The foliage around the trees seemed to move forward on legs. Eyes flashed yellow, caught by moonlight. Three long, low figures emerged. Aunt Lopa had dogs? She hadn't seen them earlier. She would ask her about them tomorrow. Her eyes closed and

she was soon asleep so did not see the shadows move back
into the trees or hear them howl as they returned to the hills
and sang to the rising moon.

Six

'*Fine Lady* will be leaving on the tide in four hours, sir.'
      William Shellard acknowledged the captain with a
brusque nod, but felt the captain's questioning gaze.

'I wanted to be early. It helps me gain my sea legs.'

His explanation for being early was utter rubbish. He'd never
experienced seasickness; in fact he'd always loved the roll of
the ship, the chopping of the bow through the Bay of Biscay.

The captain's disquiet hadn't exactly gone away; masters
of merchant vessels were always uneasy when ships' owners
were on board. The shorter the duration of their presence, the
better as far as they were concerned.

'Carry on, Captain Durham. I'll keep out of your way,'
William added.

The comment was enough to further alleviate the captain's
nervousness. Touching his cap in a rudimentary salute, he
went off to make final preparations for leaving.

In normal circumstances, William might have accompanied
him, taking note of what was going on. On the other hand,
he might have breathed an audible sigh of relief at being left
alone to enjoy the view.

However, he did none of these things. Instead the tension
he'd been experiencing all day intensified. Every muscle in
his body seemed to be stretched to breaking point and he
gripped the ship's rail as though with one squeeze he could
break it in half.

His thoughts were in turmoil. At the centre of them was
Leonora's lovely face.

But I did write, he reminded himself.

So had she read the letter? There was no alternative but to

accept that he still loved her – assuming she had actually received the letter.

He eyed the bustling quay, heard the rattling of trams and watched as barrels were offloaded from the next vessel – this one belonging to Harveys, the famous sherry house.

He became aware that someone was shouting his name.

'William!'

He took his time seeking out whoever it was.

'William! Over here!'

The upturned face of Robert Arthur Freeman shone with bonhomie and an over-infusion of strong spirits. He was not alone. Two girls barely out of school hung from each arm, their cheeks cherry red, their skirts barely reaching their knees.

William raised a hand in acknowledgement and managed a smile. 'Freeman. I see you are well.'

He trained his eyes not to divert to the whores but kept them fixed on Robert's glossy face.

'Robustly so,' beamed Robert. 'And how is your lady wife, the beautiful Diana?'

'Well enough.'

It was not in his nature to border on the rude, but Robert Arthur Freeman left a bad taste in his mouth.

Breeding and wealth do not necessarily a gentleman make. He remembered his mother bequeathing him that particular expression. Like William she'd been quiet, well mannered but gifted with great insight. He wished she'd been around when he'd fallen in love with Leonora. How would she have advised him?

He brushed the thought aside. She was long dead, ten years before their father. He missed her. He always would.

Whether Freeman had cottoned on to his rudeness, he couldn't tell and what's more, he didn't care. If the state of the man was anything to go by, he'd be hard pushed to know what day it was. In time the fortune left to him would have gone on drink and loose women; an ignominious end for what had once been a respected family name.

'Well, cheerio! Bon voyage,' Freeman shouted before moving on, his whores clinging to his arm and his coat pocket. Whatever was in there would be long gone by the time he reached his front door, but William was in no mood to warn him. There were some people he disliked intensely and Robert Arthur Freeman was one of them.

The tension he'd been experiencing returned with a vengeance at the mention of Diana. Fearing she might insist on coming with him on this trip, he had waited until she was away on one of her shopping days in Bath. As well as visiting her dressmaker, she also visited her sister while she was there. It was too good an opportunity to miss. She'd been gone less than half an hour before he'd grabbed the bag he'd had packed the night before and left her a scribbled note. A coward's way out, but he didn't regret it. Solitude would help him forgive himself for lacking the courage to face her years ago. All he hoped now was that he could find her again. He'd start at Castile Villanova.

Diana threw back her head and closed her eyes. She was sitting in front of the dressing-table mirror in a London hotel wearing nothing but a string of pink pearls.

Today, the fourth Thursday of the month, was her favourite day; the day when she excused herself from the boring house she shared with her uptight husband, saying she was going on a shopping trip. And visiting her sister, of course. None of it was true, but telling lies was worth it for what she was presently experiencing.

Her shorn hair tickled the nape of her neck along with Walter's thumbs while his fingers massaged her shoulders. This was why she looked forward so much to the fourth Thursday of the month, and today there was no rush to get home. But there was more, much more that she couldn't wait to share with her brother-in-law. She held on to the hope that he would fall in with her plans, but with Walter it was difficult to tell. All she had was hope.

'William's away and, better still, so is my sister. We've got the cottage all week. Isn't that just divine?'

Her eyes flashed open, meeting Walter's via the mirror.

'I can't do that, sweet thing,' he said to her. 'I've got a business to run.'

Diana's lips formed a tight moue. 'Oh, sweetie,' she whined. 'Can't you leave things to old man Seth?'

'No.' Without pause, Walter's hands ran down her upper arms then across to her breasts and the fine pair of dark aureoles surrounding her nipples. His touch sent her blood racing.

'Darling, you do that so well,' she breathed.

An amused smile came to Walter's wide mouth. 'Better than my brother?'

She moaned a favourable response.

Perhaps snatched moments were better than prolonged domestic bliss, she thought. Snatched moments with Walter certainly were.

She'd loved Walter since she was sixteen. He was the man who'd taken her virginity. Not once had she regretted this fact and the magic of the moment had stayed with her. She'd do anything for him, and had even married his brother at his request. Poor William. He'd never forgiven her. She couldn't tell whether he'd ever forgiven his brother. Their relationship was strangely complex; the more dominant being *allowed* to be so – at least that was how it seemed to her.

She was disappointed that Walter couldn't stay the whole week. Walter had told her that his marriage to Ellen was only a business transaction and that in time she'd probably realize that and insist on a separation. 'And that is when we'll be together,' she'd cooed into his ear.

'It's possible,' he'd responded. It was hardly a promise, but Diana chose to believe that it was.

The fact wasn't lost on her that Walter hadn't mentioned his wife as his reason for turning her offer down. But that was Walter; he had his priorities and first and foremost was making money.

Seven

The hot June sun ebbed into July then August; warm months when bees buzzed lazily over the idle landscape. Even before the sun was at its zenith the countryside looked unreal. Waves of heat rippled the horizon, and old and young folk slumbered in the shade, not venturing out until the trees cast evening shadows. September changed all that. The harvest

months saw the ripening of the grapes and a quickening pace
of life in the *quintas* and towns along the Douro Valley.

Catherine too had ripened. Her complexion had more colour
than it used to have and her legs and arms were as brown as
her great-aunt's and Francisco's. The ringlets that had once
been so rigidly curled around her nurse's finger and fixed with
sugar water, were now wild and untamed, though still glossy.

To a casual observer it would appear she'd got over her
change in circumstances. But the old life was still alive in her
mind. Each night before snuggling down in her bed beneath
the creaking roof, she knelt on the bare floorboards and said
a prayer for her mother's soul. She never included her father
in her prayers. He was one part of her past she preferred to
forget.

Thanks to the fresh air and good food, Catherine grew out
of her clothes. Aunt Lopa lengthened and let out seams on
plain dresses. She eyed the more elaborate ones of lace and
satin with outright disapproval.

'Too fancy for these parts anyway,' stated Aunt Lopa, though
she did keep one or two good dresses. After taking down the
hem and removing the over-abundance of lace and bows, she
declared them fit for Sundays. 'Use your old cotton ones for
running around in.'

Running around consisted of helping out in the fields,
crushing the grapes underfoot to produce wine for local
consumption. The grapes reserved for port – hopefully of a
fine vintage – were squeezed by mechanical presses, though
some of the older estates still kept the treading tradition alive.

Under her great-aunt's skilled instruction, Catherine became
adept at crochet, sewing and knitting. She also learned how
to make goat's cheese which she sold from her great-aunt's
stall at the local market. Aunt Lopa, blessed with a determination that this girl would survive in a hostile world, allowed
her to keep the money she made.

'Money makes money,' she told her. 'Never forget that.'

Catherine knew she would not.

In the course of that first, hot summer, Francisco Nicklau
became Catherine's friend. They ate bread and cheese together
at midday in the vineyard and in the evening he'd sometimes
come back with her to Aunt Lopa's, devouring the thick soups
and spiced rabbit legs, or whatever other food her great-aunt

put in front of him. After that they would sometimes sit outside staring up at the stars until Aunt Lopa demanded he go home.

'Have you no home to go to?' There was a scowl on her lips but her eyes danced with amusement, the corners crinkled as though holding it all in.

Nothing could dampen Francisco's warm amiability. Every day that came, Catherine would find herself looking forward to seeing that smile which, like the sunrise, was a reaffirmation of a new day.

She was drawn to him, thought she loved him, except for one niggling thing that she couldn't quite come to terms with. Francisco disapproved of 'fallen' women. Aunt Lopa said he got it from his mother.

'A sanctimonious old bat,' she said, not caring if Francisco overheard her.

It was one night in particular when his attitude particularly hurt her.

'That star is my mother,' said Catherine on one especially clear evening as they sat watching the sun go down and the stars spill on to the sky. 'See how bright it is? That's her soul,' she went on. 'She's turned into a star. That's what happens to people's souls when they die.'

She was surprised by Francisco's look of disbelief.

'Well, that depends,' he said. 'A person has to die in a state of grace before they can go to heaven, and your mother . . .' His voice petered out, not just because he was unnerved by such large beautiful eyes, but because he was repeating gossip that should not be repeated – especially to her.

Catherine turned abruptly. She detected no malice in his eyes, but what he said had confused her. 'What is this state of grace?'

This was one of those rare occasions when Francisco looked serious. He began fidgeting, which he didn't normally do until it was time to go. As yet it wasn't quite time.

'Evil people do not go to heaven. That was all I meant,' he said, diligently avoiding eye contact. 'And your mother was not an evil person, in fact not even nasty I should think. Not if she was like you, that is.'

If she noticed he was babbling, Catherine did not mention it, though the fact that his familiar smile was absent did unnerve her.

'Why are you sad?' she asked him.

Sure that the moment of awkwardness was over, his teeth flashed white. The smile was back.

'It is almost the end of September and we will not see each other for a while.'

Looking alarmed, she shook her head at him. 'I'm not going anywhere. I'll be here.'

Francisco frowned through his amiable expression. 'Then you'll be here all by yourself. Lopa Rodriguez goes travelling in the winter. The house is locked up. You can't stay here all alone.'

Catherine looked away, fixing her eyes back on the single bright star. She didn't want him to be right. This place was her bolt-hole, a little piece of heaven in a world she no longer trusted. If he was right and she couldn't stay here alone, what would happen to her?

Fear made her bridle with anger. 'I think you should go before the wolves eat you,' she said to Francisco.

He got to his feet, his eyes darting along the trees around the edge of the yard. 'Have you seen them?' He sounded excited. 'Gossip is that Aunt Lopa *does* feed the wolves. But then others say it's not true, that there are no wolves left around here. None at all.'

'Yes there are.' Catherine also got to her feet. 'But you're not going to see them. I don't want you to see them. Neither does Aunt Lopa. She won't let you! Your mother's a liar!'

Her small face was screwed up. Her voice was as loud as she could make it.

Francisco's face creased with anger. 'No she is not! She goes to church more than anyone else around here.'

'Then your mother's a sanctimonious old bat!' Catherine relished the hurt on his face. 'My Aunt Lopa said so,' she added, feeling an inner glow of satisfaction.

It was an acrimonious end to a perfect evening. He accompanied her from the goat enclosure to the farmhouse, insisting she was too young to be out by herself. 'You will be frightened,' he insisted with boyish bravado.

Now it is you who will be frightened, Catherine told herself as she watched him swing his lithe frame towards the packed mud track that passed for a road in these parts.

But he wasn't. He was whistling; his corduroy cap perched

jauntily on one side of his head. She thought how brave he looked, unafraid of whatever lurked in the darkness.

Through prayer that night she impressed on God just how wonderful her mother had been. 'Not wicked, not even nasty,' she said, remembering what Francisco had said. 'She was good. Very good. Please look after her.'

Crying softly into her pillow soon sent her to sleep, so she didn't hear Aunt Lopa calling to the wolves or see their dark forms emerge from the shadows. Neither did she hear her great-aunt tell them that the time was coming when she had to go away and that there would be no one here to feed them until Christmas.

Eight

A delaide Court overlooked the River Avon from its spot high on the Avon Gorge in the old seaport of Bristol. From here it was possible to watch the tide go in and out along with vessels from all over the world. Sir Walter's home was a place apart from the rest of the city. A high wall protected it on one side, the steep cliffs of the gorge on the other. No one entered its ornate gateway unless invited to.

The inside of Adelaide Court was as opulent as its exterior. Onyx pillars the colour of dark honey held aloft a creamy high ceiling in the reception hall. A frieze of dark honey, red and dark green separated the walls from the ceiling.

The sitting room was rich with gilt, and with interesting and valuable furniture commissioned or bought over the last hundred years.

The dining room was of the same ilk. Ruby-red wallpaper gave it a rich feel, perfectly suited to wining, dining and good conversation. No one should feel cold sitting at the long Sheraton-style dining table.

Walter Shellard sat at the head of the table and exchanged a quick smile with his wife before rising to his feet.

He used a teaspoon and a wine glass to gain his guests' attention. The conversation ceased. Some of these people depended on Walter for their livelihood. They tended to adhere to his wishes.

'Ladies and gentlemen! Tonight it gives me great pleasure to announce that my darling wife – sorry – that my wife and I, are expecting a very great treasure. The new addition to our family should arrive before next May.'

Cries of 'good luck' and frenzied hand-clapping followed.

In response to such exuberance, Walter took his wife's hand and kissed it. 'I'm the happiest man in the world,' he said, his eyes meeting hers.

'And I'm the happiest woman,' returned Ellen.

She was telling the truth. She still counted herself as being very lucky to have met and married such a man as Sir Walter Shellard.

The Lord Mayor's wife leaned across and touched her hand. 'You have a very fine house, my dear.'

'Thank you.'

'I believe you have another house in Portugal.'

Ellen nodded. 'That's quite right. It's a beautiful place. It's been in Walter's family for some time.' A faraway look came instantly to her eyes. 'I love Castile Villanova – almost as much as Walter does. It's so beautiful. So peaceful. I'm thinking of staying there until the baby is born.'

Ellen thought of what she had said. It was indeed true that her favourite times were when they were at Castile Villanova. Walter seemed less distracted there and closer to the earth in a strange, husband kind of way.

He was rarely at home when they were living in England, pulled hither and thither by business appointments – at least, that was what he told her. Business, business, business. Everything revolved around the wine trade.

Ellen took a sip of elderberry wine. Someone had told her it was good for pregnant women.

'It was a good evening,' he said when they were alone later.

'Very good,' Ellen responded as she peeled her satin evening gloves from her arms. 'The Lord Mayor's wife complimented me on our beautiful house and asked me about Castile Villanova. I told her I was going there to await the birth of the baby.'

'I insist,' said Walter, whose idea it had been.

'But you won't be there, darling,' said Ellen, leaning forward and reaching for him with a long, graceful hand. 'Will you visit?'

'Yes. When I can. Business calls.'

Ellen sighed. 'Oh, darling. At times I feel more like a mistress than a wife,' she teased.

'You have nothing to complain about, my darling Ellen. You have everything money can buy. Accept your lot in life and be grateful. I have it in mind to expand into property in a bigger way, so there will be times when I'll be away for quite long periods. And before you say it, no, you are in a delicate condition. I couldn't possibly take you with me.'

'But I could come. I'm strong as a horse,' she retorted. She hated being away from him for longer than a day, two at the most.

Walter was insistent. 'You're my wife and you'll do as I say. No travelling for you until my son and heir is at least a year old. Is that clear?'

'Who's to say that the child will be a boy? It might be a girl.'

He turned swiftly, his expression darkening. He raised his arm and pointed a finger at her, almost accusingly. 'I want a son. Is that clear?'

She nodded, unsure whether he was being serious. She stuck her neck out and managed to have the last word. 'What will be, will be.'

He was away on business for a week after that. Strangely enough, she was almost relieved. His behaviour had unnerved her. For some reason, possibly pure naïvety, she had presumed the Walter she married would act the same for ever and ever; an eternal honeymoon, his business interests and colleagues held at a distance.

'You're in love with your business,' she said to him once.

He'd looked at her silently for a moment, his face very still as though every cell in his body was being brought into play.

'No,' he said his gaze unblinking and steady. 'I'm in love with power. At the end of my life I want people to say that I was a powerful man and that I left behind a larger business than I was left by my father. And I will do that. "May the best man win" is a saying I take very seriously. I will always win, my dear. Never doubt that. I will always win because I'm the best there is.'

'Nonsense,' she said laughingly. 'At some point in your life you will be beaten by someone more ruthless, more powerful.'

He sneered, then laughed out loud. 'They would have to be well motivated to better me.'

'By an emotion?' she asked.

'By anything.'

'How about revenge,' she said plucking the word out of thin air, for no reason at all except that it was there.

He laughed again. 'He would have to be very dedicated to his cause. It wouldn't be my brother, that's for sure. He wouldn't dare come up against me – he takes after our mother.'

'Mothers can be quite powerful and even vengeful,' Ellen added. 'Hell hath no fury like a woman scorned. Is there some woman you may have wronged in the past who might be vengeful?'

His laughter melted away and a strange, questioning look darted across his eyes. What she had once interpreted as strength now manifested itself as ruthlessness.

'No. It won't happen.'

The look on his face stayed with her. It was as if a curtain had been drawn. The Walter she'd married did not wear his heart – or his thoughts – on his sleeve. They were sometimes deeply buried. She assured herself she would dig them out. In the meantime she would be the good wife and support him in all he did. This child would be a first for both of them and likely to bring them closer together. This was what she thought, though later on she wasn't quite so sure.

Nine

'Not a word! Not a word from any of you.'

Serge, the butler, had flinty eyes that fixed each servant with a gaze you could knock sparks off. They were lined up in front of the main entrance. They had been warned how to behave, what to say and what not to say.

'I know what a lot of gossips you are,' snarled Serge as he walked the line, glaring intermittently into any face he thought showed defiance or was too honest to lie.

No one dared meet his gaze. Some stared straight ahead. Some lowered their lids and looked at their shoes or a shady patch where a lizard paused before running for cover.

William thanked Serge for his welcome, though he only glanced at the thin features, the hooked nose and ramrod straightness. It had been a long time since he'd visited his family's Portuguese home, though he'd always loved this place.

'You are always welcome to come and stay,' he'd said and sounded sincere enough. But William knew his brother well. He'd had a certain look in his eyes when he'd said it, almost as though he were challenging him to visit. While Leonora was in residence his presence was not welcome at all.

'I think it's time I visited Castile Villanova. It's been a long time. I'll check on our bodega while I'm there. I might even take another look at that vineyard I noticed on my last visit. It was owned by an independent, if I remember rightly.'

He caught the look of surprise on his brother's face. It was only to be expected. On previous business visits, he'd stayed in a hotel.

'I'll send a telegram,' Walter had said.

'Thank you. And if you could explain to Diana. I feel a cad going off like this and leaving her only a note.'

'You're my brother,' Walter had said, slapping him on the shoulder and giving him that slow, controlled smile. 'I'm sure I can take a little time to tell my sister-in-law where you are. Business is business.'

Business is business. Yes, thought William with a bitter smile. He would take time to look over the bodegas and the vineyards while he was here. He'd told Walter that was his reason for coming, and it had been so long. But ultimately, he had another quest. He wanted to know Leonora's where-abouts. He wanted to be in this lovely place where she had lived, albeit as his brother's mistress.

William took his time admiring the fine lines of the Castile Villanova. Like his brother he adored the place. How well he remembered these ancient walls, the shuttered windows prom-ising shade from the summer sun. He looked up at the roof, the castellated embellishments like honeycomb cut-outs

against a crisp blue sky. He breathed in the smell of warmth,
of herbs and fruit and the dark, rich earth. He remembered a
rose garden having been planted to the north west of the house
where the shade was at its deepest and the sun weakest. His
mother had planted that garden; compensation for a life lived
in the shadow of an ambitious and powerful man. Lacking
her husband's affection, she had spent most of her time there,
rarely leaving it towards the end of her life, talking to the
flowers as if they were the love of her life.

William jerked himself out of his memories. 'Is my room
ready?'

A stupid question; of course it was. Serge was a stick of a
man, not likeable but efficient for all that.

'In the west wing,' said Serge. 'I will take you there myself.'

'The west wing,' William repeated, sounding surprised.
'When Father was alive we were always housed in the east
wing.'

'That is over the kitchen,' said Serge. 'The west wing is
better.'

'Of course. The setting sun.'

It was late afternoon and already the sun was casting indigo
shadows over the dark leaves of the lemon trees that rustled
beneath his balcony. The room was spacious having its own
settee and armchairs besides a magnificent bed of polished
mahogany. A maritime painting of huge proportions hung over
the fireplace. As a boy William had always loved this painting.
It depicted the defeat of the Turkish Armada by Don Juan of
Austria in the sixteenth century. The flags of the Knights of
St John trailed across a turquoise sea from the battling galleys.
This room was most definitely a man's room and had belonged
to his father. He felt some surprise at Walter letting him use
it, presuming he would have preferred to keep it for himself.
But there again, he thought. The Castile Villanova belonged
to Walter. It was his to do with as he wished. William envied
him.

'Will you require me to run a bath?' asked Serge, interrupting his thoughts.

William nodded, his eyes fixed on the sunlight spearing
through the trees, lengthening as the sun prepared to set.
'Serge,' he said suddenly. 'Were you here on the day Leonora
Rodriguez left?'

Because the glorious sunset held William's gaze, he did not notice the closed look descend in Serge's eyes or the tightening of his lantern jaw. 'It was my day off, I think.'

'I see,' said William quietly. 'Leave my bath. I'll run it myself later. I will dine at eight but would like a gin and lime in the orangery at a quarter to.'

'Very well, sir.'

Serge withdrew.

William kept his eyes fixed on the view beyond the balcony until he heard the door close softly behind him. Serge's answer was somehow no more than he'd expected. Perhaps one of the maids who'd served Leonora might be more forthcoming. In the meantime, this was his first time back for a very long while and he intended making the most of it.

Although the room was cool it was too warm for the fine wool jacket he was wearing. Feeling sweat beneath his arms, he stripped it off and placed it on the back of a chair.

He sighed and rubbed at his face with both hands. 'What am I doing here?'

Yes, he would look in at their business interests, but he'd come here hoping to find something out; had Leonora truly forgotten him? He was desperate to see her again, desperate to stop her becoming a nun – just like before. It was totally, totally selfish but he couldn't help himself. He was married to a woman who drank too much but looked a little like Leonora. Night and day he accused himself of making a mess of his life. Somehow, this coming back was about laying a ghost to rest, not necessarily Leonora's ghost, but the ghost of his love for her.

After visiting the bathroom and splashing water on to his face, he came back into the bedroom and looked at the painting. The sight of the galleys and the brightly coloured flags brought an old memory to mind. If he remembered rightly, there was a collection of soldiers and a fully laid-out battlefield in the nursery next to his old bedroom in the east wing. Suddenly feeling a great urge to revisit his past, he wondered if the rooms along there would be locked. For a moment he considered summoning Serge or another servant to fetch the keys. Some inner wisdom advised him to do otherwise.

Refreshed from his journey, he left his room and walked swiftly and silently along an arched corridor of cedar floors

and stone walls. Murals and silk tapestries decorated the
walls. Suits of armour stood guard in recessed alcoves.
Arched windows set into inner walls looked out over the
central courtyard.

He paused and looked down on the arcade of Moorish-style
arches surrounding the central quadrangle, the pattern of fountains forming a double clover edged with rose, brown and
yellow ochre tiles.

At the end of the corridor, he passed beneath a wider arch.
From here the corridor branched to the right and faced north.
A balcony looked out to the hills above the Douro. At this
time of day they were suffused with a mauvish mist that was
steadily turning to purple.

He turned into the north corridor, making his way to the next
wide arch and another turning to the right. This was the east
corridor, the one he remembered from his boyhood, the time
before puberty, young manhood and Leonora.

It was strange the way his spirits lifted as he neared the
bedroom he'd once slept in. He stopped before it, feeling his
palms grow clammy, his heart hammering with excitement.
The handle turned and clicked. The door opened. It wasn't
locked.

On opening it he'd expected to see the same pale-blue shutters, the whitewashed floor and blue and white rug at the side
of the bed. The bed was still there but stripped of its bedding.
The rug was gone and the shutters were painted white. There
was a pretty chest of drawers in one corner, a white rocking
chair – small enough for a child. Beside it was a second
rocking chair, even smaller, too small even for a child. Perhaps
for a doll? Of course, he thought. Silly me. Ellen has been
redecorating. This room was destined for one of her brood.

Feeling slightly alarmed that he hadn't thought of this
before, he progressed to the nursery door – or at least the
room that had been a nursery when he was young. On opening
it, he found it more or less the same as he remembered it.
Obviously Ellen hasn't got round to changing it, he thought.
Yet the room had a certain pristine emptiness about it, as
though someone had cleared out other things that had been
in there, things that had not been here in his day.

The sight of the old battle layout, the poster-painted hills
and the faded blue bay stirred his interest. Suddenly he was

a young boy again. Groping at the drawer immediately beneath the display, he found the same box of soldiers, the ships and the cannon he'd played with.

He crept on tiptoe to the door, opened it and peered out in each direction. The corridor was empty. Silently he shut it again. A few at a time, he brought the lead figures and fleet out from the box, lining them up on the painted sea in a similar fashion to the painting in his room.

Flushed with boyish excitement, he began hurrying, almost as though he were afraid of being discovered. In all honesty he did feel some trepidation; a grown man playing with toys. In his haste to get them out of the box, some slipped from his grasp and fell to the floor.

The clatter of metal against bare boards echoed around the room. He paused before reaching for them, listening in case someone had heard and was coming to investigate. He heard nothing. There were no hurried footsteps.

The toy soldiers and a fine-looking galley had fallen beneath the table, impossible to reach purely by bending down. In order to retrieve them he got down on all fours and went under the table.

Although it was only a cursory examination, as he brought them out he saw that the soldiers were intact. Their paintwork was a bit scratched, but they were basically sound and still recognizable as one subaltern and one knight of the Order of St John. The galley, however, was another matter. Something was jammed into the gap formed by its rigging and mast.

His index finger proved too large to prod or pull out the bright object. Instead he used his little finger, crooked it over the object and pulled it out, holding it up before his eyes to study it further.

It was a doll; a tiny doll made of lead and painted, but definitely not one of his toy soldiers. None of his soldiers wore pink and this tiny doll appeared to be dancing. One arm was gracefully lifted, one leg bent, the foot resting against the other.

He asked himself what he would have thought of such an object when he was a boy. The answer was speedy. A girl's toy. The tiny doll was a girl's toy.

Unsure what to make of the find, though promising himself to find out who it belonged to, he tucked the doll into his trouser pocket. First things first. There was something far more important he wanted to do. Already suspicious that the servants had been told to keep their mouths shut, there was someone else he had to see. Someone who had known Leonora as well as, if not better than, he did.

Ten

William Shellard had prolonged his stay so he could take in a visit to the Convent of our Lady of Tears.

The building was built in the Baroque style so prevalent in this part of Portugal. The front of the building was faceless; without windows or apertures to let in air. The world could not see in or the nuns see out.

Their most regular trip to the outside world was to the little chapel across the way. For some reason, at one time someone had seen fit to place a road between the two buildings; perhaps before then they'd been encapsulated in the same compound. As it was, the locals as well as the nuns went to the chapel to pray.

William stared at the steps leading up to the entrance. An old woman supported by a child of about ten was making her way slowly upwards. Placing one careful footstep in front of the other, she leaned on the child as she did so.

The child gave no indication of struggling to take her weight, not that William was really seeing them. Memories of another time blurred his sight; a vision in a blue dress and a white mantilla. Once again he relived the moment when he'd seen her eyes flash as they alighted on him. He remembered that his legs had turned to water.

Suddenly, a startled cry stirred him from his reverie. The child had cried out in Portuguese. William saw the old woman crumpled on the steps and ran to her.

He brushed the dust from his knowledge of the Portuguese language as he assisted her to her feet. 'Signora, are you all right?'

The old woman nodded. 'Thanks be to God, thanks be to the Blessed Virgin, I am not hurt. These steps,' she said, indicating the steep rise with a wave of her hand.

'I will help you,' said William.

The child, pink from exertion and panting, looked relieved.

The old woman began talking, asking him questions as to why he was there. 'Are you coming in to pray?'

'No. I intend visiting an old friend – in fact an old friend's aunt. She's a nun at the convent here.' He indicated the blank wall of sculpted images but no windows, just one stout door.

'Indeed,' said the old woman. 'I know all the sisters there and the Mother Superior. They are very good to me. What is the sister's name?'

'Her name is Sister Anna Marie.'

The old woman stopped and looked up at him, folds of flesh falling on to her brow. He saw instantly that her sight was impaired with cataracts, her eyes milky, almost totally white.

'Anna Marie? You won't find her here any more. She left the order. I don't know why.'

'Where did she go?' William asked, his head throbbing with possibilities.

Please. Don't let her be dead.

The old woman frowned as she thought about it. 'I think Pinhao or some village around there.'

'And her niece? Do you recall her niece? She may have become a nun recently. Have you heard?'

The old woman shook her head. 'There are no new postulants that I know of.' Again her brow wrinkled in concentration. 'No. No new postulants at all – not at this convent.'

He thanked the woman, who in turn thanked him. The child helped the grandmother through the church door and into the cool darkness.

William stood for a moment pondering whether to make further enquiries at the convent. He eyed the blank walls speculatively as though finding a window would be tantamount to finding Sister Anna Marie. No, he decided. Their response would be as blank as the building they lived in. Once a nun left the order she might as well be dead. But Leonora? Had she joined the order as she'd once planned to do; before he'd come along, before his brother had snatched her away?

It wasn't going to be easy to find Sister Anna Marie. Pinhao

was not as large a city as Porto, but it was large enough. There
again, the old woman had said she'd moved to that area. He
knew it well enough as a place of rich vineyards and *quintas*
that varied from the quaint to the opulent. But at least I have
something to go on, he told himself. And then I can . . .

He couldn't finish the sentence because he still didn't know
what he expected from pursuing this course of action. They'd
had such a brief time together, though so sweet, so passionate,
yet there was something deeper spurring him on. In time he
might find out what it was. In the meantime he sat among the
old men beneath a shady tree. Curious eyes squinted at him. He
did not acknowledge their interest, too busy assessing and
reassessing his reasons for this madness. Perhaps the heat of the
sun had gone to his head, for beneath the tree he began to take
stock of himself and whatever it was he was trying to find out.

Shrouded in shade, this fever that had persisted since he'd
first heard that Leonora had left Castile Villanova subsided.
He only had a few more days in Portugal before sailing home.

If she cares for me at all then she will look for me, he
thought, and if she has become a nun . . . He gazed again at
the convent so still, so sacrosanct and cloaked in shade; a
place of safety and tranquillity.

He sighed, ashamed of his selfishness. I stopped her from
taking her novice vows once before, he thought. If that is the
life she wants now, then I have no right to stand in her way.
He decided he would not contact Leonora's aunt. Satisfied he
had made the right decision, he got up and headed for home.

'School? But I've never been to school.'

Catherine felt the colour draining from her cheeks. Her eyes
were wide and focused on her mother's aunt.

'Then it will be a big adventure. It's a convent school.'

Despite her large frame, Aunt Lopa was as quick on her feet
as she was with the hands that made the lace and jerked the
crochet hook. She was surrounded by the fruits of her labour;
creamy-coloured lace and items of crochet made from multi-
coloured silks. She was folding each item before setting it on
one of many piles. Once satisfied that each pile met some mental
calculation, it was placed into the open neck of a large sack.

She spoke quickly. 'Your things are packed. One suitcase
will be enough. It has to be. I only own one. I will give you

some money for immediate needs now. The Mother Superior will hold more in case you need it.'

Catherine felt a terrible chill wash over her. 'I am to leave you? I am to go from here?'

Aunt Lopa carried on with what she was doing. 'For now. Until Christmas. I will be back then.'

Her explanation went some way to calming Catherine's fears. At least she'd be coming back. But still, she didn't want to go.

'Can't I stay here? Who will look after the goats?'

Detecting the tremor in Catherine's voice, Aunt Lopa stopped what she was doing. Her gaze was gentle as she took hold of Catherine's trembling shoulders and sat her down.

'I've to make a living, Catherine. And before you say it, goats and olives won't keep the wolf from the door. So while you're away at school, I shall be out on the road selling my wares.'

Mention of the wolf brought another useful excuse to mind. 'What about the wolves? Who will look after them?'

Aunt Lopa blinked. During the months since Catherine's arrival neither had made mention of the wolves.

Fearing rejection, Catherine had been careful not to ask too many questions. She was happy here.

A broad smile split the kindly face, but there was sadness in her eyes. 'Time they fended for themselves.'

'Why? Why are they here?'

Aunt Lopa began nodding. 'Yes, yes, yes.' It was as though she had agreed something with herself. 'I will tell you their story. A goat was found with its throat torn out. The wolf was hunted and was killed close to its lair. It was a she wolf. That is how I know it was close to its lair. I took my own goats close by to graze. I saw the cubs – and they saw me. Weak from hunger they followed me. I fed them.' She shook her head sadly. 'I should not have done, I know. I should have told the hunters. They would have killed them. I couldn't. So I took care of them. At least if they grew up they would have a chance. So I feed them. And I trained them not to kill goats. They only kill rabbits and birds. Now they are grown and must learn to live without me.'

It was on the tip of Catherine's tongue to ask if she could feed the wolves too. Aunt Lopa seemed to read her mind.

'No. Leave them be. I should have left them too. They are wild things.'

Sensing the conversation about wolves was over Catherine's attention turned to the piles of lace and crocheted things. 'They're very pretty.'

Aunt Lopa's face glowed with pride. Slapping her meaty thighs, she sat back on her heels and reached for a tablecloth. 'I've regular customers. I make them laugh. I give them good advice when they ask for it. And they pay me!' She winked mischievously. 'Some say I'm better than a visit from the parish priest or a pill from the doctor. But it pays, my sweet Catherine, it pays. I have a bank account. A big box I keep in the big chest in my bedroom. There's not much real money, but a lot of pretty papers. And one day it will all be yours. I've no one else to leave it to.'

Francisco came with the pony and trap to take her to the convent school. Aunt Lopa stood by the door waving her off. 'I will see you at Christmas.'

Feeling less than happy to be leaving, Catherine waved back, her face pale above the tight velvet collar of her coat.

'She'll be off on her trading soon,' said Francisco.

'Where will you be?' Catherine asked him.

His grin was lopsided. She stared at it, committing it to memory.

'I'll be at the school in Pinhao some days; helping with the vines on others.'

Francisco's family owned their own vineyard. They were wealthy compared to some of their neighbours.

Catherine sighed. 'I wish I could go to your school in Pinhao.'

Francisco burst out laughing. '*That* would not be allowed!'

She frowned and remembered his comment about her mother that night she'd pointed at a star. 'Am I not in a state of grace?'

Hearing the loud laughter, the horse whinnied as though it too was amused.

'No!' Francisco laughed, one hand rubbing his aching side. 'You're a girl. The school in Pinhao is run by monks. Boys only. Your school will be girls only and nuns will be teaching you.'

School was bearable, though the nuns did their best to disguise her beauty. Their main weapon in this was to tie her hair back in plaits. The plaits were meant to be strained back from her forehead, but even this severe style failed to diminish her impact. Without the curtain of hair, her facial features were more noticeable, especially her flashing eyes.

She entered the convent school as a twelve-year-old child. Each year succeeding that first one, her beauty grew. Even the nuns found themselves staring, wondering what the future held for her.

Catherine saw the admiring looks in the eyes of young men and boys. In turn she too was maturing, drawn to masculine beauty that was a mirror of her own. In this respect Umberto, at sixteen years old, was unsurpassable.

The first time she saw the altar boy he was swinging an incense burner, the sweet smoke twisting and turning its way upwards. Unfortunately, just as he got to her the intricately carved ball came away from its supporting chain. Absorbed in ritual, the priest didn't hear or notice it hit the floor and roll into the gap between Catherine's knees.

Stifling her giggles, her hands clasped in prayer, Catherine did not attempt to return the ball to the red-faced boy. Her eyes met his in mute understanding of what had to be done – or rather what he would have to do. She smiled daringly. He blushed profusely, glanced at the retreating priest, then pounced, his hands between her knees retrieving the incense burner. Somehow he managed to click the chain back into place.

He looked at her after he'd done so. She looked back, then smiled.

She'd presumed the poor boy would blush even more, but he surprised her when he smiled and kissed her on the cheek.

Daring, she thought, her face a picture of surprise. He is so daring! And she loved him for it. Of course, being a pupil at a convent school, she didn't get to see him very often; in fact only on those days they went to mass. More often than not the boy, who she found out was called Umberto, was there.

They never spoke except in whispers, but they did begin passing messages to each other. Even that was dangerous. The girls were forbidden to have anything to do with boys, but as time went on this rule became more and more difficult to obey. To be discovered would result in great shame, the cane laid across a spread palm or knuckles; all privileges, such as they were, severely curtailed. Even leave to go home at holiday time could be withdrawn and penance imposed. Catherine was not willing to give up going home to Aunt Lopa. Umberto, who was growing more handsome and more likeable with the years, was of the same mind.

With the use of whispers and gestures, they used the Bible to send each other messages by using chapter and verse numbers. If any were intercepted, all anyone would see was a series of numbers; chapter numbers and verse numbers from the Bible, but how innocent was that? To the nuns and the priests it would seem innocent enough, though if anyone had taken the trouble to check, they would have been surprised at how often lust and passion featured in Holy Scripture.

'You two are going to get caught falling into temptation one day,' said one of her friends, a girl named Theresa who aspired to become a nun but wasn't sure whether black actually suited her complexion.

Catherine was watching Umberto as he knelt and gave veneration to the altar. He did it gracefully and when he raised his eyes to the cross, for a moment she thought she detected true veneration in his eyes. As she watched she considered what Theresa had said about them both falling into temptation.

'You're probably right,' she whispered back. 'But once I've left here we're not likely to meet again.'

'It could happen here,' Theresa retorted.

Catherine grinned and nudged her friend's arm. 'Can you imagine Sister Sophia's face?'

The two girls burst into giggles. They were still girls and the future was far ahead.

Eleven

Ellen Shellard dusted the dirt from her clothes. She had been out riding, enjoying the freshness of a Portuguese spring. Her little dog, Teddy, was there to greet her, springing up at her on his sturdy, and very short, back legs.

Self-assured and worldly-wise, Ellen Shellard was of

medium height and had a womanly figure. Two children and a miscarriage had left her more curvaceous than before their birth, but she consoled herself with the fact that she still had a waistline. She wore her hair in two thick plaits, looped and fastened with a big black bow at the nape of her neck. Her hair was tawny and her complexion was freshly girlish, her cheeks naturally pink and matching her lips which formed a perfect cupid's bow.

Having been born into money, she walked with a certain confidence, which only someone without a care in the world could do.

The big passion of her life besides her husband and her children was her clothes. She loved clothes and Walter had indulged her passion, encouraging her to go on trips to Paris, London and Rome. Today she was wearing riding britches – a fact which had drawn scandalized expressions from some of the locals more used to seeing women wearing skirts and riding side saddle.

She took off her bowler hat and shook her tawny hair clear of the plaits and bow that had loosened during her ride.

Her little dog leapt and barked all the way across the stable yard, staining her britches with mud and scratching at her knees.

She bent down to pat him away. 'Teddy, you're like a bouncing ball,' she said, laughing. 'Stop it. Stop it this minute.'

The little dog was rough-coated. His eyes were black as boot buttons, and seemingly his legs were made of rubber. A groom took her horse while she made for the door that would take her past the wine vaults and into the house along the servants' corridor.

Just as she passed from sunlight into the shadow thrown by the main house, the children appeared at the back door. The youngest, Aaron, nestled in his nurse's arms. Germaine, her daughter, was jumping up and down with as much excitement as the dog.

'They've missed you,' said the children's nurse, an affable young woman with warm brown eyes that matched her hair. She had been Walter's choice. 'We need someone young to look after our children,' he'd said. 'And English. English is the only language they need to know.'

Ellen, who'd learned to accept her husband's decisions

without argument, laughed and kissed each child in turn. 'I've only been gone just over an hour,' she said, bringing her face level with her daughter.

'It was a long, long time,' Germaine responded, throwing her arms around her mother's neck.

Untangling herself, she took hold of her daughter's hand. The sun-baked yard she'd left behind was in direct contrast to the corridor and the cellars at the back of the house. Four steps on the other side of the door and the temperature dropped from too hot to too cold.

Ellen shivered. Outside she'd wanted to escape the heat. Now she missed the sun baking her shoulders and easing the sweat from her forehead.

Uncaring of cold or the company he was in, the little dog ran on ahead of them, his claws making a tick-tacking sound on the rough stone floor. His stubby white tail danced up and down as he ran.

'Have you been a good girl?' Ellen said, looking down at her daughter.

'Yes,' Germaine replied; her smile wide though toothless at the sides.

By the time Ellen looked up, Teddy and his stubby white tail had disappeared.

'Teddy!'

Ellen frowned. Walter hated the dog. He'd only allowed her to keep it as long as it didn't stray away from those rooms frequented by her and the children.

'I'll find him,' said Germaine, slipping her hand out from her mother's. 'Teddy! Where are you?' Her voice echoed along the narrow corridor where the chill of the old stone permeated the air and sent shivers down the spine.

Ellen called after her, a twinge of concern upsetting the day's equilibrium. Due to the chilly atmosphere, her imagination sometimes got the better of her along this corridor. She wondered if ghosts walked over the old stone floor in the hours of darkness. She shivered and vowed to get out of this place as quickly as possible. But first she retraced her steps in order to find Germaine and the dog.

The doors to the vaults and cellars were of stout oak and studded with iron nails in the English style. Usually they were closed, but today someone had left one of the doors ajar. The smell of cold stone, damp oak and dusty bottles hung like a curtain across the opening. Germaine dashed in.

Straightaway she could hear Germaine calling the dog. 'Teddy, I can see you.''Germaine? Where are you?'

'Teddy's stuck,' her daughter shouted back.

Ellen sighed. There was nothing else for it. She had to venture further into the cool gloom past the two barrels on either side of the door and the bottles stored in huge racks the length of the room.

Telling Mary to take Aaron back upstairs, she set off after her daughter.

The vault was colder than the corridor. She rubbed at her upper arms and suppressed a shiver.

She found Germaine trying to wedge herself between two racks of wine bottles. The racks were at least twelve bottles high and twice as wide.

Ellen had worrying visions of her daughter being buried under a heap of broken glass. Her reaction was immediate. 'Germaine. Come away from there, darling. You'll get hurt.'

Her daughter twisted her head round so she could face her mother. 'Teddy's in here. I don't know if he is *really* stuck. He's found something. He won't come out. I want what he's found!'

Ellen sighed. Just like her father, Germaine insisted on having her own way. Resigned to the task, Ellen bent down, peering between the two racks. At the same time she eased her daughter out from the gap, thankful that the racks had stayed upright, the bottles unmoved. No damage had been done.

Going down on all fours and easing her shoulders sideways between the racks, she could just about see the little dog chewing at what looked like a bundle of rags. Germaine had been telling the truth. He'd found something wedged behind one of the racks and was growling as he attempted to tug it out.

'Teddy! Teddy! Bring it here boy.'

She reached her arm in as far as it would go and gave his stumpy tail a quick tug.

'Teddy!'

The dog, who up until now had seemed totally engrossed in the bundle, now became aware of her presence and gave

one last tug. Both he and the item he'd fought so determinedly
to free from the gap popped out.

Ellen grabbed him. 'What is that?' she asked, prising the
thing from his mouth.

She felt Germaine's hand come to rest on her shoulder.
Germaine sucked in her breath. 'It's a doll!'

'It's dirty,' said Ellen, noticing that its dress was made of
pink satin, its underskirts of pure cotton trimmed with very
pretty – and extremely grubby – broderie anglaise. Its hair
was silky beneath the grime and although its straw hat was
dusty, beneath the dirt it was sunshine yellow.

Unconcerned at how filthy it was, Germaine grabbed the
doll with both hands. Seeing its grimy state, Ellen jerked it
away.

'It's filthy, darling.'

Germaine's face crumpled with disappointment, her dimples
replaced with a downturned mouth. 'I want her.'

As her mother held the doll at arm's length, Germaine did
clutching movements with her fingers.

'I want it,' she whimpered, a few seconds away from crying.

Ellen sighed. Knowing when she was beaten was something she'd learned quickly since marrying Walter. Despite
her being a girl, he had spoilt the child, though had been less
indulgent since Aaron had been born.

It's only a doll, thought Ellen, and once it's cleaned up it
shouldn't be too bad, in fact it should be quite nice. It certainly
looks of good quality.

It was easy to give in. 'Yes, you can keep it, but on one
condition. The doll and her dirty clothes have to be washed.'

Germaine scowled.

'She's covered in spiderwebs,' Ellen pointed out, guessing
this would swing her decision.

'I don't like spiders,' said her daughter, her attitude changing
in seconds, her grasping hands swiftly disappearing behind
her back. 'They're horrible. I hate them.'

'I know,' murmured Ellen, straightening up. 'I was counting
on it.'

Hand in hand they went back upstairs to the north quadrangle and the rooms she'd renovated at the time she'd been
expecting Germaine. Walter had suggested they'd best suit
children because they were cool and never received direct

sunlight on the side that faced north, and there was a corridor between the rooms and the central courtyard. She'd had no problem accepting his advice; it seemed the sensible thing to do.

The shutters of the nursery windows were left wide open. The clear white light, unadulterated by sunlight, gave the room a cool brightness. The colours she'd had it painted – a soft lemon below a painted frieze, the latter dating from the seventeenth century – were still as bright and fresh as when they'd been decorated. She'd salvaged a Chinese rug, its pastel shades muted by age but still inspiring thoughts of silk-clad, slant-eyed ladies and dangerous voyages by Portuguese merchants.

She gave the doll to the nurse to be cleaned. 'Germaine is not to have it until it is.'

'Yes, ma'am,' the nurse replied.

Germaine began to squall. 'When can I have my doll?'

Ellen had done her utmost to be a good mother, but sometimes she wondered whether she was really cut out for the job. She wasn't very good at discipline and did like a quiet life. Like now.

'We can all help wash it,' she said, aware that tantrums could still happen if Germaine wasn't involved in what was going on.

Water was boiled and a block of carbolic soap and a scrubbing board were fetched from the laundry room.

Ellen eyed the doll before handing it over to Mary and then stopped. For some inexplicable reason, she was drawn to undress it herself. Her frown deepened the further she progressed. The doll's clothes were of good quality; besides the satin dress and pretty underwear, and not forgetting the straw bonnet, the doll wore a pink pearl necklace. She examined each piece before handing it over to be dunked in warm soapy water.

As she turned each item this way and that, her frown – one of curiosity – persisted. 'Its clothes are very well made. And it doesn't look Portuguese.'

The nurse also examined the doll and its clothes. She shook her head. 'No. Most definitely not. See?'

She pointed out the name and address on the dress label: S. Brundle, Dollmaker, Redcliffe Hill, Bristol.

This was a surprise. The deep frown persisted on Ellen's

silky-smooth brow. It looked very expensive and not that old. She searched for a suitable reason for it to be here. 'It must have belonged to one of my husband's female relatives. A cousin perhaps.'

She thought it a little strange that he hadn't mentioned having had close relatives stay here. She knew William hadn't been here for years, only revisiting a few times since just after she and Walter married. There again, William didn't have any children. Diana preferred the bottle – and a few male friends – to children if rumour was correct.

It occurred to her that it might have belonged to a servant.

'Can you ask members of staff who it might have belonged to?' she said to Mary.

'I'll try, though they're not always that forthcoming with me, ma'am,' she explained. 'They treat me as though I'm a spy. Sometimes they pretend that they don't understand English, though I know full well that they do. But I'll do my best, ma'am.'

That night, once the children were in bed, Ellen took the doll, now washed, brushed and dressed in her laundered clothes and sponged-off bonnet, to show to Walter.

He was sitting behind his big desk in the library, a masculine place of dark woods and books bound in blood-red, olive-green and chocolate-brown leather. The little light that entered glittered off gilt-figured spines.

When she entered he was holding a pen in his right hand as though about to enter something on the open file before him. His head was still lowered, only his eyes regarding her with what she couldn't help but interpret as irritation. His thin lips were stretched in something that wavered between a smile and a sneer. Although she sensed her presence was unwelcome, she decided to persist.

'Hello, darling.'

He looked far from pleased to see her. 'Ellen, you know how I hate being disturbed when I'm in here.'

Apologies fell from her tongue like raindrops. 'I do apologize, darling, but Germaine was so pleased with what she'd found and wanted you to see it too! Look.' She held up the doll. 'With Teddy's help I must add.'

She smiled innocently as she glanced between the shiny clean doll and his face, curious to gauge his reaction.

Walter's eyes narrowed. The strained smile froze on his lips then defrosted – all in the space of a few seconds. The reason for this hit her immediately. The sight of the doll had unnerved him, but he didn't want her to know that. He'd covered his disquiet swiftly. The half-smile-half-sneer returned.

'Where did you get it?' He spoke casually, as though it was of little concern.

Her heartbeat quickened. 'In the first wine cellar. Teddy dragged it out from between two wine racks. It was filthy and covered with cobwebs.'

The moment of disquiet passed from his features as quickly as sun follows rain. His attention went back to the paperwork piled in front of him. 'Really.'

His expression was unyielding.

For some reason she couldn't accept his offhand manner in the matter of a simple doll. Neither could she quite understand her own misgivings. Why should the doll be affecting her like this?

A warning voice inside her head counselled her to let the matter drop. But she couldn't. For some reason she simply *could not*!

Ellen studied the strong lines of her husband's face. He was no longer in the first flush of youth, and yet he was so totally male. She remembered an old saying of her mother's in the days when Walter was courting her. 'Rather an old man's darling than a young man's slave.' She need never worry about money. He would always provide. Unfortunately, there was a price to pay. Walter brooked no opposition to anything he decided. His word was law.

But the doll rankled. She hesitated before finding the courage. 'Who did it belong to?'

His head jerked up. His features were rigid, almost as though his face had been cast in iron.

'The doll,' she said with a light laugh, pretending to think he hadn't heard. 'I was wondering who the doll belonged to.'

The cast-iron countenance loosened, but only a little. 'I would imagine one of the servants. A number of them have children.'

She was about to mention that the doll had been made in Bristol, but something held her back. She sensed he would cut her dead.

With the passage of time she had discovered that a different man lurked beneath the charming façade that had captured her heart. She had always known him to be a respected and successful businessman. She had not been prepared for his ruthless ambition and his continual need to have his own way. Sometimes she commented to him jokingly that he was married to his business. He'd laughed with her, but only lightly. The truth burned in his eyes. Power, success, wealth; they were in truth what he lived for. She often wondered what would happen if he ever had to choose between business and family.

And in the matter of this doll, judging by instinct alone she knew there was a worrying truth to be found out.

'It's just a doll,' he said, returning his attention to the work on his desk. 'Do as you will with it. I have work to do. Now go. Leave me in peace.'

She was about to open her mouth again and press the point, but suddenly his chin whipped upwards. His eyes, now full of warning, bored into hers.

'Get out, Ellen. Get out before I lose my temper.'

The doll tucked beneath her arm, Ellen felt herself flowing rather than walking to the door. Once she was outside and six paces along the hallway, she leaned against the wall, her heart pounding, her mind whirling with possibilities. One cast-iron truth had come out of this confrontation. He didn't love her. She wondered whether he ever had. She wondered whether she'd ever loved him or whether she'd merely fallen in line with what was expected of her. A woman without a man had no place in this world. That was the way it seemed.

Twelve

Seven years after leaving Castile Villanova the view above the Douro Valley was the same. So were the smells of nightfall. As the evening breeze caressed her face, Catherine Rodriguez breathed in its infusion of tilled earth and the sweetness of ripe fruit.

'No more school,' she murmured, throwing back her head. She closed her eyes. The air she breathed trickled into her throat like a mountain stream, clean and fresh and revitalizing; the taste of home. 'No more dusty classrooms, chalk and sour-faced nuns.'

'Surely they weren't that bad,' said Francisco.

She frowned at him. 'Of course they were. Do you know that Sister Sophia warned us before leaving that if we went out with a boy, we must take a newspaper with us? A very thick newspaper?'

Francisco looked at her incredulously and made a stab at the reason. 'To hit him with?'

Catherine teased him. 'No. We were to place the newspaper on the boy's lap before sitting on it.' She grinned and threw him one of her catlike expressions. 'Hence the very *thick* newspaper!'

Francisco joined her laughter, though Catherine couldn't help noticing that he'd turned slightly pink in the cheeks. Older than her he might be, but deep down he was still a boy. She found this endearing, so much so that for now she could set aside his comments regarding her mother.

They were sitting once again on the wall of the goat enclosure, looking up at the stars. Catherine had endured being a boarder at the isolated girls' school on the other side of Pinhao. The nuns had indeed considered her wild. Her summer sojourns on the vine-covered slopes were responsible for that. In the summer she did all the things she'd done that first summer; running through meadows and vineyards, enjoying the warm earth crumbling between her toes. She'd also made and sold goat's cheese. Her small treasure trove was increasing.

'What will you do with it?' her great-aunt had asked.

She'd hesitated before replying. Yes, she was resigned to marrying Francisco. She would work hard and together they would make enough money to buy Castile Villanova. It was just that she didn't want him to know that yet. She didn't want anyone to know.

'I will keep it safe until I need it,' Catherine had replied.

Autumn had come and the air was as ripe with sweetness as the vines themselves, the leaves red, orange and yellow against a cobalt sky. In the west towards the Atlantic Ocean, clouds flocked in puffball splendour like white meringue piling ever upwards.

Catherine's hurt had been healed by this place and Aunt Lopa. She stretched again and threw back her head, smiling because she knew the effect it would have on Francisco. Aunt Lopa told her she was a tease. She was probably right. And Francisco was very attractive. She observed him changing, loving his firm, brown body, the masculine muscles newly forming into adult firmness.

And he was noticing her. Even now she could feel his eyes on her. She shrugged her shoulders, which in turn sent her young, round breasts pushing against the tightness of her bodice.

Francisco was beginning to get her measure, knew she liked teasing him, making him sweat as only a young man on the threshold of manhood could sweat when a girl like her was close by. He had only meant to glance at her before laughing, but instead his eyes lingered on the silky softness of her neck. 'You have a neck like a swan,' he said softly, the words tumbling out before he could stop them.

She looked at him sidelong with flashing eyes that were slightly upturned above high cheekbones, her lashes dark and brushing her cheeks.

'White and fluffy?' she said laughingly, her laughter like water gurgling in her throat.

His chin seemed to jerk backwards, but he recovered and again bared his feelings. 'No. I meant sleek and silky,' he said.

She stroked his cheek. His jaw tensed beneath her fingers. She enjoyed that.

'All of me is sleek and silky,' she said in a tone of voice borrowed from a film star she'd seen in a movie.

'Catherine!' He tutted like an old woman and shook his head disapprovingly. A soft blush spread upwards from his throat and all over his face. 'No wonder the nuns called you wild.'

She laughed again, her eyes sparkling with happiness because she was here sitting beside Francisco in another September. And you have breasts now, she reminded herself, and your hips are wider and you are sometimes filled with the longings the girls talked about in the school dormitory. She remembered one of the girls being caught with her night-dress pulled up and her hands beneath the sheets, moaning and writhing in her sleep. The nun on dormitory duty had heard the culprit. The girl was given six strokes of the cane and her hands were tied to one of the iron railings of the bedhead after that. The poor girl.

Catherine had sunk further beneath the bedcovers, closed her eyes and thought of Umberto, the altar boy with the striking blue eyes that always strayed to her. Physical pleasure was meant to be shared, she'd decided. She'd conveyed her opinions to Theresa and the others. 'Preferably with Umberto, that gorgeous altar boy.'

Some of the girls had been shocked. Awestruck by her outrageousness, others had giggled and eyed her admiringly.

School was fine and she'd enjoyed learning. Her quick mind had absorbed lessons like a sponge.

'You're a clever girl,' said one of her favourite teachers, Sister Cristabel, who taught English. 'You really should consider university.'

Catherine had shaken her head. 'I'm no longer a girl. I'm a woman.'

She couldn't explain how she felt about her mother dying so young. All she knew was that she wanted to live to the utmost. And there was still the matter of Castile Villanova.

I'm grown-up, she told herself. This year she'd kissed Francisco in the cool shade thrown at the back of Aunt Lopa's *quinta*. Their bodies had seemed to stick together, their fingers exploring the contours of each other's face, each other's body.

Breathless, they'd sprung apart, but Francisco couldn't help coming back for more. Catherine was wary, more aware than he was of what could happen. At school, under cover of a darkened dormitory, her fellow pupils had talked of what could happen if you weren't careful. One of the girls hadn't been careful and had left the school in shame.

'You will have to marry me if you want that,' Catherine told him.

Francisco responded hotly as though she'd said something insulting. 'Of course we shall marry.'

'It's not as though we don't know each other well,' said Catherine.

'It stands to reason,' said Francisco. The wide smile she'd recalled when things at school had got too much for her, vanished. A thoughtful frown creased the face of the handsome boy who'd grown into a handsome man. 'I think my father would be pleased for us. So will Lopa Rodriguez.'

Catherine noticed he had not mentioned his mother. For a worrying moment it sounded as though he had doubts. The doubts were chased away the moment his smile returned.

'How could our families not be pleased?' he said, lightly caressing her cheek with his fingers. 'Portuguese girls are the most beautiful in the world. I will be marrying the most beautiful of the most beautiful. I will tell them tonight.'

Catherine laughed at his pronouncement. She didn't remind him that she was only half Portuguese and that her father was English. It occurred to her that she'd have to ask for her father's permission. She frowned at the prospect. Why should he have any say at all? In all the time she'd lived here, her father had not written or even sent a card or present for her birthday. In the vain hope that it might make a difference, she'd added a codicil to her nightly prayers. *'Lord, give my father the reward he justly deserves for his sins.'*

She never hinted to God of what that reward should be, presuming that he'd know only too well how badly her father had behaved towards her mother.

After she and Francisco had parted with a kiss and a lingering clasping of hands, she went into the house where Aunt Lopa's crochet hook was flying through yet another batch of tray cloths, doilies and tablecloths. She looked up and smiled as Catherine came in the door.

Catherine didn't let on that she'd guessed Aunt Lopa had been watching them through a crack in the shutters. In Portugal unmarried girls were closely chaperoned until they were safely married. Aunt Lopa was only doing her duty.

'So! Have you fixed the date yet?'

Catherine found herself blushing. Aunt Lopa was nothing if not blunt.

'No. Not yet. He has to tell his parents.'

The way his voice had wobbled slightly came back to her. What about his mother? Donna Nicklau gave the appearance of being a pious and overly respectable woman. And that, in effect, was exactly what she was, though her piety bordered on sanctimonious hypocrisy.

Catherine assured herself once again that this would be no problem. Francisco had told her himself that it would be no problem, so that was the way it would be. Wouldn't it?

But no matter how many times she tried to tell herself this, a nagging doubt remained.

The crochet hook paused in mid-stitch as Aunt Lopa nodded her head sagely. 'Francisco will do things properly. And you will be a wife. You will be happy.'

Loose and glossy, Catherine's hair fell forward like a curtain, hiding a blush of deeper intensity. 'I will be happy. I'm sure I shall.'

The crochet hook failed to continue its diving in and out of the pattern already made. Aunt Lopa's eyes were fixed on her. Her wide face and small mouth were in stiff repose as though she were holding something back, something that needed to be said, something she didn't want to say.

'Consider carefully, Catherine. Be sure it is what you want. What is good at sixteen is not necessarily as good at twenty-six or even thirty-six.'

Catherine lowered her eyes. Marrying Francisco seemed such an obvious step forward in her life. She would be settled for the rest of her days and she'd expected her aunt to be overjoyed at the prospect. The fact that she was urging caution threw her completely off balance.

'I thought you'd be pleased,' she said, frowning and picking nonchalantly at the unpicked wools lying in a heap on the table among bone knitting needles and crochet hooks.

Aunt Lopa leaned forward. A shadow seemed to cross her face, giving her fresh-coloured features a chill, greyish tint. 'Don't throw your life away until you have lived a little. I thought I knew what I wanted. It suited for a while but then I became restless and questioned my reasons for doing what I was doing. I found out that I had far too questioning a mind for what I'd thought I'd wanted at sixteen. There was no longer satisfaction or spiritual peace in what I was doing. Whatever your mother did – and some condemn her – she was doing what she wanted to do.' She sighed reflectively, old wounds along with old memories dulling her eyes. 'Love is like a young vine; plant it in the wrong soil and you reap a sour fruit, a bitter harvest.'

That night as she lay staring out at the sky, Catherine thought about what Aunt Lopa had said. She had refrained from retorting that her mother should not have loved 'that man' because it was his fault she was dead. Shifting slightly, she pushed the window open a little more so she could smell the night and hear the sound of creatures flying or scurrying in the darkness.

Up until now it had seemed a logical step to marry Francisco; was it because he was the only boy she knew intimately around here? Or was it really because she loved him and wanted to be with him for the rest of her life? And what, indeed, was passion?

If a certain twist of fate had not occurred, she would never have discovered the answer until later on in her life.

The news that old Father Benedict had died and that a new priest was taking over came to them three days later. Three days after that, the new priest appeared. He was cycling through the shade thrown by the lemon trees at the side of the road, appearing as a black shape in sunlit spots and disappearing completely in the shadows.

Catherine and her great-aunt waited patiently as the priest propped his bicycle against a stone wall, shook the dust from his robe and straightened his hat.

Catherine sucked in her breath. There was something familiar about this young, agile priest, something that brought back the vision of a gloomy chapel and being surrounded by sniffing girls in dusty school uniforms.

'Good morning, ladies,' he said, sweeping his hat from his head like some latter-day cavalier – minus the feather, of course. 'I am your new priest, Father Umberto . . .'

Thirteen

'My thanks for your vote of confidence,' said Walter Shellard with a businesslike smile. He hid his pleasure behind a pall of cigar smoke. He had their backing for company expansion – not that he'd expected otherwise.

At the far end of the table, Seth Armitage, his financial director, cleared his throat and raised one snowy eyebrow above a cerulean eye. 'It's well deserved, Walter. Your plan to carry the company forward is well timed. It makes sense to increase our holdings in Spain at this time. Like the rest of Europe, its economy floundered somewhat after 1918 and land prices have plummeted. However, in view of the impending political unrest, I stress again the need to spread the liability. Who knows what the future holds. If you can achieve that, which you say you can, then we can expect success. Everyone is in agreement,' he said, his all-seeing bright blue eye alighting on each of those present, as though daring anyone to find fault with the plan.

Philip Marks, their diminutive Jewish bank manager who had earned the position on the board due to past financial support, leaned forward over clasped hands – a sure sign he wished to speak. 'It's a pity these two vineyards are some miles apart. I understand the land in between is also under vine cultivation. Is there any chance that we can purchase this too?'

Although Walter smiled, his eyes hardened. If anyone was going to point out the factor that had proved to be a thorn in his side, it would be Philip.

Ronald Parker, Walter's brother-in-law, interjected. 'I've been having discussions with the owner. He wants twice what we're offering. He can't have it. If we paid him what he wanted, it wouldn't be worth our while.'

Philip frowned. 'Pity. If there were some way of persuading him, the bank would find it easier to supply the necessary backing. I'm not saying that we won't. I'm merely saying that the returns on investment are likely to be greater.' He looked pointedly at Walter and knew immediately that both the problem and its solving had already been considered.

No frown creased his brow. No sweat spotted his forehead. He made a snap statement of intent that took everyone, except Philip, by surprise.

'No need to fret, Philip. I'm taking personal charge of the negotiations. The vineyards – all of the vineyards – will be ours. I'm going to make Arthur Freeman an offer he can't refuse.'

Ronald looked devastated. He had a long face that length-ened further when he was disappointed. 'But Walter, I was doing . . .'

'Nothing,' Walter snapped. Then more congenially, 'You did what you could,' he added. Walter sounded pleasant enough, but those around the table knew he was criticizing Ronald's capabilities. Although well brought up, well educated and wealthy, he lacked experience and sheer gut instinct. Most of them thought he'd only got the job by virtue of his sister, Ellen, being married to Walter. For the most part, they were right.

The meeting was brought to an end. A red-faced Ronald asked to speak to Walter alone. His eyes were moist, as though he were on the verge of tears.

'Not now, Ronald. I have to speak to Seth.'

Seth noted the comment and stayed seated, shuffling papers until Ronald was safely out of the room.

Walter stubbed his cigar into an ashtray and slipped his hands into his trouser pockets. He looked out of the window. The window looked out on Trenchard Street, an old part of the city where wine warehouses had proliferated since the sixteenth century. The warehouses of W.W. Shellard and Company backed on to those of Harveys, purveyors of the famous Bristol Cream.

Walter watched men unloading crates of clinking bottles. There were close on two hundred in the load and there were three trucks, each waiting to be unloaded. And there could be more. 'So, Robert Arthur Freeman is proving difficult. How unfortunate that he owns the vineyard sitting between our two latest acquisitions. Think how efficient our operation would be if we controlled all three.'

'I think we need to offer him something more,' said Seth, who had been wracking his brains for a suitable solution. Offering too much would make the deal too costly and effect-ively nullify the plans they'd been entertaining. He watched Walter Shellard with one eye almost closed, as was his manner when scrutinizing a man or a business proposition. He knew from experience that Walter's mind was racing, dashing about hither and dither. Like Philip, he knew him well enough to guess that he'd already reached a satisfactory conclusion.

'An amalgamation of interests perhaps would do as well as an outright purchase,' said Walter, who'd made up his mind that this plan would go through – on his terms, of course.

'And it would leave us with excess capital,' Seth Armitage replied, showing no sign of being surprised. The Shellard family had long ceased to surprise him. Especially Walter. When it came to business, Walter Shellard was second to none; like his father but even more so. Sometimes his ruthlessness quite frightened Seth, but he told himself that it was what was needed in this modern world. Hopefully it would replace war; he'd lost both sons, one in 1914 and one a year later. His wife had died shortly afterwards. Staying on as a director of Shellards helped him keep sane. Without it, he'd die.

Walter's gaze stayed fixed on the old stone warehouse opposite. 'Look at it,' he said, a self-satisfied smile on his lips, his eyes narrowing as they swept from window to window, floor to floor. 'My family built that. My father's great-great-grandfather was a common seaman. By making the right decisions – and the right marriage, it has to be said – he got the show on the road.' He chuckled and shook his head. 'The right wine, the right time and the right wife. A shrewd man. A very shrewd man.'

Seth Armitage made no response, but perceived that this nostalgia had a purpose. Everything Walter said led some-where. But he made no comment about the family's history. Walter Shellard received enough flattering comments without him adding to them. The truth was that he was the shrewdest and perhaps the cleverest of his line.

'Presuming you've got something in mind, I've sent Arthur Freeman a note for you to meet at your club,' said Seth.

Walter half turned and half smiled. 'You have the knack of precipitating my next move, Seth. How come you know me that well?'

Seth lifted that snowy eyebrow again and fixed him with his own half-smile. 'You forget. I served your father before you. You're just like him and though I'm old I still think on my feet. Pity I won't be around to give the same service to your son.'

Walter laughed and slapped his old friend on the shoulder. 'You'll live to be a hundred, Seth.'

Seth shook his head. 'I doubt it.'

'Right,' said Walter, his mind already working out a plan of action, a plan that would give him more vineyards, more power, more wealth. 'What time?'

'Eleven.'

'Eleven. I'll be there.'

'He hasn't confirmed yet.'

'He'll be there. I'll guarantee it.'

Seth Armitage didn't doubt it. When it came to business, a cunning look came to Walter's eyes as easily as his smile. Like a fox he was out to make a kill, and also like the fox he measured his risks, not committing himself unless he was 100 per cent sure of success.

'I doubt whether he'd consider a directorship in exchange for a half-interest. No matter what you offer, he's likely to drive a hard bargain.' Walter's eyes narrowed. Again he thought of that long-dead ancestor and how a marriage to a moneyed woman had founded a dynasty. Seth couldn't read his thoughts, so continued imparting sound, but repetitive advice. 'He'll require some kind of affirmation of title; a surety that he'd still have some say in the running of the company. And a guarantee of income, of course. He's looking for long-term benefit. That's the only way we'll get him on board. Do you have something in mind?'

Walter was still looking out of the window. The city light made sharper the already sculpted brow, high cheeks and strong chin. There was no emotion in his voice when he spoke, only determination and an unfailing belief in himself. 'Like kings and queens of old, my family made favourable marriages in their time. There are great advantages in making your opponent your business partner and a family member – albeit a very minor one.'

Clifton Gentlemen's Club smelled of beeswax, brandy and hair oil. Black-suited retainers padded over the shiny brown floor carrying a single glass on a silver tray.

Walter was sitting in a leather armchair reading *The Times*. One of these neat suited men had brought him a single malt. He'd sipped sedately as he waited, appearing engrossed in his newspaper. In truth his eyes never missed a thing.

A mouthful of malt remained in the glass sitting on the small circular table at his side; just enough to swallow in one gulp before ordering another. The object of this visit entered without being aware that Walter had spotted him. Robert Arthur Freeman had arrived. Though his shadow had fallen over him, Walter gave no sign that he noticed. Best to let Freeman make the first move, he decided.

'Shellard. I hear you wanted to see me.'

'Good timing, Robert,' said Walter, laying down his paper. 'I was just about to order another drink.'

Saying that, he drained his glass and ordered a malt for himself and a gin for his guest.

One glance and he had committed Arthur Freeman's details to memory. Average height, grey suit, overlong hair; he had a handsome face, boyish almost, although he was around forty years old. His mouth was wide and betrayed his sensual nature. He wore a rose in his lapel and carried a silver-topped walking stick and was foppish edging on the melodramatic. His reputation went before him. He loved the good things in life; women – very young women – wine and an opulent lifestyle.

So did Walter, though he never allowed any of those things to intrude on his ambitions. Power, wealth and the acquisition thereof would always be the prime movers in his life.

'I haven't got time for preamble,' said Arthur Freeman, after swallowing a third of his drink. 'I've stated my price.'

Walter was not rattled by his brusqueness. On the contrary, his behaviour was exactly as predicted; success in business was all about good research and knowing your opponent.

'Quite so,' said Walter, his fingers interlaced across his chest in the manner of an older man, like Seth perhaps, as though checking the beating of an ageing heart. 'An amalgamation of our Spanish properties would be advantageous to both of us.'

Robert tipped more of the clear liquid into his mouth and swallowed. 'At the right price,' he said, draining his glass and calling for another. 'On my account,' he said to the waiter.

The waiter looked nervous. 'I'm sorry, sir, but it has to be . . .'

'Here.' Robert threw him two half-crowns before the embarrassed-looking man had a chance to say that his account was large and in need of being cleared.

Walter missed nothing. He already knew Robert's situation. The man had debts everywhere. Those two half-crowns were probably all he'd had in his pocket. He needed money, as much money as possible. He was a widower with children, a household, an extravagant lifestyle, but no wife, no wealthy fiancée in the offing. He smiled to himself. Walter understood that one of this man's children was the issue of a barmaid in

King Street. If he thought he was going to bluster his way
into getting more money from Shellard and Co, he had another
think coming.

'I've decided not to buy your Spanish vineyards.'

Although he tried to hide it, Walter could see that Freeman
was taken aback. He drained his glass swiftly – a common
ruse to hide a dismayed expression.

He's gathering his thoughts, thought Walter, worrying as to
how he can reopen negotiations without losing face.

'But I thought you favoured owning the land that divides
your acquisitions. What made you change your mind?'

Walter had no intention of elaborating. While waiting, he'd
firmed up an option that had come to him the night before.

'Keep your vineyards. They're your birthright, after all. But
what say you we amalgamate our resources? All three vineyards can work in tandem using the same labour, the same
transport and the same fermentation arrangements. And of
course, your family started the business with wine rather than
port as my family did. As I think Seth Armitage told you,
we're looking to expand in both Portugal and Spain. The time
is ripe – the war's seen to that. We'll look at expanding our
operation in other European countries – including Germany.
Their white wines have great potential. Shellard and Company
has already been renamed Shellard Enterprises. We are going
to grow very big. Very big indeed.'

Robert eyed him warily. For a split second he appeared to
give the offer favourable consideration before his hooded eyes
narrowed as though he were concentrating more deeply. But
Walter had judged his prey well. The thought of expansion
and an increasing fortune would reel him in.

'Are you offering me a directorship?' He looked slightly
nervous asking.

Walter took a deep breath and a sip of his drink before
shaking his head. 'No. I was thinking of a more "personal"
arrangement.'

This man, who Walter had decided was a wastrel and a
fool, frowned as he tried to work things out.

He's wondering what I'm offering, thought Walter and felt
a surge of excitement. Business excited him in the way that
racing, or adventure or even a beautiful woman excited other
men. Business was everything, the force that drove him on.

With the resultant money he could not only maintain his lifestyle, but enhance it further. First and foremost, extra money would go to maintaining and refurbishing his beloved Castile Villanova.

'Continue,' said Robert, looking seriously interested.

Now was not a time for embarrassing moments, so Walter ordered and paid for another drink. Not for himself. He intended to keep a clear head and only sipped at his drink, sometimes not swallowing anything but merely keeping up the pretence. In his experience the opponent would continue, the drink dulling the intellect and therefore the judgement.

'I understand you are a widower,' said Walter.

Robert eyed him curiously. 'Yes.'

'What if we became related? Isn't that the strongest reason for men to work together? For businesses to combine as one? You are a man of the world,' said Walter, looking at Robert as though they both had secrets to share. 'What if you were to marry someone of my family, someone who would bring a dowry with her? We would then be related. So would our vineyards, though yours would still be yours. I could instruct that your property is run in conjunction with my own. Your costs would thus be less than they presently are, which of course would generate greater profits. What do you say?'

Looking as though he'd been hit by a steam train, Robert Arthur Freeman blinked rapidly and sucked in his lips.

Walter guessed that his mouth was dry. This was a man who wanted more money but also wanted the prestige of owning a vineyard that his family had left to him through his mother's line.

He didn't ask for time to think it over. Walter had not expected him to.

'This relative of yours, is she pretty?'

Walter nodded. 'Pretty, ripe and just eighteen years old.' He wasn't too sure he had the age right, but it didn't matter. Eighteen was old enough to be married, but young enough to whet Robert's appetite. Walter had heard the rumours; Robert liked them young, the younger the better. Each man to his own predilection, he counselled. This was business and Leonora's daughter – his daughter – was no longer a child.

'And the dowry?'

'A substantial sum. Shall we say half of what I originally

offered you? Just think, half of that plus keeping your own property. In time of course, when we are dead and gone, everything will go to your heir – who will also be heir to a large segment of the Shellard Company.'

Walter waited, watching as the hooded lids flicked over the unusually flecked eyes.

At last, Robert stopped considering and made a decision. Walter had no doubt that it would be the right one; right as far as he was concerned, that is.

Fourteen

Rain clouds were gathering in the west, piling like mountains as more and more surged in from the far Atlantic Ocean. The rain was heavy enough to beat leaves from trees and grapes from the vine. Arrows of rain speared into the dry earth, puffs of dust shooting upward with each hit. Soon the dust had turned to mud, and although the rain ceased, the sky remained overcast. The rain returned, beating on the sodden earth and the drooping vines.

Catherine stared out at the marbled clouds and the driving rain. Dust-covered leaves drooped wet and dripping from trees. The world had turned grey. She told herself that the weather was the reason that Francisco didn't come. In the back of her mind his mother's presence lurked like a malign shadow.

A strong hand landed on her shoulder, disturbing her thoughts. 'It's just the weather. He will come.'

Catherine placed her own soft fingers on the work-worn ones of Aunt Lopa. Silently she stared out at the lonely landscape seeking that one form, that one smile certain to brighten the day. He never came that day, or the day after or the one after that. In the meantime the weather brightened a little, though not for long. More clouds were accumulating in the west and the thunder rolled across the valley.

Francisco was her salvation. Marrying him would save her

from the terrible temptations that had darkened her soul on the day Father Umberto had dismounted from his bicycle and raised his hat.

Their eyes had locked for a split second, and although they had recognized each other, neither had acknowledged this fact. It was as if they were back again in that gloomy chapel, sending messages with their eyes or scribbled on to scraps of paper hidden between the pages of a Bible.

Aunt Lopa had taken to the young priest immediately, inviting him for meals and also taking him into her confidence regarding her will and the contents of the iron-bound coffer.

'I've made him executor of my will in place of Father Benedict. If anything happens to me, he's promised to take care of you.'

Catherine had refrained from blushing at the thought of what Umberto's interpretation of 'looking after' her might be. Sometimes at night, to her great shame, it was his ultramarine eyes she saw in her dozing moments, not the burnt sienna of Francisco's. Her school friend's comment about temptation also came back to her.

She rolled over in her bed, folding the bedclothes up under her chin. Soon, I will be safely married and out of the way of temptation. This was what she had hoped for, but still Francisco did not come.

The bad weather showed no sign of abating. The track to the *quinta* remained slick with water and empty. Even Father Umberto stayed away, preferring the more easily accessible parishioners further down the slope.

At night her body writhed with longing. She felt his hands on her, though in fact they were her own. In her dream she opened her eyes, looked up into his and saw they were not brown, but blue, and the young man was Umberto and not Francisco.

Lopa was aware of her great-niece's melancholic moods. Sometimes Catherine caught her looking at her, her wide face bathed in concern and a strange worldly look in her eyes. 'Whatever will be, will be,' she'd say once Catherine had caught her looking. 'Whatever will be. Yes. That will be so.' And she'd nodded and dropped her attention back to her busy fingers.

At night when she was saying her prayers, her great-aunt would call up, one foot braced on the bottom rung of the ladder.

'Ask God to do something about the weather,' she said before retreating to tend the goats prior to going to bed. 'Otherwise I will.'

The comment brought a smile to Catherine's face. She could imagine Aunt Lopa giving God a good talking-to if he didn't do something to change the weather.

The only person who did get through the mud and down-pour was an old man who made goat's cheese in a *quinta* some way back down the track. It was he who brought Aunt Lopa a letter, a letter that she read quickly before tucking it down the front of her blouse.

Catherine was wrapping her own home-made goat's cheese in scraps of muslin when she saw her do it. 'Is it important?' she asked, mildly curious.

'No!' Aunt Lopa was abrupt, much more so than usual. Instead of sitting down with her lacemaking and crochet hook as she usually did late afternoon, she went out to milk the goats – even though they'd been given a good measure that very morning and it wasn't yet sunset, their designated time.

Aunt Lopa remained strangely silent at suppertime, her lips tightly closed; her conversation more abrupt than usual.

Catherine eyed her from beneath a lock of fallen hair as she spooned vegetable soup into her mouth. She was no fool and calculated when this mood had first manifested itself. The arrival of the letter had started it. Before that she'd been chirpy enough, not that Catherine was that concerned. The only question that filled every waking moment was how Francisco had fared telling his parents about their plans to marry. And then I'll be safe, she told herself, the rest of my life mapped out.

Sometimes the life she envisaged seemed mundane, without sparkle, without adventure. And what about romance? Marriage is about being comfortable with someone and she was certainly comfortable with Francisco. Staring at the rain reminded her of her mother's tears when her father had been expected and he hadn't turned up. Her mother had always been crying, so it seemed. But I won't, she told herself. I'll be happily married. Francisco is totally dependable and a lovely boy. As for the only boy to have inflamed her passions,

Umberto . . . well . . . he'd chosen his vocation. He'd married the church.

It still surprised her how circumspect they'd both been when he'd turned up at Aunt Lopa's. Their attitude had remained the same on future visits, not once acknowledging each other as old acquaintances. Sometimes she laughed and wondered what Aunt Lopa would say if she knew about their dark lingering looks and secret messages during mass! Horrified or amused. It was difficult to say. Aunt Lopa could be either as far as religion was concerned. It was as though two factions were fighting for her soul.

The ongoing storm intensified until the sky was so dark lamps were lit an hour before they were due. The old farmhouse trembled with each roll of thunder and the rain found ancient fissures in the walls and roof until there weren't enough vessels in which to catch the drips.

Catherine cleared up the dishes in a methodical manner. Just for once she wanted to immerse herself in simple chores so she didn't have to think. There was no room in her thoughts for anything or anyone but Francisco and this spurious future of hers.

'Catherine!'

At the sound of her name, Catherine jumped and a metal dish clattered across the floor.

Aunt Lopa was apologetic. 'I'm sorry. But there is something I have to do. I'm going over to see Francisco. I think it's the only solution that will have you looking cheery again.' The nervous chuckle that followed made Catherine think that she wasn't telling the whole truth.

'Nothing to worry about,' said Aunt Lopa. 'Stay here and clear up.' She patted Catherine's hand. 'Leave things to me.' She winked in the mischievous way Catherine had become accustomed to.

Catherine didn't need to ask where she was going and why. The only question that remained was why now? They'd both been concerned that Francisco had not returned, but why go over there now it was dark? Did the letter she'd received have something to do with it?

'I don't want you to go,' Catherine blurted suddenly.

'Nonsense! Nonsense!' Her great-aunt waved both hands as though she were swatting at flies.

Catherine persisted. 'You said the roads are dangerous in this weather. Tell me why you have to go now.'

Aunt Lopa was not one to lose control for very long, and if she didn't want to tell then tell she most certainly would not!

'I know this country better than you. It's not so dangerous for me. Sit there until I come back,' she commanded, pressing Catherine into a chair with both meaty hands. Her eyes flickered on seeing the questioning fear in Catherine's eyes. 'Then we will talk.' Her eyes shone with sadness.

Catherine sighed. 'All right, all right. But give him my love. You will, won't you?'

Aunt Lopa smiled and said she would. Then she heaved on her old work coat and shoved her oversized feet into a pair of man-size working boots – the ones she always wore for work around the farmhouse. She tied the laces vigorously so the boots were tight around her ankles. Clods of mud not reached by the boot scraper dropped off to be scrunched underfoot on her way to the door.

'I'll sweep it up,' offered Catherine.

Aunt Lopa nodded. 'Yes. Yes.' Though the door was half open and the damp seeping in, she paused. There was a gentle look in the deep-set eyes. 'You're a good girl, Catherine.' And then she was gone.

Catherine held a lamp up to the window and watched the strong, tall form make its way across the yard, through the gate and out on to the track. A flash of lightning suddenly lit up the landscape. For one fleeting moment darkness became daylight. Aunt Lopa's large frame was bowed against the wind. The rain beat more heavily than it had in the previous days. The lightning flashed again, making strange shapes from things that were nothing in daylight. Black trees were outlined in silver, stone walls starkly brought into relief. Catherine narrowed her eyes and waited for more lightning to turn the night back to day. When it flashed again there was nothing.

Catherine slept fitfully in her great-aunt's rocking chair. Rain fell like handfuls of copper nails flung on to the clay-tiled roof. Shutters rattled in their frames and wind-driven leaves scuttled across the stone floor.

By dawn the storm was close to blowing itself out. Blue

sky appeared among the grey, like bright patches sewn on to a curate's gown.

Wrapping a brightly crocheted blanket around her shoulders, Catherine knelt before her bedroom window. She'd left the shutters open all night and left the oil lamp burning. The lamp was out now and the wooden floorboards in front of the open window were sodden. The damp air, still strung out with rain, played with her hair and turned her pale cheeks pink.

Narrowing her eyes, she looked out, aching to see Aunt Lopa's broad figure making her way home. The freshness of morning air eased her weariness, but did nothing to placate her concern. Where was she?

Despite all that, her stomach rumbled, but she couldn't bear the thought of preparing food for just herself. Make something for both of us. Yes! She should prepare something hot. Aunt Lopa would be hungry when she got back. Cold too.

She made her way down the rough wooden ladder, her bare toes curling over each rung until she'd gained the ground. The stone floor was cold beneath her feet as she darted across to the old wood-burning stove on which they cooked their simple food. The fire was still in, though the ash had been blown around the room.

She sliced bread, warmed up yesterday's stew and placed a kettle on the hob. In reality she could have done nothing to stop her great-aunt going out on such a filthy night, but still she felt guilty. And why the urgency?

She paused, the bread knife still in her hand. The reason came suddenly. Her father. The letter was from her father. But why now?

Keeping busy helped her stop worrying that something bad might have happened. There were many reasons why her great-aunt wasn't home yet. The Nicklaus may have insisted she stayed overnight because of the storm. Yes, that had to be it.

'Catherine Rodriguez!'

The sudden shout was accompanied by loud hammering on the rough wooden door.

Flying across the room, she lifted the latch and swung the door wide open. Her face paled at the sight that greeted her.

'We made a stretcher from our coats,' said one of the two men carrying Aunt Lopa. She recognized the men as itinerant workers who journeyed from place to place depending on the

season and the abundance of grapes to be harvested or vines
to be planted.

Their explanation, their very presence, flew over Catherine's
head. Her eyes were fixed on the big strong woman she'd met
only seven years before. No longer ruddy featured or sprightly
of step, her face was a mess of torn and shuddering flesh; her
torn clothes saturated with blood.

'Wolves,' said one of the men, his eyes full of fear.

The shapes in the shadows.

'Here,' said Catherine, rushing to the rustic bed hidden
behind a thick woollen curtain. 'Here.' Words were a luxury.
Action! There had to be action! Her whole body was shaking,
but she had enough presence of mind to rip up a sheet and
fetch a bowl and boiling water. She leaned over the woman
who had taken her in, shown her kindness and cared for her
mother.

'Aunt Lopa?'

She looked down expecting to see some semblance of the
familiar face. It was far from familiar. The stuff of nightmares.

One eye opened. Catherine shivered. She dared not let her
gaze stray to where the other eye had been. That part of Aunt
Lopa's face was raw and bereft of features. One side of her
mouth seemed to have been ripped away exposing her teeth.

Catherine swallowed the nausea rising in her throat. This
face! Half a face! A terrible mangling of flesh!

'You're going to be all right,' she said, gulping back her
revulsion.

Is she going to be all right?

Her hands shook as she tugged blankets over Aunt Lopa's
ripped body.

'You're going to feel much better once the doctor's been,'
she murmured; yet she knew it would not, could not, be so.

Aunt Lopa knew too. That wise owl look was on what was
left of her face when she shook her head, her one eye fixing
on Catherine's face.

'Three of us found her,' said one of the men. 'José went
for the doctor.'

'And the priest,' said the other man, crossing himself as he
said it.

Catherine barely acknowledged him. Her attention was fixed
on this dear woman who had taken care of her. Aunt Lopa's

heart was as big as her frame. Catherine loved her, just as she had loved her mother. Now this woman too was being torn from her life.

The man who had spoken had seen her pallor and the despair in her eyes. He jerked his head at the door. 'We'll wait outside.'

She neglected to thank them. For the first time in a long while, she closed her eyes, clasped her hands together and prayed.

'Our Father . . .' She bit her bottom lip to stop it trembling and tried again. 'Our Father . . .' It was no good. Her lips would not stop trembling, so she prayed as her great-aunt had told her to pray – with her heart. The words of the Lord's Prayer rang through her head and were sincerely meant. Again and again, with every tear shed, she ran silently through the same prayer, the familiar lines interspersed with entreaties to not let her beloved Aunt Lopa die.

The inside of the house was darkened, the shutters drawn. By the time two women known for their laying-out and midwifery skills had come up from the village, Catherine was stiff. She'd been sitting in the same position for hours, had had nothing to eat, nor anything to drink.

One of the villagers eased her away from the dying woman's side and into the old rocking chair.

'Sit here, me dear. Leave her cleaning up to us. Here. Take a drink.'

Catherine barely felt the beaker pressed against her lips and declined to take hold of it. She sipped but the water ran down the side of her mouth. She waved the beaker away.

'What are you doing?' she asked them, a sudden panic taking hold of her.

The old woman's voice was gentle. 'Cleaning her up, my child. The priest is on his way. Anna Marie would want to be respectable.'

'Not Anna Marie. I mean Aunt Lopa,' said Catherine, presuming in her despair that they were referring to someone else.

'She is your aunt,' said the old woman kindly, her work-worn hand resting on Catherine's shoulder. 'She used to be Sister Anna Marie when she was with the order. She only became Lopa because of her feeding the wolves.'

Lopa! From the Latin for wolf.

'She said animals acted closer to God's laws than humans,' Catherine retorted defensively.

The two women exchanged startled looks, clamped their mouths tightly shut and got on with what they had to do.

Catherine sat stunned, her hands tightly clasped in her lap. The fact that her great-aunt had once been a nun came as something of a surprise. In happier circumstances she would have demanded to know more. But not now. All that mattered was what was happening to her now in this old farmhouse kitchen smelling of burned stew, polish and fresh wool.

She watched the old women, wanting to help but feeling weak and terribly inconsequential. They worked quickly and silently, and so very, very gently. One carried a bowl that slopped pinkish water as she moved away from the bed. The other was bundling up blood-soaked linen.

Aunt Lopa was bound around with strips of cloth; her body, her arms, her face. The blood pulsed through the bandages from flesh that had once been covered by skin. Even her hands had been ravaged. Lifting what was left of a finger, she gestured for her great-niece to come closer.

'You mustn't speak,' said Catherine, her slim fingers hovering over Aunt Lopa's lips. She couldn't bear to touch the torn flesh and exposed teeth. She saw the anguish in pale eyes that had once been bright, replaced by gritty determination. Her stomach churned as the torn mouth spoke muffled words she didn't understand.

She leaned closer. 'What was that? What was that you said?'

Forcing herself to listen meant almost drowning in the smell of blood and dying breath. But she steeled herself to be steady, to be strong. This time she heard what was said.

'The things in my treasure chest are yours.' Specks of crimson spittle spattered her face; she stayed her hand from rubbing it off. Her eyes were swimming with tears.

'The chest. Yes.'

She kept the iron-bound chest at the foot of her bed. It was battered, the edges of its lid eroded by worm. Aunt Lopa had referred to it as her treasure chest.

Again the stalk of finger gestured her to come even closer. 'The letter . . .' Bubbles erupted with words. Her breath came in short sharp gasps, as though even her lungs were torn and ragged.

She raised a bloodied hand to her breast and laid it there.

Catherine stared at what was left of the stout fingers. They'd been chewed to the bone. She imagined her aunt lying help-less, the wolves tearing at her flesh, eating her alive. Her whole body shivered and turned cold as death.

'The letter,' Aunt Lopa whispered. She stared up at Catherine unblinking. It had been her habit to secrete letters, notes and money into her bodice. That's what she was saying now; the letter she'd received the day before was in her bodice. The letter that had triggered her to set out in bad weather.

'You want me to read it?' asked Catherine, her lustrous eyes big and wide. She would gladly do so, but the thought of first moving the chewed fingers was grossly unpalatable.

Aunt Lopa's sigh was long and drawn out, like a draught falling down an empty chimney. The one eye still in its socket stayed fixed and open.

'Aunt Lopa?'

Catherine didn't know why she suddenly looked up at the rafters. It was something to do with a strange emptiness coming to the room, as though larger-than-life Aunt Lopa had shrunk in size and could no longer fill it as she once had.

The single eye continued to stare. The day brightened as Catherine sat there and the fire went out. The women had gone, leaving the door open to let in the fresh air and the warmth of a drier day. There was no one to retrieve the letter except her.

Catherine was far from happy to reach through the blood and gore. Someone else, she prayed. Please let someone else do it.

The sudden clunking of boots on the stone floor of the veranda heralded the arrival of Father Umberto.

'My apologies,' he said, rushing to her side, already adopting the vestments necessary for the task he was sure to perform. 'My bicycle got stuck. I got a lift on a donkey.'

She looked away, preferring to hear him say the last rites rather than actually seeing it done.

He might just as well have been old Father Benedict for all the notice she took of him and he of her. And yet she remembered her aunt commenting on his beauty.

'Too handsome to be a priest,' Aunt Lopa had said, never

one to mince her words. 'There'll be many temptations put in that young man's way along the road to salvation.'

They'd both laughed and Catherine had made a great effort not to turn red. Aunt Lopa was as outspoken about sex as she was about religion. She'd instructed Catherine as to how babies were made, using the goats when they were mating as an example of what went on between a man and a woman. Her views had gone beyond that.

'A man can take a vow to be celibate, but that doesn't take away his natural urges. God made him that way and why should God have all the handsomest men? The same applies to women.'

For some reason Catherine had been sure she was referring to her mother. 'Your mother had a passionate nature,' her great-aunt had added as though reading her thoughts.

Suddenly Lopa Rodriguez, otherwise known as Sister Anna Marie, gave a great sigh.

It was as though a cold wind had blown in through the door and out again just as quickly.

'Her soul has flown,' said Catherine. 'If there is such a thing.'

'Of course there is.' She felt his eyes on her. It was the first time he'd spoken or looked at her so directly.

She did not return his look.

The sound of gunfire filtered through the still air. Local men were already out hunting the perpetrators of this terrible deed. Catherine thought of the dark shadows she'd seen when she'd first arrived here, their dark coats, their yellow eyes . . .

The weight of his hand fell on her shoulder. Startled, she gasped and sprang to her feet.

Father Umberto looked as startled as she did. 'I'm sorry . . . I did not mean to frighten you. My child?'

He said it questioningly and looked apologetic, like a small boy who has forgotten to buy his mother a birthday gift. This boyishness only served to strengthen the memories of the boy she'd once known.

She stared at him round-eyed. She felt so confused, so totally cold and separate from everything going on around her. 'She's dead,' she managed to say. Her upturned eyes were suddenly challenging. 'Where were you, priest?'

He looked taken aback. 'I'm sorry I was not here earlier, but I had another of my flock to attend to.'

'It doesn't matter,' said Catherine, her pallor now replaced with an angry flush. 'Aunt Lopa isn't . . . wasn't terribly religious. She used to say that if there's a God, why does he let such terrible things happen in this world.' It was only a half-truth and she trusted she wouldn't be cursed for saying such a thing. And hadn't the old women just told her that Aunt Lopa used to be a nun? She was taking some time accepting that fact – if it were true, she reminded herself.

'She was of two persuasions,' said Umberto, his eyes now averted from her face and fixed on that of the dead woman. 'She used to be a nun. Did you know that?'

Catherine started and stared at him. So he knew too? Why hadn't her great-aunt confided in her? 'Yes, I knew. Why did she stop being a nun?'

She chanced looking sidelong through her tears, seeing the bluish tinge of the strong jaw, the firm lines of his shoulders and the way his hair curled over his collar.

'She decided that the best way to serve God was to live the life he'd given her and to stop reaching for the unreachable. Those were her words, not mine.'

Catherine forced herself to drag her eyes away from him and back to her great-aunt whose hand was still clasped over the letter that lay at the heart of this tragedy. A bitter taste came to her mouth. This letter was to blame for everything; not just the wolves. They'd only been acting as nature intended. But it was the letter that had made Aunt Lopa venture out in this foul weather.

'Father. One thing.' Her voice sounded small. Frightened. But she forced herself to be brave, taking a great lungful of air and holding it in.

'Whatever.' Hands clasped in the accepted style, he stood waiting for her to enlighten him.

She exhaled her breath. 'Can you move her hand? There's a letter in her bodice. She told me I must read it, but her fingers . . .' She couldn't say anything more about her fingers, but no explanation was needed. Umberto understood.

While still at the seminary, he'd assisted an army chaplain and also administered in a hospital. He was used to gory sights. With gentle respectfulness, he lifted Aunt Lopa's hand, undid two or three buttons and brought out the letter, handing it to the young woman sitting there.

Her hair fell forward as she read it. He fancied he saw her shoulders tense then shake. Was it despair or fear? He couldn't tell. Generally speaking, his job was to help if she wished it. On the occasion of Lopa Rodriguez' death he was required to give more. The woman had confided in him and asked him to befriend her niece should anything untoward happen to her. He'd promised her that he would, though the thought of being alone with such a young and beautiful girl did worry him. And of course, Lopa Rodriguez had known nothing of their previous meetings – some years ago now. In the dark hours of the night, it was Catherine who came to tempt him. Seeing her again had shocked him to the core. He had thought his passion for her was behind him along with his adolescence. That creamy complexion and those eyes like dark pools had acquired a breathtaking maturity. Although he'd tried hard not to notice the feminine form bursting against the childish clothes, the hems lengthened, the seams let out to accommodate her transformation to womanhood, the task was impossible. He had tried consoling himself with the fact that Catherine Rodriguez was his single temptation. He must resist. *He must resist.*

He'd tried not to be affected by the way her hair fell forward like a black silk veil, nor to notice the way she parted her lips exposing clean, white teeth. It was even harder to hold his breath and not breathe in her scent. She smelled like young shoots bursting through rich soil; young buds about to burst into flower; sweet grapes ripening on the vine.

He pushed the thoughts away; such troubling thoughts. Powerful urges that still plagued his loins and his dreams. His punishment for such lustful thoughts was crude and the only thing he could think of. Tonight he would retrieve the knotted rope from its hiding place and chastise himself until all trace of the urge to sin had faded from his body.

'Be her friend,' Lopa had said.

He had agreed, even though Lopa could not possibly be aware what agony that would be. Or perhaps she did know, he thought. Anna Marie was clever and incredibly shrewd. He asked himself whether he'd fallen into a trap.

In the short term, befriending Catherine would have to wait until he had regained his self-control. He would do as he'd promised, but not yet, he counselled. Not until after the first clod of earth had been thrown on the coffin.

He crossed himself, rose from his knees and concentrated on putting his accoutrements away. He refrained from looking at her – never had he known his urges to be so strong. All he wanted to do was clasp her to his chest, to comfort her, to kiss her, and much, much more.

Instead he settled for pulling the sheet back up over the face of the dead woman. Once that was done, he glanced over his shoulder to see if Catherine had finished reading the letter. She had.

Her eyes were wide and seemed too big for her very pale face. The contents of the letter were explicit.

'Is it bad news?' he asked.

'Yes. My father wants me back.'

'I see.' He nodded. Something inside him screamed to tell her to stay, but he quelled the sound with inner prayers and promises of penance. 'And you do not wish to go.' His voice was steady, without a hint of trembling.

She shook her head. 'My life is here. Francisco and I wish to marry. Perhaps we can live in this house now that my aunt . . . If I were married, he could not force me to go.'

'True.'

She lifted her head and brought the full force of eyes swimming with tears to meet his. 'That's why Aunt Lopa set out so quickly to go to the Nicklaus.' If I were married he couldn't take me away, Catherine thought. It's his fault that she's dead. His fault too that my mother died. It's he who deserves to die, not them. Him, for the evil man that he is.'

The dryness in Umberto's throat spread throughout his body. He saw vengeance blazing in her eyes and it frightened him. Give solace, said a small voice deep inside. He approached her, his hands clasped in prayer.

'Would you like to pray for your aunt's soul, Catherine?'

Still sitting in the same rocking chair, she turned her face away from him and looked towards the door. The setting sun gave her complexion a fiery glow. She didn't answer him, but continued to sit, alone with her thoughts.

He fell to his knees and silently gave up prayers on her behalf. When he'd finished she was still sitting and staring.

The terrible urge to take her into his arms – just as he did in his dreams – threatened to overwhelm him.

'I'd better go,' he said.

Her eyelids flickered in a barely perceptible nod.

Umberto got to his feet. Once outside he took huge gulps of the cool air wafting his hot cheeks. Like a man in a dream he remounted his bicycle. The horror of Lopa Rodriguez' death was enough to give him nightmares, but it was Catherine Rodriguez who would haunt his dreams.

That evening he went about his duties as a man in a daze. No matter how much he prayed, how much he chastised himself and tried putting her and the past behind him, he found he could not.

Alone that night and before lying down to sleep, he took the scourge from its locked cabinet and beat his back until the pain and bleeding were greater than the urgings of his loins.

Fifteen

The sky seemed full of rainbows in those days following Aunt Lopa's death. Like a painted bridge they spanned the Douro Valley from one side to the other. The sunsets that followed each day were just as vivid; as though God is trying to compensate me for my loss. But nothing could.

She saw Francisco at the funeral. At first her spirits rose at the sight of him, though not for long. His stiff-boned mother was with him. His father, shoulders rounded against the dull wind as well as in response to the warning looks from his dominant wife, mumbled his sympathy.

Guessing he would attend, she'd made a great effort to look her best. Her glorious hair was caught up in a tortoise-shell comb topped with a black lace mantilla. Her dress had been hastily contrived overnight, cut from her great-aunt's own mourning outfit kept for such occasions. She'd kept the cut simple; a scooped neckline, three-quarter sleeves and a slim sheath of a dress with only a hint of waistline. The only black shoes she owned were left over from her schooldays. They were flat and buckled around the ankle, but would have to do. She was aware of the veiled looks from those attending the funeral and had quivered at what they might be thinking.

She's shabby. A peasant.

The moment he set eyes on her, Father Umberto looked taken aback, seeming to draw in his breath though his eyes appeared loath to leave her face. His professional face reasserted itself, masking his reaction.

'Señora Rodriguez. My profound sympathy.'

His eyes seemed to flash before he lowered them.

She nodded her appreciation.

Umberto smiled, though sadly. 'Your aunt would have been proud of you,' he said.

Catherine didn't understand what he meant at first, but the look in his eyes and the tone of his voice stayed with her.

Umberto regretted his outburst, for outburst it certainly was. Punishing his body each time she came to mind had done nothing to subdue his desire. It is only right and proper that I offer my condolences and officiate in a proper manner, he'd told himself before the funeral. The moment he'd set eyes on her his fortitude had begun to crumble. The simplicity of her outfit was very suitable for the occasion and, what was more, enhanced her beauty. Plain black accentuated the creaminess of her skin and the darkness of her eyes, like pools, deep and moist, full of unshed tears.

Confused by her own feelings, Catherine turned swiftly back to Francisco. He had stiffened the moment he saw her and had hesitated before falling away from the family party.

Catherine waited patiently, pretending the tortoiseshell clasp of her clutch bag was far more interesting than this handsome young man.

He finally escaped the family crowd. 'Catherine.' He sounded nervous.

She smiled up at him; saw the redness of his hair caught in the sunlight. 'Francisco, I'm glad you came.'

He gave a small nod and offered his sympathy, eyes half hidden beneath lids and a lock of reddish dark hair. Although she ached to smooth the stray lock back on to his forehead, she held back. Would her action be appreciated? She sensed Father Umberto watching her, but resisted looking in his direction.

She searched Francisco's face for some sign that his feelings had not changed. No trace of that affable smile, or even a slightly sad one, stirred his features. Despite this being a solemn occasion, it puzzled her. It was as though there was something left unsaid between them, or perhaps he found the circumstances awkward. She preferred to believe the latter. Death was such an unwelcome intruder in life. In the midst of life we are in death; life a little island in eternity and death an unwelcome reminder of our own mortality.

'I haven't seen you for ages,' she said, her lips feeling strangely stiff, her throat dry and aching to cough. 'Where have you been?'

Not wanting him to pity her, she refused to cough, moderated her tone and managed a ghost of a smile.

Francisco glanced nervously to where his mother watched with crow-black eyes.

Catherine saw this. 'Tell me what you've been up to, Francisco. I won't bite you,' she said. 'And I won't hold you to anything.'

The last few words seemed to unlock his courage despite his mother's glower. He made the effort to explain. 'My father sent me up to the vineyards in the north. The weather was bad. I couldn't get back. The roads were blocked. I'd come round tonight, but . . .'

The full meaning of what he said flashed between them. He could come round, but in the circumstances a chaperone was needed.

'My mother disapproves of our plans,' he said, his breath turning to steam in the chill morning air.

There was a rustling like dry leaves as women in stiff taffeta – so beloved for mourning in these parts – and men in dark serge drifted in their direction. Already their behaviour was being monitored. Their chaperones, in the form of Francisco's large family, were like a flock of black crows with beaky faces and plumped-up plumage. Like crows they were out to protect their young and peck an unwelcome intruder to death. Some muttered their disapproval.

'*Making cow eyes at her great-aunt's funeral. So disrespectful.*'

'*She'll end up the same as her mother.*'

She understood everything they were saying, but couldn't believe that people could act so badly on such a sad occasion.

This was a tight-knit community where things were still done 'properly' and with propriety. Her English father had spirited her beautiful mother away from their world of tight corsets and regular visits to the confessional. Some of their glances were almost contemptuous, flying at her like vicious sparks and swiftly igniting a raging flame of defiance.

'I don't care to have a chaperone!' She smiled up at him. 'Tell your family this. After all, we are going to get married, aren't we? My mother would have approved. And Aunt Lopa certainly did. She was on her way to propose the matter to your mother. She never got there.'

He hanged his head, his eyes hidden. 'So I understand.'

Her heart turned black at the thought of the letter her father had sent. Yet again he was responsible for the death of someone she cherished. She wished he were dead.

She brought herself back to the present. Francisco was fidgeting, his eyes flitting nervously between her and his family.

'Well?' she demanded, her head held high. 'It's up to us to carry on. We have to get on with our lives. We can't turn back the clock.'

It sounded harsh, almost uncaring. Inside her grief mixed with her fear for the future.

'There's just us,' she whispered, her deep, dark eyes holding his. If a look could hold a man to her, then this was just that look. She did not want to leave this place, and to remain here she must marry Francisco.

One side of his mouth turned upwards. The smile – and the love – came back to his eyes.

'I'll come.' He said it sharply, like a sudden jump over a cliff.

'Then kiss me,' she demanded. 'Kiss me now.'

Looks as dark as mourning clothes flew like daggers in their direction. But they didn't care – Catherine certainly did not. In her mind she could see Aunt Lopa egging them on, laughing at those who dared condemn.

Black looks, black hearts.

Tonight he would come. Was she foolish to believe him? Strange that the prospect of a safe and respectable future was slightly unnerving. Was that really what she wanted?

That evening after feeding the goats, Catherine sat in her favourite spot and watched as a more seasonal sun dipped into the horizon. Her eyes were fixed on the track between the trees. The sound of a distant gunshot cracked into the cooling air. Men were still out hunting the wolves blamed for Aunt Lopa's death. Another shot followed. The wolves would all be dead by morning. None would be left in Portugal at least. Perhaps survivors would limp back into Spain, probably from where they'd come in the first place, straying down from the foothills of the Pyrenees, across the border in search of food.

The contents of the letter to Aunt Lopa resonated in her mind. If Francisco were to marry her, then it would have to happen soon. If not she might just as well be dead.

The hours, the minutes, the seconds ticked by and still there was no sign of Francisco and his horse-drawn trap. Her spirits began to sink with the sunset.

She'd expected him to arrive before sunset. This had always been their favourite time of day when the earth gave up its heat to cooler air. A series of excuses came to mind as to why he hadn't arrived. Perhaps his family had insisted on a chaperone and he was searching one out. Perhaps her intention to throw caution to the wind had shown on her face.

Whatever, her frown deepened as sunset ebbed into twilight, blue clouds shifting like veils across a bed of crimson sky.

She was dressed in her favourite blue dress. It was cotton and trimmed with silk around the arms, neckline and hem. It had no bows, no buttons, no over-decoration, but it fitted her well. It was one of Aunt Lopa's cut-downs. Catherine remembered her grumbling as she'd done the alterations, complaining that Walter Shellard should have been more generous with his allowance.

'A young woman needs good clothes if she is to make a splash in the world.'

Catherine had laughed and said this made her sound like a

fish. She smiled at the memory and for a moment the pain of loss was at least subdued, though not for long. Never for long.

Dusk gathered like a cloud of soot blotting out the daylight and the details of smaller things. The moon was beginning to rise, and by its light she saw a lone figure coming her way.

Her heart leapt in her chest. Francisco! It had to be him.

Blood racing, she rose to her feet, her eyes narrowing as she attempted to establish the identity of her visitor. It looked as though the person was wearing some kind of fluctuating skirt. She almost laughed out loud at the thought of it. Then she saw it wasn't a skirt, but a bicycle and a fluttering robe. Father Umberto was paying her another visit.

Though she told herself that he was visiting in his capacity as a parish priest, a tingling nervousness spread like a cobweb over her body.

She forestalled this by telling herself that he'd visited her great-aunt far more frequently than the old priest had ever done.

Aunt Lopa's chuckle echoed in her ear. 'Now is that to do with wishing to see more of me or more of you?'

Catherine had been surprised by the comment. Surely her great-aunt had not detected the fact that she and the priest had met before?

Although taken aback, Catherine had hidden her feelings and remarked that he was very dedicated. It had never been in Catherine's nature to blush like a silly girl. Umberto the altar boy had looked at her as though he wanted to strip her clothes from her body. Umberto the priest avoided looking at her.

She'd tried to analyse what was really going on behind the strong face, the heavy black robe.

'He's still a man for all that,' Aunt Lopa had observed, a half-smile hovering above the ever-clicking knitting needles.

The priest dismounted just before the gate into the yard, pushing his bicycle the rest of the way and finally resting it against the stone shed in the corner.

He lifted his head. His expression was thoughtful and he was frowning.

'Good evening.'

'Good evening,' she responded, with a swift incline of her head.

The temptress in her emerged from the sadness. She eyed him boldly and leisurely, wanting him to see her do so, perhaps to turn and run.

He smiled, as though he knew. The breeze ruffled his hair. His long lashes brushed high, strong cheekbones and his eyes flashed like sapphires. As an altar boy he'd been handsome; as a priest he was strikingly beautiful. Heavenly.

'Catherine?'

She smiled. He spoke her name as though it were a question. She recalled the dim past when they'd exchanged sly, longing glances and silly, childish notes.

Her eyes locked with his. 'Can I offer you a drink, Father?' Her voice was soft, hesitant.

He looked startled when their eyes met. 'Just water.'

'Come into the house.'

She turned abruptly away. His footsteps followed her in.

Their conversation started innocently enough. As he drank, they spoke of the funeral and how well it had gone, and wasn't it wonderful that so many people had turned out to pay their last respects. Still, they did not mention having met before. Like water, the past was dammed up, waiting until the weight and height of desire got too high and overflowed, threatening to drown them both.

'And so wonderful that your aunt made such a generous settlement on St Magda's,' Father Umberto added.

Catherine gave a brief nod of her head. This was all news to her, distinctly surprising. It appeared Aunt Lopa was more religious in death than she had been in life – or the life of her latter years; a reversion perhaps to the years spent in a convent. As she mused over these things, Father Umberto unfurled a stiff piece of paper; Aunt Lopa's will.

'Your great-aunt instructed me to ensure the contents of her coffer – and the coffer itself, of course – passed to you on her demise. Do you wish to inspect the contents?'

Her first inclination was to look inside, but the fact that Francisco had not appeared this evening had stung her deeply. Afterwards she'd question why she'd said it, but for now the statement came out without forethought. 'I won't open it until Francisco and I are married.'

Father Umberto was stumped for words. He set the will out on the desk, flattening its edges with the palms of his hands.

He nodded sagely. 'I see. A suitable marriage dowry, I have no doubt. Lopa Rodriguez was a frugal person. She told me herself she kept her valuables there, and I can well believe they are quite a useful amount. Your great-aunt wasted nothing.'

A dowry. Yes. She liked the thought of that. Perhaps a dowry would help ease the Nicklaus' opposition to the marriage.

Father Umberto looked down at his clasped hands. His brow was furrowed as he considered the weighty matters needful of his careful consideration. 'Would you like me to act as go-between in the matter of your wedding? I could negotiate the marriage contract on your behalf seeing as you have no living relative to hand.'

'Will you inform his family that I have a dowry?'

'If you wish.'

She nodded. 'Yes. Because . . .'

She looked up abruptly, but when he raised his deep-blue eyes, she lowered her own. Looking at each other was becoming dangerous.

Still contemplating his clasped hands, he asked how long he had to arrange things.

Catherine sighed. 'One month. My father's given me one month to lay Aunt Lopa and her matters to rest. If I am to be married, he won't take me away. I'm sure of it.'

Umberto nodded that he understood. If she was sure of her father's response, he was most certainly not. There were ways around a contractual agreement, but he was less than familiar with that kind of thing. But he had to do what he could.

For her part, Catherine felt devastated; in fact she had not felt so low since the day her mother died. In her mind she roasted her father over white-hot coals for what he had done. She'd never forgive him. And now he wanted her back.

The formal way the letter was termed stuck in her mind: *. . . one month is long enough to bury your mother's aunt and resolve what small matters might need attending to . . .*

No words of sympathy. No asking whether she herself was keeping well. It was the first letter in seven years and might just as well never have arrived.

'May I disclose the contents of the chest?' he asked.

Catherine stiffened. 'I haven't opened it yet.'

There was something now in his eyes that made her feel

uncomfortable, almost as though he were reading her mind and knew she was lying – or something close to lying.

'No,' she said sharply. 'They must take it on trust.'

He looked surprised. 'If Francisco truly wants me, then he'll accept that. If not . . .' She shrugged. 'I'll trust to fate. Who knows what's in store.'

Umberto narrowed his eyes into chilly blue slits. Strange how she could read him just as well as he read her. She knew what would come next.

'You already know what's in the chest. Am I right?'

She smiled enigmatically. She had a small sum of her own. The contents of the chest could remain a secret for now.

Sixteen

Father Umberto hid his nervousness well as he was offered the best chair in the room at the *quinta* of José Nicklau, Francisco's father. The room was opulent by local standards, having more than one room on the ground floor, the stone paving covered with thick rugs. The chair was upholstered in tan-coloured leather and had rosewood arms carved to resemble lions' paws.

'Fetch the priest's cup,' said José to his youngest daughter. The girl ran to a painted cupboard and got out a silver cup.

'Wine?' asked José, his manner deferential, his features ruddy by virtue of his outdoor life and the fact that he tested too much of the port wine he produced.

'Just lemonade,' said Umberto. 'It was a warm ride,' he said, excusing his own slightly flushed complexion as he raised the silver cup to his mouth. Donna Nicklau always kept a separate cup for the priest, whoever he might be.

Before taking a sip, Umberto tried not to pull a face at the thought of his predecessor having shared the same cup. The old man had been dribbling somewhat come the end, so he'd heard. He consoled himself with the fact that Donna Nicklau was a house-proud woman. Doubtless it had been washed many times since the old man had last taken a sip. All the same, it was hard to blank the vision from his mind.

'Much appreciated,' said Father Umberto, returning the silver cup to José's waiting hand.

'Your visit is unexpected,' began José, an anxious look in eyes that were brown and bordered with a yellowish white. 'But of course we are always pleased to see you. Was there something special you came to see us about?'

José looked worried; concerned perhaps that it had been at least six weeks since his last confession. Acting as go-between in this matter of the marriage of Catherine Rodriguez seemed a penance to the young priest. He could not have her, but Francisco could, and in order to alleviate his own desires, it made sense to put all his energies into the task of getting them married. However, it would not be easy. Francisco's mother would see to that.

He rubbed the palms of his hands over the chair arms, eyes lowered as he considered his words. He had a moment to do so. Francisco was already here, but his father had gone upstairs to fetch his mother.

'Do you know why I am here?' the priest asked.

Francisco nodded. He was pacing up and down before the wrought-iron gates dividing the main room from the roofed courtyard, the light at his back. His shoulders were tense, yet there was agitation in the way he took three steps that way, three steps back.

Francisco pushed back a dark lock of hair that had fallen on to his forehead. His thick brows met in a deep frown above the bridge of his nose. He looked worried, and had every right to be. His mother was not an amiable woman. Neither was she handsome in the way of most women. While Francisco's looks were perfect but rigid; just like a statue of a saint, there was a weakness about the chin that to Umberto's mind declared him to be a man who took the easy path. No doubt he took after his father. Perhaps in years to come he'd take to drink.

Father Umberto pursed his lips and tried not to feel envious of this callow youth, this weakling who could not stand up to his mother. 'And you have told your parents this?'

Francisco stopped pacing, took his hands out of his pockets, throwing them in the air in exasperation. 'There's nothing I

can do about it. She retreats to her bed every time I mention
the matter.'

'I see.'

It was exactly how the priest thought it would be. Donna
Nicklau was not an easy woman to persuade about anything.
She adhered to traditional values and expected great things
of her family. Francisco was her eldest son. Besides that,
Donna Nicklau was a staunch defender of traditional
Catholicism. She was not likely to tolerate him marrying the
daughter of a woman who'd killed herself.

'I will see what I can do to persuade her,' said Father
Umberto. In his heart of hearts, he wasn't confident of being
able to do anything to change Donna Nicklau's mind. The
Pope himself would be hard pushed to do that. But Francisco
looked so troubled, thin and pale. There was also Catherine
to consider, and himself of course. A married woman, especially if she had children, would be less accessible.

Donna Nicklau preceded her husband into the room, just
as, for the most part, she preceded him in life. She was
shrouded from head to toe in black, her dress a dark sheath
shaped like a dagger. A silver crucifix dangled on her chest.
Dressed like a widow before her time, thought the priest, as
though she was looking forward to a singularly bereaved state.

She greeted the priest with a show of respect most people
saved for a cardinal or even the Pope, bowing over his hand,
her lips brushing his fingers.

Father Umberto was uncomfortable with such a display. He
couldn't get the notion out of his head that she reminded him
of sulphur. It was purely a personal thing. He had a habit of
applying colours to people. Priests were black of course; young
people were lime green like leaves in springtime. Donna
Nicklau was unique. She was yellow. Her skin was the colour
of old parchment; her eyes golden and fluid like olive oil. A
black headscarf covered hair that had once been flame-coloured
but was now streaked with grey. No one dared suggest to
Donna Nicklau that such hair was evidence of non-Portuguese
ancestry. She was fervently nationalistic and sanctimonious
as well as being staunchly Catholic.

The usual pleasantries were exchanged and drink and food
were offered. Father Umberto declined.

'Perhaps it is best that I get straight to the point,' he said and perceived an instant drop in temperature. They knew why he was here; there were no secrets in the countryside. He soldiered on. 'For some time now your son has been close to a certain young lady, namely Catherine Rodriguez. In the absence of any locally living relative I act on her behalf.'

He went on to formulate the suggestion as favourably to Catherine as possible. At the end of it he sat back against the cool leather, knuckles whitening as his hands tightened over the chair arms. It was now that he regretted refusing a second drink; not just because his mouth was dry, but tipping a glass before his face would protect him from Donna Nicklau's fierce glare.

Husband and son looked to the one woman standing alone among them. Father Umberto felt as threatened as they did. Sulphur, he thought to himself. Donna Nicklau is most definitely the yellow of sulphur.

She said not a word, but listened with pursed lips as the colour drained from her face.

Father Umberto prepared himself for the worst. The worst happened. Donna Nicklau raised her hand to her chest and emitted a high-pitched wail. As those around her panicked, there followed a closing of eyes then a thud as she fell to the floor. The action was followed by outright pandemonium. A pitcher of water was called for; a pillow was placed beneath her head.

'I . . . am . . . dying,' groaned Donna Nicklau, her eyes rolling in her head. 'My son . . . he breaks my heart . . .'

Amid her wailing, José Nicklau was shouting for a second pillow and a blanket. 'And where is that water? Fetch water! Fetch a doctor!'

Father Umberto had sprung from his chair. Mouth agape, he caught the look on Francisco's face.

I told you so.

The woman's cries became more hysterical. Father Umberto's expression clouded when she began calling for a priest. He hesitated. Her demand changed.

'My son! Where is my son?'

Poor Francisco. He looked so helpless – as though, Umberto guessed, two factions were waging war inside his head.

Looking like a frightened boy, Francisco knelt at his mother's side. 'I'm here, mother.'

Donna Nicklau reached for his hand. 'I see death in the shadows, Francisco.' Her eyes became round and staring, focused on some point beyond her son and her husband.

Father Umberto, feeling suddenly vulnerable to her accusing gaze, moved out of her line of vision. But he needn't have worried. Softening now, her eyes went back to her son.

'You mustn't let the shadows get me, Francisco. You mustn't upset me so.'

In danger of saying too many things he shouldn't say, Father Umberto made slowly and softly for the outer vestibule, a stone structure leading to the front of the house. He should have conferred a blessing before leaving but, with grim-faced determination, he'd decided she didn't deserve one.

The fine day did nothing to lift his spirits. Just as he was mounting his bicycle, Francisco called to him. He waited, one foot poised on a pedal. There was a haunted look in his eyes.

'Father. You can see how it is.'

Umberto nodded. 'What will you do? Adhere to your mother's wishes, or marry the young woman you love?'

'I want to marry Catherine, but I do not want to be responsible for my mother's death.'

Umberto bristled. He blurted out the truth even though he should appear impartial. 'Your mother is as strong as an ox. I get the impression she is not in favour of this union. Am I right?'

Francisco blinked nervously. Umberto sensed his panic and outright confusion. He swallowed the contemptuous bile that rose from his stomach. Francisco wasn't the first man to be controlled by his mother and he certainly wouldn't be the last.

'Please convey my regrets to Catherine. Ask her to give me time. If all else fails, I'll come for her. We'll run away.'

Father Umberto said nothing. He wasn't supposed to advise people to run away together. His job was to solemnize their promise to each other in a marriage ceremony. He was also unnerved by two things; that Catherine needed support in this time of trouble, and also that if Francisco could be so weak-willed, he was not the right man for her.

So who is? he asked himself and buried the immediate answer.

It is not your place.

He made ready to push off, about to heave himself on to the saddle. Francisco continued to follow.

'Please understand,' he said.

Umberto sighed and looked at him. Although twenty years old, Francisco looked gangly and youthful, his arms too long for his body, his hands continually seeking out the deep pockets of his trousers.

'Will you tell her I love her?' His expression was strained; appealing.

Umberto stopped. 'Why not tell her yourself? Why not go over there?'

'Not today. I mean, how do I know for sure that my mother isn't seriously ill? The doctor says her heart may not be very strong. Please, ask Catherine to give me time.'

Father Umberto pedalled away without promising any such thing. Francisco had made him angry – very angry! He frowned as Catherine's lovely face came to mind; disappointment moistening those beautiful eyes. If he was Francisco he'd run away with her tomorrow!

'Damn Donna Nicklau to hell!' he yelled as he sped down a stony hill.

Seventeen

Catherine sat in her favourite spot watching the sun go down. She was close to giving up waiting for Francisco to come to her and began wondering what would happen if she travelled to Porto as her father's solicitors had instructed.

Her expression clouded at the thought of him.

I'd probably kill him. Or shout; tell him exactly how much I hate him.

Her heart was heavy and her eyes sore from staring at the road for so long. A figure appeared in the distance; Father Umberto, the front wheel of his bicycle bouncing over the hardened mud and stones.

She stood up and waited, the setting sun bathing her in a warm, amber glow. She tried to look welcoming, but for the life of her she couldn't countenance a smile. What news would he bring? Her heart raced at the thought of it. Somehow, she guessed it wasn't good and her stomach tightened into a nervous knot.

She remembered his gracefulness as an altar boy; he was still the same, his body seeming to flow with movement, even in the simple task of riding his bicycle.

He glanced at her briefly, then bent to give close inspection to his front wheel. 'That road is worse since the rains. It needs resurfacing.'

'Would you like a drink, Father?'

He shook his head. 'No. I'm fine. I had one with José Nicklau.'

Folding her arms, she willed herself to show no emotion.

His eyes flickered then widened before he looked away, bending low to brush the mud from his robe.

Catherine guessed he was giving himself time to decide how to break the news as gently as possible. She trembled inside, but would not show it.

'You know, Catherine, people can sometimes think they want something and when it's denied them, they are upset; but years later they realize—'

'Just tell me,' she snapped.

He looked surprised by her bluntness and the defiant stance. His eyes widened. In that brief moment she perceived that he was taking in every detail of her face, her hair, her body. He looked away, his gaze rising to the eaves where the tail of a swallow twitched from a hidden nest.

'I'm afraid there will be no marriage. I'm sorry.'

'They do not approve of me?'

A lesser man would have licked dry lips and wrung his hands. Father Umberto stood straight and tall, his broad shoulders catching the last redness of sunset. 'Donna Nicklau is very possessive of her only son.'

'The woman's a witch!'

The priest's lips twitched with a barely concealed smile. His blue eyes twinkled. 'I wouldn't go quite so far as to say that.'

Catherine glared at the deserted road where weeds and tufts of grass were pushing through the dislodged stones. Her thoughts fluttered to and fro like a butterfly beating its wings against a glass window in its efforts to escape. 'And Francisco? What does he have to say about this?' Her voice was firm. She would not, could not, allow it to tremble.

'He asks that you give him time.'

His eyes did not meet hers. She sensed there was something else he could have said but was unwilling to do so. She asked the obvious. 'Have they arranged a marriage for him?'

She was aware that her voice had an unfamiliar shrillness about it. Her heart was the cause of it, beating so loudly it was ringing in her ears, drowning out her voice.

The priest's eyes were full of concern. 'I don't think so.'

Catherine searched his expression for one of those small signs that betray what a person is really thinking. A sudden blink, a nervous constriction of the throat as though swallowing guilt. At the same time she noticed the fact that the hem of his black robe had caught on his bicycle, was ripped and spattered with mud.

Her gaze dropped to his fingers tapping nervously across his stomach.

'There was something else. Something you disapproved of?'

Surprised by her words and forthright expression, the priest seemed to hold his breath before meeting her eyes. 'I cannot lie,' he said.

'Of course you can't. You're a priest.'

'Francisco is a coward. I don't think you'll ever see him again.' He looked down at his torn hem, grimacing as he fed it through long, sensitive fingers. 'More sewing to do.' He shook his head. 'I hate sewing.'

'Perhaps it's you that needs a wife,' said Catherine with a wry smile. 'Come into the house. I'll find a needle and some thread.'

He looked panic-stricken. 'Oh, no. Not indoors. Couldn't you mend it out here?'

She raised a quizzical eyebrow, sensing he feared being alone with her – just as she feared being alone with him.

'I wasn't going to mend it. You were. Never mind. It makes no difference. I'll fetch the needle and thread. You can do it out here if you like.'

'Oh, yes.' He looked abashed. 'Of course,' he said, recovering his equilibrium. 'Of course I will do it.'

She threw him a half-smile. 'Wait a moment.'

Once inside the house she raised her hand to her face and felt the warmth of her cheek. This was silly. They really should be acting more grown-up.

But you are. And there lies the problem.

She found what she was looking for in her aunt's workbox, an elegant tripod table of cured walnut into which a linen bag had been stitched. The tabletop formed a lid, fixed with brass hinges to the frame.

She took a deep breath before diving in to find black cotton and a needle. This will do, she thought, and closed the lid.

When she got back outside he was running his fingers along the hem. His eyes met hers and he smiled.

'I've sorted it out. I think I can manage without needing to mend it.'

'So typical of a man! Of course it must be mended.' She hit his hands aside as he reached for the needle and thread. 'I'll do it.'

First she threaded the needle, turning the eye to the setting sun and finding it almost magical when a single ray seemed to split the steel on target. Licking the end of the thread, she eased it through at the first attempt.

She was feeling numb with an inner coldness that left little room for emotion. Francisco had taken her warmth away. 'Take off your robe.' She'd done everything with swift, staccato movements, not looking at him, not showing emotion. Her voice and stance remained purposely abrupt.

Father Umberto's eyebrows rose questioningly.

'Or I could kneel at your feet,' she said just as sharply as before, 'if that's what you want.'

He hesitated before silently disrobing down to his singlet and trousers. 'It's very dirty,' he added. 'I trust you can cope.'

She took the robe from him as though it were nothing, as though she were unaffected by his presence. Perhaps that might have been true if she hadn't felt the warmth of the cloth, the slight smell of fresh, masculine sweat. There was usually only a dusty, slightly mildewed smell to priests' robes. The smell of Father Umberto's robe was not at all like that. His physical presence was imbued in the yarn itself.

She found herself forgetting he was a priest, thinking of another time, another place and the boy she'd desired before he'd become a priest. The fact that he was sitting there in singlet and trousers – like a normal man – didn't help.

With veiled glances, she discerned that the body beneath the white cotton was firm and his shoulder muscles and upper arms were well developed as though he chopped wood when he wasn't saying mass.

'There's a bottle of late vintage in that cabinet behind you,' she said suddenly. 'Those glasses are fairly clean. I washed them in the well.'

From beneath lowered lashes, she saw him glance into each glass before pulling the cork and pouring.

'Not for me,' she said as he filled the second glass.

He looked at her. 'No?'

She shook her head. 'I don't like it.'

He laughed lightly. 'Your father wouldn't like to hear you say that.'

Her mouth tightened. 'I doubt that my father would recognize my voice.'

He understood her bitterness. Her great-aunt had told him something of her history.

Catherine carried on. 'He abandoned me. He hasn't seen me for years. And before you make comment,' she said, 'I know he's rich and he could have a wonderful life planned out for me. But why now?' She stopped pushing the needle into the dense material and raised her eyes to meet his. 'I can't help thinking that he's got an ulterior motive. One thing I do remember from the Castile Villanova is overhearing servants discussing his ruthless reputation. His actions confirm those whispers.'

'It's a very rich taste,' the priest said suddenly, holding his glass of port up to the sun. 'It looks like blood with the sunlight shining through it.'

She looked and saw that it was. 'Perhaps I should get to like it,' she said. 'Is that a good one?'

His smile lit up his face. 'Your aunt wouldn't have anything second-rate. Taste it,' he said, handing her the glass. 'But don't swallow it right away. Taste it with the front of your tongue, then each side, then the back. Your tongue is divided into different areas for different sensations. Sugar, salt, bitterness, dryness . . . Savour each as you drink.'

Their fingers brushed as she took the glass. It surprised her when he didn't snatch his hand away as she'd seen some priests do in response to female contact.

In the past she'd sipped and disliked. Now, under his instruction, she *savoured* and learned. She did as he'd instructed, rolling the liquid around on her tongue. She found it amazing that one flavour was in fact made up of many.

'You're right. It divides into different tastes.'

'So does wine,' he said, his face glowing with pleasure. 'Although of course it is less rich than port or sherry.'

He pretended to examine the repair, though his eyes followed her. 'Thank you. I couldn't have done better myself,' he added with a twinkle in his eyes. 'I really mean that.'

Despite everything, she laughed. Initially he'd come with bad news, but ultimately he'd lifted her spirits purely by way of his quiet, deep voice, the way his eyes twinkled, the way his wide mouth curved into a smile. She felt very satisfied that she had waited all these years to hear his voice. The voice of the boy would have been nothing compared to that of the man.

'I'm glad to have you as a friend,' she said to him. 'And I don't mind being your part-time wife. I'm quite good at sewing.'

The words had tumbled from her mouth. She bit her bottom lip and looked down into her glass, wishing she hadn't been so impulsive.

He seemed to hold his breath before responding. His eyes flickered. 'I'm glad too.'

He quickly pulled his robe over his head without undoing any buttons. If he was at all embarrassed by her comment, any betrayal in his expression was hidden.

She turned abruptly away, watching as the last sliver of sunlight shimmered above the horizon.

There followed a moment of silence. She presumed that he too was watching the day dip into twilight. When she turned she saw that his clear blue eyes were examining her in a disturbing manner.

Why shouldn't he? After all, he is only a man!

Aunt Lopa again. The woman was in her brain. And always would be, said that same, small voice.

All the same, that look and her own reaction came as something of a surprise. Unlike most people, she had known him as a boy – although from something of a distance – so accepted that a man existed beneath the black cassock. The garment was meant to create a demarcation between the religious and the secular. It did its work well. And now, although the robe was mended, she fancied something else was ripped.

For a moment they had seemed frozen in time.

'It's time I was going.' He looked at the sunset rather than at the watch he wore on his wrist. 'I will see you again.'

'Yes. Thank you for coming.'

Gone were the two people chatting amiably about the port wine they were consuming, enjoying the texture of the goat's cheese, the freshness of the bread.

He has replaced his uniform and returned to being a priest, she told herself. She wasn't sure what she'd returned to, only that she felt cold and lonely and wished he could stay. Francisco was the second man in her life to let her down. The first had been her father. At least the priest had never let her down, but would he? She wondered if that fleeting moment would affect the frequency of his visits.

Would he visit and listen in the same slightly vague manner he listens to all his flock, or would he *really* listen, *really* take on board her hopes and fears and the bitterness towards men, born when she was just twelve years old. Suddenly she couldn't bear the thought of him never coming again, and yet, instinctively, she knew that to encourage could lead to both their downfalls.

Her impulse won over common sense.

'Will you come again?' she called after him.

He stopped in his tracks. She couldn't read the look in his eyes, but the way his face reflected the roseate glow, she sensed a softening, a look of outright wonder.

'Of course,' he said quickly.

Father Umberto tied the hem of his robe between his legs, reminding her of a peasant woman off to do her laundry. If Aunt Lopa was still alive she would have laughed and told him so.

His movements were quicker than usual although he tried to disguise the fact, unwilling to seem in a hurry to get away.

As she watched, she thought of the smell of his priestly robe, the hair growing on his arms and chest, the thickness of his neck. Francisco had aroused a similar response, but never as powerfully as this. Had she really loved him, or was her affection a result of her growing into a woman?

She didn't quite know but resolved not to be frightened of it. That night she dreamed of the way Umberto's hair curled over his stiff collar and the cowlick that flopped on to his forehead. Like a picture of Lord Byron at the front of a book her mother had given her.

Mentally he was indeed a good priest. Physically, he was still a man, a handsome man. The black robe was indeed a formidable barrier, but Mother Nature and man's nature were ever stronger.

Eighteen

Walter Shellard was seeing a vision. In his vision he did not see the man of careless good looks and impeccable tailoring, but row upon row of vines ripening in the sun; not just hundreds of them, but thousands standing in close-grouped battalions all the way to the horizon. Three huge vineyards, one beside the other, and trucks of course; lots of trucks loaded with grapes on their way to the pressings, or bottles and barrels on their way to bodegas and eventually on to ships for passage to England and other burgeoning markets.

The trigger for his musings of greater estates and greater wealth was standing in front of him. Robert Arthur Freeman was here in his study at his home overlooking the Avon Gorge. Although the man beamed with confidence, Walter glimpsed something else in the darting eyes. If viewed from the perspective of the Ten Commandments, Freeman was guilty of covetousness, greed, envy, lust – and perhaps of breaking a few other God-given rules.

Envious of the wealth of others, such men attempted to acquire the same, but were too lazy to achieve business success; the majority suffered from lack of business acumen. Arthur

Freeman fell into this last category, though he was too arrogant – or too ignorant – ever to admit his failings.

'I've called to take my leave of you,' he said, smoothing away a perceived smut from the cuff of his jacket.

Walter's tone of voice matched his eyes; measured, clear-cut and straight to the point. 'Jolly good. I trust you have a good trip.'

'Thank you.'

He could see the man looked a little uneasy about something.

'I trust you've received the ten per cent promised you?'

The eyes of Robert Arthur Freeman flickered nervously. 'Yes. Yes, I have, but of course the warehousing side of the business was in need of an infusion of capital, and then I had a little investment I had to take care of . . .'

A horse running in the three fifteen at Newmarket more like.

Having foreseen this eventuality, Walter took out an envelope from a desk drawer.

'Here. That should cover your expenses,' he said, flinging the bulging envelope across the desk. Contempt like bile easing up his throat, he watched as his visitor reached for it, his greedy fingers flicking through the contents followed by a brief weighing of the envelope in his right hand, then his left. Satisfied with the sum – some five hundred pounds – he opened the sharply cut jacket he was wearing, sliding it into an inside pocket.

'Wonderful!' He said it in a rush of breath, as though the money had relieved a shortage of air.

'Anything else?' asked Walter. He disliked hesitation in business. He also disliked it in men's general character. Get to the point. That was his motto. 'The man who dithers, dies, Robert. Spit it out.'

Although they'd never been close business associates – Walter had done more business with Robert's father – he had taken to calling him by his Christian name. And why shouldn't he? After all, the man was marrying his daughter – though the girl didn't know that yet.

Robert frowned suddenly. 'I must admit to some concern about your daughter's reticence to come to Porto. Do you think I depart too early?'

Walter shook his head. 'The sooner you get there the better.

The trip will take you a week and I have arranged for you to visit a number of my estates in Portugal and to see what progress we're making in Spain. I think you should have some input into that.'

Robert nodded. 'I just wonder whether she'll like me enough to marry me.'

The same thought had occurred to Walter. It was just a case of persuading her, he'd decided. Sanchia Juventa would see to that once she'd returned from a shopping trip to Paris.

'Rest assured my agent will deal with the matter and will meet you there to ensure you are presented to my daughter in a favourable light.'

If there was one person he could count on to do his bidding, it was Sanchia. She was strong-minded, independent and totally loyal. Besides that, she still had a firm body and curves a man could slide down.

Seemingly satisfied, Robert nodded. 'It appears you have everything covered, except . . .'

Walter was beginning to get restless. How far did this man's greed go?

'Time you were going, Robert.'

His patience was running out. He reached for a sheaf of papers, and made it obvious that he'd finished with their interview.

'I take it we will be included in family gatherings?'

Walter fixed him with unblinking eyes of steel-bright blue. 'Have you disobeyed my instructions?'

A deep flush spread swiftly over a complexion that would have been as fitting for a girl as a man. 'No. I've kept silent. Except with Armitage, of course.'

'I'd trust Armitage over my own brother. You've told no one?'

Robert shook his head. 'No.'

'Fine. You'll both be introduced to my family when the time is right.'

Robert frowned. 'Of course . . .' He hesitated. 'I understand from Armitage that the family are unaware of Catherine's existence.'

Walter slammed the desk with the flat of his hand, sending papers quivering and a pen rolling across a blotting pad.

'Damn it, man! She's the child of a past liaison before I was married. Her mother died years ago. My wife will be informed when I feel the time is right.'

To Walter it was perfectly logical. Robert Arthur Freeman had been told that Catherine Rodriguez was his daughter. Ellen had not. He saw no need to tell her and no need for her to get agitated. Where was the problem? William would probably find out too, but that was neither here nor there. He told William nothing unless it was of the utmost importance, and only Shellard Enterprises fell into that category.

'Then I'll be going.'

They shook hands. After Robert had gone, he took out the details of land, yield and accessibility for the ex-army trucks he'd bought at a knock-down price. The vines were being grown in the old way, but some other things were moving on. Robert Arthur Freeman could not know that without his property, access to the Shellard vineyards would have been difficult – if not impossible.

As for the costs? Walter smiled to himself. First rule in negotiation; know your opponent's weak points. In Robert Arthur Freeman's case it was ignorance. According to his informants, nothing much had changed on Robert's estate since his father had died. He didn't make it his business to visit in order to see what was happening but left managers in situ. He took it as read, relying on other people. All Robert Arthur Freeman wanted to do was enjoy himself. He had the usual weaknesses; wine and women, both in equal quantities, and he was also a man of the turf. On top of his weaknesses, he had dependents: three children and no wife. Reeling him in had been easy and, by the looks of the projections, would turn out to be extremely profitable.

The only concern he felt after their meeting was the fact that Seth Armitage had disclosed that the family were unaware of Catherine's existence. This surprised him. Seth had never been so careless with the family's personal details before. His look darkened as he replaced the top on his fountain pen and laid it neatly at the head of the blotting pad. Seth was getting old. Perhaps a younger man was needed; one more dynamic and in tune with the times.

Yes, he decided getting to his feet. The time may have come to put the old warhorse out to pasture. It's time I was looking for a replacement.

Nineteen

Pride kept Catherine from tramping the road to face Francisco and his family, though she did have moments of weakness when she wanted to run to him and throw herself on her knees before his parents.

It was hard to come to terms with the fact that Francisco had not made any attempt to seek her out and explain. It hurt. He'd been her friend since the day she'd arrived at the train station and he'd driven her to Aunt Lopa's *quinta*. She had not realized how strongly his mother had objected to their relationship, though she should have guessed. She remembered the tight expression and even tighter mouth, no more than a thin line in a narrow face. Yet he had continued to be her friend.

Down in the nearby village she listened intently to the conversations going back and forth. It was said that Francisco had been sent away to his uncle's vineyards. Sympathetic eyes and also those who relished the misfortune of others watched her as the gossip was passed from one person to another. Yet again he'd run away from disobeying his mother.

Market day was in full swing, simple stalls set up on upturned buckets and boxes, live chickens and rabbits in cages, a few fluffy kids tethered to carts and bleating for their mothers.

She was making purchases from a man who brought in supplies from Pinhao for sale at the local market. Everyone who knew her and everyone she knew visited his stall at some point.

'Donna Nicklau is determined that her son will be a priest,' said the robust woman who was delighting in telling her the unwelcome news. 'And knowing Donna Nicklau that is exactly what he will be, whether he likes it or not.'

Catherine kept her eyes fixed on the brown paper bag into which the stallholder was tipping scoopfuls of sugar.

'I'll take another,' she said, her face reddening. She didn't really need another bag of sugar, but pretending to be preoccupied helped her cope. Without meeting the woman's expression, she placed the last of her purchases into her basket. As much as she tried to keep it in, the obvious question popped out. 'And if he does not wish to become a priest?'

The woman, a widow judging by the black she wore from head to toe, frowned as though Catherine's question was an outright blasphemy. 'In my day a young man thought himself privileged to be called to God.'

Catherine couldn't hold back what was in her mind. 'He's not being called. He's being pushed!'

The woman's frown deepened. 'But he'll be a *priest*.' She emphasized the last word as though it were sacred within its own right.

Catherine retaliated. 'And beneath the black he will still be a man!'

Eyes wide with shock, the woman crossed herself. 'Holy Mother of God! What a terrible thing to say.'

One or two of the other women followed suit. Others stayed their hands, winsome and secretive smiles twitching at the corners of their mouths.

'It's not so terrible at all. They're all men before they become priests! A priest is a man for all that!' Catherine pushed away from them, her eyes brilliant with defiance. A chorus of condemning chatter broke out behind her.

She became aware of footsteps. Her heart skipped a beat. Were they following her intent on punishing her blasphemy? Were people already gossiping about Father Umberto's frequent visits?

She glanced over her shoulder. An old woman, the very oldest of the group gathered back there, did her best to keep pace with her.

She attempted to lengthen her stride, but the small woman, her back hunched with years, interspersed her scurry with a series of half-skips, half-runs.

'Dear lady,' she cried between gasps of scrappy breath. 'I hear your aunt's influence in what you said back there.'

At mention of Aunt Lopa, Catherine came to a halt and looked at the woman.

Bright eyes that might have been dark grey, the colour of

dulled pewter, looked out at her from a face burrowed and furrowed with a profusion of such deep lines and folds, that it was hard to discern their true colour. Her skin was parchment brown, not so much tanned by the sun but stained by age and hard work. The wrinkles reminded her of the convolutions of a walnut; deeply gouged and as though cut with a knife.

Catherine recognized her as Rosa. Although she tried, she failed to remember her other name. She'd only met her once or twice before and that was many years ago when she'd first come here. In latter years, her great-aunt used to visit the woman rather than the other way round. Rosa could not heave herself up into a cart or on to the back of a donkey, and long journeys tired her.

'I knew a priest once,' said Rosa. Pinpoints of nostalgia misted her deep-set eyes. 'He was beautiful. We were both young and we became lovers.'

Catherine's jaw dropped and she only barely stopped herself from blushing. Had she said something she shouldn't? Had she betrayed her thoughts in some way? She shook the silliness away. Of course she hadn't. This was Rosa and she was old. Perhaps her mind was wandering. Perhaps Catherine herself had misheard.

'You're Rosa,' she said, looking down into the aged face and smiling. 'I'm sorry. I didn't recognize you.'

Rosa grinned, exposing a series of infrequent, loose and very small teeth. 'I can understand that you did not. We only met once or twice, and anyway, I was taller then. My bones are now shrinking inside my flesh.' She laughed and took hold of a fold of her wrinkled face, pulling it outward. 'See? My skin is too big for my body.'

The effect was unattractive but effective. Catherine smiled. 'My aunt thought well of you.'

The old head nodded on a skinny, wrinkled neck and the deep-set eyes sparkled like water at the bottom of a well. 'Aye.' She nodded and the intensity of her thoughts was reflected in those storm-grey eyes. 'We'd both lived a long time – me longer than her. In fact, I remember when your queen came to the throne. She was eighteen years old.' She paused.

Catherine realized she meant Queen Victoria who'd

ascended the throne in 1837. She herself had forgotten about
one half of her antecedents being English, even though she
did speak the language. The locals had not forgotten. What
struck her even more than that was that if Rosa was telling
the truth about her age she was now well over ninety!

'Back then, we were all young,' Rosa added, hanging her
head and lowering her eyes as though overcome by memories.

Catherine looked to where the road wound up from the
village towards home. It was three miles hence and although
she wanted to be back before dark, it would be discourteous
to hurry away.

'Was there something you wanted to tell me?' she asked Rosa.

The nut-brown face creased into a different pattern of lines
and furrows as she smiled. Her skin shone as she turned it to
the light flowing from the west. 'I knew a priest once. And what
you said back there is true,' she said, jerking her head in the
direction of the market stall. 'A man's a man regardless of what
he's dressed in. My priest was most definitely a man,' she said
softly, a gentle gleam in her eyes. 'He was passionate about
Christ, but his passion didn't end there. Your Francisco may
indeed end up as a priest, but his manly desires will still be
intact.'

Catherine tried to think of something suitable to say, but
her mouth was too dry. She recalled an English saying of not
judging a book by its cover. This saying certainly applied to
Rosa, she thought as she scrutinized the old face, the bent
limbs and the hunched back.

'I see you're surprised,' remarked Rosa. 'That's because I
shocked you.' She sighed deeply. 'You see before you an old
woman, crabbed with age.' That smile again. 'But I wasn't
born old. And there will be other men for you just as there
were for me. Enjoy the passion. Enjoy the moment, and
remember it's only the Church that makes the rules, not the
men they make them for.'

The three miles back up to the *quinta* flew by, simply because
Catherine was simmering with anger. It wasn't just Donna
Nicklau who was taking Francisco away from her; so was the
Church. Added to that, the women at the market who had
made her feel dirty and incredibly rebellious.

The hurt and the anger stayed with her. Only once she set

eyes on the long, white *quinta* nestled among stone pens and fruit trees, did she begin to calm down.

Blasted with the sun and rain of a hundred summers and just as many winters, the dried-out door was smooth to the touch as she pushed it open. The old house was silent except for a few cicadas singing in the rafters and the scurrying of a lizard in response to her footfall. Life is unkind, she thought as she placed her basket of purchases on the kitchen table. Only in those formative years at the Castile Villanova had she been really happy and sure of her place in life and now that was gone. It was only a matter of time before this place too, this place where she had also been happy, would fade into her past.

Hiding was what she felt like doing. There was no future for her with Francisco and she did not want to face her father. On the other hand, she wasn't entirely sure she wanted to stay here.

Being jilted would be the subject of gossip every time she was seen in the village. She could almost hear their comments. Most of them true. She was the girl rejected by the respectable family of the man she loved – or thought she loved. Being illegitimate was bad enough, but being also the great-niece of Lopa Rodriguez didn't help. Some people viewed Aunt Lopa feeding wolves and going from door to door selling her home-made goods as merely eccentric. Others considered her mad.

What worried her more was her growing relationship with Umberto. In her mind she no longer referred to him as Father Umberto. His title, his vocation no longer mattered to her. What was happening between them was far stronger, and far older than any church. It was as though the years in between, including his ordination as a priest, had never happened. She tried to counsel herself that it was unwise to continue what could only end in tears – or more gossip.

She sighed and opened the shutters, flakes of green paint fluttering like snow as they slammed against the outside walls.

Twenty-four hours seemed more like forty-eight living alone with little human contact. The time was spent looking after the goats, tending the vegetable patch and tidying up the house. All these things kept her hands busy, though her mind was with Umberto. Each day she looked out at the track expect-antly, narrowing her eyes against the glare of a metallic-blue sky, seeing his figure in the twisted shadows of a tree, a flash of birds against the horizon, the shape of a scudding cloud. With each passing day that he didn't show up, her bitterness increased. Why did life give her such happiness only to snatch it away? There is only the moment, she decided. Only the here and now to enjoy, and there was only herself to rely on.

Twenty

Via a lawyer in Pinhao, Catherine received a letter from her father referring to the previous letter he'd sent to her great-aunt and demanding she travel to Porto by the end of October. The letter came with a handful of money: *Enough for your transport requirements.* She fancied it was a lot more than she'd need to get there. A note at the bottom of the letter suggested she purchase some suitable travelling clothes.

She thought of the shabby items, lengthened and let out over the years, now folded in a box in her bedroom.

'Any reply?' asked the courier who had brought it, an elderly man from Pinhao who just happened to own a horse and liked riding. Delivering letters suited his lifestyle.

'No,' she replied once she'd read it, her lips tight with defiance. 'None at all.' Once he'd gone, she tore it into shreds, opened the door of the bread oven and watched it turn to ash.

The storms that had flattened the vines were long gone, and the air now smelled of fruit and dark earth and was warm again, though slightly oppressive due to the gradual evaporation of moisture from waterlogged plants and ground.

The road that had been a muddy track leading to the *quinta* was now brick-hard after days of baking heat, though like a piecrust a rich gravy of mud sloughed just beneath the surface.

Father Umberto visited of an evening when the air was heavy with the smell of ripe fruit. She made no mention of the day she'd sewn the hem of his robe.

Catherine had still not unlocked the padlocks of the iron-bound chest. The contents were to have been her dowry; there no longer seemed much point in opening it.

'I'll open it when I'm ready.'

The priest did not seem to accept her decision as final, but continued to visit, offering arguments as to why she should.

'If there is money in the box, you can use it to fund your own lifestyle and not need to follow your father's wishes.'

The suggestion was appealing; all the same she was strangely reluctant. 'Are you not curious about its contents?' he asked.

She thought about it, her eyelids and the fall of her hair masking her thoughts. She narrowed her eyes, taking pleasure in watching the clouds scudding across the sky. The wind was coming from the west, bringing the smell of rain and the salty freshness of the Atlantic Ocean.

It was difficult to put into words how she felt about opening the wormy, iron-bound coffer, but she made a stab at it anyway.

'Do you know of the legend of Pandora's box?'

He nodded. 'Yes. I do. Pandora was told not to open the box entrusted to her care, but curiosity overwhelmed her. She opened the box and vented evil on to the world.'

'Yes. All the ills of the world were set free. I don't want to do that with my box. I want to be sure that I'm opening it at the right time and that I'm not allowing any troubles to escape – or to enter.'

'You're worried,' he observed one sunset as they sat outside sipping port.

He was right about that. Yet she'd said nothing. His ability to read her face and the look in her eyes was born of a growing familiarity. She wondered how long it would be before the old wives in the village noticed the frequency of his visits and began to gossip. She shivered at the thought of their condemnation – especially of him.

'I've had a letter from my father. He demands that I travel to Porto.'

'Have you written back to him?'

She shook her head and raised her wary eyes to his face. 'No. I hate him.'

'Perhaps you should reconsider. He is your father. Perhaps he is seeking your forgiveness.'

'Your father beat you. Have you forgiven him?'

Umberto heaved a deep sigh and set his glass steadfastly down on the table. 'I do not wish to talk about that. We're talking about you. How old are you?'

'Nineteen.'

He nodded sagely, his eyes darting between her and his drink. He adopted a serious, professional expression, the sort he used when counselling people who were older – though not necessarily wiser than he was.

'I believe the age of majority in England is twenty-one.'

'I don't have to go, do I?'

She knew by the way his eyes flickered that she wasn't going to like the answer.

For his part, Umberto had considered his response very carefully. He had to remind himself that she was not his and could not be his, though these visits and being her only source of support made it seem otherwise. His blood raced, so he had to do something. Counting how many clouds were presently crossing the sky helped fill the pause before he could properly respond.

'Your father has legal rights over you. You are not yet of age to be your own woman.'

'You said I should use the contents of Aunt Lopa's old box to run away.'

Umberto hung his head, wished he could cut off his tongue, and shook his head.

'I should not have said that. It was wrong of me.'

'I will stay here. I can manage quite well by myself,' she said hotly.

He looked away and, smiling, said, 'You are not entirely alone. I visit you.'

She glowered at him as though she hated his smug expression when the opposite was true. He looked vulnerable at such times, like a nervous suitor rather than a kindly priest. They'd both become amazed at how much they had in common; they could talk about history, literature or politics for hours, or merely sit in silence admiring the view. *In silence is true friendship.*

The saying was certainly apt. They experienced long periods when neither of them spoke, both gazing at the setting sun and drinking in the scenery.

When they did speak again, the conversation always went back to her father and his sudden reappearance in her life.

She sipped port and shook her head, her eyes still fixed on the trails of salmon pink dissecting the evening sky. 'He didn't want me before. Why now?'

Father Umberto took another sip of port and smacked his lips before attempting to explain. It was at times like these, times when he preferred to keep his true feelings to himself, that he used the well-tried platitudes of generations of tempted priests. He was telling her it was her duty to honour her father, and by the same token her father was attempting to honour her, to plan for her future, to ensure that she was happy.

She pretended to listen, but he could see by the faint dents above her eyebrows that she was seeing through his act. He felt himself blushing.

'I hear Francisco's mother wants him to be a priest,' she said to him.

He tried not to fidget. To fidget would further proclaim just how uncomfortable she made him feel.

'I had heard that,' he answered.

She nodded slowly, her eyes not once dropping from his.

'Do you think a man can be too passionate to be a priest? After all, celibacy is required, and for some men—'

He cut in quickly, not wanting her to finish the sentence. 'Well, it is a matter of discipline.'

He clasped his hands together, his gaze dropping downwards, seeking something inconsequential to look at; anything but her features, her body.

His eyes scrutinized the rough planks from which the floor of the veranda was made, but alighted instead on her knee. Its firm curve was only inches away from his. He could feel her warmth diffusing through the thin fabric of her cotton skirt. The skirt was mauve scattered with purple and green flowers. It was faded where the hem had been taken down to cover her lengthening legs.

But he wasn't really seeing the material or the neat needlework hemming the faded alteration. He was seeing the shape of her knees, her calves, her thighs, and every fibre in his body was screaming.

He went on to answer her questioning of a man's role in the priesthood.

'If a man is commit . . . committed . . .' he went on, hiding his stuttering words behind a mild clearing of his throat, 'then he will do everything to bury his natural urges, to dedicate himself to the life he has chosen, despite everything.'

He looked up at her face again. Her eyes were still fixed on his face, more intently now. It was then that he knew she hated the Church for taking Francisco. A sense of panic came over him. He did not want her to hate him.

'At the end of the day, Francisco will make up his own mind,' he blurted out.

'Father, if I make you nervous, you shouldn't come here.'

He looked shocked that she'd seen through him so easily. 'I . . .' He tried to find the right words, but the pot of platitudes was completely empty.

Catherine smiled. Her expression changed. A minute ago she had adopted the expression of a temptress. Now she clasped her hands in prayer, lowered her eyes and bowed her head.

'Father, bless me for I have sinned. Will you hear my confession?'

'I don't think . . .'

She raised her eyes. 'Are you not a priest?'

He thought about getting on his bicycle and riding away. But he couldn't. She was challenging him to stay and do his priestly duties no matter how difficult.

He nodded. 'Yes, my child.'

She bowed her head again and sank to her knees.

Father Umberto looked down on the top of her head. Her hair smelled of lavender. His blood raced. Worse still, his knees were now only inches from her breasts. Holding his breath for a moment, he gathered as much self-control as he still possessed and carried on.

'You don't need to be on your knees . . .'

'Yes, I do.'

He couldn't find the strength to contradict her.

Closing her eyes, Catherine recited the details of her affair with Francisco. There wasn't much to tell really, so she invented some.

'We went swimming naked in the river, and when we got out . . . we lay naked on the bank. The grass was cool against my back. The sky was so bright. I was dazzled, but Francisco protected me from the worst of the glare, holding his naked body over me, shielding me from the sun . . .'

He felt himself reddening and lowered his hand. He saw the laughter in her eyes and the smile flickering at the corners of her mouth. Bitch! His look hardened. 'You're lying. You're doing this on purpose!'

Face contorted with fury, he stormed off in the direction of his bicycle. It was leaning against the goat pen. One of the goats was standing on its hind legs nibbling at the bicycle's torn leather seat.

Father Umberto lashed out. 'Get away, you stupid goat!'

Without tying up his robe, he mounted his bicycle. Just for this once, he didn't look back.

Catherine's amusement melted away as she watched him go. She'd been cruel to him, almost wicked, and she regretted it. He'd shown her and her aunt nothing but kindness. She asked herself why she'd done it. The answers came in an irregular order. The Church was taking Francisco and Father Umberto represented the Church. On top of that, she was lonely, not that she wanted to walk down to the village every day and swap gossip with the local women. So, if you're lonely go to Porto as your father has ordered, she said to herself.

But she couldn't do that. Her father figured too prominently in the deaths of the two people she'd loved the most.

Another reason swirled around in her head and her blood, its heat more fiery than the setting sun. She'd seen the priest without his cassock. Aunt Lopa's measured words came tumbling back. He was kind, he was considerate, but he was also a man. The unguarded moments; a look, a brushing of hands that had been quickly retrieved, had increased along with the deepening of their relationship.

She told herself to put aside these strange feelings, that they could only lead to trouble, but it wasn't easy. Like an underground stream filling up with freshly fallen rain, their attraction was only just beneath the surface. Eventually, unless he stopped coming, it would burst through.

'I'll tell him not to come any more,' she said when he was no more than a speck at the end of the road. Yes, she decided. That was exactly what she had to do; that, or leave for Porto.

Twenty-One

Another letter arrived.
'Nothing for years and then one letter after another,' she muttered.

She opened it, read it and did the same with it as she'd done with the others. The old iron stove sucked the pieces of paper into its glowing embers. Her father's lawyers – not her father directly – was ordering her to use the money to travel to Porto. They were threatening to send an agent to collect her if she did not conform to his wishes.

'*We would respectfully remind you that you are still a minor and therefore subject to your father's wishes . . .*'

After all this time! The nerve of the man. He made her blood boil. In order to cool down she poured herself lemonade, took it out on to the porch and waited for Father Umberto.

He waved to her when he came, propping his old bicycle against the fence before joining her.

The evening was drawing in, the last of the summer swallows swooping from the eaves to head skywards for Egypt. The shadows thrown by an early October sun were bluish black; like blobs of paint across the green and brown landscape.

Twilight was turning the old walls from pink to pale mauve. The sound of crickets was replacing the sound of bees and the air was thick with myriad scents. 'I never want to leave here,' she said wistfully.

Father Umberto regarded her silently. He'd been thoughtful ever since he'd arrived, his eyes carefully avoiding hers each time she looked at him.

They were sitting outside on rickety old chairs set beside a table with log legs. Two rough planks formed the tabletop.

Catherine poured freshly made lemonade into clay beakers. She handed one to Father Umberto and caught the look in his eyes. She recalled him wearing that same look on the day he'd come to tell her about Francisco's mother objecting to their marriage.

'Bad news. You've brought me bad news.'

Sighing, he rested his elbows on the table and took hold of the beaker with both hands. Seemingly making a sudden decision, he set his drink down on the table. 'José Nicklau has asked me to give you notice. You have to be out of here within the month. He has a new tenant for this place.'

It felt as though her whole world had come tumbling down. This place was her last link with the past and the familiar. Being evicted was not something she had contemplated. 'But I could be his tenant,' she blurted. 'I have money. My father sent money. And then there's my cheese money and Aunt Lopa's chest . . .'

She could tell by the way the priest was shaking his head that this wasn't just about money.

The silky cowlick fell forward as he frowned. He pushed it back impatiently, his eyes darting from her to the freshly made lemonade she had squeezed especially for him that morning, to the house and beyond. She sensed his unease.

'He says he has a tenant willing to work the vineyard and pay him twice as much as your aunt was paying.'

'But I could . . .'

Father Umberto held up his hand, palm outwards. 'Stop there, Catherine. This man has three sons all willing to work in the vineyard. Good, experienced help is hard to come by.'

'And they have no daughter likely to steal Donna Nicklau's precious son,' snarled Catherine.

'Don't!' Soft fingertips touched her face. 'You look ugly when you do that.' His voice was soft and full of restrained emotion.

She shook his hand away and covered her face with both hands. 'Where will I go?'

'To your father? Perhaps it would be better for everyone.'

The words were like an arrow. Catherine opened her hands like shutters and fixed him with wide, angry eyes. 'Including you, I suppose. It would be better for you too because you wouldn't feel obliged to come here. Don't you understand? My father killed my mother! I won't go to him. Not ever.'

Catherine covered her face again, not wanting to see him or the world around her. She'd wanted to marry Francisco, but had settled for staying on here in the hope that their day would eventually come. That's what she told herself, though the truth was that Umberto had been like balm to her emotional wounds – and more besides.

One solitary sob broke from her throat, a sob that changed everything. Father Umberto took hold of her hands. His look was intense, full of emotion – and something else.

'Catherine, we must face life head-on. Everything changes, but God stays the same.'

She smelled the dampness of his woollen cassock and turned herself so that her forehead touched his chest. 'All the people I ever loved have been taken from me. And now I'm to leave this place where I've been happy. I'm so afraid.'

The distance between them closed. If the priest noticed, he did nothing to stop it closing. The slight hint of fresh masculine sweat took precedence over the damp wool, reaching out to her, pulling her closer. Warm fingers stroked the nape of her neck.

'Catherine,' he said simply, his other arm lying heavy around her waist.

Laying her cheek against his chest, she closed her eyes and listened to the beating of his heart. It was racing, drumming against her ear.

'Catherine,' he said again, his voice hushed and trembling.

She could have helped him fight his conscience; drawn back and become flustered. She could have acted embarrassed that she'd been party to him stepping through the barrier presented by the long dark robe. But she didn't. She was caught by the tide and nothing would stop it throwing her up on to an unknown shore. This was her solace for all that had happened, one tender moment she would not be denied.

They stayed there like that in the gathering darkness; he stroking her hair and she with her eyes closed. The rhythm of his racing heart steadied. Hers did not. She wanted to drown in his smell and his warmth. And she dared not look up at him. Judging by his present stance his expression would either be one of sympathy for her predicament or surrender to his own physical need. Either way she felt guilty. She had leaned on him following her great-aunt's death.

The moon appeared from behind a rip in the clouds. A

silver mist flowed over the landscape. The only sound was of the wind stirring the trees. There were no more wolves. The hunters had seen to that.

Umberto cupped her face in his hands, his thumbs brushing away imagined tears. He'd thought she was crying, though she hadn't been.

The light of the moon touched her face. She saw its effect in the priest's eyes and the way his lips parted as he fought his inner battle.

'I must go,' he said, tearing his gaze from her and turning swiftly away. 'But I will pray for you,' he added, grabbing his hat before retying his robe between his legs and throwing his leg over his bicycle.

He paused for an instant, looked at her and then up at the stars. 'It's a golden night,' he said. 'And you are golden.'

She shook her head. 'No. I'm devastated. Just like my mother was. I can understand why she killed herself. It's not such a bad thing. I could do it. I might. I don't think it's that much of a sin. Do you?'

His expression froze. 'You must not think that way!'

Catherine stuck out her chin. She *wanted* to be argumentative. 'I'll think as I like! When you've no one left in the world, what are you to think?'

'I have to go,' he said, pulling the brim of his hat over his eyes, his hands trembling as he reached for the handlebars.

Nodding a last goodbye, he mounted his bicycle. She caught the expression in his eyes. He wanted to stay just in case she meant what she'd said. But if he stayed he was lost.

Twenty-Two

The next night a fine drizzle was falling. The goats had got out and devoured a whole row of late-ripening tomatoes. Freedom had made them skittish and disinclined to be caught. Catherine had spent three hours rounding them up, then another two hours mending the fence and saving what she could of her vegetables.

After eating a bowl of soup, cheese and a slab of dark bread, she drank water and wine, then clambered up to her bed meaning merely to change the sheets. She did exactly that, but after doing so couldn't resist taking off her clothes and lying down, enjoying the freshness of newly laundered bedding against her skin.

She dozed for a while but awoke abruptly. Something had disturbed her. The wind, she thought, or the rain pattering on the window. The light spilling on to the bedclothes told her otherwise. The rain had cleared. She looked out on a star-spangled heaven.

The noise she'd heard was merely the wind rattling the old shutters. She lay back, closed her eyes and folded her arms over her chest, each hand resting on the opposite shoulder. Her eyes flicked open briefly, staring at the ceiling. The last time she'd seen her mother she was lying just like this; cold and white and wearing a wreath of bloodstained lilies.

Tired out by fretful emotions and working around the farm-house, she dozed. In her dreams she and Francisco were running barefoot through the vineyards. Aunt Lopa was cheering them on, her hands resting on the heads of two wolves standing by her side.

'No! Please God, no!'

The voice was not in her dream.

Catherine's eyes flashed open.

Father Umberto stood on the ladder at the entrance to her room. While asleep, she'd pushed the bedclothes down to her midriff. Her breasts were exposed, white as alabaster in the moonlight. He stared at her, his mouth open like a man gasping for a last breath of air before drowning. 'Mother of God! I thought you were dead.' His expression changed to relief and then something else. She read what was there. Her heart skipped a beat. He looked entranced.

She made no attempt to cover herself. Their eyes locked. The moment had come and neither was moving away from it.

It happened quickly. He was at the side of the bed where he fell to his knees, stroking her hair back from her face. His breath was warm. As usual his cassock smelled of damp wool.

She didn't want him to go. She wanted him closer. She

closed her eyes and swallowed. Could she lie? Yes, if it meant he would stay here.

'I wanted to end it all. I've no one left in the world.' Her eyes flashed open. 'Only you. You're all that's left.'

He stared, his breathing erratic as he fought the age-old battle between the spiritual and the physical. The physical, the man he was, won the battle.

Francisco's kiss was like that of a child compared to Umberto's. His hand, large, square and rough as a peasant's caressed her breast. He broke his kiss for a moment to gaze into her eyes, his fingers stroking the line of her jaw, her eyebrows, her nose and her mouth.

Catherine stayed silent, closed her eyes and let the inevitable happen, convinced that to do otherwise would break the spell. Yes, she had coerced, she'd lied, but was it so bad? Hadn't he come to her aid? And surely what was happening could only help heal the hurt.

She told herself afterwards that she should have felt ashamed. The truth was that she didn't. There would be no confession to cleanse her wicked soul because she didn't think she had been wicked. What had happened had happened spontaneously, naturally. The lie didn't matter either, although it was indeed the reason why he'd come.

Umberto had been concerned that she'd mentioned feeling as her mother had done. He'd brooded and prayed in turn that night; wanting to go back to make sure she was all right, but not daring to. 'I wouldn't have left until morning if I had.'

Her eyes asked the question. *And now?*

'I couldn't help it,' he whispered.

She tried to work out how she was feeling. Deep down she was glad this had happened. She'd got under that dull black robe and found a man, a man who was even closer to her now than he had been. She'd also found the crusted ridges across his back. He winced as she touched them.

'For my sins,' he said.

She didn't ask what sins he was referring to. She already knew.

With a sense of wonder she stroked his strong body, the line of his jaw, the misalignment of his collarbone which he'd broken as a child.

'Did you fall off a bicycle?' she asked him.

He shook his head. 'No. My father did it.'

He went on to tell her about his parents, his violent father, his six brothers and sisters.

Catherine was impressed. 'You have such a big family!'

'Yes. Though not perfect.'

Catherine immediately envied him. 'But you *have* a family,' she repeated. 'It must be wonderful . . .'

'Not so. We were always fighting. There was always shouting and hitting. I sought solace. I found it in the Church. Unfortunately I did not leave all earthly pleasures at the door.'

'Is that what I am?'

He looked at her. She saw the amusement in his eyes, though the rest of his face was stiffly serious. 'You are such a typical woman. You seek flattery. You want me to say that you are beautiful and that I love you.'

'Do you?'

The amusement in his eyes spread to his lips. 'I give people colours. Favourite people have favourite colours. I couldn't think which colour I should give you. It was like wrestling with a rainbow. So I decided on gold.'

Umberto's visits became more frequent, though he arrived a little later on those evenings when his duty was required elsewhere. One of those duties was to counsel José Nicklau to adopt restraint in the matter of the new tenant. He'd asked him to give Catherine a little time while she finalized her great-aunt's affairs and made arrangements for her own future.

Catherine was grateful, but that was not the reason she slept with him. He was a good lover, considerate and gentle, consumed by a passion he'd kept bottled up for years. In her heart of hearts she longed for somebody to be close to again. Some kind of family. Any kind of family.

'What shall we do?' she asked him as they lay looking out at the stars.

'Do?'

She could tell by the tone of his voice, the stiffening of his body that he understood what she was saying. But he wouldn't answer, so she answered for him.

'Shall we open my aunt's treasure chest and run away together?'

He didn't answer and she felt a further stiffening of his body. She answered for him. 'You won't stay with me. You'll continue to be a priest.'

'Yes.'

Squeezing her eyes shut to hold back the tears, she kissed a dark brown mole on his shoulder blade. 'Never mind. You've healed my soul. Isn't that what you're supposed to do?'

It wasn't true. She wanted him for always, but yet again he was someone who would not stay. Why did she lose all those she loved?

A low deep chuckle sounded at the back of his throat. 'I'm not sure the bishop would see it that way.'

She wriggled against him, her loins pressing against his buttocks, her hand wandering over his belly so she could bury her fingers in his pubic hair.

'Will you hear my confession, Father Umberto?'

He groaned and half turned. 'What? Now?'

Catherine smiled, withdrew her hand and threw back the bedclothes. She lay on her back looking up at the ceiling. The light coming in the window fell over her nakedness like a soft gauze veil.

Umberto turned round on to his other side. She heard his breath catch in his throat, saw his eyes widen at the sight of her. She sighed when he reached for her, running his hand down over her shoulder. A thumb strayed to her breast before sliding over her waist and the rise of her hip.

'What do you wish to confess, my child,' he said, the words catching in his throat, strangled by the stirring of his loins.

For the first time in her life, Catherine was filled with a feeling of having power over someone else. She'd thought she'd had power over Francisco, but their relationship had been as children compared to this.

'I wasn't really going to kill myself – like my mother.'

She saw a more guarded look come to his eyes. 'You lied to me?'

'But I couldn't help it,' she whispered.

He inched away, but her hand remained on his shoulder and the roughness of healing scars, all that remained of his efforts to purge her from his system.

She felt his muscles tense, but kept her hand in place,

needing to stay connected to him. Those whom she'd loved had left her alone too often.

He raised his head suddenly. 'What was that?'

Raising herself on one arm, she peered over his shoulder. 'Nothing. Just moonlight and shadows.'

She lay down again, curving her body against his.

He moaned and closed his eyes, his body stiffening in a different way. His blood pounded beneath the touch of her fingers. Like her he could not help himself. The rules of man were not the rules of nature. He rolled over on to her, and she opened up to him.

'We'll be condemned for this,' he said later as he got ready to leave.

He opened the door. The moon was high, its light flooding the room.

Catherine followed him, a thin sheet flung loosely round her shoulders, her loins bare. The world outside was as bright as the room behind them. He caught a handful of her hair, bent her head back and kissed the hollow of her throat.

As she gasped, the sheet fell from her shoulders and around her hips, like a lovely Greek statue.

The night air was crisp, the sky clear and the moon wore a silver aureole, a forewarning of a chilly night. Catherine admired it. Umberto, however, was looking elsewhere.

Suddenly the front of the house, the humble yard and the goat pen were lit up as though by day.

They froze, looking out into the night. A figure stood beside a car with shiny headlights. The smell of cigarette smoke joined that of a hot exhaust.

Catherine felt her stomach tightening. She grabbed the sheet and covered herself, bringing it up beneath her chin.

Umberto was frozen to the spot and all the colour had drained from his face. They could have demanded who was this person leaning against the car, but they'd both been surprised, shocked out of the fantasy world they'd locked themselves in.

The woman – Catherine could see it was a woman – slowly raised her head. A pale, handsome face appeared from beneath the brim of a trilby-style travelling hat. The moonlight was such that she could see pencilled eyebrows, thickly lashed eyes and bright-red lipstick. The black stalk of a cigarillo protruded from the side of her mouth. Her eyes flicked from the half-naked girl to the highly embarrassed priest.

'Your name?' she said, addressing Umberto.

Umberto gave his name.

'Yes. The local priest.'

Umberto looked terrified. 'Yes.' His voice sounded fragile, far away.

'I've caught you sinning. I heard locally that you visit here often – too often.'

Umberto suddenly seemed to collect himself. 'Who are you?'

Unsmiling, the woman threw him a haughty glare. 'I'm the witness to sin who can ruin both your lives. Now get out of here.'

She turned her gaze back to Catherine. 'Get dressed. We need to talk.'

Even though the woman had not given her name or stated her business, her manner and her sudden appearance in a very fine motor car gave her credence.

Despite the circumstances, Catherine was awestruck. The woman was wearing a woollen suit with a dropped waistline. A silver fox fur adorned her shoulders. A black bow perched like a dead bird on one side of her broad-brimmed trilby. Everything was expensive and shouted city life. She'd seen no such clothes as these since leaving Castile Villanova.

Catherine concluded she was tough; how else had she managed to drive on such a ruined road?

Umberto was edging into the shadows.

The fear of being left alone threatened to overwhelm her.

'Umberto.'

Umberto stalled.

'Go,' said the woman in a threatening manner. 'Leave before I inform your superiors of your shocking behaviour. I can assure you that your career in the Church will be short-lived if I have to do that.'

There was a moment – a fleeting moment reminiscent of the time when Catherine had been a schoolgirl and Umberto an altar boy and a figure of girlish romance. As they had back then, their eyes met with unspoken words.

'Inside,' said the woman in the rich clothes.

The room, which earlier had seemed so warm, felt cold as Catherine backed into it. She shivered and watched as the woman's eyes searched the humble farmhouse; a look of pity laced with contempt.

'My name is Sanchia Juventa.'

As she spoke the woman lifted the lace-trimmed edge of a curtain between the thumb and forefinger of her kid-gloved hand, examined it and let it drop again.

'This was your aunt's place?' She spoke quickly and economically, no ten-letter word used where a three-letter word would do.

She found herself stuttering as she explained. 'My mother's aunt . . . Aunt Lopa was my mother's aunt.'

The woman glided over the stone-paved floor, her shiny presence making the old place look shabbier by the minute.

Catherine thought of the motor car outside. She didn't know that much about cars, but it looked fine, very fine – which she interpreted as costing a lot of money. The woman was well dressed, definitely not from any of the farms or vine-yards, and probably not from Pinhao. The suit was made of some kind of tweed, a plain mustard trim bordering the neck and hem of the jacket. She frowned.

'Did you drive here from Porto?'

The woman nodded in the same manner as she spoke; sharply and swiftly. 'Yes.'

With a sinking heart, Catherine came to the obvious conclusion. 'My father sent you.'

'Yes.'

'I won't go.'

She flinched under the threatening look in the woman's greenish eyes. 'I think you will.' Her tone of voice was bereft of emotion. This was a woman who got things done, who stuck to the facts and never, ever wore her heart on her sleeve.

'Will I go to live with my father?' She gathered the sheet more closely around her in response to the look in the woman's eyes.

'You will do as your father says.'

The woman appeared unconcerned about what Catherine wanted or didn't want. Her contemptuous gaze was still scru-tinizing the basic furniture and primitive interior of the dwelling house.

'My father abandoned me!'

Her words were filled with fire and based on fact. She barely remembered the man responsible for her mother's death. An obstinacy borne of anger shot through her.

'We're going. Tonight,' said Sanchia Juventa, speaking in English that to Catherine's attuned ear hinted at Spanish being her native language.

Catherine snorted defiantly. 'Then you'll have to take me as I am,' she said, dropping the sheet and standing there stark naked.

Sanchia Juventa raised one thin eyebrow. 'If you like. I really don't care.'

'I'm not leaving right away.'

'Right away.' The tone was dismissive. Her word was law.

Catherine recognized this was a battle of wills. She had no intention of giving in to this woman and sensed if she won this battle, the rest of her life would run in much the same vein.

Sanchia Juventa was elegant, cultured and not the sort to get involved in physical work. And that, thought Catherine, is her weakness. 'Are you terribly strong?'

Arched eyebrows lifted a little higher on the powdered forehead.

'That chest is my inheritance.' Catherine pointed at the old coffer. It looked heavy and *was* heavy. 'I can't leave it here. A new tenant and his sons are moving in. The contents are quite valuable. That's besides my clothes and personal items. We'd have to load it into your car between us – unless you have a chauffeur hidden beneath the back seat.'

Catherine had only seen the woman; a woman beautifully dressed and driving a shining motor car. She wouldn't show it, but she was mightily impressed. This was an independence to be admired.

The Spanish woman took only a few seconds to come to a decision. 'Is there someone who can do this for us?'

'A boy comes tomorrow to milk the goats. He'll fetch someone.'

Dawn came too soon. Catherine's eyes clicked open. Pigeons were still roosting above her in the rafters of the room she had loved at first sight. The view outside the window was the

same as it had been yesterday except for the men man-
handling her luggage, including Aunt Lopa's chest, on to the
back of the motor car. And there was Sanchia Juventa over-
seeing everything.

The Spanish woman had wanted to leave immediately, but
Catherine had been stubborn, citing her dowry – the iron-
bound – chest as a reason.

'Unless we lift it between us. Then there's my other luggage,
and the road being so bad in daylight let alone darkness . . .'

She'd won the argument. The truth of the matter was that
they could have handled everything between them quite well,
but Sanchia was not the sort of woman used to getting her
gloved or ungloved hands dirty.

Exactly as Catherine had promised, the boy who came to
help with the goats was sent to fetch help. Everything had been
loaded – the few dresses, some of Aunt Lopa's favourite
crocheted pieces; Catherine handled them carefully, remembering the clicking of that hook and her great-aunt's homespun
wisdom.

Although she had won a significant battle with Sanchia
Juventa, she sensed that her ordeal was far from over. There
were more battles yet; for the moment she was still smarting
from the fact that Umberto had been ordered from the house.
More than that, Sanchia had *known* about their liaison. Had
tongues already been wagging?

Poor Umberto. What would happen to him? She asked
Sanchia.

'He's being moved to another parish.'

Three, Catherine thought to herself. Three people had now
been taken away from her, although Umberto at least was
alive. God has his way, she thought to herself, except that her
father had more to do with it than God ever had.

She lingered in the old house, wandering through each room
and smelling again the old leather, fresh straw and ash from
apple logs left in the fireplace.

She'd attempted to stand her ground the night before, but
that was when Sanchia Juventa had stated the obvious. If she
stayed or if she ran away, the priest would be ruined.

'Your father would see to that,' Sanchia had said in no
uncertain terms.

Catherine had glowered at her, hating the way the woman

smoked cigarettes; the long ebony holder like a witch's wand.
But she knew what gossip could do. She'd heard whispered
tales of women like her who'd been stoned or dragged out of
their homes to have their head shaved and their naked bodies
covered in animal filth. She'd heard of priests sent away to
rot in perpetual seclusion.

'His sin would be forgiven but not forgotten. He would
remain a priest. All ambition thwarted. Would he like that, do
you think?'

Sanchia had a cruel way of smiling. Catherine decided she
would actually *enjoy* observing the consequences if she did
rebel.

No. She couldn't bring herself to do that to Umberto. He
meant a lot to her and always would, but like others she'd
loved, he was gone.

'Catherine!'

Holding back the tears, Catherine backed out of the shady
house into bright sunshine, but she did not feel bright. One
world was closing behind her, another was about to present
itself.

She remained staring at one particular shutter squealing on
its hinges like a baby crying for its mother.

Sanchia paid off the men – though not enough, it seemed.

'We came at short notice,' they said grudgingly.

'Fine,' said Sanchia. 'And you only worked a short time.'

The metal clasp of her handbag snapped shut. She turned
to Catherine, frowning as she looked her up and down.

'What is this outfit?'

Catherine shrugged. Her coat was too tight, her dress frayed
at the hem and she was wearing her work boots which had
no laces.

'My father never sent pretty things from the city. We made
do with what we had.'

Sanchia seemed to bristle at this.

'Your father has more important things to spend his money
on.'

Now it was Catherine who eyed *her* up and down. 'So I
see.'

Sanchia's dark expression darkened some more. 'I meant
business.'

'I didn't.'

As a child, she'd sometimes imagined meeting her father again, finding him penniless and in dire need of her assistance. In her imagination she refused to assist him even though he begged for her help on bended knees and asked to know why she treated him so.

Her response was always the same. 'Because you killed my mother.' In her vision he would turn away, fading into the greying fog of destitution and death.

Twenty-Three

Ellen Shellard sat in front of her dressing table, staring at her reflection without really seeing it. Germaine had stormed out of the room after throwing a doll on to the floor. The tantrum had been about her wanting to go away to boarding school in England. Walter was insisting and had informed his daughter that this was what he wanted, and this was exactly what she would do.

Germaine had whined and pleaded, and although she hadn't actually agreed to her father's demands, she gave the impression that she did.

However, once she was alone with her mother, it was Ellen who got the blame. Germaine's bluish-grey eyes had turned as steely cold as those of her father.

'It's you who wants me to go away. Not my daddy. My daddy would never send me away to school.'

In a vain attempt to support her husband, Ellen had insisted that the idea *was* her father's, and that Germaine shouldn't be quite so hostile about it. 'You'll probably enjoy it when you get to Red Maids. You'll make lots of new friends.'

'I've got lots of new friends here,' she'd retorted, her long ringlets bouncing and her cheeks an unhealthy shade of crimson.

'You haven't really,' said her mother. 'You spend most of your time with your dolls.'

Germaine's crystal-blue eyes seemed to send out sparks of electricity. 'I have friends! Not just dolls!'

With a last torrent of angry words Germaine flung the doll she was carrying across the room, where it thudded against the bottom drawer of her mother's dressing table.

Alone with her thoughts, Ellen had sighed and closed her eyes; although Germaine was her own flesh and blood, there were times when she harboured a most definite dislike for the girl. Her father had indulged her far too much; what she wanted, Germaine got. Now she could not believe it was her father's idea to send her away because it wasn't what she wanted.

Ellen had picked up the doll and sat it on her dressing table. She recognized it as being the same doll they'd found in the wine cellar some years before. Back then she'd wondered who it had belonged to. It was some months after finding it that she'd discovered the truth about its owner.

She'd been walking along the corridor above the kitchen when she'd heard a commotion from down below. A woman was demanding to know how her darling Catherine was doing.

Intrigued, she'd gone down to confront whoever it was. The kitchen staff had turned round askance when she'd asked what was going on.

'Just a worrisome local woman. She wants to know about . . .'

The woman, restrained by the gardener's son, was strongly built and had no trouble in flinging the lanky youth aside.

'Catherine,' she said, her eyes wild and her plump face as dark and polished as a church pew. 'Master sent away my little one and promised he'd send me word of her. He never did. I know he's a busy man, but 'tis his own flesh and blood after all . . .'

Ellen had remembered how cold she'd suddenly felt. On seeing her pallor, the kitchen staff had made another attempt to eject the woman from the premises.

'Mistress,' implored the plump woman. 'Mistress. I beg you to help me.'

It was not in Ellen's nature to be unkind and the woman had looked so desperately unhappy. She had the look of a peasant, though she was cleanly dressed and had a kind face.

Her shoes seemed too large for her feet and slapped on the stone floor with each step, like the paddles of a waterwheel.

Ellen had taken charge. 'Leave her. Come,' she'd said, taking hold of the woman's arm. 'Let's seek some fresh air.'

With her hand cupping the woman's meaty elbow, she'd guided her out into the cool passage that led from the servants' quarters to the stable yard.

'This Catherine. You said she was my husband's flesh and blood?'

The woman thrust out a square, work-worn hand and leaned against the wall. ''Tis my joints,' she said breathlessly. 'My legs are no good. And I need to catch my breath.'

Ellen was touched by the forlorn expression in the woman's eyes and the fact that the corners of her mouth seemed permanently pointing downwards. Overall her demeanour was one of abject sorrow.

'He promised,' she said, her eyes now full of pleading. 'Her mother died of a broken heart and then her father, the master, sent her away.'

Up until now the woman had gushed with emotion. Now her expression became more guarded, as though she'd said too much – and more than that, she'd spoken openly to someone she'd never met before.

'Did you know Leonora?' she asked pensively.

Ellen could barely control the dizziness brought on by the woman's words. She reasoned there must be a perfectly sound explanation, and yet, deep down she already feared the worst. Leonora had lived in this house before she had. What was more, the child Catherine had been her daughter – hers and Walter's.

Ellen looked down into the woman's face. 'Would you like a drink? To sit down?'

The woman shook her head.

'Perhaps you could tell me your name?'

'Conceptua Delamora. I was Catherine's nurse.'

Ellen nodded her head slowly, her eyes wide with a mix of curiosity and sheer fright. Over the years she'd begun to guess that her husband was not the handsome, though mature, Prince Charming she'd been led to believe. His word was law, but he was not only ruthless but more selfish than she'd ever imagined. His family, the world at large and everything else took second place to Shellard Enterprises. His company was swiftly becoming a monster created by and controlled by her husband.

Walter allowed no one and nothing to stand in his way. The love she'd borne him had faded away to a dull though dutiful physical routine. If he noticed her frequent absence from his bed, he did not mention it. Not long ago she'd come to the conclusion that he was acquiring satisfaction elsewhere. Like other long-suffering wives who knew, she swept it under the carpet and maintained the public face of a very successful and respectable family. Her mother had told her to turn a blind eye and think herself lucky. Happiness didn't enter the equation.

Ellen's mouth turned dry before she could answer the question that burned her tongue although she'd already worked out the answer. But she wanted it confirmed. 'Who was Catherine?'

The old nurse looked up into her face as though she'd been abruptly awoken from a very deep and satisfying sleep. 'I've already told you, signora. Leonora's child, of course. Leonora Rodriguez. Catherine was sent away after her mother died. I took her up to Pinhao where she was met by someone who took her to her aunt's farmhouse. A boy came to fetch her,' she said, turning thoughtful. 'A boy with reddish hair and a pony and trap.'

Ellen barely heard her.

Catherine Rodriguez.

The name burned into her brain.

'How did her mother die?'

The old nurse's face clouded. 'I have said too much.'

Ellen grabbed her shoulder. 'Tell me.'

Conceptua told her the circumstances, the place and the date. Ellen felt numb, as though her blood had turned to ice.

'I go now,' said Conceptua, everything about her now slower, more silent, and sadder.

Ellen rummaged in her pocket for a few escudos. 'Here. Take these.'

Conceptua looked suddenly alarmed. 'I want no money. I want Catherine . . .'

Ellen clasped both the woman's horny hands in her own softly refined ones. 'I promise I will find out where she is and how she's doing. I promise.'

She smiled a hesitant though sincere smile, tears stinging

at the corners of her eyes. Her pity was not just for the old woman, but also for herself. Life, it seemed, had dealt both of them a hard blow. Now she had to decide how best to deal with it. She wasn't a coward, but she knew her husband well. Confronting him would do no good at all. He might admit the existence of an illegitimate child, but he wouldn't go into detail. He would leave her stewing, in fact she was almost sure that he *enjoyed* torturing her in that way.

In the meantime she stared at the doll and tried to work out the best way forward. Who was close enough to Walter to know about this child? Not his mistresses, the women who shared his bed. Seth Armitage knew everything there was to know about the family, but Seth had been put out to pasture and replaced with a smart stockbroking type from Surrey.

William! It had to be William.

Taking her diary from a drawer, she counted the days until they returned to England. Seven days. Seven days and then she would arrange a meeting with her brother-in-law. If anyone knew of this Catherine and her mother, Leonora, it would be him. And she preferred talking to him rather than Walter. Walter would be dismissive. 'Water under the bridge, my dear. I can't waste time talking about what's long past. I have a business merger to deal with.'

Basically he wouldn't care whether she knew or not. She was merely his wife and the gilt had worn off with the ongoing years. But Ellen was intrigued.

That evening she entered the locked room next to the nursery in the north wing. She stood there a while, imagining she could smell Leonora's perfume and hear her tinkling laughter.

Dusk turned into darkness before she found the will to leave the room, closing the door softly behind her, as though she were loath to awaken old ghosts.

On the contrary, she wished very much to know more about the woman who had died in that room. She wanted to know about Leonora and was overcome with a great urge to try and put right whatever wrong had been inflicted.

Twenty-Four

'I want to meet him today,' Catherine said to Sanchia. 'I insist.'

Sanchia raised a beautifully plucked and arched eyebrow, part of a look of pure disdain.

'You cannot.' She sniffed, her nostrils flaring like those of a well-bred horse. 'He is not ready for you. Besides, you need a bath.'

'I'm not having one until he agrees to meet me.' She slumped down on to the satin-covered bed. 'I'm not moving from here until he does. And I'm not bathing.'

Sanchia's nostrils seemed to quiver at the prospect of her natural smell, unadulterated by French perfumes or soap, but she was not one to give in easily.

The haughty countenance was transformed by a hearty, and uncharacteristic, smile. 'Your father has given me money to take you shopping. You can buy as many pretty dresses as you wish plus lacy, silky underwear, stockings, shoes and accessories. Other girls of your age will be envious. Won't that be wonderful?'

Catherine narrowed her eyes until they were catlike slits. She scowled.

Sanchia faltered and her smile slipped from her face like melting butter.

'Well?' said Catherine.

Sanchia pursed her crimson lips as she thought it through. 'It may be possible.'

Catherine threw herself back on the bed, lying full stretch, arms above her head.

Sanchia threw back her head, exclaiming her exasperation in Spanish through clenched and very white teeth.

'All right. I will see what I can do. Will you get up? Will you bathe?'

Catherine turned her head and looked at her. She saw Sanchia flinch – perhaps at the intensity of her look and the dark-grey eyes – or perhaps it was something else.

'Will you promise?'

Sanchia's lips parted. Catherine discerned that she was wondering whether to lie; whether to promise in order to achieve what she wanted, then go back on her word.

'Don't promise unless you mean it. Otherwise I'll run away.'

A moment of panic flashed in the Spanish eyes. 'You do not know this city. There are dangers.'

Catherine turned away. 'There are dangers all over this world. Not just here.' She jerked her head back again, her eyes opened wide. 'My aunt fed wolves. Did you know that? They killed her in the end. Ripped half her face off and chewed her fingers. Did you know that?'

It gave her great pleasure to see Sanchia's sophistication distorted by horror.

'Liar!'

Catherine rolled over on to her stomach and began picking at a loose thread in the quilted satin.

'I relate, I never lie, and when I promise I keep my word.' She glanced over her shoulder. 'Do you?'

Even before she said it, Catherine knew she had won. Sanchia presented herself as a confident and sophisticated woman. Underneath it she was the same as most women, obeying the orders of the man in her life. She was everything she was because of him whereas Catherine was herself, would love where she wished and be what she wanted. Of that she was now certain.

Sanchia promised; just as Catherine had expected her to. Before leaving she promised to ring him from her room.

'I'll wait to hear from you.'

Sanchia was not the sort to sigh in surrender – at least not to another woman. She knew when she was beaten, not just because of Catherine's strategy, but because of the determined look in those dark-grey eyes. It confirmed beyond doubt that Catherine Rodriguez was indeed her father's daughter.

She thought of these things as she walked the sumptuous corridor of the hotel. Oblongs of chocolate brown with dropped corners broke up the plain beige walls. Each wall light consisted of three upturned triangles outlined in a darker chocolate. Normally she would have admired such a forward-thinking style inside a Baroque exterior. Today she was oblivious to the fashionable décor, the newly installed wall lights matching the same art deco style.

Sweeping past the room she had been allocated, she made for the elevator and instructed the bellboy to take her to the fifteenth floor. He'd recognized who she was so didn't question her choice. Hotel guests were not given the choice of going there. The official letting rooms available to the general public stopped at floor fourteen.

Sanchia watched the stiff needle of the crescent-shaped indicator above the door. It finally came to rest on fifteen. The hotel was the loftiest in Porto. If the lower floors were sumptuous, the fifteenth was breathtaking. Burnished copper strips replaced the chocolate brown of the lower floors. The walls glowed with a colour just a few shades lighter than clay.

Walter's butler, Hopkins, a bland-faced man with pale eyes and greying hair, awaited her.

'Is Mr Walter expecting you?'

'No,' Sanchia snapped. She'd mentioned to Walter that Hopkins' habit of calling him Mr Walter irritated her.

'He's been with the family a long time. I am Mr Walter and my brother is Mr William. It's his habit.'

He'd given no indication that this was likely to change. Despite everything, Walter was very defensive about his family name and traditions. Like this hotel; he'd intimated that he didn't want too many people to know he'd entered the hotel business. She'd never quite understood why; she'd presumed it was because he preferred to be known for wine – and port wine in particular. Not that it mattered to her. She loved Walter and she loved the luxuries he showered on her. How he made it was of no consequence.

The butler peered at her in an unassuming yet puzzled way, like a tortoise poking its head out after a long winter's sleep.

'Do you wish me to disturb him?'

He sounded quite concerned at the thought.

'No. I will,' Sanchia snapped.

She swept past him in a flurry of perfume and swishing skirt, her arms swinging at her side.

'Walter?'

She found him dictating to his secretary, a frump of a woman named Miss Vincent.

On seeing her, Walter's face clouded. He jerked his head at his secretary. 'That will be all for now, Joyce. Get those letters out and we'll go back to the report later.'

'Yes, sir.' Miss Vincent adjusted her spectacles, tucked her notebook under her arm and nodded a brief acknowledgement to Sanchia on her way out.

Walter got up from behind his desk and opened the adjacent cocktail cabinet. 'Drink?' he asked, raising a decanter of blood-red liquid.

Sanchia frowned. 'You don't usually drink before midday.'

He glanced at her, an expensive cigar clenched at the corner of his mouth. 'You look as though you need one. Go on. Spit it out.'

He passed her a glass. She drained it.

'Aren't you having one?' she asked, her eyes widening questioningly as he placed the decanter back in the cabinet.

His smile was rueful, almost triumphant. 'You know me, my darling. I never drink until after sunset. It's not good business practice.'

She felt immediately that he had her at a disadvantage and that he'd done it on purpose. He'd caught her off guard, just as he did many people.

'Your daughter wishes to meet you. She's demanding you both meet now, today, right away!'

He looked surprised. 'Does she now! How very interesting.'

'I tried to put her off. She's very determined. She made me promise.'

He turned away from her, slowly closing the cabinet doors. She watched him, taking the opportunity to scrutinize the mane of iron-grey hair tamed back from a widow's peak at the centre of his forehead. At this angle she could not determine the expression in the cool, dark-grey eyes, but for some odd reason she fancied he was flustered. It came to her that she'd never seen him flustered; never known him to be thrown off balance by anyone or anything. And yet for a split second she'd thought she'd seen him hesitate. Someone not as intimate with his habits and movements as she was would not have detected it; but she knew him well. She'd known him for eighteen years; since she was twenty years old. Two years and she would be forty, a fact she tried hard not to think about; not the years themselves but the fear that, despite her lasting beauty, Walter might turn to younger women. There were many of a 'modern' turn of mind who would willingly take her place. She would do her best to keep rivals at bay.

He turned to face her. He was wearing a navy-blue three-piece suit. A gold wristwatch of the latest Swiss design flashed at his wrist. His shirt was impeccably white and the strong face above the neat collar had not yet lost its firm lines, even though he was in his fifties.

Even now, after all these years, her legs turned to water at the sight of him.

'What shall I do?'

His eyes were unblinking. A sly smile hovered on his lips. 'Well, Sanchia my dear. Best not break a promise.'

The rigid shoulders relaxed. Internally, Sanchia breathed a sigh of relief as the tension she'd breezed in with left her.

'Perhaps tea?' she asked, her tone of voice reflecting her sense of relief.

'Tea would be fine,' Walter's mouth stretched into a smile. His teeth still clenching at his fine Havana.

'I saw her getting out of the car. She looks pretty. Her clothes look dreadful. You'll have to do something about that before we introduce her to Arthur Freeman.'

'I can make a clothes horse look alluring,' Sanchia exclaimed, throwing back her head and expelling a heavy sigh.

She threw her arms around his shoulders and kissed him longingly and deeply. The moment her lips met his, she wanted more . . . much more.

She paused briefly for breath. 'Darling, I should stay,' she said, running her hand down his chest to his waist where he caught it before she could stray lower.

'You heard me tell Miss Vincent that we have a report to write. Business before pleasure, my darling. Now run along and fix a teatime meeting with my daughter. I'll see you later.'

Sanchia positively blossomed at his words. The proud exterior turned humble once his hands were upon her, although in bed he reckoned she became a tigress. Outside the bedroom, Walter was like a ringmaster and the tigress in her was tamed.

After she left, he went through to the small office where Miss Vincent tapped away on her new Imperial typewriter.

'We'll get back to that report later, Miss Vincent.' He looked tellingly at his watch. 'I have a luncheon appointment in my apartment. We'll resume the report at two.'

His luncheon guest arrived at twelve noon precisely, as arranged. Hopkins ushered her in.

'Miss Maria Elrosa,' Hopkins intoned, his face implacable and giving no sign whatsoever of how he might feel about this girl.

Walter smiled and offered his hand. As the girl took it he appraised her anew. She'd applied for a job as a waitress just two days ago. He's spotted her in passing making an appointment with the concierge. The black hair coiled high on her head had immediately grabbed his attention. He disliked the new style for women to have their hair cut short. He loved the way a woman's hair fell when released from its confines of pins and combs or from beneath a veil or hat. Short hair could not do that; neither could it replace the trailing of long tresses over naked flesh, one of the most sensual pleasures he'd ever experienced.

'So, how much have we offered you to work here as a waitress,' he asked, at the same time appraising her long legs, her rising bosom and the flare of her hips beneath the shapeless dress.

She told him how much in a soft, lilting English. Owners of bodegas and others in the port wine trade stayed here quite frequently; speaking English was a definite advantage and he told her so. He also told her that she was pretty and would most definitely prove a great asset to the establishment.

'Thank you,' she said, blushing profusely. The light of interest sparkled in her eyes.

'Yes,' he said, 'I think you will do very well.'

In his mind he was finding a new position for Sanchia, perhaps in some venture away from Portugal, from Spain and from him. She was getting older. It was time for casting his net and seeing what could be caught.

Twenty-Five

Ellen Shellard couldn't help fidgeting. Simpson's was full and she was sitting alone at a table for two. Brushing her fingers across the blazing white tablecloth, she briefly wondered what other diners must think of her; did they wonder if she had a liaison? Don't be silly, she told herself. You're nearing thirty-five years old. Act your age. You're here to meet your brother-in-law.

But the jitters were endemic and she tapped her fingers, shifted in her seat, and played around with cutlery. In the process of doing all this, she dropped her handbag, a very expensive item from Harrods and made of Blue Nile croco-dile – or so she'd been told. Walter had bought it for her for Christmas. On reaching down to retrieve it, she knocked a spoon and fork from the table and dipped down a second time to pick these up. As she did so, her foot brushed against the brown paper carrier bag she'd brought with her. It contained the doll she'd discovered at Castile Villanova.

'No need to bow and scrape, Ellen. I'm pleased to be here.'

The dangling end of the tablecloth caught beneath the sole of her shoe. 'Oh, blast!'

'Let me.'

While Ellen disentangled her shoe, William rested one hand on the tablecloth to stop it slipping further.

'Are you all right?' He kissed her cheek.

Ellen sighed like a deflated balloon. 'My health is fine, if that's what you mean. It's everything else that isn't quite right.'

A waiter pulled out a chair and William sat down and ordered drinks.

William had been blessed with the same good looks as his brother, but more softly endowed. Almost as though, thought Ellen, there hadn't been quite enough metal left over to make him of the same iron hardness. William was softer and, although she'd never admit it, she found this quite endearing.

He offered her a cigarette from a gold case monogrammed with his initials. They lit up, drew in the acrid smoke then like a mutual sigh, let it out again simultaneously.

'Tell me all about it, sis,' he said to her, his eyes full of concern in a way Walter's never were.

The waiter brought menus. Before looking at them, Ellen drew the carrier bag out from under the table.

'I've got something to show you.'

'You've bought me a present?'

His face was bright with merriment. He was joking but he loved it. Humour was never very high on Walter's agenda, so Ellen welcomed it.

'No,' she said, and brought out the doll.

William frowned. 'It's a doll.'

Deep dimples appeared at the sides of Ellen's mouth. Even though she was feeling far from her best, William never failed to make her smile.

'I didn't buy it for you. It's Germaine's, but I didn't buy it for her either. We found it behind a stack of bottles at Castile Villanova.'

He took it with both hands. Looked at it. Made a non-descript face and shrugged. 'So? What's the significance? It's a nice-looking doll. I expect one of the servants' children left it there.'

Ellen made a cat's cradle of fingers, on to which she rested her chin. 'It was made in Bristol by a very expensive doll maker.'

She saw his eyes flicker and a small frown pucker his hand-some forehead. 'So it wasn't for a servant.'

Lowering her eyes, then her hands, to start playing with the cutlery again, she said, 'No. It most certainly was not. I believe the doll belonged to my husband's daughter.'

Ellen was astonished at William's transformation. Up until now he'd been the attentive though impassive recipient of her conversation. Now he was changed; far from impassive, indeed, she'd never seen such a pained expression in his eyes.

'Walter's daughter! Is she with her mother? Did you see Leonora?'

She glanced down at her hands. For a brief and very strange

moment she'd almost believed that her hands were around his throat; so husky, so full of emotion did he sound. His eyes had drifted from her face. He looked lost; lost and far, far away.

Ellen felt immediately worried about him. 'William.' She reached for his hand, clasping it between both of hers regardless of what anyone watching might think. His look was such that she couldn't care less about social conventions. 'William. Leonora's dead. She shot herself when she found out Walter had married me.'

Mouth open, face pale as white flour, William shook his head. 'No,' he said, in a muted voice. 'No.'

Ellen gauged everything about his reaction.

'I understand Leonora lived with Walter for a number of years.'

His eyes flickered at the mention of her name. Mouth gaping still, he nodded.

Ellen ordered a waiter to bring tea and some food. 'Just a light lunch. The chef's recommendation will do,' she said quickly. She'd ordered the food merely to buy them time, certain they would not eat it.

'I knew her before Walter did. It's my fault she lived with him,' he said at last. 'But I didn't know about the child.'

'I see.'

She waited for him to continue. He told her about Leonora Rodriguez and how he'd fallen in love with her. 'She was going to be a nun, so I stepped back and let her do as she pleased, though I loved her . . . I sorely loved her. She was so beautiful. Heavenly in looks and spirit. In a fit of melancholy – and too much to drink – I confided my feelings to Walter. It was the worst thing I could have done. He was intrigued and sought her out. What Walter wants, Walter gets. You should know that.'

He told her the whole story and how he had felt afterwards, also how he had ended up marrying Diana.

'I never visited the Castile Villanova while she was installed there.'

Ellen had listened attentively, all the time condemning herself for marrying Walter, for thinking she could be happy with such a man. You accepted him, she thought to herself, and in return a woman killed herself and a child was turned out of her home. She felt responsible.

'I want to find this child,' she said, her voice firm with conviction. 'I want to put things right for my own peace of mind.'

William nodded. He suddenly looked a lot younger than his forty-eight years. Ellen automatically reached out and covered one of his hands with one of hers.

'You loved her deeply.'

He nodded. 'I tried to find her after Walter married you. He told me she'd decided at last to enter a convent, but I didn't believe him. All the same, it was pretty feasible. Her aunt was a nun. I enquired about her at the convent where she used to be. I thought she'd know where Leonora was. I learned that she'd left. No one seemed to know where she'd gone except that it was north, up in the Douro Valley.'

Ellen sighed reflectively. 'I haven't mentioned any of this to Walter.'

William shrugged disconsolately. 'There wouldn't be much point. He'd just shrug it all off and wouldn't tell you anything. Once something's done, my brother quickly relegates it to the past.'

'Exactly.'

They sipped silently at their tea, both engrossed in their own private thoughts.

'And he wouldn't give a damn if you knew,' William said suddenly.

'No. He wouldn't,' returned Ellen and knew it was true. 'When I next go to Portugal I intend seeking out the woman who brought this to my attention.'

William's face lit up. 'Who is she?'

'The child's nurse. Her name is Conceptua Delamora.'

'When do you go to Porto again?'

'In two weeks. Walter has arranged for the children and me to holiday there for the summer. He's too busy to come.'

William nodded, his eyes heavily lidded in a similar, though more open, way than his brother's when he was planning and scheming.

'I'll meet you there. We'll search her out together.'

Twenty-Six

U nlike the splendidly well-groomed Sanchia, and certainly against her advice, Catherine had purposely hooked out her ugliest dress in a weak attempt to proclaim her disdain for everything her father stood for. Green had never been her colour. Blue would have better complimented her dark-grey eyes.

'You dress carelessly,' Sanchia had said, her arched brows meeting like an arrowhead above her straight nose.

'I don't think so,' Catherine had retorted.

She was speaking the truth. She had thought carefully about what she should wear to meet her father. The choice was difficult. On the one hand she wanted to go to him bathed in defiance so he would look at her and rue the day he'd set aside both her and her mother. On the other hand she wanted him to think her childish, even a peasant, and not want anything to do with her.

The latter was preferable. The dress, washed and worn a thousand times, was now a very light green that made her look sallow, almost as though she were sickening for something.

Sanchia stared at her feet. 'Those shoes!'

'They're all I have.'

Sanchia's jaw dropped in dismay and her frown deepened. 'They are dreadful.'

'They're my school shoes.'

She said it blithely, though secretly she blessed the flat black creations with the ankle strap. Like a pair of chameleons, they could be flattering with the right dress and extremely ugly with the wrong one.

Sanchia sighed. 'At least your hair is presentable.'

Catherine grimaced. She'd bound her hair into plaits. Naturally silky, escaped fronds fell around her face relieving the tightly torturous look of her hairline. Her features too were unalterable; there was nothing she could do about the colour of her eyes or the way they reflected the light like flashes of highly polished silver. Her cheekbones were high, her mouth wide and sensual.

She followed Sanchia up to the fifteenth floor.

'My father lives here?' she asked, taking in the quality surroundings and the pale-eyed man who greeted them.

'Yes,' said Sanchia.

She found herself impressed. 'He owns this?'

'Yes,' snapped Sanchia as they followed the butler through a pair of double doors.

'How rich is my father?'

'Very rich. Now stop asking questions.'

She had no need to ask any more questions. Other questions, other answers and ensuing plans were forming in her brain. Castile Villanova was the most luxurious place she'd ever lived in and he owned that too. And all this would be hers if he'd married her mother. In response to this sudden truth, she not only felt resentment but also a great urge to recover what should rightly have been hers.

The room she found herself in was broad yet had been decorated and furnished in such a way as to focus on what appeared to be a glass wall immediately ahead of them. Beyond this glass was a balcony and on the balcony was a dark-suited figure.

Her heart began to palpitate as he turned and entered the room. Before he'd entered, the room had seemed spacious and clean-cut, decorated as it was in the modern style. Once he'd entered, it felt cluttered, small and almost stifling.

Catherine found herself holding her breath. She clenched her hands behind her back as she studied him, determined she would not smile, would not like him.

Her mind worked quickly, assessing from the way he moved whether he would offer her his hand. She decided not and was proved right. Once he was close enough, she studied his face. His eyes shocked her most of all. They were dark grey. Fixing on them alone was like looking at her reflection. His face, however, was not like hers. She was reminded of a linocut print she'd seen of Napoleon Bonaparte that had been defaced by a school friend who'd insisted he should smile. Her father smiled just like that – and, as in the case of Napoleon, it didn't belong.

He stood with his legs braced as he looked her up and down. 'Well!' he said at last. 'You're Leonora's daughter.'

In a split second before she responded, Catherine changed her mind about his eyes. They weren't exactly like hers. There was no warmth. What light she'd seen in them was reflected from a mirror that in turn had reflected the light from the windows.

'I understand I'm yours as well,' she retorted and purposely copied the tone he himself had used.

If he was at all taken aback, he didn't show it.

'You look a little like her.'

'But I have your eyes.'

He flinched, seemingly surprised that she had noticed and he had not. So! Walter Shellard was not infallible.

There was an arrogant tilt to his jaw, a purposeful look in his angular features. She decided his face had always been totally bereft of curved lines or soft flesh. Everything about him was hard and would be hard for a very long time. Not until he was really old bones – perhaps in his eighties – would deep lines score the corners of his mouth or his flesh droop, hanging like limp lichen from his cheek-bones.

'Those clothes,' he said, preferring to forego her features and return to the less palatable subject. 'You're wearing them specifically to annoy me?'

'They're all I have. I've had to make do and mend over the years. You never sent Aunt Lopa any money for my keep.' She didn't know whether it was the truth or not, but didn't care. He deserved to be the target for every grievance she could think of.

His eyebrows rose in surprise. 'Aunt Lopa?' He laughed, not a big, manly laugh, but a sly, low sound deep in his throat. 'You mean Anna Marie Rodriguez. I hear she was slightly touched. Runs in the family, I think. That's why your mother killed herself.'

Although her coldness cut her like a knife, she refused to show any emotion. 'Really? I thought you drove her to it.' Her delivery was as cold as her father's had been.

He shrugged. 'I did what I had to do. Now sit down,' he said, indicating a square-armed sofa of a green only a few shades darker than her dress. 'But carefully, so I can see where I've left you. That dress is almost the same colour as the sofa. We might not be able to find you again.' He laughed at his own joke.

Every nerve ending in her body tingled as Catherine sat on the sofa aware of the soft fabric surrounding her, the thick carpet beneath her feet. In some odd way each luxury item seemed an affront to her mother's memory; such opulence, such ostentation directly in opposition to the empty hollowness of death.

Her father seated himself in a chair directly opposite. Sanchia lowered herself into a chair covered in gold brocade. As usual she was elegance personified in a claret-red silk jacket and a close-fitting skirt. A stiff visor of black net drooped over her eyes from a hat that matched her outfit. She took an ebony cigarette holder from her handbag. Her eyes were fixed on Walter Shellard, Catherine's father.

'Put that away,' he said, pointing at the unlit cigarette.

Sanchia obeyed instantly.

Catherine observed, sucking in information like a sponge. Inside she was squirming, but outwardly she was calm. She fixed her eyes on him, wanting to know more about him, but only in order to destroy him. She'd read somewhere that revenge should be savoured cold. To do that she had to control her deep-seated emotions.

Sanchia poured tea and handed cups around. Her father sipped at his tea like a gentleman, yet Catherine sensed the steely hardiness of a common seaman at the core of his soul.

'You read my letters so know why you're here,' he said after replacing his empty cup in its saucer.

'No. I burned them.'

'You're at a vulnerable age and you're my responsibility until you are twenty-one. From what I gather you are most definitely in need of moral guidance. You either live under my roof or under that of a husband. At least with a husband you would be mistress of your own house – your own life to a great extent.' He looked her up and down. 'Though I doubt anyone would have you dressed like that.'

The idea of having some kind of independence from her

father – from everyone – was attractive. But she wouldn't tell him that. Although he tried not to show it, her behaviour and shoddy appearance was irritating. She decided to go one step further and be shocking. 'A husband would expect a virgin bride,' Catherine said, her eyes flaring with defiance.

Her father's response was less than pleasing. His lips spread in something resembling a smile. 'That is true for Portugal and other Catholic countries. An English husband would not be so choosy.'

'I think I too will be a nun. Like my Aunt Lopa.'

He slapped his hip with an air of exasperation. His patience was swiftly running out.

'Stop being so irritating, Catherine. Go with Sanchia and buy some new clothes. We can't have you going to England looking like a poor peasant.' His manner was dismissive, as though she were no more than an annoying fly buzzing around his ears. He glanced at his watch.

Angered by this, as he looked up, she said, 'I suppose you have to be somewhere else. You never did have much time for me.'

For a moment her sharpness seemed to put him off balance, though not for long.

'You're spirited.' He sounded surprised.

'Like my mother?'

He paused and a small frown creased his brow, then it was gone. 'No. Not like her at all.'

She disliked the way his gaze held hers, as though he were trying to glean what she was beneath the scruffy exterior. But she would not lower her eyes. She detected a seed of concern in his mind and instantly knew what it was. She was not like her mother, but he'd expected her to be. And if she was not like her mother, then she must be like him. She liked the thought that it worried him.

Sanchia passed him a buff-coloured folder, opening it for him before sitting back down. He proceeded to read from it. 'As your official guardian . . .'

Guardian? Not father?

'I've made reservations for you and Sanchia on the packet to England. The ship leaves in two weeks. Be on it.'

Catherine glowered. 'I don't want to go to England. I want to stay here.'

The set of her father's features were as stiff as a marble statue. His voice was devoid of emotion. 'You will do as I say.'

She felt as though she were drowning in a sea of panic, but still she reined in her voice and the emotion that drove it. 'I have my own money. I saved money from selling cheese. And I think my aunt left me shares.'

An amused smile crossed his face. 'A few may be in some ne'er-do-well Iberian companies. Not enough to live on, my dear Catherine.'

He glanced again at his watch. His tone was clipped and matter-of-fact.

'You've no choice. Your mother was not respectable. And neither are you. I've no time to argue. Everything's been arranged. If you continue to refuse, then that priest fellow will bear the consequences. My credit is good. Sanchia will go shopping with you. You cannot go to England dressed like a peasant. Bristol is not London, but it does have some standards.'

The hated country! The hated city! A rough seaport on the western coast. 'I don't want to go to England! It's your place. The place that killed my mother.'

His eyes rose sharply to meet hers. 'Your mother killed herself! Anyway, that's beside the point. I thought I made it clear. You have no choice. You're young but will adjust quickly.' His eyes narrowed suddenly. 'Besides, you wouldn't want to be responsible for a defrocked priest, would you? I know the bishop in that area and the cardinal above him. I could ruin him with a word in the right ear.'

Those cold eyes were like needles sticking into her mind. She knew he meant what he said and she couldn't be responsible for Umberto's destruction. Although she wished it were otherwise, she knew the priest would confess his sins – or perhaps not – and get over her. He would return to being a celibate priest, dedicated to God's work, though perhaps more intensely now because he had known the face of temptation and could put it behind him. She knew exactly what Walter Shellard was saying to her. Do as he said and Father Umberto would continue in his chosen vocation. Disobey and he'd be destroyed.

Twenty-Seven

Walter Shellard slid his arms into his silk-lined dressing gown. With practised movements, his manservant brought one edge of the gown over the other, smoothing the front flat before tying the silk cord.

'That will be all, Cedric,' said Walter.

His manservant backed away, dipping to pick up his master's shoes on the way out. The door made a comforting click behind him.

Walter Shellard let out a great sigh of relief. Alone at last. He enjoyed his own company. It gave him time to think and he had a lot to think about. Acquiring more vineyards both in Portugal and other wine-producing regions occupied most of his mind. His daughter, the offspring of him and the sloe-eyed beauty he'd accosted on her way from church all those years ago, occupied a lesser portion.

To help him think he lit up a cigar. He had them made in Havana, his name embossed on the label; the cigars matched everything else in his life. He insisted on only the best.

Feeling his eyes watering in response to the intense smoke, he opened the pale-green shutters and stepped out on to a red-tiled balcony. Narrowing his eyes he surveyed the hotchpotch of clay roofs glowing with the last rays of the setting sun. Old buildings creaked as they breathed out the warmth of the day, cooling with the promise of evening.

The sky was still blue in places, like icy pools among hills of snow. Blue brought Leonora to mind. She had been little more than seventeen when he'd met her; he'd been twenty years her senior and married. Literally bumping into her as she descended the steps of the local church, her dark hair swathed in a white mantilla, her blue dress floating around her like a piece of fallen sky, she had taken his breath away. She'd been everything William had said she was, and although she insisted that she was to become a novice in the local convent, Walter had pursued her. Unlike his brother, he had refused to take 'no' for an answer but worn down her resistance until she'd finally given in.

The time had been right for both of them. He had been ripe for love, not just his usual indulgences with fleeting fancies, but affection as well as passion.

At the time marriage was not suiting either himself or his first wife. Gertrude had turned into an invalid just a few months after their wedding once she had discovered the secrets of the marriage bed and found them not to her liking. Her attitude towards Portugal was pretty much the same and based on just one visit. 'I have no wish to ever see Portugal again. I shall stay here,' she had announced in the bedroom of their home in Clifton. Things, opulent things, were more to Gertrude's taste. She'd surrounded herself with clutter that suited her taste but did nothing for his. China-faced dolls with painted eyes and pouting mouths sat in tiers against one wall. In a fit of anger one day, he'd stolen one of those dolls, taken it to Portugal and given it to Catherine. Whether Gertrude ever missed it, she didn't say. Anyway, he relished the small act of cruelty that he'd given something of hers to his mistress's child.

The house in Clifton, a superior area of the city of Bristol, suited Gertrude very well, though thankfully he succeeded in curtailing her dubious taste to her own suite of rooms. The Georgian façade and interior of Adelaide Court remained elegant and, for the most part, unembellished in its lofty spot overlooking the Avon Gorge and the ships journeying up the river.

Feeling cheated and burning with the urges that no young man worth his salt could ignore, for a while he had considered whether he could endure the monk-like celibacy of a married man who is married only in name. But his blood had run hot; it still did.

He did not seek her approval of him taking a mistress. Somehow he knew that she would not care very much at all – as long as such an arrangement was discreet.

There had been many women over the years, but only Leonora had shared his home. Variety, he'd found, suited his nature. But always there had been Leonora. He smiled as he remembered their early passion.

Dark and sensual, Leonora had expressed fear at a ruined reputation. Portugal, like the rest of Europe, was narrow-minded back then. It still was. He'd taken her from her family and her village; a place high above the River Douro where vineyards fell like green ribbons into the valley and folk were simple and honest. Only months after their first meeting, she had moved in under his roof. A year or so later she had given birth to a daughter.

He'd considered himself a fortunate man. He had the best of both worlds; a legal spouse far away in a smart town house in Bristol, lying sick and fragile – at least, she was when he was home in Bristol – and a graceful and passionate young woman in Porto.

'Gertrude fades every time I see her,' he'd told Leonora. 'One day, my dear, one day you will take her place.'

He'd been right about Gertrude fading away. Bloated and pale, she had drawn her last breath on the couch where she spent most of her waking day complaining of headaches. The reason for the headaches became clear the day after her death when a servant had cleared out the bottles beneath her couch. Inactivity and the fruits of the vine had proved her downfall along with Fry's chocolate and Cheddar cheese bought by the truckle from a farm near the town of the same name. She also drank Somerset cider, a heady dark-green brew festering with the pips and cores of the apples from which it was made.

They'd lived apart for years, so he didn't miss her and therefore did not grieve. There'd been no love, no physical contact and no mutual respect. They'd agreed over the years to tolerate each other, toleration made easier by distance. With hindsight, he should never have promised. His frown deepened at the thought of it, but he brightened again when he thought of Ellen and the children she'd borne him. Everything had worked out fine in the end – for him.

'You're a lucky man, Walter Shellard,' he said to himself. 'Keep lucky. Keep going, old man.'

He did not turn at the sound of a key unlocking the door to his suite. He knew who it was and turned to face her.

'She's stubborn,' said Sanchia, flinging aside her handbag. 'Like you,' she murmured. Her hat followed the handbag. 'I take it she's too old to be spanked.'

Her words tumbled from between plush red lips at the same

time as her unpinned hair tumbled around her shoulders. After unbuttoning her red jacket she tossed it to one side, exposing the upper half of a tightly boned basque. Her skirt followed. She let it fall around her ankles, stepping out of it as though it wasn't there.

Walter smiled and arched one eyebrow. His thoughts had caught on her idea. Sanchia had a most glorious backside, twin orbs as firm as ripe melons. Her waist was tiny, her breasts as voluptuous as her buttocks.

'Where is my daughter?'

Sanchia, his lady of Cordoba, took her time answering. By the time she reached him she was clad only in her corset, French knickers, stockings and high-heeled shoes. 'In her room, staring out of the window. She does not want to be here. I think she prefers goats to civilized company.'

She pursed her lips and sucked on his, her arm sliding around his waist. Encased in pink and coffee-cream lace, her breasts pulsed against his chest. He would have covered one swelling mound with his hand, but there was something he had to arrange before they went to bed.

Walter smiled to himself. 'You're right about one thing. She's very like me.'

His smile diminished at the thought of it. The fact that she was so like him was surprising, but nothing to worry about. After all, she could never rival him. She was a woman. Women were annexed to men. That's the way it always had been, and in his opinion that was the way it would stay.

Sanchia looked peeved at his declaration. 'I expected her to be like her mother; insipid and slightly deranged.'

Walter clenched his jaw. Her description irritated but did not anger. She knew very well that she was one of many. If the situation didn't suit, why did she stay? As always, his voice was as straight as an arrow and did not reveal his reaction.

'Now, now my dear. It's bad luck to speak ill of the dead.'

The red lips pouted. The dark eyes looked soulful. 'I'm sorry.'

'Good,' he said slowly prior to voicing the plan forming in his mind. 'I want you to be a friend to Catherine.'

'A friend?' Now it was Sanchia's eyebrows that were raised in surprise.

'A surrogate mother if you like.'

She looked puzzled by his request; this pleased him. He'd half expected her to explode like a volcano. She was the exact opposite of the fragile and gentle Leonora. Leonora had been subservient and dependent on him. Sanchia, on the other hand, was self-sufficient, strong and incredibly passionate. She was a red rose to Leonora's white lily, and that's what he liked; contrast, at least among his women.

Sanchia flinched as the hand holding the cigar cupped one side of her face.

'No need to be jealous, my dear. You're still here and I need you. I need you to help form my daughter's future,' said Walter, stroking her cheekbone with his thumb.

A dark cloud of shingled hair sloughed around Sanchia's face as she tilted her head. Her eyes sparkled and pearl-white teeth showed from between vermillion lips as she smiled up at him. 'I will do anything you want – for your daughter and for you,' she said huskily. Her pink tongue slid slowly and salaciously along her bottom lip, leaving it glistening. Her hands ran up and down his back, her fingers feathering out over his buttocks, her fingernails raking his flesh.

'You're distracting me,' he murmured.

'I know.'

'I want you to concentrate.'

She adopted that sultry smile he knew so well. 'Is that what you are calling it now?'

She gasped as he took hold of a chunk of her hair, bending her head back so that she had to be still, she had to listen.

His breath fell on her face, his eyes bored into hers. Even after all this time, she could still arouse him, though these days she had to work at it. Younger women did not, and in time they would take her place. But this was now and she was loyal and efficient.

He began outlining what he wanted her to do. 'I like things to be tidy in my life. I am responsible for Catherine. I have to do what is best for her, and you will help me do that.' His statement was far from the truth. Control of Robert Arthur Freeman's company was within his grasp and the poor fool would hardly even notice.

Sanchia attempted to nod, her white teeth biting into her bottom lip, half with pain, half with pleasure.

'Say you will,' he said, jerking her head back that bit more. Sanchia gasped. 'Yes! Oh, yes.'

'I do not want her turning up at Castile Villanova. I do not want my wife knowing of her existence. I am shortly vacating my house in Bristol and moving to London so it's not likely she'll find out about her. In the meantime, there's nowhere for her to go. Catherine is young, but old enough to get married. I would have left it a bit longer if Lopa Rodriguez hadn't got herself chewed to death. I wish my plans to run smoothly. I want her to marry this man.'

'Of course you do,' said Sanchia, relaxing slightly as he released his grip. Her hand slipped beneath the silk dressing gown to do delicious things to his flesh.

'She's wilful and, as you say, stubborn. Arthur Freeman has been over here a few weeks and has probably spent the money I advanced. Luckily, he's a charmer. It's just a case of outlining what he should say to her and what he shouldn't say. Meet the man and instruct him. I know you can do that.'

'Of course,' she replied as she began to sink lower down his body.

'Not yet,' he said, his mind elsewhere for the moment as it tended to be when he wished to exert his will over others. 'It's imperative that you get him to act out a part – even if you have to resort to your most lethal powers of persuasion.'

He saw her expression change. She knew exactly what he was asking of her. How few women would actually adhere to that? He answered his own question. Few. Very few.

She knew him well enough to know when he was being serious and looked up at him over his loins, his belly and his chest.

His eyes filled with cunning. 'As for Catherine, become her companion. Gain her trust. This will work well on the boat trip over to England.'

The wide smile returned to Sanchia's face. Her hair now released, she pressed her body tightly against his. 'And my reward for this service?'

Walter smiled. 'What is it you want?'

'You.'

'You should know better than that.' He shook his head. 'You women. You always want most that which you cannot have.'

She rubbed the curve of her cheek into his palm. 'Or that taken in rebellion that is bad for us. That is our nature. You know women well, my darling Walter.'

His smile was enigmatic, almost cruel. 'Much to my advantage.'

Defiance flared in her eyes before subsiding to be super-seded by helpless adoration. He'd always had that effect on women. His thoughts returned to his daughter. The little bitch had it in her to be defiant. He'd seen himself in her dark anger and could almost smell the need for revenge burning beneath the surface. Nothing would come of it; if he put a stop to it now. She was young; as a wife her character would be moulded by her husband, if not wholly, then partially.

'And for my reward?' breathed Sanchia, her voice as rich and thick as melted chocolate.

Walter sighed, bent his head and kissed the creamy orb of bosom swelling above the tight corset. 'You, my dear, will receive your just desserts.'

Twenty-Eight

A week before departure, an army of seamstresses was employed in altering dresses purchased in Porto. Catherine sat having her long locks shingled into the latest 'elfin' cut. The result fitted her head like a glossy black cap and made her eyes look huge in her heart-shaped face.

While the shorn hair was brushed from around her feet, she watched as Sanchia examined each and every outfit again and again.

She struck a commanding picture, her long arms stabbing at the air like a musical conductor in charge of an off-key orchestra. Curt and to the point, she snapped out exactly what was wanted, insisting that full skirts were cut to take account of current fashion. 'Have none of you seen a Hollywood film?' she shouted. 'Have none of you seen *Mary Pickford*? Take

out the seams. Flatten the bosom. Shorten the hem. A glimpse
of knee. Not ankle! Knee!'

The women, most of whom were of late middle-age,
exchanged shocked, round-eyed looks. Their own hemlines
still reached the floor; their skirts were bulky over bulging
hips.

'Like this,' shouted Sanchia, slapping open the pages of a
fashion magazine, yet another featuring an article on
Hollywood movie stars.

On seeing the short-skirted 'flappers' the women exchanged
more shocked glances before catching sight of Douglas
Fairbanks. Their expressions softened noticeably and they
began fingering the pages with hesitant interest.

It was hard not to smile. The hairdresser intervened and so
prevented the smile from becoming too wide. '*Voilà*,' she said,
teasing Catherine's hair into feathery tufts around her face.

Catherine eyed her reflection. Her glossy black hair framed
her face. Her eyes looked huge, her lips too red against her
creamy complexion. If things had been different she would
have been pleased. As it was . . .

'Do you like it?' asked Sanchia.

Catherine shrugged but said nothing. She was *letting* this
happen to her; she told herself this in defiance. Secretly she
was pleased with the transformation. If she was ever to
command the sort of respect Sanchia received, she had to look
the part – only more so. Being confident and smartly turned
out would enable her to take control of her own life, her own
destiny.

Occasionally she considered delving into Aunt Lopa's
chest to check exactly how much 'pretty paper' was in there.
Fear of disappointment stayed her hand. Wait until you have
no choice, she told herself. Wait until those bits of paper
– small sums as they may – are your only way out of a
difficult situation.

'It suits very well. I like it,' said Sanchia to the hairdresser.
It sounded to Catherine's ears as though it were the hairdresser's
crimped glory she was referring to, not the glum-looking girl
sitting silently in the chair.

'Perhaps the young lady would like to go outside a moment.
The hair will brush into place so much more easily once it's
drier,' said the hairdresser.

'Yes,' said Sanchia, gushing with unexpected enthusiasm. 'I think that is a very good idea. Go on, Catherine. You may go to the courtyard. Sit there a while.'

The hotel had become very familiar during the extent of her stay. Catherine knew very well where the courtyard was. She'd discovered it two days ago. It was pleasant to sit in, away from all these arrangements. Better still, she'd found someone to talk to.

'Hello,' he'd said, appearing from around the corner of a flowering shrub. He'd been whistling, so hadn't taken her by surprise.

She'd said hello back, although she hadn't really been in the mood to strike up a conversation. She needn't have worried. He asked for her permission to sit next to her and from then on he'd done the talking.

At first the conversation had been about him. He'd told her that he was an inveterate wanderer, a man who had travelled all over the world.

Catherine had never met anyone who had travelled the world and was immediately intrigued. 'Are you a famous explorer?'

He shook his head. Fine lines appeared at the corners of his eyes when he smiled. 'No. I don't travel to discover high mountains or deep rivers. I suppose you could say that I travel to discover myself.'

His answer intrigued her. She immediately wanted to know more.

'My name's Catherine Rodriguez,' she said, offering him her hand.

She noted his palm was very warm. Her hand encased in it was very cool.

'Call me Arthur.'

'Arthur,' she repeated, liking the sound of his name. 'You're so lucky to travel. I've never travelled anywhere except from Porto to my great-aunt's farm. Tell me more,' she said. 'Tell me about the places you've visited. Tell me about the people.'

His eyes held hers. He smiled as though much satisfied that she'd asked him.

'Very well, Catherine Rodriguez. I will tell you. I've seen the pyramids at sunset, dawn over the high Himalayas, and gold-covered statues in Siamese temples. I've ridden horses, camels and elephants; I even attempted to ride a zebra in

Rhodesia, but that didn't prove very successful. It kicked like a mule!'

'You fell off?' she asked, suddenly amused despite her depressed spirits.

His eyes were a strange greyish green flecked with hazel and danced when he smiled. 'Absolutely! Straight into a steaming pancake laid sometime earlier by a passing water buffalo.'

She laughed at his meaning. 'A very large one?'

'Very! I have avoided zebras ever since. And as for the people; some were veiled from head to foot, and some were nigh on naked – begging your pardon, miss.'

He doffed his hat when he apologized. It was a white panama with a black band. His suit was light-coloured and he wore a matching waistcoat with a gold watch chain that sparkled in the sunlight. He carried a silver-topped walking stick that he leaned on with both hands once his hat was back on his head.

They were sitting beneath a cluster of shady palms. She guessed her new companion was at least ten years older than she was, perhaps more, but she didn't care. He'd certainly put her at ease and she'd never known anyone quite so interesting.

Throwing back her head she enjoyed the alternating pattern of sun and shade dancing over her eyelids.

'I wish I could stay here for ever,' she said, wanting desperately to hold on to the moment and her uplifting companion.

He made an agreeable sound deep in his throat and looked around him. 'It's not bad.'

Her eyes shone when she looked at him. He'd filled her head with such tales and fired up her imagination. 'Did you ever enter a harem?'

'Young lady!' he said, taking on a shocked expression. 'I'm surprised you know of such things.'

Catherine narrowed her eyes. She could see a smile twitching around his lips. She shook her head. 'You don't mean that?'

He pretended to be insulted, his chin seeming to recede into his collar. 'Of course I do!'

The afternoon had worn on and Sanchia had not come to fetch her, and she was sure she'd seen a flash of yellow dress lurking in the shadows. No matter. She readily agreed when he asked if he could see her again.

So here she was, shrugging her shoulders in order to alleviate the itching around her neck.

As she made her way to where they had sat, she shook her head, finding it strange that her neck felt so exposed to the air. Deep down she knew the fashionable haircut suited her, but she'd never admit that to anyone, least of all to Sanchia.

Just as she'd hoped, her 'explorer' was sitting on the bench beneath the clutch of dark-leaved palms, his head back, eyes closed and mouth slightly ajar.

Her spirits soared, though for a split second she paused and a small cloud of concern flashed over her face. Should she proceed? After all, so many of her acquaintances disappeared once she cared for them too much. Was it wise to enjoy the company of a man who would soon bid her farewell?

No, she decided. One part of her wanted to go forward, to sit and laugh and talk with him as she'd done these few days past. The other was afraid, pleading with her to go, making her feet tap as she considered what was best.

'You smell strange,' he said suddenly. 'Quite pretty, though.' He opened one eye and regarded her along the length of his nose.

'You've had your hair cut.'

She had the instant impression that he didn't like what he saw. 'It's the latest fashion,' she blurted out. It sounded so lame, such a pathetic excuse for cutting off hair that had never been cut before. 'I used to be able to sit on it,' she said, sounding extremely apologetic.

'Well you can't stick it back on again,' he said, shifting to sit up straight as he fixed his eyes on her. 'Promise me that you'll never cut it again.'

Overwhelmed by his charm, she promised him.

'I didn't have it done by choice. Sanchia insisted,' she said, sitting down beside him. She touched her shorn locks. 'I hate it. I hate everything that's happening to me. Have you ever felt like that? Hating what was happening but not being able to do anything about it? I don't doubt that becoming a modern woman has its advantages. But there are sacrifices, like putting up with people you don't really want anything to do with. I wish I wasn't here.'

He pulled a face as he appeared to think about it. 'Sometimes I've wanted to run up a mountain and get away from it all.

To do something outrageous to cleanse my system no matter what anyone else might think. Is that what you mean?'

She nodded, her eyes shining at having met a kindred spirit, someone who would understand.

'That's exactly it. I don't want to be the same as other people. My mother wasn't the same.'

'You mean she didn't conform. I take it she was just as beautiful as you?'

Catherine smiled enigmatically. This man was such a flatterer and was expecting her to blush; an impossibility on account of his comment. The most beautiful vision of her mother was of her lying in her coffin wearing a wreath of bloodstained lilies.

'She was,' she replied. 'But I'm only like her in some ways. Looks, mostly.'

She knew she was speaking the truth. Looks were one thing, but in other ways they were very different. Her mother had been submissive. She'd lived for Walter and through him.

Catherine was beginning to realize that her weakness was not in being submissive but in being passionate. She had enjoyed her time with both Francisco and Umberto. Since leaving them both behind, she had had the chance to analyse the difference between the two. If his mother had acquiesced, Francisco would have given her the security of a wife and her passion would have been sated in the marriage bed. As it was, he'd let her down. Her relationship with Umberto had been something grabbed on the spur of the moment. She had also been the spur to his repressed sex drive – in that his passion had matched her own. Looking at her father and the fiery Sanchia, she knew from whence it had been inherited.

'Now tell me what you're going to do with your life,' he said suddenly.

There were a number of possible answers. She stared at him, trying to gauge from his expression whether he expected a maidenly answer. Maidenly! A maid was the last thing she could be.

She countered his question with one of her own. 'What did you do when you were young?'

'I travelled,' he said abruptly, his flecked green eyes fixing on a wasp and a droplet of sap oozing from a lemon tree.

'Yes, of course. I wish I could travel, but my father has made other plans,' she replied.

Arthur related more of his travels. Catherine listened, enraptured by his tales of distant lands and strange peoples.

'I'm going to England,' she said suddenly. It was likely to be the only travelling she would ever do.

'I am *from* England,' he said with a smile. 'I'm travelling back to the old homestead shortly. Can't say I'm keen on the idea, but there; I do have responsibilities and business matters to deal with.'

It occurred to Catherine that they might be travelling back on the same ship. That would be nice, she thought to herself, but should I ask him? No! Asking would sound too needy. Being casual, almost indifferent to his plans, would suit her better.

'If fate allows, we might meet up in England.'

He smiled. 'That is indeed a possibility, although . . .' He frowned and shook his head. 'I doubt that I'll linger there too long, just enough to sort things out and then I'm off to pastures new. Our meeting would necessarily be brief. Foreign shores and foreign folk would beckon, I'm afraid.' A heavy sigh was followed by a wry smile. 'I would then have no recourse but to take you with me. How would you like that?'

She tried not to show any reaction on her face, though her excitement might have gleamed in her eyes. The urge to throw her arms around him then and there was tempered by her determined self-control. Give in to such a suggestion and she'd give in to anything. And his eyes and his smile were so alluring . . . No, she warned. Be calm. Be careful.

Her words were guarded. What did she know about travel? However, the thought of it intrigued her.

'Travel? I've never ever left Portugal, though I know of England, of course. Because of my father. He has business and a house in both London and Bristol. And of course I can speak English.'

'When do you sail?'

'Tomorrow.'

'I see.' His sage expression and a resolute straightness to his mouth made him seem much older. She wondered she hadn't noticed before.

'I'm not looking forward to it.' She refrained from

mentioning the details of why she was travelling to England. Not that it mattered to her. Basking in the company of such a charming, well-travelled man helped keep her mind off her future.

'No doubt we shall meet again,' he said, the softening of his features regaining a few years of the youth she'd initially seen there. 'But for now . . . parting is such sweet sorrow . . .'

Taking hold of both her hands with his, he got to his feet. 'Alas, we must part.'

If he sounded dramatic, if his actions were theatrical, it didn't really register – not until later, much later.

'Goodbye, sweet Kate.'

He kissed her cheek and took his leave, striding from her swiftly, as though he wanted to distance himself from her as fast as he could.

'Good travelling,' she called.

He flung a casual wave over his shoulder.

And then he was gone. If she felt hollow inside, her outside was as fragile as an eggshell and easily crushed. Meeting him had helped her cope with what was happening to her. Now she would have to cope alone.

Some miles away Father Umberto lay dying in the cool ward of a hospice where soft-footed nuns padded over stone floors, the hems of their habits whispering as they moved. The sister in charge had allowed them five minutes. 'No more,' she'd hissed like a wary snake when William Shellard had asked for ten. 'Father Umberto is suffering from blood poisoning brought on by his wounds.'

William was curious. 'How was he wounded?' He figured an accident; certainly no war was going on in the vicinity and the word 'wound' was more specific to that. Should she have said 'injuries'?

The sister's jaw stiffened. Thin lines radiated from her pursed lips. 'By his own hand,' she said. 'And now he must bear the consequences of overzealous self-flagellation. Blood poisoning, I'm afraid.'

Her long white fingers swept across her chest in the sign of the cross before asking them to follow her.

The priest was lying in a small cell bereft of ornament or

decoration. The walls were glaringly white and the floor chillingly cold as the stone echoed with hollow footsteps.

Ellen Shellard followed William. The sister swept out with a rustle of habit, though not before warning them yet again that they could have only five minutes.

The priest's face glistened with sweat. His breathing was laboured. He had the look of a dying man, one who no longer cared whether he lived or died.

Ellen Shellard sucked in her breath. His face was not merely handsome; he was beautiful. She found herself thinking that if he'd been her priest, she would have gone to confession every day – mostly to have him forgive her for feeling desirous of him.

Stifling her instant reaction, Ellen leaned forward and whispered, 'Father Umberto?'

Blue eyes flickered in puzzlement, stunning her even more.

His eyes glanced over her and went to her brother-in-law. He frowned. 'I don't know you.'

Ellen threw William a warning glance when he seemed likely to introduce himself. After all, they had only five minutes. She leaned closer.

'Father Umberto, I believe you knew my stepdaughter, Catherine – Catherine Rodriguez.'

His eyes flickered in a livelier manner than before. 'Have you seen her?' A froth of blood and spittle bubbling from one corner of his mouth.

Ellen shook her head. If she could have told him, she would. 'No. We're looking for her. Do you know where she is?'

He blinked as though he didn't believe her. Or perhaps he didn't hear properly, she thought, so she repeated her question.

'A woman came,' he said. 'She took her. The last letter she received said someone would come if she didn't obey her father. He wanted her to make her way to Porto.'

Ellen and William exchanged surprised glances. William shrugged helplessly, was about to say that his brother knew a lot of women but remembered he was with his sister-in-law.

'Do you know the woman's name?' Ellen asked.

'No,' said the priest, his deep-set eyes closing as though his lids were made of lead.

Ellen frowned and turned to William, who was looking

uncomfortable and had been intermittently ever since he'd found out that Leonora was dead and that she had given birth to a daughter.

Once the smell of sickness and carbolic soap was behind them, Ellen pulled on her gloves, a determined look in her eyes. 'I'm going to confront Walter. He must know where she is.'

William was looking down at the ground, a troubled frown diminishing his amiable features.

'Are you coming with me?'

He looked thoughtful, then nodded. 'Yes.'

'A fine vintage.'

Walter handed the sampling spoon to one of his retainers. The man, who was Portuguese, wiped it with a scrap of linen before handing it back.

A few steps along the red-brick floor and they were waiting at the next barrel.

There were twelve huge barrels in this section alone, the blood-red liquid settling and fermenting before it was sent to be bottled.

The tap was opened. Port, the fortified wine made from brandy and Portuguese vintage, poured slowly into the sampling spoon.

Walter Shellard, as master of the wine lodge, had the honour of the first taste.

Just as he was about to take the spoon, one half of the main door, a huge thing made of oak, slammed open. He raised his eyes and without pausing for a single beat, he sipped, tasted and spat into a silver ice bucket.

Ellen was marching towards him like a soldier off to do battle. 'Walter! I wish to talk to you.'

He hid his immediate reaction and adopted a false if edifying smile. 'Why, Ellen. I didn't expect to see you here. Would you like a taste?'

He nodded at the man who had custody of the sampling spoon. In response the tap was reopened, the spoon refilled.

'That's not what I've come to discuss,' she said, her hands tightly clutching her handbag.

Walter's smile was sardonic, even mocking. He eyed the crushed crocodile handbag. 'My, my, Ellen. You're strangling that bag as though it were someone's neck. Is it mine, by any chance?'

'I want to talk to you.'

There was no mistaking the anger in her eyes. Walter refrained from showing surprise.

'Then talk,' he said, taking a second sample of the vintage he'd already tried, although this time he did not spit but swallowed.

For a moment she was unnerved. 'Here?'

'If you must,' Walter responded.

The nerves passed. She seemed to come to an instant decision.

'All right. It's about Leonora's daughter, Catherine. I want to know where she is.'

'I see.'

He spoke in such a cool, unflappable manner, that she was immediately taken aback. For a moment he was almost sure that she was going to turn away with a promise to talk about it later. To his surprise, the second of the day, she did not.

There was no point in beating about the bush. He decided to be forthright. 'She's on her way to England. Her aunt died so I took her under my wing.'

He could tell by Ellen's face that she was in two minds about this now.

'Where is she going?'

'Rest assured, she won't be living with us,' he went on. 'She's going to be married.'

His strategy had worked. She looked deflated, but also shocked. 'Who is she marrying?'

'A business partner of mine. Robert Arthur Freeman. I think you've met him, dear.'

She shook her head.

Walter smiled to himself. Of course she hadn't, but it was never easy to recall nondescript people, people that did not easily fit the social scene. 'She'll be well looked after and very settled. Isn't that what every girl wants?'

Ellen phoned her brother-in-law from Castile Villanova. She felt a fool as she repeated what Walter had told her. He went silent the moment she'd told him.

'William? Are you still there?'

'This can't be right. I know Walter's far from moral, but no man would marry off his daughter to a man like that.'

'So why has he?'

William sighed. 'The usual reason. That's bad enough. But him! Robert Arthur Freeman.'

The name meant nothing to her. 'Do I know him?'

'No,' he replied. 'And you don't want to.'

Twenty-Nine

The coastline of Portugal was no more than a mauve strip lying between a dark-blue sea and a bright-blue sky.

Catherine committed this last sight of it to memory, waiting for the moment when it finally disappeared. She swiped at her eyes with a white-gloved hand, determined not to be seen crying. The wind tousled her shiny hair and almost succeeded in snatching her pale-lemon hat. The hat matched her outfit; the dress was a fine network of different-coloured lemons and yellows. The jacket was of the same colour as her hat and the bandeau fashionably circling her hips. She wasn't sure the style suited her generous curves, but Sanchia had been adamant. On reflection the fiery Spanish woman had been right. She looked fresh and alluring, a fact confirmed by the appraisals she'd noticed while boarding the ship. Sailors had rushed to carry her luggage; officers had saluted as she'd passed.

A thought came to her. How far would men go to please a beautiful woman? And how far could you push them?

Sanchia, rather than watch the vanishing country, had taken to her cabin.

'*Mal de mer*,' she'd said with a doleful expression.

The last of the land-based seagulls screeched and dived over the white-topped waves. The shadow of the ship glided along, turning the indigo sea to a darker shade of green. She saw her own shadow outlined against the rail, a solitary figure, willing to brave the breeze for a last glimpse of home.

A seagull swooping down on an unsuspecting fish drew her attention away from the shadow of the ship. When she next looked her shadow was no longer alone.

'Kate?'

Her spirits lifted at the sound of his voice. Again that smile, the creases at the corners of his eyes and his mouth, his tanned complexion emphasizing the colour of his eyes.

She became aware that her mouth was opening and closing like a fish catching flies. 'How did you know I'd be on this ship?'

His lips twitched in a smile. 'I didn't, though I did hope, of course.' His smile widened. 'Fate is favourable to us, don't you think?'

The truth was she didn't know what to think. On first coming aboard, she'd looked round the tiny single cabin and remembered that lizard hiding in the wall of the house. The cabin was comparable with its secret niche, but in her mind she was free. Rather than dwell on the negatives, she purposely confronted the positive side of her father's plans. In England she had the chance to study him; to work out his weaknesses, to plot his downfall. And he most definitely has weaknesses, she thought – as do we all.

In the meantime she toyed with Sanchia's sense of duty to a man she was obviously in love with.

'He asked you to befriend me,' she said. 'Why is that?'

Sanchia looked at her with heavy-lidded eyes. 'He feels you should have some close company until you are married. He would like you to marry.'

'Someone of his choice? I wouldn't do that. I'd kill myself rather than marry someone he'd chosen for me.'

'A young girl has not the experience to make her own choice.'

'Well, this one does!'

Pleased with her defiance, she couldn't stop smiling at that moment on deck, looking out at the sea.

Arthur beamed. 'You look pleased to see me.'

Although she had resolved to be hard-headed and as elegant as an older woman, her enthusiasm bubbled over. 'Oh, yes!' It came out in a silly, girlish way and made her blush. Such was loneliness, she told herself. The most pragmatic plans can be pushed aside by something emotionally trivial – like being lonely.

He looked around and over her shoulder. 'Where is your chaperone?'

Catherine grinned. 'She's not feeling well.'

'Seasick?'

She nodded. 'Strangely enough, yes. I wouldn't have thought Sanchia had a weak stomach, but . . .' She shrugged casually.

The breeze chose that moment to tug more vigorously at her hat, lifting it from her head. Arthur stopped it flying off, clamping two hands down on the crown so it sat firmly, though a bit squashed, on her head.

Catherine laughed. Arthur's hands slipped slightly so they were cupping her face.

His hazel flecked eyes bored into hers. His smile widened to show perfect white teeth. 'I'm so glad we met up. I think we get on really well together, don't you?'

She nodded. 'Yes. We seem quite well suited.'

His smile lessened. There was a moment's silence as he turned thoughtful. 'Would you like to come to my cabin?'

Dimples appeared alongside Catherine's wicked smile. 'Sanchia wouldn't like it.'

His mouth widened into a smile. 'Of course. And then there's the tarnishing of your reputation to consider. All the more reason?'

His amusement was contagious and the fact that he was daring her made her feel like a naughty child. And she wanted to be naughty. She wanted to tarnish her reputation so much that her father would be mortified and shamed before his peers. What price reputation to a man like that, she wondered.

She grinned broadly. 'Why not?'

He took hold of her hand and led her to his cabin.

'My word,' she exclaimed, looking around. It was probably the best on the ship and much larger than her own. The ship itself only carried a few passengers, its main business being to carry port wine from Porto to Bristol.

A double berth took up half the length of the cabin. The rest of the space was taken up with a washstand and a small chest of drawers. There was a desk, a closet and a two-seater settee against the other wall.

After inviting her to sit down, he took out a bottle and two glasses from a bracket fixed to the wall above the chest of drawers. She guessed the device on gimballed fixings kept the bottles upright on the open sea.

She turned her attention back to the dark-red liquid as it glugged into the glasses. She felt she had regained something of her freedom – if only to make mistakes or get into trouble. The woman watched her most of the time, though not back at the hotel nor here on the ship. If it seemed odd, she paid it no account. Only later did it all add up.

Arthur's eyes fixed on hers over the top of his glass. 'Is the port to your taste? Some people find it a little too sweet and sickly and won't touch it unless it's accompanied by a wedge of Stilton, crusty bread or a few biscuits. Are you enjoying this?'

'My father has a bodega. I've drunk watered-down port since childhood.' Back in Castile Villanova, she reminded herself. Only back there.

His eyes narrowed. His look intensified. 'That's not what I meant. I meant you're enjoying being alone with me.'

She felt a thrill warming her as much as the smoothly swallowed port. 'I like danger.'

He laughed. 'I thought as much. I consider myself a good judge of character. I know a wild, adventurous woman when I see one. You've got the attributes of the women who followed their men to India, or those who crossed the great prairies of North America. My instinct is that you're not really cut out to run a household or supervise a nursery, though I dare say you'd make a great success of it if you did.'

She hung on to his words. They were like pearls spilling from the interior of an oyster shell and gleaming with potential. He was charming and made her feel special. Arthur lacked the animal magnetism of Umberto and the familiarity of Francisco, but he did know how to make a woman feel good. His tales of exotic places had a lot to do with it.

'I want to travel. Like you,' she exclaimed, her eyes shining with excitement.

He sat beside her on the two-seater settee, his knee touching hers. He gazed into her eyes. 'Let's drink to an exciting future.'

His voice was melodious, designed to charm. Her legs turned to jelly.

They sipped from their glasses, though little slipped through Catherine's lips. Arthur had fired up her imagination with his tales of travel. The thought of settling in England was a nightmare she was loath to face. She made a snap decision. 'I want to travel with you.'

He didn't look as surprised as she'd expected him to be. Neither did he proclaim the idea to be preposterous.

'Eyebrows will be raised. An eligible man and a single lady,' he said, his eyes twinkling with what she could only interpret as wickedness.

Her eyes twinkled as a thought occurred to her. 'We could get married.' It seemed the obvious conclusion.

He gulped back the contents of his glass.

'Well,' she said when he failed to make any comment, waiting for him to laugh or call her a silly goose.

'Well, indeed,' he replied while pouring himself another measure from the plum-coloured contents of the decanter.

Her heart raced as she waited. At last he raised his eyes and his smile was wide enough to split his face.

'I think it's a positively wicked idea. Shall we drink to that?'

Feeling triumphant, Catherine raised her glass. 'To wicked men.'

Arthur followed suit. 'To wicked women!'

The sound of their laughter and the clink of one glass against the other was interrupted by a loud hammering on the cabin door.

'Catherine! Catherine? Come out this moment. I know you're in there!'

Catherine's expression was something between a grin and a grimace. 'My chaperone.'

Arthur laid his hand on her shoulder. 'Stay there.' He got up and opened the door.

Sanchia blustered in, her eyes blazing. She looked directly at Catherine.

'Catherine. Get out of here.'

She stabbed a long fingernail in the direction of the cabin door.

Catherine stayed seated, bristling with defiance. 'Why?'

Sanchia looked fit to burst at this sign of rebellion. 'Because I say so!'

'I don't want to go.'

Sanchia's face clouded with a deep frown. 'You are aware of the consequences if you do not?'

Yes, she was aware. Umberto. But Father Umberto was far away now. Surely her father wouldn't trouble himself to ruin the poor young man's career?

Catherine weighed up the chances of this happening. Suddenly the prospect seemed remote, part of the past and another country.

She looked up at Arthur, reached out and stroked the half-smile on his face. 'I'm going to marry this man.'

'Don't be ridiculous.'

Arthur's eyes shot between the two women, weighing up who would win this contest of wills.

'I'm staying here,' Catherine said at last, her eyes meeting Arthur's. 'I'm going to travel the world. That's what I want to do.'

Sanchia looked as though she were about to explode. 'We shall see about that! I will contact your father! A message can be sent.'

She stormed off, the door slamming behind her.

'Ah!' said Arthur after she'd gone. 'I think you've upset her.'

Rather than be taken aback at this turn of events, the clever-looking eyes danced with amusement.

Catherine studied his face. 'You didn't tell her it was nonsense.'

'About getting married and travelling the world?'

She nodded.

'I think the sooner we marry the better, purely to keep your father happy.'

'The moment we get to England?'

She eyed this charming man and asked herself whether she could lie with him as she had with Umberto. The prospect was not distasteful, but neither was she enthused with desire.

Arthur sighed and looked thoughtful. 'Of course, there's no need to wait. The captain can marry us.'

'What a romantic idea,' she whooped, her head swimming due to the amount of port she'd just drunk. 'Let's!'

'Right now?' he asked.

Head still swimming – far more so than it ever had when drinking farmhouse port – she went with him.

Sanchia gulped when they told her. Catherine stood slightly in front of Arthur waiting for the fireworks to start. She was used to the Spanish woman's temper. Arthur might buckle beneath the expected onslaught, and she didn't want him to buckle. His presence and the life he offered were a golden path that would take her away from her father. The further she travelled away from him, the less chance she had of destroying him. For the moment, at least, revenge didn't seem to matter.

There was a crack as, huffing and puffing, Sanchia unfolded a black-lace fan and wafted it in front of her aquiline nose.

'Your father will be furious.'

'Good.'

Sanchia bristled. Her black eyes glowered at her rebellious charge. 'I'm shocked. Shocked and surprised, Catherine. But if that is what you desire . . . and as I have your father's authority . . .'

It all seemed so straightforward. So simple. Perhaps if she'd been more sober she might have been suspicious. But for now she was carried along with the sheer excitement of the idea.

'Shall we have a celebratory drink?' Arthur suggested.

Sanchia seemed strangely reticent about the whole affair, though she only sipped at her drink. Arthur insisted that Catherine have an extra glass.

'Dutch courage,' said Arthur, and sank a third glassful.

Catherine's head was reeling and she was having some difficulty focusing. The ship's captain beamed when they told him and remarked that he would be delighted. Sanchia and a fellow passenger witnessed the ceremony.

'Catherine Leonora Rodriguez, do you take this man . . . ?'

Of course she did. As she looked up into his eyes she imagined all the places they would see, the people they would meet. She said 'yes'.

'Robert Arthur Freeman, do you take this woman . . . ?'

Sanchia looked triumphant. 'Your father will be pleased.'

'So am I,' said Robert.

It didn't register at first. Catherine frowned, looking from one to the other to try and understand. When it finally clicked, she felt sick.

The final confirmation of what had actually occurred came to her when the captain congratulated her. 'So convenient that you already had your father's approval and a copy of the marriage contract with you,' he said affably. 'All nicely arranged in advance.'

Catherine couldn't believe what she was hearing. She looked at Arthur – Robert Arthur Freeman.

He laughed. 'I had your father's blessing weeks ago. We had to make sure,' he said, grinning broadly as though it were all a huge joke. And the joke was on her.

There was one last vestige of the dream she wished to hold on to, yet even before she asked she guessed what the answer would be. 'Are we going to travel?'

He looked smug. It was as though a mask had fallen from his face. 'Only to England. My cabin first, though – after I've celebrated with a few drinks.

He made a clicking sound at the side of his mouth and pinched her chin. She stared at him in wide-eyed alarm. She felt such a fool and so angry that she'd been outmanoeuvred; not so much by these two, but by her father. Yet again he was responsible for a shift in her life. How could she have been deceived, she who had formed relationships with the opposite sex on her own terms?

It was as though her blood had turned to iced water, her legs seemingly encased in iron. So heavy, so cold did she feel.

'You tricked me,' she said to Sanchia once Arthur – Robert Arthur Freeman – was laughing and drinking with the other men.

Sanchia's eyes narrowed like a cat that's just swallowed a whole sparrow. 'I know men. I know women. We are easily fooled. We hitch our destiny to unsuitable men, men who lie easily, who charm us with their far-fetched tales.'

Sanchia had told the truth. All lies.

Catherine made a dash for the door, wanting solitude, wanting to be anywhere but here. She paused before leaving. Her dark-grey eyes smouldered like burning coals.

'And you should know about unsuitable men, Sanchia, men who charm and lie. My father charmed and lied to my mother – and to you?'

Sanchia's perfect features froze but, as is the way with women who are lost in love, the thaw came quickly. She gave a little nervous laugh. 'Don't be silly.'

Catherine looked at her more soberly than ever before. For the first time since they'd met, she was seeing a more vulnerable woman beneath the classic confidence. The clothes, the perfect grooming and that aloof self-assurance were all a veneer. Beneath it all Sanchia was addicted – yes, that was the right word, thought Catherine. She's addicted to an unsuitable and selfish man.

Suddenly it was as though she'd aged five years in one small ceremony. Her head still ached, but not as much as her heart. She glared at Sanchia. Her words were like ice.

'My youth and inexperience go some way to excusing my foolishness. It's a hard lesson to learn, but learn by it I will. But what's your excuse, Sanchia? What's your excuse for still trusting my father after all these years?'

Sanchia looked dumbstruck. The age-defying complexion and firm jawline sagged beneath the weight of the spoken truth.

'At least you have all those beautiful clothes I chose with you,' Sanchia shouted after her as she dashed out of the door. Her voice lacked its former strength.

A turning point for both of us, Catherine thought as she raced for her cabin.

Once inside she stared at the old coffer that she was so loath to open. First she had held off its opening until she was married to Francisco. Now she was married to Arthur – she hadn't got used to calling him Robert. But still she could not bring herself to spring open its rusted hinges. Opening that box would be like the last throw of a dice. She told herself she could cope for now, though not for ever added a small, still voice.

Her new husband had tricked her. He admitted it. He did travel, though only within the confines of the wine trade and then only infrequently. Their marriage was based on a series of lies. He was not the man she had thought. Their future would not be as she'd envisaged.

She sat there staring into space, wondering if there was some way she could get out of this. At around six o'clock he came for her.

'We're expected to dine – as the happily married couple,' he said, his hair slickly oiled back, a bemused look in those dancing eyes. 'And this is no longer your cabin – not at night anyway.'

His tone was intimidating, as though he wanted her to feel apprehensive about their first night. She shook her head in an effort to dislodge her disquiet. Her head ached but was clearing.

She vowed to drink some more. She wanted oblivion. She wanted not to know what would happen next.

The steward offered her wine with her meal. She drank white with the fish course, red with the meat and champagne with the dessert and even port with the cheese course. Not that she ate very much. The wine would dull her senses; lying with her husband would pass in a rushed blur – at least that's what she hoped.

The time she was dreading eventually came. Robert got to his feet and made his excuses. More toasts were drunk to the 'happy couple'.

'Come, my darling,' said Robert, his pupils somewhat diminished, black dots in a hot and florid face, a face that she'd once considered calm and kindly. He took hold of her hand.

She felt the sweatiness of his palm through her thin cotton glove. His arm encircled her waist once they were outside the door, his fingers curving upwards over her ribcage and touching her breast.

'Everything is ready for us,' he murmured, his breath hot and moist against her ear lobe. 'Tonight I take you. It may hurt a little, but it has to be done. You may want to scream, but as the walls of this vessel are rather thin, I will have to place my hand over your mouth to stifle the noise. But hey ho,' he said, straightening. 'I shall enjoy it nonetheless.'

Dizzy with drink, Catherine looked at him, studying the flushed countenance, the sweated brow and the incredible excitement burning in his eyes. Robert Arthur Freeman was convinced he'd got himself a virgin bride. Well, did she have news for him!

The wine might have blurred her senses, but she was still astute enough to know that there were two ways she could play this. Tell him the truth, or act the part of the untouched maiden.

Heart pounding and a small man with a hammer beating at the inside of her skull, she toppled against him.

'Now come along, young lady. Behave yourself or Daddy will have to smack your bottom.'

He said it in a soothing, silly voice, just as if he were indeed speaking to a child.

Perhaps if she'd been more sober she would have coped better; understood better. As it was, she wanted to say to him that he was speaking nonsense and that she was a grown woman – nineteen was old enough to be considered a woman. As a woman she knew what had to come next. It was just a case of what form it would take.

The truth of the matter was that she'd fully expected Robert to rip off her clothes and ravish her. Instead he gently unbuttoned her cream-coloured dress and the wide peach-coloured sash fastened around her hips. The whole ensemble fell on to her two-tone shoes. Next he took off her jewellery, her earrings, her necklace, her bracelet and her wristwatch. After laying everything to one side, he pressed her down into a chair and to her amazement began to wipe at her make-up with a damp flannel – not that she wore that much anyway.

'I'll do it,' she said, attempting to take the flannel.

'No,' he said, smacking her hand away. 'I'll do it. And don't ever wear *any* face paint again. Daddy doesn't like it.'

The flannel was cool upon her heated face.

'My head,' she said, opening her eyes.

'Never mind, my darling,' said Robert, flattening the flannel and laying it across her forehead. 'You hold that there. I'll brush your hair and then we'll get you undressed and into bed.'

The cool wetness and the gentle brushing of her hair helped her aching head. Robert Arthur Freeman was proving less predictable than she'd thought. Suddenly she wasn't dreading going to bed with him. On the contrary, she was beginning to look forward to cuddling up to his worthwhile physique. As for the other thing; well, purely out of consideration, tonight he might leave her alone. Even so, she reasoned that once the drink had worn off, he would be gentler taking her than she'd presumed. Or was she forgetting something? What was that he'd said about stifling her screams? She closed her eyes and the room spun again. She couldn't remember. She just couldn't remember.

'Come along,' he said, his fingers curving around her wrist. 'Let's get you to bed.'

He spoke softly yet urgently in a way that reminded her of Aunt Lopa. She'd come home once from the convent school with a fever and her aunt had insisted she go straight to bed. She'd felt too weak to undress herself, so Aunt Lopa had helped her. Robert was just like that. But she didn't care. Even when he turned her to face away from him and stripped off her under-wear, she didn't try to cover herself. After all, it was only her bottom showing anyway. It didn't occur to her that most men would keep her facing the front so they could drink in the sight of her breasts and the deep 'v' of pubic hair between her thighs. Nothing really made much sense until later.

'Let's get you into your nightdress,' he said.

Holding her arms up, she felt the freshness of white cotton fall over her. The nightgown was high-necked and fell to her ankles. It had long sleeves and a stitched bodice that flattened her chest.

He turned her back round to face him.

'There. My little girl,' he said, his eyes shining and a slimy wetness on his lips.

Catherine rubbed at her eyes as she tried to make sense of what was happening here. Where was the beautiful peignoir Sanchia had bought for her? She remembered it being black and pink, riotously enticing. She'd hated it, but this shapeless cotton thing made her uneasy. It was more suited to a child than a wife.

She was aware of him leading her to the bed, drawing back the sheets and plumping up the pillows.

'There you are. Now lay down on your stomach. It will be better that way.'

'Hmmm!' she murmured, not caring how she lay down as long as it did her aching head some good. The moment her head hit the pillow, she closed her eyes. A trio of lights whirled around behind her closed lids. The bed seemed to be moving, spinning on its iron legs. But she would not, could not, open her eyes. She wanted sleep. She wanted this dizziness to be gone. Fresh air would be good. She thought about asking Robert to open the porthole, but her lips were half buried in the pillow. Besides, she couldn't possibly find the energy to lift her head.

The cool air came anyway. She could feel it on her bottom and the backs of her legs. She murmured a vague thank-you.

She heard Robert say something and felt pillows being forced beneath her thighs. Her bottom rose higher than her shoulders and felt incredibly cooled, unfettered by nightdress or bedclothes. Her knees dug into the mattress as the front of Robert's thighs brushed against the back of hers.

She didn't care what he was doing. All she wanted to do was sleep, but her sleep was vague and disturbing. She felt the weight of his body, his hand dividing her legs before he burrowed into her.

'There, there, there. This is what naughty girls deserve.'

It made no sense. Not then. Her eyelids were heavy. She fell asleep.

It wasn't until the morning that she tried to analyse exactly what had happened, though her head was throbbing so nothing made much sense.

She opened her eyes and saw him looking at her. His eyes were unblinking, like flecked glass in a carved face.

'Before breakfast comes,' Robert said seeming to come to a sudden decision. He reached across, drawing her near, then turning her over on to her stomach.

'No,' she said, as he tried to push the pillows beneath her hips. 'That isn't how I want it.' She swung her legs out of bed and saw she was still wearing the hideous cotton gown.

'What is this?' she said, holding the voluminous garment out to either side of her.

Robert only gave the nightdress a cursory glance as though he were searching for something. Apparently he didn't find it, so that same glance settled on the bedcovers. He inspected the sheet. He frowned. 'No blood?'

Catherine stared at him. 'What?'

'You're a young girl. A virgin.' He sounded concerned, his eyes taking on a darkness that she'd never seen there before.

Suddenly everything came together. Catherine began to laugh. 'So that's the reason for this charade!'

Robert swung his legs out of his side of the bed. He was naked, his hair was plastered to his head and his mouth was bowed with disappointment. She tried to ignore his body, the fair skin, the freckled chest and the thin layer of pubic hair. The sight of it failed to arouse her. With a pang of regretful memory, she recalled the body of her passionate priest.

His expression darkened further. 'Why didn't you scream?'

'I'm not a *blushing* bride,' she said, her eyes blazing.

'You've had other men?'

'Yes.'

She was taken aback when his face contorted with anger.

Two strides and he'd crossed the cabin floor. Her ears rang as he slapped one side of her face then the other.

'You are never to mention them again. Is that clear?'

She felt the heat of her face as she covered both cheeks with her hands. She stared, unable to find her voice.

His smile was dangerous. He took hold of her chin. 'Yes. You will forget they ever existed. You will turn back the clock and become the untouched little girl you were before they led you astray.'

She wanted to say that she'd been driven by passion as much as they had been; that she was her mother's daughter, and didn't he know that? But some womanly instinct told her to hold her tongue. The man who had captured her imagination was no longer affable and good-natured. His true character was emerging and it sickened her.

The only redeeming feature that kept her spirits up was the thought of living close to her father, learning his ways – his weaknesses. Now it seemed she would have to be in earnest learning the further weaknesses of her husband. Indolence, she decided, would be his downfall. And she'd be there to take full advantage of it.

Thirty

B ecause of its size, the ship docked at the Bristol Channel port of Avonmouth, which was more capable of taking bigger ships than the city docks; the latter could only be reached by navigating the twisting, tidal river.

As barrels of wine were swung over the side on to waiting barges, their personal luggage was loaded into a taxi with dark-blue paintwork and large brass headlamps. Robert was making an effort to supervise the operation, though only in a desultory fashion, waving his walking stick between taking languorous draws on his cigar.

Catherine proceeded down the gangway and on to the shore

where she proceeded to survey the broad quay for sight of a chauffeur-driven car. Sanchia had left the ship early to stay at a hotel in the city for a few nights before reboarding the ship back to Porto.

There had been many times when Catherine had felt alone in her life, but never more so than she did now. At the same time she felt she had aged on this short voyage and gained greater insight into humanity and especially into men. She blamed herself for the situation she found herself in; she'd been naïve, silly. But never again, she promised herself. Never, ever again.

Stiffened by her new resolve, she tried not to dwell on the more intimate details of her marriage to Robert Arthur Freeman.

'Catherine!'

Robert took hold her elbow and guided her towards the same taxi that was being loaded with their luggage including Aunt Lopa's iron-bound box. Most of the boxes and bags had been tied on to the rear of the vehicle, but some were piled up beside the driver.

'There's not much more room, sir,' said the taxi driver. 'Would you and the missus like to go in another taxi?'

Robert looked astounded. 'Certainly not! Unless one fare covers both taxis.'

'I can't do that, sir,' said the whiskered man, his greatcoat straining across his broad belly, his stout legs clothed in oilskin gaiters. 'If you don't mind that box there sitting on the back seat with you, that would take care of all your luggage.' He indicated the stout iron-bound box.

'That?' said Robert.

Judging by the look on his face, he would have been satisfied to see the box thrown into the river.

'It's coming with us,' said Catherine firmly, addressing the taxi driver. 'Put it on the back seat. We can manage.'

Robert shrugged as though he didn't care one way or another. While they waited he took a sip from a silver hip flask and shrugged his shoulders. 'As you wish. You'll be the one squashed in the middle, not me.'

Robert, she'd learned, had a very casual attitude to most things. The faraway look she'd often seen in his eyes had more to do with his imbibing of alcoholic spirits than the possession of a poetic spirit. His carefree attitude was more akin to carelessness, an indifference to anyone's feelings but his own.

It was a tight squeeze travelling along while squashed between the wooden coffer and her husband, and unpleasant in more ways than one.

'This is very cosy,' he said, his hand resting on her knee, his fingers moving like a spider's legs, gathering up her hem.

Catherine blushed scarlet. 'Stop it,' she hissed, her eyes flashing between him and the back of the driver's head.

She winced as Robert gripped her knee and glanced tellingly at the driver. 'He's on the other side of the glass. He can't hear,' said Robert.

'I don't care,' she muttered, using her own fingers to try and dislodge his hand.

In response, Robert gripped her knee even more tightly. 'You're my wife. I can do as I please and that unremarkable little man up front will say and do nothing. He's just a servant. Like a horse is a servant.'

Catherine could not believe what she was hearing. Even her fingers stayed still, locked over those of the man she had married.

'If you do not remove your hand and allow me to continue, I will slap your face here and now in public.'

Catherine weighed up in her mind all that she knew about Robert Arthur Freeman. What did she know that would give her some form of defence against him? Whose opinion did he fear above all others? The answer came in a flash.

She steeled her expression and lowered her voice. 'If you do not desist instantly, I will inform my father in public of what an uncouth lout you are!'

She saw his eyes flicker, a sudden fear flash through them. The fingernails digging into her knee loosened and then retreated. In that single moment Robert Arthur Freeman had told her more about himself than he had ever put into words. He both feared and admired men who were more powerful and wealthier than he was. She'd also seen something else in that petulant, jealous expression, the reason above all else that he had married her. He wanted to be like her father. He wanted to be powerful. Although inexperienced in matters of business, she was and always had been an astute judge of character.

Her husband would never be as successful as her father or any man like him.

The rest of the journey passed in comparative comfort, though she edged herself closer to Aunt Lopa's box than Robert. The only time he spoke to her was to ask what was in the box. To sit beside something familiar was strangely comforting, inanimate though that object might be.

'Family mementoes,' she replied, and returned her dark gaze to the view from the window. Now she had found Robert's Achilles heel she contented herself with thoughts of the grand house he had boasted of. At least she would have something reminiscent of Castile Villanova, that beautiful house in Porto.

In reality, it was not so.

Cornwallis House overlooked St Michael's Hill, a long sweep of eighteenth-century houses curving down to the main road. Catherine eyed the mix of ginger clay and blue-slate roofs with glum resignation; none of them glowed with borrowed sunlight like they had in Portugal. The sky was only a few shades lighter than the rooftops, clouds swirling like grey porridge against a pewter palate.

At a distance Cornwallis House took her breath away. Four Palladian pillars supported a central pediment. Lofty windows, each with their own pediment, were set at equal intervals along each floor level. They entered through iron gates that looked as though they hadn't seen a lick of paint in years. Long grass whispered like bent silk beneath clusters of oak, ash and stately elm.

Halfway up the drive, a flash of colour to her right caught her eye. A posse of sunburned faces stared in their direction. They were standing in front of three brightly coloured gypsy caravans. Piebald and skewbald horses were tethered close by and a hoard of scruffy children were playing in the dirt.

Robert noticed her looking. 'Ah! So you've seen our tame gypsies. Their animals keep the grass down and they pay me for being here.'

'Strange,' she murmured. Patient, knowledgeable men tended the gardens at Castile Villanova, nipping buds, planting and weeding, seeding and hoeing in the rich, dark earth.

Catherine got out of the taxi to get a better look at the frontage of the house itself. She was vaguely aware that figures of various sizes had filed out of the front door and were waiting to greet them. But for the moment, her gaze fixed on the house, the house she had visualized as imposing, elegant and awaiting the attention of an interested woman.

Once upon a time the building must have been quite splendid. Now fallen into neglect, there were patches where the original stucco had fallen from the pillars. The same had happened on the upper floor, where water incursion had caused bricks to be exposed and weeds to flourish.

On closer inspection, she saw that panes were missing from windows, catches were broken, the casements leaning out at odd angles. Paint flaked from frames and some broken panes had been boarded up rather than replaced. An air of neglect lay over everything.

The figures she'd perceived filing out of the front door stood in a line to greet them. There were just four. For a house of this size? A nervous knot began to tighten in her belly. Nothing was making sense.

Inside Cornwallis House was just as bad. Stained walls testified to square gaps where pictures had once hung. Furniture was old and neglected, curtains faded. In the dining room a beautiful Sheraton dining table and chairs were ill polished, lacked lustre and were patterned with sticky fingermarks. A sweet smell of long-laid dirt, old food and mouse droppings filled the air.

Catherine explored each room, her jaw slack, her mouth hanging open. Dirty windows meant murky rooms smelling of dust and lacking fresh air.

Cornwallis House was indeed a place of past glories. Catherine could imagine how it had once been; polished furniture, richly coloured wall hangings and the sounds of a bustling household rising to its lofty ceilings. Now it echoed from the lack of both.

'It needs a woman's touch,' said Robert with a casual wave of his hand, indicating nothing in particular.

'It needs cleaning.'

'You can take care of that,' he said with an air of finality.

Alarmed at the prospect she might have to do this all by herself, she looked up at him. 'Do we have any more servants than those four?'

He looked slightly amused. 'Just the four. Do you think I'm made of money? If you need any more, go along and see your father. Tell him he owes me credit for supplying damaged goods.' He looked pointedly at her.

She frowned and then understood. Clasping her hands in front of her, she looked away, trying to keep from blushing. Obviously Robert had wanted a young virgin. She had failed to fulfil his expectations.

'You were not a virgin,' he said suddenly, blasting the fact into her ears.

'And you are hardly a gentleman,' she shouted back at him. 'In fact you're the most obnoxious man I have ever met.'

'You didn't say that back in Portugal!'

Her eyes were like flames, full of all the pent-up anger resulting from how others had treated her.

'You're a sick man, Robert Arthur Freeman. Tell me the truth. Have you ever satisfied a fully-grown woman? Well? Have you?'

She'd followed his own example and said it loud enough for the servants to hear. His eyes stared. His face reddened.

She smiled triumphantly to herself and at him. 'See? Tread carefully Robert or you'll end up stepping in your own filth.'

Catherine knew at that moment that she'd see little of her husband in future; certainly he'd stay away from her bed. She'd shamed him. In the space of a few weeks she had grown from a girl into a woman. Girls he could cope with. Women – especially strong-minded women – he could not.

And what of the rest of my predicament? she asked herself.

The selfish, impressionable girl who'd been swayed by Robert's easy charm had died halfway across the sea on the journey here. The new Catherine would have to take her place and make the best of a bad job. His comment about getting money from her father didn't fall on deaf ears. Her father owed her much more than he owed her husband. And what of his new wife? Did she know he had a daughter?

Robert looked at his watch. 'The children are waiting to meet you. We'd better see them now.'

Her head spun round. She looked at him askance. 'Children?'

She presumed he meant the servants' children. 'Wonderful. They can help get this disgusting ruin into shape.'

'They're not the servants' children. They're my children,' he said indignantly.

They were walking on Turkish carpets that had long since seen better days. Her foot stuck in a particularly large hole as they came to a sudden halt.

'They are most definitely *my* children,' said Robert again, looking quite gleeful that she'd tripped over. 'They are answerable to you when I am not around, but when I am around, they are answerable only to me – as you are. Is that clear?'

'You never told me you had children.'

'I didn't need to,' he said sharply. 'You married me, not my children. Well there you are. You wanted a husband without encumbrances and I wanted a virgin and your father wanted access through my vineyard in Spain to two of his own. Strikes me we've both ended up with something less than we'd hoped for – except your father, that is.'

'You're a liar.'

'So are you.'

Feeling cheated and glaring at his back, she followed him along the shabby carpets and past the shabby curtains and furniture to the place where his children were waiting. But she couldn't really blame him for wanting a wife. Yet again it was her father who was at fault. Everything led back to her father and she hated him for it.

Thirty-One

Ellen Shellard waved to her children from beneath the arched colonnade of the Castile Villanova. They were sitting in the back of a small trap pulled by a white pony and looking pleased to be going off for a ride.

Her smile felt stiff and behind her contented mask, her thoughts were in turmoil.

The driver flicked the reins, made a clicking sound to the pony and away they went. Ellen watched them go. She regretted that her two children were growing up. They'd both started boarding school, and though her heart ached for them,

Walter was insistent. She missed them badly when they were away and had determined to make the best of the holiday. But her heart was heavy. The world was not the beautiful place she'd always been led to believe. In her mind she could still see the tortured priest. She'd left her gloves at his bedside. When she'd returned to fetch them, the nuns had turned the young priest over on to his stomach and were bathing his back. Her blood had run cold at the sight of the encrusted wheals running across his back, the mix of black blood and yellow pus. She recognized that he'd been purging his soul, but from what?

The purging of souls swiftly led her to thoughts of her husband. Things had gone from bad to worse between them. She could barely stand being in the same room with him, let alone having him touch her.

Years ago she had admired her husband's strong features, the way his mouth set in a determined line when he wanted something. Even though his hair no longer grew in leonine splendour from his high forehead, it had only grown thinner and not disappeared altogether. His eyes were his most dominant feature. He had a very direct way of looking at people and rarely seemed to blink unless he was caught off balance, and that happened only rarely. He'd blinked when she'd mentioned the doll. It had been such a swift fluttering, perhaps someone not so familiar with his looks and ways would have missed it. But Ellen had not. A split second – that was all it was – and she'd noticed. However, he'd admitted nothing, and neither would he. Her husband, Walter Shellard, was one of the most successful businessmen in the city. What was a doll in comparison with a million-pound deal? Nothing!

Holding the doll in both hands, she eyed its staring eyes and yellow hair. The grubby dress was now a fresh shade of lemon and the crumpled petticoat was white again.

Placing the doll to one side, she sat on a velvet stool before her dressing-table mirror. Turning her head this way and that, she studied her reflection. Her tawny-coloured hair was cut in the latest fashion close to her head and her complexion was creamy white. Plucked brows arched above clear grey eyes. Pearl earrings matched a three-strand necklace. Today she was wearing a peach-coloured dress trimmed with fawn satin. Although the colour was cheerful, it did nothing to alleviate the pinpoints of apprehension in her eyes. Ellen sighed and eyed the doll sidelong. It was beautiful, almost too beautiful to ever have been played with. Someone in the house must know who it had belonged to.

She sat back and eyed her reflection. Her clear eyes looked brilliant and decidedly brave.

'Right,' she said to her reflection. 'I'm going to show this little pretty to several of the servants, those who have been here for a number of years.'

Her reflection nodded back at her. My, my, she thought, I look so pale, so out of place in this country. The thought that she didn't quite fit in had haunted her for a while. It had occurred to her to put aside her sunshade, lie out in the sun and tan herself to *their* skin tone. But I'd probably end up the colour of a cooked crab, she told herself. Horrible! And she shuddered.

Even this room of hers reflected her Englishness. Walter had given her carte blanche to decorate her own sitting and dressing room as she wished. Gone were the colourful tiles and walls painted the colour of crushed rose petals. Everything was cream-coloured now and teamed with fawns and pale greens. The dark-green shutters were cream; the paintwork was cream, and even the carpet was cream. The carpet covered the hardwood floor – far too dark for modern tastes, Ellen had decided. The only thing about this room she would not change for the world was the view. From a stone balcony paved with red and black tiles, she could look out over the garden, see the distant blue hills and smell the mix of perfumes and damp earth. Like the glorious women of the region, it was vibrant with colour and rich, earthy scents.

She'd mentioned her observations on Latin women to Walter after meeting the daughter of one of his Spanish business associates at a social event.

'She's stunningly colourful and makes me feel washed out,' she'd said to him.

Walter's eyes had followed the girl. Ellen had sensed he'd tensed suddenly, almost as though an electric shock had passed through him, or someone had pricked him with a needle.

'Don't you think so?' she'd said, studying his face intently for any sign of something she did not want to see; his approval, his desire for someone so different in looks from her.

He'd laughed. 'You women.'

That was all he'd said. *'You women.'*

Yet again she went over and over the same nagging suspicions. She looked again at the staring eyes of the doll.

'Stupid, stupid, stupid,' she muttered, slamming it down on the dressing table hard enough to make her perfume and cosmetic bottles rattle.

Just at that moment, a knock came at her dressing-room door and her maid entered. Around thirty years old with pale skin and dark, deep-set eyes, Honoria came in with a dress draped over her arm.

'The dress is repaired, madam.'

Ellen instructed her to hang it up in the wardrobe. She was just in time to see her put it in the wrong place. The dress was of a soft lavender colour, but Honoria was hanging it next to a navy-blue dress scattered with tiny pink rosebuds.

'Not there, Honoria. Mauves with other mauves and similar shades. Such as purple, for instance.'

The maid apologized and did as requested. Ellen's eyes went to the doll. It was a long shot as, although Honoria had been at Castile Villanova for several years and now travelled regularly with them back and forth, she was not a servant of long standing.

Ellen wound her fingers around the doll's white stockings. She held it up. 'Have you seen this doll before, Honoria?'

Honoria closed the wardrobe door and came closer. She looked at the doll. 'Is it one of Miss Germaine's?'

'No. It's not. Germaine found it in the cellar. I wondered if it belonged to a servant's child.'

Honoria shook her head, her thick eyebrows meeting in a sudden 'v' before dividing again. 'I don't think so, madam.'

Ellen nodded vaguely and pushed the doll back in the drawer. What was the point? She wanted to talk to him properly about Leonora and Catherine, but Walter was as dismissive about her wishes as he'd been at the bodega. William was cautious. 'Don't start an argument until I've had chance to meet her face to face. I want to see Catherine first,' he'd said.

Honoria started when she felt a hand on her shoulder.

Walter Shellard smiled. 'I'm sorry, my dear. I didn't mean to startle you.'

Honoria managed a nervous smile in return. She'd never felt at ease with the master of the house. Yes, he smiled at his servants, but the hardness in Walter Shellard's eyes was always there. His smile was like a smear of potter's clay that could be pulled around to suit. The man behind that congenial countenance was never caught off guard. He was always on full alert, assessing what people were thinking and calculating how to turn the mundane to his advantage.

'Is everything to my wife's liking?' he asked her. His lips moved as he spoke, though his teeth seemed to stay the same; clamped together, the inner part of a rictus smile. His grey eyes held hers.

'Yes, sir.' She bobbed a curtsey, though her legs felt like jelly.

His smile remained. 'What did my wife want?'

'I was just returning a dress that had been repaired, sir.'

The non-wavering smile continued. 'Is that all? Was there anything else she wanted you to do, my dear?' His eyes seemed to burn into her brain.

Unable to drag her eyes away from those teeth, Honoria shook her head so hard, the tiny white frill she wore on her head shifted to one side. 'No, sir.'

'Now, now, Honoria. No need to take on so. See? You've shaken this pretty little frill off your head. Let me put that straight for you.'

His hands brushed against her forehead as he pinned the frill more securely on her glossy black hair.

Honoria hated snakes and for some reason had assumed that Walter Shellard's touch would be like that of a snake. However, she did manage to control a sudden shudder, and once she'd got used to the idea, she noticed that his hands were really quite warm. Not sweaty. Just warm. She found that quite surprising. She'd heard gossip in the kitchen. She'd heard that the master had had quite a reputation before he had married his second wife. She'd heard about the other woman who'd lived here, a beautiful woman from somewhere around Pinhao. And she had a child. The other servants had gossiped in hushed, shocked tones, though in all honesty they relished the lurid details, made more lurid in the repetition of telling over the years.

He placed his hands on her shoulders in a fatherly manner

and looked searchingly into her eyes. 'Did my wife ask you any specific question?'

There was a certain set to his mouth, not so much a smile as an enquiring grimace, and although his voice was pleasant enough, it had undertones. Her fear of snakes returned, the curved shape of their mouths, and they certainly were not smiling. Neither was Walter Shellard. Not really.

It was the question she was dreading, and yet she reasoned, it had been such a little question, not really very important at all, so why was she trembling?

'She showed me a doll.'

Walter Shellard's smile had frozen, making his square jaw look even squarer, his teeth more even.

'Tell me the rest.'

His voice remained pitched at the same level, no word varying from the one that went before.

Lowering her eyes, Honoria forced herself to continue. 'It was just a doll. She asked me whether I'd ever seen it before. I said I had not.'

He nodded and the frozen smile defrosted a little, twitching at the corners of his mouth.

Honoria began to visibly quake in her shoes. She valued her job. She had a mother and a dullard of a younger brother to support. She was vehement in her attempt to remain in his favour. 'I said nothing, sir. Just as instructed. I said nothing.'

His light eyes were stone cold and paler than alabaster. A lesser man might have blinked more frequently than he did, but Walter Shellard was a man who could not bear to miss anything. He'd actually trained himself to keep his eyes wide open, to fix his opponent or enemy with a cold, searching stare. Becoming what he was had not happened overnight. He had trained himself to be successful, to have the upper hand over anyone who opposed his wishes. Family mattered, but only as long as they towed the line. He would not countenance opposition from within his business concerns or his family, and that included his wife.

Thirty-Two

The nursery at Cornwallis House was nothing more than a shabby but very large room. A pine table with chipped corners occupied the area closest to the window. A bookcase leaned against the wall at one end and a fire of damp coal steamed in the grate of a white marble fireplace.

England was cold and this house was colder. Catherine shivered at the fire's ineffectiveness and vowed she would do something about it. In the meantime, she made a superior effort to control her nerves, concentrating on the room's details as a kind of precursor to confronting its occupants.

There was a blackboard and easel on the other side of the room; a rocking horse with faded paintwork and a tangled mane; a selection of dolls sitting in tiers, propped up against the wall and looking for all the world as though they were posing for a photograph. There was also a model yacht; a metal automaton of a monkey complete with tin drum and a pair of cymbals; bats, balls and a brown doll's pram with wooden wheels.

A brass fender sporting a leather-covered seat at each corner was set in front of the fireplace. A girl with a flat face and straight brown hair was sitting on one of these corner seats toasting a doorstep of bread on a brass toasting fork. The girl turned round and looked her up and down then diverted her gaze and returned her attention to the toast that was beginning to colour.

'This is Jennifer. My eldest,' said Robert. He said it heartily with a great sweeping out of one arm and a flashing of even white teeth.

He was met with silence.

Outright rudeness, thought Catherine and tried to read the look on Robert's face; there was pride in his features, but something else, a sparkle in his eyes. He adored his eldest child. No! More than that. The form his affection might take made her shiver.

The girl was not much more than fourteen, four or five years younger than Catherine. Robert's daughter had little to commend her; seemingly she'd been in the humdrum middle of the queue when attractiveness was being given out.

Jennifer's most outstanding feature was her hair. Although mousy in colour, it was prodigious, bouncy and big. Curls that had been teased since babyhood were unruly and dry. Her flat face was framed by a deluge of fuzziness.

She's a beige person, thought Catherine, remembering Father Umberto and his habit of colour coding. Just as she thought it, she saw Jennifer's knuckles whiten as she tightened her grip on the toasting fork.

'And this is Evelyn,' said Robert, breaking into her confused thoughts.

She watched as he placed his hands on the shoulders of his second daughter. Her hair was dark and hung in thick skeins, falling forward and hiding her face. Her arms were resting on the mantelpiece. Her head was nestled within her arms as she leaned forward and watched her sister toasting bread.

Unlike her sister, who was sturdy and a little unfeminine, Evelyn was taller, sleeker of form, but just as distant, if not more so, than her sister. She gave no acknowledgement that she had heard but continued to regard her sister slide the bread from the fork and place it on top of another piece. Both were set on a willow-patterned plate within the grate. A butter dish and a honey pot sat there too.

'My girls, this is Catherine, my new wife. Your stepmother.'

'A *wicked* stepmother,' said Jennifer without turning round, her voice low and without warmth.

Evelyn said nothing, her face still buried in her arms.

'They'll get used to you,' Robert said breezily, taking her arm and turning her away. 'And you'll get used to them.'

It sounded like an order. Catherine wasn't at all sure that she would and felt a stirring of unease. Neither of his daughters was much younger than she was and although she wasn't exactly afraid of them, she wasn't comfortable. She knew instinctively that they'd never regard her as an adult when there were so few years between them.

She wished he'd told her he had children.

Robert let go of her arms, his head swivelling so he could look all around the room.

'Where's Charlie?'

Evelyn shrugged. Jennifer stabbed at yet another hunk of bread. 'Around somewhere.'

Her voice sounded hollow, bereft of emotion or interest.

Going on first impressions alone, Catherine disliked both girls intensely. If this rude welcome was anything to go by, they were spoilt and loved too much.

A loud wail suddenly sounded, gaining in intensity until it almost became a hysterical scream. The sound came from a cupboard set against the same wall as the collection of toys.

'Girls!' Robert said the word in a reproachful fashion but looked highly amused. Taking long, quick strides, he went to the cupboard, turned the key and threw open the door. Still wailing, a small boy crouched among toy bricks and a set of junior croquet mallets. He held out his arms.

The contents of the cupboard clattered outwards on to the floor as Robert swept the boy up into his arms.

'There, there, my fine young fellow,' he said.

The boy wound his arms around his father's neck and buried his head in his shoulder.

Catherine was immediately aware of the close bond between the two. She was also aware that the key to the cupboard had been turned. The poor boy was still trembling from his ordeal at the hands of his sisters.

She caught the two girls exchange a cruel smirk and made comment before thinking.

'You two should be ashamed of yourselves, treating your little brother like that. Surely as older sisters you should be taking care of him.'

The smirks turned stony. Jennifer glared, uncaring that her latest hunk of bread was turning black and smoking.

Evelyn, the younger girl, was almost screaming. 'We are not his sisters! He is not our brother! His mother was a whore. Our father wasn't married to her,' she shouted. 'He didn't love her like he did our mother, did you, Daddy? And you don't love him like you do us.'

'Now, now, my beautiful girls . . .'

Catherine felt sickened by Robert's smile. His eyes, and

apparently his love, were all for 'his' girls. Poor Charlie didn't seem to stand a chance.

Jennifer seemed to have contracted the hysterical mood of her sister. 'And you're not our mother either!' she shouted, running up to shout into Catherine's face, then running backwards away from her. 'And any brat of yours won't be our brother or sister. So there!'

'Jennifer. My darling, beautiful Jennifer,' wheedled Robert as the room filled with smoke.

Catherine raced to the fireplace and knocked the toasting fork from Jennifer's hand. The fork clattered against the brass fender and the blackened bread fell off the end and into the fire where it was swiftly consumed by flames. From there she ran to the window and threw it open.

Once all that was done, she turned to face this new family of hers. Each of them was regarding her with differing expressions. Even the pale-faced, sandy-haired Charlie was eyeing her with undisguised curiosity. His arms were still firmly wrapped around his father's neck.

The two girls were glowering, as though they had the right to burn the whole house down if they wished. Their expressions were bad enough, yet it was Robert's that worried her more. It wasn't anger and neither was it gratefulness. It was more as though he'd reached a realization about her that he hadn't been prepared for.

The moment passed. He snapped out of it quickly, concentrating his energy and attention on the young boy in his arms, tickling him and swinging him around at head height.

As she watched the goings-on, Catherine felt more and more like an outsider in this run-down, tired old house and her first inclination was to head for the door and run as far away from here as possible. But she couldn't do that. She was alone in a city she did not know and surrounded by people she did not like. Even now she could feel Jennifer's and Evelyn's eyes stabbing her in the back. She resolved not to look at them but to escape somewhere else. This house was to be her world. Getting to know it seemed the right and proper thing to do. She told Robert this.

'As I'm to be mistress of this house, then I should get to know the staff and the areas they work in,' she said as brightly as she could, though she was hardly feeling bright.

'You won't have much to organize,' said Robert. 'I won't be having dinner here tonight. I'll be at my club.' He grabbed her arm before she could get away and leaned close, whispering so no one else could hear. 'And then we'll make our own baby when I get back.'

'I doubt that,' she said, fixing him with a hard glare. 'Only a man, a real man, can make a baby with me.'

Her new, forthright attitude shook him. He winced and she knew immediately that tonight, at least, she would not be disturbed.

Later that night, she sat in a chair in her dressing room, a place that in a few short days had become something of a retreat from the crumbling house and the dysfunctional family.

Unseeing, she stared out of the window as dusk curtained the garden and an evening mist obliterated the near distance. Twilight fell into darkness, and still she stared.

Anyone discovering her there would think she was a picture of desolation, resigning herself to the way things were in this family and this house. But solitude had never found her feeling sorry for herself. Nothing, no situation was beyond redemption.

Plans for revenge and building a new life came thick and fast. She took courage from the fact that she'd inherited a substantial portion of Walter Shellard's quick-wittedness. She'd also inherited his strength, and she trusted that would always save her – even from herself.

Following her mother's death, she had not wallowed in grief. Neither had she retreated into herself on arrival at Aunt Lopa's *quinta*. And in the days following her great-aunt's death, she had proved she could manage by herself. By the same token, all her ills had been engineered by her father, and this marriage was the latest of his evil doings. Although she did not dwell on her misfortune or fall into despair, the anger she felt was always there, simmering beneath the surface.

Where will I start? she asked herself. For whom or what does he harbour great affection? The answer came easily. No person, but most definitely a place. Castile Villanova. Yes! That was what she would set out to take from him. Someday and somehow she would take the Castile Villanova.

It was a tall order, a far-fetched promise, but she owed it to herself and also to her mother.

Thirty-Three

Walter Shellard was in his office, a masculine room of dark woods, dark colours and a total lack of feminine frippery. The windows were bordered by solid elm shutters; the oak floorboards were varnished and the walls panelled. Walter regarded rich woods and a dark palette as an aid to plain thinking. Anything decorative smacked of an emotional response, and in business emotion of any kind was a luxury.

He glanced at the face of the black marble clock sitting on the mantelpiece. He had a board meeting shortly. Robert Arthur Freeman had upset his schedule.

'What did you wish to see me about?'

His daughter's husband had helped himself to a chair. Robert made a great show of crossing one leg over the other and brushed a speck of something from the soft grey material. 'I apologize.'

Walter gave no sign that the apology was accepted. 'We do have a board meeting. You could have saved it till then.'

Robert held his chin in a superior manner as he began voiding his hands of a pair of soft kid gloves.

Walter watched impassively. The smile that spread across Robert's face reminded him of hair oil, slick and best used sparingly.

'I doubt whether you would want family, indeed personal, matters aired at a business meeting,' said Robert, lowering his voice.

Walter maintained an implacable expression. He regarded Robert as a wastrel. No ordinary man would want him as a son-in-law – even on a clandestine basis. Only a few knew Catherine was his daughter. He wouldn't broadcast the news. He regretted that Ellen had found out before he could make good with the truth – the truth as he saw it. Her brittle attitude irritated, but did not trouble him unduly. Neither did his brother's loss of temper. 'How could you have married her off to that monster?'

His answer had been considered and delivered with cool, calm efficiency. 'Nothing personal. It was business. Purely business.'

He'd wanted that vineyard, the one that lay between the two he'd bought at a very good price. His plan was already paying off. It was early days, but the profit ratio had already increased thanks to the decrease in journey times and the general amalgamation of resources.

'Go on,' said Walter, resigned to hearing that this man sitting before him, a man he detested, wanted more money.

'Well,' said Robert, shifting in his chair and looking slightly abashed. 'I don't know quite how to put this rather delicate matter . . .'

He looked sidelong, as though waiting for Walter to urge him on.

Walter recognized the signs, but had no intention of doing so. Instead he sat back in his chair, steepled his fingers and waited.

'The fact is,' Robert went on once he'd worked out that he wasn't going to receive any encouragement. 'I was led to believe that Catherine was an innocent young girl. But . . .' His eyes fluttered and although his cheeks turned a little pink, Walter decided the change did not reflect the man's true feelings. Embarrassed he was not. A conniving scoundrel he most certainly was.

'So you're looking for compensation,' said Walter. His expression remained implacable. His eyes stayed fixed on Robert's limpid looks. He saw a flash of relief in the other man's eyes. He espied weakness and a certain deviant feminism about Robert's facial features and air of careless gentility. In past times he might have been a poet; he had that look about him. Of course he would have needed the private income to support him. Not that money would have lasted him long. Robert knew best how to spend money. He was useless at making it.

He saw the relief on Robert's face and knew he'd hit the nail on the head.

'I think two thousand would be a satisfactory sum,' said

Robert, his face glistening, his mouth almost salivating at the prospect of more money – money unearned.

Walter remained sitting in his big leather chair behind his equally large mahogany desk giving no hint whatsoever of his thoughts. Both desk and chair were set on raised dais not readily visible to visitors. No matter the size and status of those sitting in the chairs on the other side, Walter always looked down on them; as he did now. Especially now.

Silence hung in the air. Walter enjoyed making people wait, imagining what thoughts were going through their heads. Robert would be wondering whether he'd asked for too much, whether the ensuing silence meant he had overstepped the mark. He remained silent for quite a while, waiting for the moment when Robert started to squirm.

He congratulated himself on his superior judgement as Robert shifted in his seat, recrossing his legs and brushing at yet another imagined speck on the exquisitely tailored trousers.

'Ummm . . . perhaps I've been too hasty,' he began.

Walter took immediate advantage. 'What will you do if I refuse to compensate you for something that I myself regard as not being of any specific value?'

Robert's mouth dropped open. His initial surprise gave way to a frown. 'I'm not quite sure what you mean . . .' His voice trailed away.

Walter almost smiled to himself, but refrained from such a luxury. He preferred to remain unreadable. That way he maintained the advantage.

'What will you do if I refuse to pay you?'

It pleased him to see Robert's further discomfiture, the sudden agitation evidenced by the beads of sweat breaking out on his brow.

'I think . . . I think that would be very remiss of you,' said Robert, rushing his words.

Walter got up from his chair, turned his back and stood looking out of the window. His office was in an old building towards the end of King Street opposite the old almshouses which dated from Tudor times. If he looked one way he could see the façade of the Theatre Royal, home to Bristol Old Vic. In the other direction were an old black and white inn and a view of the river, ships and barges. The scene was no more than a pictorial backdrop to the scene going on inside his office. He could almost *taste* Robert's apprehension. What should he say? Would he back down or would he issue some threat meant to put him, Walter Shellard, in his place. A threat would at least be challenging, but was Robert brave enough to do that? And what form would a threat take?

'I shall inform your wife,' Robert said suddenly.

Walter paused, then turned slowly. His expression was unaltered, his steely eyes fixed and unblinking. His enjoyment of the situation was slightly irked by this pronouncement. As if such a threat held water. It almost made him smile.

'Do so,' he said abruptly.

He saw the consternation in Robert's eyes. My God, this man was an open book. No wonder the fortune left to him by his father was diminishing by the day. The man was a pushover.

Robert gathered up what resolve he had left. 'But your wife . . .'

'I provide my wife and children with a very comfortable lifestyle. Without me, she'd have nothing. No money. No status. No children.'

He glanced again at the clock, giving the distinct impression that he'd lost patience and that Robert Arthur Freeman was out of time. Four minutes to eleven. 'Shall we make our way to the boardroom?'

Robert was speechless, as dejected as a squashed insect trodden underfoot. Which was what he was – on both counts.

Walter wanted to laugh out loud at Robert Arthur Freeman's face. The man had a long face and a large jaw that looked longer now and very pale. Whatever confidence the man had come in with, was lying flat and battered on the floor.

'Look,' said Robert, getting suddenly to his feet, a restraining hand reaching for Walter's arm. 'I have some rather large debts. I'm desperately in need of funds . . .'

Walter couldn't help the contempt that crept into his eyes, not that Robert was likely to notice. He didn't ask for details of the debts. He already knew what they were; women, drink and gambling.

'We all have weaknesses,' he said.

'I'm afraid so,' said Robert, his eyes downcast as he nodded vehemently. 'Just a temporary problem,' he said with a nervous laugh.

'I'll transfer the funds into your account.'

At his sudden reversal of fortune, Robert's face brightened and the apprehension left his eyes. 'That's wonderful, Walter.'

'In return Shellard Enterprises will take another ten per cent of your interest in the St Monica Vineyard.'

Robert's mouth dropped open. This hadn't been part of the plan.

Later, once the board meeting was over, Seth Armitage came to his office. Ten years older than Walter, he had white hair and eyebrows and a slightly amused look in his eyes. They'd been business partners for many years and had known each other for many more. He'd been co-opted on to the board as an advisor following his retirement. It was something but not enough. He'd lived for Shellard Enterprises. He wasn't happy about being sidelined.

Seth chose a chair and let out a sigh of satisfaction as he sat down in it before turning his attention to Walter.

'Sometimes you frighten me, Walter Shellard.'

One side of Walter's mouth lifted in a half-smile. His eyes were unchanged. They never changed, always steel-grey, always observant, searching for the other man's, or woman's, weakness.

'Whisky?'

Seth nodded. 'Why not?'

'I take it you're referring to Arthur Freeman.' He deferred from mentioning the man's first name. It hinted at intimacy. Walter felt no intimacy towards Robert Arthur Freeman, only disdain. He handed Seth his drink and sipped at his own.

'The man spends money like water,' said Seth.

'To the advantage of Shellard Enterprises,' said Walter, raising his glass in a toast.

Seth reciprocated. 'He's arrogant and stupid, not at all like his father. You wouldn't have pulled the wool over his eyes.'

Walter was already paying only minimum attention to what Seth was saying. He had no time for nostalgia. It was the moment that counted, and in turn the future. There was nothing that could be done about the past.

'By the time I've finished with him, Shellard Enterprises will own his whole business outright.'

Seth raised his eyebrows. 'All his business interests?'

'Why not? He doesn't seem to attach much value to them and, in the right hands, they could make a fortune.'

Seth shook his head and his look hardened. He'd considered himself as close to Walter Shellard as anyone could be and just as hard-headed. But of late, knowing some of Walter's more closely guarded secrets, he'd realized there was a widening gulf between them. For a start he would never have given one of his daughters – even an illegitimate daughter, if he had one – to someone like Robert Arthur Freeman. He'd heard some rumours – some very sickening rumours.

'Increase his credit at the gambling club.'

'If you say so,' said Seth.

'I'll pull the rug out from under him when I see fit,' said Walter.

He showed no sign of any consideration, and neither did he allow emotion to enter his cut-throat dealings. And that, thought Seth, is why he's so successful.

'You'd make a good gambler,' Seth Armitage said as he swigged back the last of the whisky before getting to his feet.

Walter's expression was unaltered. 'I never gamble. I only back dead certs.' He allowed himself a strangely self-conscious smile. 'I'm luckier than most men who merely gain a son-in-law. I've gained a son-in-law and a ready-made business.'

Seth nodded and ambled towards the door.

'Seth?'

The old man turned round.

'I've noticed you're slowing down of late. Understandable, of course – at your age. You're no spring chicken; it's time you stood down completely.'

Seth looked shell-shocked. Just for once, both his snowy eyebrows rose to the same level.

'I don't want to stand down, Walter. Shellard Enterprises is my life.'

Walter appeared to be concentrating all his efforts on lighting a fresh cigar from the still burning stub of an old one. 'There's plenty in the graveyard who thought their work was their life, Seth. Step aside, and don't worry about someone taking your place. It's all taken care of.'

Thirty-Four

It was a new challenge and excited her. Catherine had made up her mind to get Cornwallis House into some sort of order. She had a vision that she could make it something to be proud of – something to rival Castile Villanova. To this end she summoned the four servants the house depended on to a meeting.

She gathered them in the drawing room, the lightest and most dust-free room in the whole house, and ordered that they come with a tray of tea and biscuits.

Once everyone was settled, she proceeded to pour the tea herself. Four surprised-looking faces stared at her. Conclusions were expressed with swiftly exchanged looks. It was left to the butler to make comment.

'Mrs Arthur Freeman, it's for us to be doing this,' said Gerald Collier, who as butler had acquired the job of servants' spokesman.

'I'm quite capable of pouring tea,' said Catherine. 'I'm not helpless. Now please take a biscuit if you want one.'

She felt their eyes upon her before shifting their gaze sideways, exchanging more surprised looks as they sipped at their tea.

'Now,' said Catherine, who had rehearsed what she intended saying in front of the dressing-table mirror; a mirror as besmirched with grime and dirt as the rest of the house. 'I've only been here a short time, but in that time I could not help noting that Cornwallis House is in a state of neglect. Now don't think I'm picking fault because I'm used to living in grander places. Indeed, I lived in quite a rustic environment before coming here. So what I have to ask is why things are in such a bad way and whether anyone can enlighten me?'

More looks before Gerald Collier made an attempt to

explain. He cleared his throat first. 'Begging your pardon, ma'am, but there's only four of us and this is a big house to keep in order. And as you can see, we're all of . . .' He paused and exchanged worried frowns with his colleagues before continuing. 'We're all getting on a bit. Truth is we started work here with the old master and mistress. Things were different then,' he said, his face lighting up at memories of better times. 'There were twenty-four of us then. And we were young. Then when Master Robert took over . . .' He lowered his eyes and his words melted.

Catherine took a deep breath. 'And my husband has proceeded to waste his inheritance.'

She didn't need anyone to explain any further about Robert's shortcomings. It had become obvious that he squandered money more quickly than it was earned. She sighed audibly. 'I plan to engage some young blood to help you. Until I find someone suitable, we shall finish our tea and then you can fetch me beeswax and polish. I'm going to attack that dining-room table. It's far too good to leave unpolished.'

Gerald Collier's pale eyes opened wide in surprise. '*You're* going to do it?'

Catherine smiled at the old man whose wispy white hair barely covered his pate. 'I'm not afraid to get my hands dirty.' She held out her hands as she said it, scrutinizing their softness and remembering how they'd often been grimy from planting vegetables, or sticky from milking a goat. 'And as you say, this place needs some serious attention.'

The three women, not one of whom was a day below sixty, looked at each other before one of them came to a conclusion.

'I'll give 'e a hand,' said Polly. She got to her feet in two stages; getting up from her chair, her bones creaking in protest, then straightening her legs, an action accompanied by yet more creaking.

The other two, Florence the cook and Betty who doubled as maid and help to Florence when needed, followed her lead.

'I'll get these washed and put away,' said Florence. 'Though it's not really my job,' she added in case someone should forget her higher status.

'I've got laundry to do,' said Betty. 'And if I don't set to right away, there'll be none clean and none ironed, and dirty sheets on the bed.'

Catherine remembered the women who'd collected and laundered linens at Castile Villanova then brought them back when they were clean. She made a mental note to find out whether there were similar women hereabouts; but not yet, she counselled. Best to proceed slowly until she'd gained the servants' trust and found out how much such a service might cost.

Gerald Collier lingered, his loose bottom lip quivering as though he had something further to say.

'If you don't mind me saying something, madam; I wouldn't want to be speaking out of turn . . .'

'Please go on.'

She wondered what was on his mind and prayed that, at least for a time, he wasn't considering retirement.

'Do you think there's any hope of employing a gardener like we used to? It's not just that the vegetable garden is in a mess, there's also the sheep to consider. They're leaving a mess all the way down the driveway and they've been getting into the vegetable garden and eating up what little remains there. I know Mr Freeman brought the sheep in to keep the grass down, but couldn't we have a lawnmower like other people?'

The vegetable garden was enclosed behind a high brick wall. Catherine had noticed the broken gate and the air of dereliction, both in the garden itself and the greenhouse adjoining it. The sheep had been noticeable since the very first day along with the gypsy encampment on the other side of the copse. Presumably Robert had considered employing the sheep to keep the grass down rather than purchase a lawnmower or, more likely considering the size of the grounds, pay an army of men with scythes or a man with a tractor to keep the grass down to size.

'Presumably the gypsies pay something for their grazing and their campsite?'

'They butcher a sheep now and again and bring it to the kitchen.'

She jotted this information down on the paper in front of her. 'I see.' Indeed, she did see. A whole sheep was not to be sniffed at.

'Will that be all, madam?'

'Yes, thank you, Collier.' She nodded thoughtfully, still looking at the list of possible actions to bring the house back up to a reasonable condition.

'That really do look a picture,' said Polly once they'd polished the Sheraton-style table to the point where they could see their faces in the honey-brown surface.

Polly was small and wiry, and did everything at breakneck speed, quite a feat for a woman of her age. She told Catherine she was seventy-three years old.

'I got called back into service at the end of the Great War.' She shook her head despairingly. 'Young women ain't so keen on going into service nowadays. They can make more money in factories making paper bags or chocolate or cigarettes. No pride in domestic service any more.'

The strength of her voice seemed to falter towards the end of what she was saying, and Catherine was sure she heard her give a little sigh. Looking up from polishing the very last chair, she saw that Polly's pink face had turned pale and her head had fallen to one side.

Flinging her duster aside, she ran and knelt at Polly's side, took hold of her hand and patted her cheek.

'Polly? Can you hear me? Polly?'

Polly's mouth was open. She was making short, cackling noises.

'Oh, God,' muttered Catherine, panicking.

She heard someone enter the room and looked over her shoulder. It was Betty.

'Polly's not well,' she shouted. 'Quick. Fetch a doctor.'

'No, no, no.' Betty shook her head and came running instead. 'She's just having one of her turns,' she said. 'If you can help me get her up to her bed, ma'am.'

Each took one of Polly's arms and placed it around their shoulders. Between them they began ascending the stairs to the very top of the house. There were six flights and, although she was far from heavy, Polly's feet were off the ground and they really were carrying her, so that their calves ached by the time they reached her room.

'Good job she's got a room to herself,' said Betty as they lay her on the bed.

The room was small, had plain brown wallpaper and rose-patterned curtains at the small, square window. A chest of drawers stood against one wall with a small chair to either side. A silver crucifix hung above the bed. A small rug was set beside the bed on dark-green linoleum.

'I should think she would have it to herself,' Catherine remarked. 'It's only big enough for one.'

Betty made a chortling sound. 'It used to sleep two years ago when there were more of us. Not now, though.'

'Really?'

Betty explained. 'It were a tight squeeze, though fun at the time. Hard work, but then we was young and not afraid of hard work nor nothing.'

'I get the impression that Robert's parents were good employers.'

'So I hear,' Betty interjected, her round eyes brown and soft as a cow's and her lips rubbery, always on the move. 'I couldn't vouch for it meself. I didn't come 'ere till later. I was a lady's maid to Mrs Gertrude Shellard, the first Mrs Shellard. You must know them; Shellard the wine people. Biggest wine people in the city, they are. I left when she died on account of there being no woman at Adelaide Court, so no job. I was out. So I came here.'

Betty could not possibly guess what effect her words had had. Nobody in the household knew who her father was. Catherine felt herself turning cold. She could not look at Betty in case she saw the consternation in her eyes. Instead she fixed her gaze on Polly, sitting on the side of the bed, holding her hand as she slowly came round. She'd reached her own conclusion regarding the cause of Polly's 'funny turn'.

Polly's eyes flickered open. 'Did I go queer?' she asked.

Catherine leaned closer. 'It's my fault. I think that polishing was too much for you.'

Polly's eyes opened wide with alarm. 'But, missus, don't turn me out. I've only got a small pension.'

'That isn't what I meant,' said Catherine, already back-tracking on suggesting that Polly might consider going back into retirement. Obviously such a suggestion would not be welcome.

'I think you need some help. A young girl, perhaps, in need of a wage. And training, of course. She could learn a lot from you. Do you think you could do that?'

Although Polly's eyes didn't exactly sparkle, there was a definite improvement in her colour.

'I expect so,' she said, as she closed her eyes and fell asleep.

She did not mention her plans to Robert, firstly because she didn't think there was any point, and secondly he was rarely home until the early hours of the morning and wouldn't care much anyway.

He usually came in noisily, smelling of drink and cheap perfume. 'But I only love you, darling,' he slurred, his breath falling over her in thick, porous fumes in one of those infrequent moments when he found his way to her bedroom.

Most of the time, she pretended to be asleep when he fumbled beneath the hideous nightdress she had worn on their honeymoon. He hadn't yet twigged that because of its size, she could tie the back of the hem to the front. Stone-cold sober he'd be hard pressed to find his way to her body. Inebriated and already satiated by some cheap tart from a dockside inn, he gave up easily and was swiftly snoring.

All the same, Catherine had made up her mind that she would not let things continue like this. She loathed him touching her, but sometimes a dominant veneer was not enough and intimacy could not be avoided. In order to limit their intimate relations, she'd decided to move into the room at the end of the corridor. She wouldn't be completely out of his grasp, but he lacked energy and commitment when he came home drunk. She'd have some respite, and for that she would be grateful. She needed space to think and to make plans.

Betty and Doris, a local girl, helped her get the room into some order. They brought a brass bed and a mattress down from the attic and found some cotton twill sheets and a silk counterpane lying forgotten on the top shelf of a linen press. The silk counterpane was a lovely shade of pale turquoise embroidered around the edge with pink flowers and pale-green leaves. The existing curtains were plain and of a similar colour and would have looked quite nice, except that Betty had found a laundry woman to wash them.

'They were too old,' said Betty, lifting what was left of the fragile curtains.

'Too rotten,' said Catherine on inspecting the torn fabric. Even as she inspected the hem, another tear appeared. 'Throw them out,' she sighed. 'I'll have to make do with what I've got.'

The door opened suddenly and Robert appeared. 'I'm going out,' he said abruptly. 'I'm taking the girls shopping in my motor car.'

He didn't ask whether she wanted to come. Neither did he question what she was doing. For that she was grateful.

The house was beginning to come together and although windowpanes were still missing and the gypsies' sheep were still messing up the driveway, she'd spent only frugally. Robert, on the other hand, had bought himself a motor car and was already contemplating hiring a chauffeur. Catherine wondered where the sudden windfall had come from, though wouldn't ask him. Their relationship had deteriorated beyond mending. Their social life in the city was non-existent and the only time they shared any intimacies was when he was sober enough to join her in bed. Thankfully that particular scenario didn't happen very often.

As for the children – they kept out of her way, and it saddened her. Up until now the house had totally occupied every waking moment. There was so much to do; but conversely, except for the servants, she lacked human contact. She still had some money left over from the sum her father had sent her via his solicitors plus her cheese money. Sullenly, she'd counted it out. The Portuguese equivalent had been changed by the bank into twenty-five pounds. Not really enough to do much with. She sighed. She had to make a start somewhere. And little things can grow into big ones; Aunt Lopa had told her that. 'You'd be surprised how the few coins I earn for my crochet work grow like mushrooms into crisp dollar bills.'

Dollars? She smiled. Her great-aunt had used varied turns of phrase, but for some reason whenever she referred to money, it was always in dollars. The chest! She got to her feet, overcome by the sudden feeling that there was money in the chest – possibly in dollars.

Thirty-Five

Catherine was standing on the top landing near the door leading to the servants' quarters, waiting for the right moment to open her great-aunt's chest. Her heart thudded at the prospect of finally unlocking that battered old box. It might contain the dollar equivalent of a few hundred pounds, a sum she could do so much with.

It was silly to feel excited about such a mundane happening, but she'd put it off for so long. To that end she couldn't help treating the event with something approaching reverence – like a mass, but far more exciting.

As a result, she craved privacy for doing this, waiting until after dinner, until the children were in bed and Robert had left to pursue his nocturnal habits.

The top-floor landing had become a significant refuge where she could gather her thoughts and try to work out the best way forward.

She'd worked out that it would take a great deal of money to return the house to its former glory. Her problem was that Robert spent money like water and their income from the vineyards and warehouses appeared strangely erratic. She'd worked out that an upturn occurred in their bank account immediately following one of Robert's boardroom appearances at Shellard Enterprises.

Unblinking, she stared at the gathering darkness. Robert stayed out most of the night and lingered in bed until midday. Rarely did he put in an appearance at the warehouse and she wasn't convinced that his appearances at Shellard Enterprises had anything whatsoever to do with business. Robert was allergic to work; that much was obvious. Hence the state of the house; which matches the man, she thought to herself and sighed. She remembered her life how it used to be; the warm walls of the Castile Villanova, the fresh air around Aunt Lopa's *quinta* high above the Douro Valley. Both were beautiful in their own way, and both were cherished. Robert had no affection for anyone or anything but himself – with the possible exception of his children, especially the girls.

Money was always a contentious matter with Robert. He raided the children's piggy banks. He raided money set aside to pay the greengrocer and the butcher.

She never failed to tackle him about his nefarious ways. 'And what about the housekeeping?'

'Your father won't let you starve.'

She bridled at that sort of comment. 'You have to make money yourself, Robert. You have a business that should be thriving.'

'Stop nagging, woman. It takes care of itself,' he said with a dismissive wave.

'No business does that,' she retorted.

Her sharp retorts, and the fact that he was beginning to discover that her mind was sharper than his, unsettled him. To that end, he'd taken to avoiding her more and more.

'I'm going out,' he said. And he'd gone.

Hearing thudding feet on the landing immediately below her, she moved sideways so she could peer down unseen. She heard someone whispering.

'Have you got keys?'

There was no mistaking the childish voice; Jennifer, Robert's elder daughter, speaking in a loud whisper.

'Of course I have!' It was Jennifer's sister, Evelyn, who responded. Jennifer was fourteen and Evelyn twelve. She felt like an interloper, an intrusion into their world. That's why she liked it up here. All the same, she leaned forward straining to hear. She had an inkling of what they were up to.

There followed a jangling of iron against iron as one key after another was inserted into the lock before one finally turned.

She heard other footsteps, softer, smaller ones.

'What are you doing?' asked a small voice.

'Never mind what we're doing. What are you doing here, turnip? Go away! Go away now!' She recognized Jennifer's voice.

'Don't call me that. I'm not a turnip. What are you doing?'

Catherine recognized Charlie's voice. Charlie was seven years old and the result of Robert's liaison with a barmaid at the Llandoger Trow, an old inn on the Welsh Back at the end of King Street.

There followed the sound of a slap. 'Yes, you are a turnip. I said you are and so you are.'

Jennifer was fond of treating the boy cruelly. Robert seemed oblivious to her behaviour. To him she was the apple of his eye and spoilt to distraction.

'Why don't you let me play with you?' Charlie whimpered. He sounded close to tears. Catherine imagined him rubbing at the redness on his cheek. Her first instinct was to rush down the stairs and intervene at once. Robert's instructions that she stay clear of his children held her back.

There followed a series of whispers. 'All right. You can come with us. We're going to look at *her* things. But you have to keep quiet.'

It was no surprise to Catherine that Jennifer had referred to her with as much contempt as she treated Charlie. She heard the door to her room groan on its hinges as they opened it and went in.

This was too much! A wave of anger swept over her. If Robert wasn't going to correct his daughter, then she certainly was.

She was about to leave her hiding place when Betty came running from the direction of the servants' rooms.

'Oh, madam, come quickly. It's Polly. I think she's having another of her funny turns.'

Catherine looked down to where the children had disappeared into her room. She was in two minds about what to do, but made a snap decision.

'If you could come, madam,' said a worried-looking Betty.

'I'll be right there. Keep her quiet for the moment.'

'I see,' said Betty, sounding just as put-out as she looked. 'Hmm! No appreciation nowadays.' With that, she stormed off.

There was no time to explain that the children were rummaging in the small dressing room adjoining her and Robert's bedroom, intent on looking through her personal things. It didn't do to share family problems with servants. Robert had been adamant about that. Besides, she didn't want their prying fingers inside the old coffer that she'd still not opened. Just looking at it brought a lump to her throat and, for now, she couldn't bring herself to open it; not until her life improved; not until she felt happy again.

Catherine swung out on to the landing and rushed down the stairs. She found the two girls hunched over the coffer arguing over which key they should try next. Their heads spun round when they heard her.

She snatched the keys. 'Get away from that!'

Surprised at first, they swiftly recovered. Jennifer, her pudding face framed by a lion's mane of uncontrollable hair, recovered first. Her small mouth pursed, she sprang to her feet.

'Those aren't yours.'

Catherine stood her ground, her fists bunched on her hips. 'Whose are they then?'

Jennifer glared back defiantly. 'They're my father's.'

'And I am your father's wife!'

'He only married because you came with a discount. That's what he said. Shellard gave me a big discount on his wine for marrying his daughter. My father's a businessman. That's why he married you!'

Catherine was dumbstruck. To have this . . . this . . . *child* . . . telling her . . .

'That's a lie!'

Only it wasn't. Deep inside she knew it wasn't. Robert had reeled her in like a fish on the line. The whole scenario of her brief courtship had been designed to snare her into the marriage arranged by her father.

'He doesn't love you,' her younger sister added. 'He loved our mother. *That's* who he loved.'

Catherine looked up at the ceiling. 'Why am I arguing with these *children*? Get out,' she ordered, pointing at the door. 'Get out of here right now!'

'We're going,' snapped Jennifer, giving a toss of her unruly mane. 'Come along, Evelyn.'

Catherine shut the door after them. Leaning against the door she considered whether her father had brokered a business deal. It made no difference to her estimation of her father; she still hated him. On further consideration it made little difference to her estimation of Robert. He'd sprung too many surprises on her; she didn't hate him, but she certainly didn't trust him.

It came to her suddenly that Charlie had been with the girls. Where was he now?

'Charlie?'

She heard a bumping sound from within a mahogany wardrobe. On opening it, she found Charlie inside, rubbing at red raw eyes. Her heart went out to him.

'Oh, Charlie. Come out from there. Let me give you a cuddle.'

He came out willingly, but took a step back when she attempted to throw her arms around him.

'They said I'm not to cuddle you. They'll beat me if I do. They said they would.'

Clasping her hands behind her back, Catherine told him she understood. 'I wouldn't want them to do that,' she said. 'I'll wait until you're older and bigger before I mother you.'

He looked at her round-eyed. 'They say my mother, my real mother, is nothing but a cheap tart.'

'They would say that. They're jealous.'

He thought about that for a moment. 'She works in a bar.'

'That doesn't mean to say she's not a good mother.'

'So why did she give me to my father?'

Catherine understood how he felt, but managed a smile of reassurance along with a viable explanation. 'She thought she was doing the best for you. Your father can afford to give you a decent education. Won't you be going away to school shortly?'

He nodded. 'I'm frightened of going to school, but I want to. I don't like Jennifer and Evelyn. They're horrible.'

Catherine considered the alternative. 'You'll be among other boys of your own age. Let's face it, are they likely to be any worse than your half-sisters?'

His tight little face stiffened into a brief moment of contemplation. 'I think I would prefer the other boys to them,' he said vehemently.

Catherine brushed his hair from his eyes and smiled at him. 'I think you would too.'

Suddenly he reached up for her. 'Daddy said he was having second thoughts about sending me away. I'll hug you if you promise to persuade Daddy to send me away to school.'

Her heart went out to this little boy. How sad he must be if he actually wanted to be sent away from home.

'I promise,' she said, and they hugged as she thought how best to live up to her promise.

Having decided that opening the coffer was on hold for the moment, she went to check that Polly had recovered and then went to bed feeling tired and drained by her mixed emotions. She did most of her thinking lying alone in bed; her mental list of things to be done as clear as the one she'd written on paper. Twenty-five pounds was not enough to buy a quarter of Castile Villanova let alone the whole place. She had to find a way to make money. She certainly couldn't rely on her husband. Robert was a gentleman in the old sense; he liked income but hated work. He never went near his study if he could help it. The running of the warehouse which received produce from his own vineyard was left to a manager. How stupid to leave one's livelihood in the hands of an employee, she thought. How stupid not to keep an eye on what was going on, and how stupid to spend money you didn't necessarily have. Someone should take things in hand.

'You,' she muttered.

Swinging her legs out of bed, she reached for her dressing gown, tied the silk cord tightly around her waist, donned her slippers and headed for the study.

Because Robert rarely used the study, it wasn't likely to be locked. Luke Townsend, the warehouse manager, had brought a copy of the month's transactions just the other day. And there were bound to be other records; details of the property lease or freehold – employees, equipment – everything she could need.

On slippered feet, she padded over the thick brown carpet. Moonlight diffused through a thick lace curtain. She pulled it back and the heavy furniture and bookcases were silvered with light. For added efficiency, she turned on a green-shaded, brass-stemmed desk light.

The latest batch of company records was slung in an unlocked drawer. Portfolios of property owned – plus debts owed – were filed in dark wooden cabinets. They were neatly stacked and labelled, though not by Robert. A clerk, a Mr Maddingly, came in once a week to ensure things were in order.

File after file, ledger after ledger, page after page, she checked through Robert's business records. When her eyes were too tired to continue, she sat back in the brown leather chair and closed them. The details of what she'd been reading were imprinted on the back of her eyelids. The main warehouse was in an old building in Colston Avenue. The main storage consisted of deep cellars on two levels running beneath the road at the front of the property. The offices of Arthur Freeman and Son were situated at street level and also on the first floor. There were two floors above that appeared to be used only for storage. Above that was an attic floor which was not used for anything.

Sales were made via commercial travellers who took lists around to wine shops and other varied outlets. Delivery was by way of two bull-nosed black Morris vans with white lettering on their sides.

Catherine rubbed at her eyes. Going over the details had made her tired, but had also inspired her. Tomorrow she would go and inspect the premises. Should I ask Robert for permission? she asked herself. She decided not to. Mr Townsend, the manager, would be arriving by taxi tomorrow with copies of the latest records for her husband. She'd go and visit the warehouse with him.

Thirty-Six

The next morning Catherine found herself being given a guided tour of the tall property that served as warehouse and business premises in the very centre of the city.

Townsend explained to her that the area now referred to as the Tramways Centre and covering a vast oval in the city centre, had once been open to shipping.

'All covered in now,' he said to her.

She couldn't help but notice how he seemed in awe of her, as no one had taken any interest in the business for ages, and he'd resigned himself to seeing it run swiftly and surely down-hill.

'I take it that's why it's so chilly down here,' she commented, shivering as they traversed the dark cellars that ran between the building and the river.

'But not damp,' said Mr Townsend. 'Wouldn't do to store port wine and suchlike in damp conditions.'

Catherine brushed at a spider's web that had chanced to cling to the sleeve of her navy-blue jacket. The jacket had a nautical look about it, a blue and red stripe running around the cuffs and brass buttons fastening a neatly fitted jacket.

She'd been aware of the men in the warehouse pausing in their work to take a look at their employer's wife. Far from being impervious to their approving looks, Catherine had felt a great surge of confidence rush through her. She'd smiled at them and wished them a good morning. They'd looked surprised and had responded in kind.

'My, my, Mrs Arthur Freeman. You'll have them eating out of your hand with that kind of treatment,' said Mr Townsend, his face slightly pink when she caught him studying her.

'Being civil costs nothing,' she replied.

'Aye. Yer right there.'

He nodded and looked totally approving. He even looked far happier than when she'd first inveigled him into accompanying her.

'This way to the office and general loading area.'

She followed him as he slowly climbed the stairs back up to street level. The front office was an untidy place of desks, paperwork and odd crates serving as makeshift desks. Sheets of brown paper covered the broad window of what was essentially a shopfront. Catherine wrinkled her nose. The room smelled of dust and neglect.

'It needs cleaning,' she said, swiping at a dusty shelf with a pair of kid gloves.

Mr Townsend sighed and leaned against a bookshelf. 'The old place is past its best.'

A small, wiry clerk was flitting in and out with order sheets, darting out to the backyard where a van was being loaded, and darting back in again, down the stairs to the cellar, up again and back out to the van.

Seeing her looking, Mr Townsend asked her if she'd like to go through to the back.

'It's only a yard,' he explained. 'And that fellow you saw running in and out was Mr Maddingly.'

Catherine, with her usual observance, noticed a lot more than 'just a yard'.

'What's that?' she asked, jerking her chin at a pair of wooden doors set at a slant between the building and the ground.

'Cellar doors,' said Mr Townsend.

Catherine could not possibly know it, but Townsend was experiencing a nervous anticipation. Ever since Robert Arthur Freeman had inherited his father's business, he'd been asking permission to open those trap doors. Mr Arthur Freeman had been quite adamant about keeping them closed.

'The steps are broken going down from the doors and in need of repair,' Townsend had told him on one of his visits to Cornwallis House. The fact was they'd rotted away and a new set was needed.

'I've no money for bloody wooden steps,' his employer had retorted. 'Manage as best you can.'

Catherine looked from the cellar doors to the backyard, her scrutiny shifting to the wiry clerk and the men loading the van. All of them were walking miles in order to check and load an order. It seemed ridiculous when there were cellar doors here waiting to be opened.

'Why don't you use them?' she asked.

Townsend explained. 'It would cost at least two pounds two shillings and sixpence to replace the stairs,' he added.

Without him having to tell her, Catherine knew Robert had refused to fund the repair.

'Just a minute,' she said, and got a notepad and pen out of her handbag. She made a note regarding her thoughts about the front office, the broken stairs and the fact that the front shop was used as a storeroom-cum-office.

Townsend, a man of her father's age who had worked for Robert's father, seemed to come alive in response to her interest, 'Would you like to see the upper floors?' His face was brighter, and the aimless air of despair she'd surmised on his visits to Cornwallis House had lessened. His shoulders were less rounded; his step a little lighter.

After informing him that she would very much like to inspect the other floors, she followed him up the stairs.

The landing on the first floor was bright by virtue of a sash window letting in the morning light. The sun was shining brightly, the window was open and the screams of wheeling seagulls added life to what would otherwise have been a dead space.

'There seems to be a lot of space up here,' she said, whirling from room to room, one plan succeeding another in her fertile brain.

'Six rooms.'

'Six! And only one of them used as an office.' She sounded and felt utterly astounded. She noted the details. In her mind she was questioning why Robert was not making the best use of these rooms. A small return was better than none at all; her Aunt Lopa had told her that, she of the many items of crochet she'd sold door to door.

By the time she'd reached the attic rooms and saw the long iron staircase going down from a small door to the yard below, the building she saw bore no resemblance at all to the one in her mind.

'Can we sit somewhere and talk in private, Mr Townsend? Perhaps you can get someone to bring us tea?'

Mr Townsend's face was a picture. His pale-blue eyes twinkled with renewed faith. Someone in the family had finally shown an interest in the source of their income.

His voice was as big as his body. 'Indeed I will, Mrs Arthur Freeman.'

Earlier she'd noticed a stoop to his shoulders. Now, there was none.

There was a table and two long-forgotten chairs in one of the first-floor rooms. Light flooded into the room from an uncommonly lovely oriole-style window at the front of the building.

'It's Elizabethan,' he said on noticing her interest.

'It's a lovely view.' Bending her head back to her notes, she sipped tea from a chipped china cup. It didn't matter that it was chipped. All that mattered to her at this moment was this building, the fact that they weren't selling enough wine to cover their outgoings, and that the amount produced at the vineyard in Spain was greater than the amount being sold from their own premises.

Accounts had never been her strong point, but a naturally enquiring mind had brought her to one basic truth. Wine was being filtered off at source. It was being produced but not reaching the warehouse. At present she couldn't investigate why that was; not until she addressed this end of the business. These premises had to make a profit purely to ensure their survival. Run-down as it was, Cornwallis House could be very grand if the money were there to refurbish it.

'I've worked out a plan,' said Catherine after another hasty sip of hot tea.

'I'm glad of that,' said a smiling Townsend, his eyes fixed on her, his arms folded on the tabletop. The glow of admiration shone on his face. He couldn't believe that this flood of ideas was coming from a slip of a girl.

She found the way he looked at her quite amusing. She felt like God handing down the Ten Commandments and sensed he would do everything that she asked of him.

'First, we need to get a new set of steps made for the cellar. At present time is being wasted going to and fro through the shop and up and down the internal steps.'

The man sitting opposite her nodded his head slowly, his eyes filled with a kind of wonder. 'I'll hire a carpenter, though you must know, ma'am, that he'll want paying up front. I'm afraid Mr Arthur Freeman is a bit tardy in paying tradesmen on time.'

In response Catherine swiftly snapped open her bag. 'Take this,' she said handing him a five-pound note. 'And hire a stonemason to make the steps, not a carpenter. This time we'll have something that lasts.'

Townsend's jaw dropped before a winning smile came to his mouth. 'I'll do that, ma'am. Indeed I will!'

He sounded so exuberant, as though with a wave of her hand she could make everything right.

Start as you mean to go on.

She had to be honest with him. 'I've little money at present, Mr Townsend. As I'm sure you are aware, the business is in dire straits. My husband is otherwise engaged elsewhere, so I will take over. You will say nothing of this to my husband or any of his agents. You will answer directly to me. Is that clear?'

Her look was intense, her voice strong.

His mouth still gaped when he nodded.

'Now. We will concentrate on making good what we have; things that cost little or nothing to improve. First things first, I want the brown paper stripped from the window of the front office. Do we have any paint?'

'There's some pots of dark green somewhere.'

She nodded brusquely. 'Good. I want the outside of the shopfront painted. If there's enough left over, I want the inside painted too.

'Aye, ma'am.'

She smiled suddenly and looked into his eyes. 'And stop calling me ma'am. You're my manager. Mrs Arthur Freeman if you must be formal; or Catherine if we are to become firm friends.'

Townsend frowned. 'Isn't the downstairs office going to lack privacy if we get rid of the brown paper?'

Catherine sat up straight and beamed at him. 'I noticed two good rooms on this floor at the back of the building. Those will be the new offices. One general office, and one for you.' She looked out through the oriole window at the church spires on the other side of the Tramways Centre. 'I shall have this office. I like to see what's going on in the world.'

She went on to explain her plans for what was presently the office. 'We're going to have a shop,' she explained. 'There's too much stock lying around in the cellar. We need to move it more quickly and seeing as we have a large shop frontage and good passing trade, a shop it shall be. In fact, I think we'll attract a lot of new customers. Don't you?'

Townsend seemed to expand in size as he poured praise on her scheme. 'I've often said that this place was wasted,' he said, beaming from ear to ear.

She could not read his mind, but Townsend appeared mightily impressed. He kept asking himself how she saw things so clearly. It must be in the blood, he thought to himself.

'And the other rooms?'

Catherine was scribbling a small design on her pad. 'There's a fire escape serving the attic and the second floor. Altogether that makes eight rooms that could easily be converted into office units we could rent out to people like lawyers and accountants. They prefer being in the city centre and rarely require to buy their premises. Do you live in a house, Mr Townsend?'

He nodded. 'Yes.'

'How much rent do you pay?'

'Ten shillings per week.'

'Good,' she said, multiplying that sum by four. She wrote it down and, with a final flourish, added a full stop.

Townsend suddenly turned thoughtful.

She leaned closer to him, fixing him with her dark-grey, lustrous eyes. 'Is there anything that concerns you about my plan?'

He frowned. 'Shouldn't we have shopfitters in to put up shelving and suchlike?'

Catherine's thoughts were already loading some of the less attractive furniture from Cornwallis House on to a cart. No doubt the gypsies would transport it from one place to another once she'd crossed their palms with silver.

'Leave that to me,' she said.

One of the van drivers gave her a lift back to Cornwallis House. She made sure he dropped her at the top of Bridge Valley Road. 'I'll walk the rest of the way,' she said to him. 'It's a fine night.'

Robert caught her as she came through the door. He eyed her suspiciously. 'Where have you been?'

She averted her eyes as she took off her hat. 'I went to look at some new material to make curtains for the drawing room. It was going quite cheap.'

'It would have to be,' he said gloomily.

She noticed he smelled of drink.

'Did you go to the warehouse today?'

'Christ, no!' he exclaimed, glaring at her as though she'd thrown him the worst insult she possibly could.

'I see,' she said.

'Where are you going now?' he asked as she headed for the door.

She turned to face him and couldn't help smiling. Robert looked so disconcerted, almost afraid. He had reason to be. Going to the warehouse was the best thing she'd ever done. Unlike her husband, she had loved being there. It was as though she could smell the challenge presented to her. In accepting that challenge of running the business, something inside her had changed.

'I'm seeing the children, arranging dinner, then afterwards I may read for a while. What are you doing tonight?'

He looked at her as though she were mad. 'I'm off out, of course! To my club,' he added.

She surmised that he was lying. It didn't matter. She didn't care. Something new and far more exciting than him had entered her life.

Thirty-Seven

William had watched the slim, lovely young girl entering the tired-looking building that housed Arthur Freeman's business. Believing all he'd heard about Robert, he'd fully expected to see a nervous, downtrodden child bride. The reality had surprised him. Yes, she was very young, and at first he'd been dumbstruck by her resemblance to her mother.

He'd doffed his hat at her as she'd passed by. Although seemingly preoccupied, she'd acknowledged him with a small smile. That was when he'd seen her eyes. He remembered Leonora's eyes as being brown; though time can dim the memory, he told himself. But brown they most definitely had been. Catherine's were dark grey like his brother's and like his own.

It became his habit to stop the car outside the neglected frontage of Arthur Freeman on his way to his office at Shellard Enterprises. The brown paper was removed from the shop frontage; two employees were painting the elegant window frame and shop door. The upper-floor windows were open, letting in the fresh air, and he could have sworn he saw Catherine – and the Arthur Freeman children – cleaning the upper windows and wielding brooms.

He smiled to himself. Robert Arthur Freeman had made a better match than he could possibly imagine. His smile faded. The rumours sickened him. As for Walter, he'd always respected his brother's business acumen, but to more or less sell his own daughter to someone like Robert was going too far.

He was about to tell his chauffeur to drive on, when he saw her come out of the shop door. She was carrying two enamel mugs, and aimed a bright smile at the two men finishing off repainting the frontage.

She was wearing a grey woollen two piece over which she had tied a very large and very white apron. The fact that she could be so considerate towards her workforce brought a lump to his throat. Leonora had been a kind person; too kind for this world, he thought with a pang of remorse. Why, oh, why hadn't he left her alone to enter the silent world she'd craved?

The answer was easy. He'd fallen in love with her and liked to think, even after all this time, that she'd loved him too.

He saw that same kindness in Catherine, but was also aware of something else, some inner strength that was very much closer to home.

On reaching the office, he phoned Ellen on the new system the firm had recently had installed. He told her he'd seen Catherine and asked whether she'd finally managed to tie Walter down.

'Yes,' she answered. 'He's been trying to avoid me since I challenged him in Portugal. Not that I got very far. He said it didn't matter. His liaison with Catherine's mother ended before we were married.' She sighed. 'The thing is, William, I feel much sorrier for that girl than I do for myself. How did he manage to persuade her to marry a man like that?'

William gulped back what he knew about Robert; the fact that he liked young girls and knew how to charm them into trusting him. 'I suppose she didn't have anyone else in the world.'

'I suppose not,' said Ellen. She hesitated, as though she were thinking something through.

William tried to guess what was on her mind. 'Are you thinking of befriending her?'

'It did cross my mind.'

'I don't think you should.

'I know what you're saying, William. She could spit in my face. But I feel I have to try and gain her trust.'

William didn't try to dissuade her any further.

There was a board meeting arranged later that morning

where the latest report from their new estates in Spain was being presented. So far they'd avoided going into direct competition with the great firm of Harveys and their Bristol Cream Sherry. Instead they'd concentrated their efforts on quality wines and the setting up of a holding company with a French partnership.

'People's perception is that French wine is the best. We need to take advantage of that,' said Walter.

His proposal was that their current volume of French production would be boosted by the infusion of a Spanish blend.

'Is that ethical?' asked one of the board.

Walter had grinned. 'The French won't think so, but we're not in this business to please them. We're in it to make a profit. The fact is that the grapes in Spain are cheaper to produce than they are in France. A little cross-border participation can only be to our advantage.'

Shellard and Company, wine merchants, was now widely known as Shellard Enterprises. This name change was to cover their diversification into hotels and property. The subject therefore changed to hotels.

William only half listened. Shellard Enterprises moved from success to success.

The main board were dismissed; the brothers and their new financial director talked about where the company went next. Seth Armitage, their father's old friend, had been put out to pasture just the week before. He'd proved harder to dislodge than Walter had bargained for, but eventually a settlement had been reached. William had seen the old man eye his brother with outright dislike, if not hatred.

'You'll have to watch your back,' William had said to his brother.

Walter had smirked contemptuously. 'I have a broad back.'

The boardroom was getting stuffy. William opened a window.

Walter concentrated his dark-grey eyes on his new financial director. 'So how goes our progress with regard to our Colston Avenue holdings?'

With the air of a man with a vastly inflated ego, Peter Reading opened the file in front of him.

'We are still in negotiation for the lease on number seven; numbers eleven and twelve we already own. Purchase of the property between these others is irrelevant as they already belong to a board member.'

Walter's killer smile slid over his lips. 'The property of Robert Arthur Freeman. How much does he owe?'

William sat silently as Reading answered. 'Too much. The property is mortgaged to the hilt.'

The board meeting had been a pretty general affair, but this was different. For this William was highly alert.

His brother was looking pretty pleased with himself. 'My, my. Robert certainly knows how to spend a pound – or rather a few thousand. Buy the debt. We might as well be his main creditor as anyone else. Keep it in the family, so to speak.'

This last comment was meant for his brother. William ignored it. 'These are very old properties. And they're the ones you plan to knock down and replace with a hotel?'

'Of course,' said Walter.

'Some people might object on the grounds of historic value.'

Walter's look hardened. 'There's no room for sentiment in business, William. And that also goes for Robert. I'm no expert, but doesn't it say in the Bible, reap as ye have sown? I think you'll agree, Robert has more than sown the seeds of his own destruction.'

Thirty-Eight

Buoyant with satisfaction, Catherine surveyed the interior of what had been a scruffy, run-down office. The boxes the wine bottles arrived in had been set on their sides and hammered into rustic but very attractive shelving. Red and white gingham cloths had been set on small tables at regular intervals. On these she'd set wine glasses for sampling plus a price list of current stock. George Maddingly, the wiry little clerk she'd seen running to and fro, had typed each out on his iron-keyed Imperial typewriter.

'It looks a picture, Mrs Arthur Freeman,' said Mr Townsend, his face reflecting the enthusiasm in his voice.

Fists resting on her hips, Catherine turned in a full circle. Already she'd seen people glancing in and stopping to take in the fresh paint, the swept floors and the clean glass of the huge window. Looking out of the window across the Tramways Centre to the buildings on the other side, it seemed the whole world was bathed in light.

The clackety-clack of the typewriter sounded from upstairs where she'd relocated the office. George was typing out more price lists to serve them until the printers delivered. The printers had demanded immediate payment. The cash flow of the Arthur Freeman wine company was getting worse. Another three pounds six shillings and sixpence had gone from her dwindling cash reserve.

The price lists were to take around to restaurants and hotels; Catherine had decided that passers-by and private households might form the basis of their business, but the commercial trade was worth pursuing.

'You mean you want jam on yer bread as well as butter,' said an amused Mr Townsend.

Things had been worrying at first when he'd told her that they didn't have enough staff to carry out the alterations she'd planned. To his amazement, she'd not only rolled up her own sleeves and picked up a broom, but she'd brought the children in to help out.

'They'll get the benefit of the money earned, so it won't hurt them to work for it,' she'd stated, her pretty face set with determination.

The two girls had been less than enthusiastic about helping out. The boy had taken to it like a trooper. He'd also taken to following Townsend about once he'd finished one job, asking – no – demanding he be given another.

Townsend had chuckled. He hadn't seen the old place so lively, or so attractive, for many a long year.

He'd fallen in easily with her plans. 'So when is Mr Robert coming to inspect?'

She'd immediately fallen silent.

Townsend interpreted the look on her face. 'Oh!'

'When was the last time my husband dropped in?'

Townsend scratched his head. 'I can't really say ...'

'He never looks at the paperwork Maddingly brings. It's filed and that's it. He's only good at spending money, Mr Townsend, not working for it. I decided to take charge before we're all out starving on the streets.'

Townsend didn't question further. He knew as well as she did that even if Robert did drop in, he wouldn't care that she'd taken over responsibility.

In one corner of the window, she'd advertised offices to rent. Within no time an accountant and a newly qualified solicitor had expressed their interest. The latter had in fact already paid a deposit with the promise of paying six months' rental in advance. As she knew no other solicitor in the city and didn't wish to use the family lawyer, she allowed Mr James Birkett to draw up his own contract.

He'd beamed at the prospect. 'It seems I have my first client,' he'd said.

She'd smiled back. 'And I my very own lawyer.'

The shop began to do very well, especially when she became sales assistant. The news that a pretty young woman of foreign extraction and great quality was in situ spread like wildfire. Even the managers of upmarket hotels came in to see who was supplying their new wine range. In no time at all they were dropping in for the odd bottle for personal use.

Her father did not drop in, though she'd half expected him to. She wanted him to see how well she was doing, to acknowledge that she was worthy of being his daughter. Not that an acknowledgement would make any difference to her hatred. She hated him coldly, she hated him hotly; in all ways that she could hate.

One month after it opened, the doorbell jangled. As was her habit, she looked up and her ready smile froze on her face. It was her father, and yet it wasn't; the face beneath the black fedora was less hard, the wide mouth less pitiless. Though his eyes were the same colour as her own.

The man smiled, bid her good day and took off his hat.

'Can I help you?'

'I'm William Shellard. We need to talk.'

He said it in a rush, as though he had to get it over with. Catherine frowned.

'I'm Walter's brother.'

Her heart was racing. She'd not expected a brother – an

uncle. She'd only recently heard there was one. But why was he here?

He'd thrown her off balance. She reminded herself that he was still a Shellard. She stood her ground, her chin held defiantly, her hands clasped in front of her.

'What do you want?'

Long, sensitive fingers fiddled with the brim of his hat. She sensed his unease, but did not allow herself to be sympathetic.

'Can we talk in private?' he asked.

'Here is good enough.' Her voice was sharp. She saw him wince.

He glanced at the open door between the shop and the passageway to the stockrooms used to bring bottles of red wine up to room temperature. Beyond that was the backyard where the vans loaded.

Catherine shut the door and stood in front of it. 'Go ahead. Talk.'

His eyes wandered over the gleaming bottles and the shelves made from wooden crates. 'Very imaginative. It looks very attractive.'

She folded her arms across her chest. 'I'm sure you didn't come here to discuss the décor. What is it you want?'

'I knew your mother,' he said in a soft, halting voice. 'I loved her.'

Catherine felt numb. There were a number of things she thought about saying, but none of them suited the moment. She waited for him to continue.

He took a deep breath. 'I didn't mean to say that. I suppose it was bound to come out sometime. But not yet.' He looked directly at her. Again she saw those eyes that were hers yet not hers. 'I came to warn you and to help if I can. This building ...' He gestured with the hand holding his hat. 'It's mortgaged to the hilt. My brother – Shellard Enterprises – intends buying the debt. He owns the neighbouring buildings and intends knocking them all down to build a brand-new hotel. This building is the key to doing that.'

Catherine felt her blood draining from her face. 'He can't!'

Now it was her saying something stupid. Of course he could.

'I could help. I've some property of my own and some personal wealth.'

'No!' Her response was immediate and not without reason.

She couldn't find it in herself to accept help from the brother of the man responsible for her mother's death and she told him so.

He nodded. 'I understand.'

She turned away from him, her thoughts racing. Finally the contents of Aunt Lopa's coffer were about to come into their own. She only hoped there was enough in there to get her out of this.

That afternoon she arrived home early and went straight to her dressing room. Her heart pounded as she eyed the iron-bound chest. Her great-aunt had told her that her mother's diary was in that chest along with 'some valuable bits of pretty paper, a few investments made years ago from my crochet money.'

Having locked the dressing-room door behind her, she took the key from its hiding place on a hook in the wardrobe and pushed it into the lock.

Apprehensive as to what she would find, she opened it slowly. It held surprisingly little; a blue silk dress, a white mantilla, a silver crucifix, a series of diaries and a brown cardboard file box.

It was this last box she guessed contained her supposed fortune, a fortune made from peddling crochet, other handicraft and the odd goat's cheese from door to door. Using both hands, she lifted it, shaking it in order to gauge its weight. It didn't feel as though it held a lot of money. Feeling slightly disappointed, she set it down and ran her hands around the inside of the coffer, searching for some secret compartment containing jewels perhaps. There was nothing.

Her gaze fell on the diaries. She fingered the rough leather, opened a front cover, but let it fall again. No. She wasn't ready to read them. Not yet. Perhaps she never would be.

With a disappointed sigh, she turned her attention back to the file box, undid the cord bound around it and opened it. Just as her great-aunt had described, there were indeed 'pretty bits of paper'. 'Just a few share certificates.' Catherine understood more or less what they were. She took in the large bundle wrapped around with pink embroidery thread. This was more than a few!

On top of the paper was an envelope addressed to 'My dearest Catherine'.

Catherine opened the envelope and read the contents.

> To my dearest Catherine,
>
> If you are reading this, then I am surely departed for Paradise. I trust I have been a good guardian, for indeed you have been a joy to my soul.
>
> As promised, I have left you your inheritance which includes your mother's diaries, bless her soul.
>
> Your inheritance is not quite as you may have expected. You know me as a person who has always done things with her hands and sold on what she's made. I did this even before I entered a convent. I had the good fortune to attract the attention of an elderly banker. His wife was incapacitated and I helped him look after her. We both had a great love of animals. His wife had never shared his love. He also advised me on where to invest the little bit of money I made from selling my work. As you can see, years before 1914 I began investing in Standard Oil and the Ford Motor Company.
>
> My banker's wife died and he died shortly afterwards. That was when I entered the convent, though I found the life didn't suit me.
>
> I love you very much and hope you'll be able to do something with the share certificates. I don't know how much they're worth. Good luck, and have a good life.
>
> Affectionately,
> Anna Marie Rodriguez

A heavy knocking sounded on the door. 'Catherine? Are you in there?'

Robert!

She quickly put everything back into the box.

'I'm coming.'

She said a swift prayer before opening the door. Robert hadn't spent a night home in ages and hadn't bothered her in bed. She'd thought it strange for a man like him, but she was grateful. Her gratefulness shone in her face when she opened the door.

'Robert,' she said brightly, taking in the fact that he was already dressed to go out.

Thank God!

At first he looked at her with eyes full of suspicion, but the look passed swiftly. 'I'm going out.' His eyes dropped to the pulling on of his gloves. 'I need some money.'

She opened her mouth to protest that she didn't have much housekeeping left – only enough to pay the greengrocer, who refused to supply them unless he was paid up front. But she too wanted to go out tonight and the last thing she wanted was for him to stay home.

'I'll see what I've got,' she said, plastering a smile on her face.

She waited until he was gone before phoning James Birkett and explaining what she'd found.

'Phew!' said Birkett, his exclamation whistling down the phone. 'How many do you think there are?'

'I'm not sure. Lots. A few hundred of them, perhaps more.' She told him the name of the companies.

Her tenant and new-found solicitor fell to silence. At last he found his voice. 'We could be looking at thousands of pounds.'

'I need to sell them – or at least some of them. I have an immediate need for some money to pay off the mortgage on the property.'

She'd had the foresight to check the records in Robert's study. She'd gasped in dismay at the sight of the size of the mortgage. Five thousand pounds!

'I need five thousand pounds almost immediately. Can it be done?'

James was adamant that the best course was to find a ready buyer. 'I have someone in mind,' he said. 'There's a well-heeled old gent who's become a client. My second! He comes in to buy wine now and again. Thinks you're the prettiest thing on two legs – as do we all,' he added with a light laugh.

Dimples appeared at the sides of Catherine's mouth. She knew James had a thing for her and liked him well enough. However, this was business and she'd found that she was surprisingly good at separating one aspect of a relationship from another while still using her attractiveness to her advantage.

James continued. 'This old gent doesn't seem to go much on the Shellards. Think he used to work for them. His name's Seth Armitage. I'll get on to him right away.'

Thirty-Nine

Even though the windows were tightly shut and a cast-iron radiator thrummed with heat, the atmosphere in the board-room of Shellard Enterprises was decidedly chilly.

Peter Reading had lost a little of the self-confidence he had exuded on achieving the post left vacant by Seth Armitage.

'I don't know how it happened,' he said, beads of sweat breaking out on his broad brow, a stray lock detaching itself from his oiled hair.

William Shellard smiled behind steepled fingers.

Reading looked like someone about to get his head chopped off – which was extremely likely judging by the look on Walter's face.

To Walter's credit, he never lost his temper. His razor-sharp mind saw no profit in the heat of anger. Cold, calculated revenge was more his style.

Walter's unblinking gaze was fixed on his flustered financial director. His eyes were as cold as his anger. 'Of course you don't, Peter. But you should.'

'I know the name of the company who have bought the property and paid off the mortgage. Wolverine! Wolverine Investments!'

Poor man, thought William, recognizing Peter Reading's desperation to get back into Walter's good books.

Walter was unmoved. 'Approach them. Offer whatever they want. Now get out.'

Looking as nervous as a whipped dog, Reading left the boardroom. Only Walter and William remained.

William knew Walter was no fool and that he'd probably noticed the sparkle in his brother's eyes.

A chill ran down William's spine when Walter's eyes fell on him.

'Is Diana pregnant by any chance?'

William was caught off balance. 'No.' He frowned. 'What makes you say that?'

'You look happy,' said Walter, his own expression far from being so.

'Diana's staying on the south coast near Portsmouth. She's got a cousin there.'

Walter's mouth curved upwards in a cruel smile. His eyes glittered. 'You should watch her, my dear William. There are a lot of sailors in Portsmouth.'

Walter had hit a raw nerve and its ache stayed with William as he made his way from the office to Catherine's wine shop. The crisp air of autumn was turning swiftly into a frost-laden winter, but the light from the shop window made him feel warmer.

He had intended going in to congratulate Catherine on outwitting his brother. He paused on hearing laughter. Keeping back so he wouldn't be seen, he looked in. Four people were raising their glasses in a triumphant toast. One of them was Catherine, of course. There was also a young man in a dark suit; he recognized him as the lawyer who rented offices on the second floor. The third man was Townsend, the manager. The fourth was Seth Armitage, the man most likely to be the prime mover behind Wolverine Investments.

Dear Catherine, he thought as he walked away, turning up his collar against the chilly air. She was just a woman after all. Seth Armitage was the one who'd forestalled Walter's plans.

Catherine felt drunk with power.

She called for more champagne. Townsend did the honours.

'It's all mine,' she said, her eyes glowing as she read the deed for what must be the seventeenth time. 'Thank you for doing what you did, Mr Armitage.'

When he smiled, his bright-red cheeks turned as glossy as freshly picked apples and his eyes twinkled. 'My dear, it was a pleasure. I'd have loved to be a fly on the wall when Walter discovered this property had slipped through his hands.'

'What will he do now?' she asked, her face flushed as much with triumph as with champagne.

'Make you an offer you can't refuse.'

'Which you *will* refuse,' added James, who was also feeling as though he were rising in the world. The word was going round that he did a good job for his clients, *and* that one of them was no less than Seth Armitage, formerly of Shellard Enterprises. Things could only go from good to better.

Catherine was strangely silent, looking down into her champagne. 'That depends.'

The three men looked at her. Two of them looked puzzled, but not Seth Armitage.

'You have a quick mind young lady. Dare I say it, but you remind me of your . . .' He paused. 'Your grandfather. I take it you're going to wait for their offer and double it.'

He flinched at the brightness of her eyes when she looked up at him from beneath the long dark lashes.

'Perhaps.' She turned that same vibrant look on James. 'As representative of Wolverine Investments, you will suggest a partnership. Shares in Shellard Enterprises in return for use of our premises – but not to knock down and build anew. I think Wolverine would prefer to convert the existing buildings into a hotel – a hotel with a period feel. I think I would like that. Never mind art deco and modern trends. Let's offer the traditional; take advantage of people's nostalgia for the old days.'

The three men stared at her silently. At last, Seth Armitage put down his glass and clapped. 'Well done, young lady. I was right about you taking after your grandfather. He'd be proud of you, as I most certainly am. I can see nothing to stand in the way of your success.'

The three men raised their glasses again and toasted her. Catherine smiled, but behind that smile lurked thoughts of the one person who could stand in the way of her plans. Robert.

Forty

Diana was never around and William had no family that he wished to spend his leisure with – certainly not his brother – and so he'd made Catherine his cause célèbre. That was why he was following Robert Arthur Freeman.

The only person he confided in was Ellen, Walter's wife.

'That man's a monster,' he'd said, cracking his knuckles as he fought to suppress his anger. 'I'd quite happily kill him. Fortunately Catherine is rapidly growing into a woman, hence his loss of interest in her. He has a new love interest. I believe she's about twelve years old.'

Ellen had turned quite white as the brevity of what he had said sank in. 'You won't do anything silly, will you, William?'

He hadn't answered, just hung his head.

The chill air of the last few days had metamorphosed into a white mist made thicker by the smoke and steam from thousands of coal fires and coke furnaces.

By day it was bad enough, but by night city landmarks were made invisible by the thickening fog.

Gas streetlights flickered as though gasping for air, their meagre light doing little to alleviate the gloom.

William heard Robert's laughter. 'Come on, Susan. Be nice to me.'

He heard the girl protest, though laughingly like young people, as though she wasn't quite sure what he was asking her to do.

Careful not to be seen, William stopped when they stopped. More laughter. The larger grey shape – Robert – glanced over his shoulder. William was positive he hadn't been seen. He had become quite adroit at merging with the shadows. At times he asked himself what he proposed doing should Robert realize he was being followed. He wasn't quite sure. So far he'd been lucky, but who knows how long luck would last?

He heard Robert offer the girl a sovereign. 'A gold sovereign.'

'I don't know,' the girl responded, her words muffled by the mist. 'My father will kill me if I let you do that.'

'Of course he won't. Anyway, you've already let me do it to you. One more time isn't going to hurt, is it?'

Again he heard that girlish, nervous laugh. The two figures combined into an amorphous blob and fell into a shop doorway.

He drew closer and listened. At first there was the rustling of clothes, then the throaty cries of the girl, the urgent grunts of Robert as he began doing what he'd paid for.

William thought of Catherine. She was young. Too young to be married to a man like that. It wasn't right. He saw Ellen's strained expression, the look of horror in her eyes, but most of all he saw Leonora's eyes. He owed it to her to stop this, to end what he saw as Catherine's imprisonment.

Blinded by anger and fog, he charged into the doorway. Robert's back was towards him. The girl's white, under-developed thighs shone through the murky darkness.

William raised his cane. Again and again he brought it down on the back of Robert's head.

He heard the girl's muffled shout. 'Get off! Yer too heavy!'

Whatever happened next, he wasn't sure. The girl began to scream. Perhaps she'd felt the warm sticky blood falling on her face.

William didn't stop to find out. He ran before she could see him, before she had fully realized what had happened.

The police told Catherine that he'd been beaten to death. They interpreted her lack of tears as shock and didn't press for details of where she'd been that night. Not that it would have mattered. She'd been at home attempting to understand why Robert's daughters locked their bedroom door against her. It was young Charlie who'd enlightened her. 'It's because father visits them in the night when he's drunk. They don't like it.'

'He was with a young woman,' said one of the police officers, coughing behind a closed hand before he went on to explain further. 'Begging your pardon, ma'am, but we don't know too much about why they were together . . .'

She'd nodded quietly. Of course they knew and so did she. It was James who told her that they'd arrested the girl's father on suspicion of smashing Robert's head in.

'Robert got what he deserved,' said Catherine without regret.

It was some days after Robert's funeral that she had un-expected visitors. She was in the garden standing over a bonfire. The leaves, twigs and dried-up flowers of late autumn had not yet produced a suitable flame for her purpose. She was prodding it with a stick when Polly came trotting over to tell her that Mr Birkett and Mr Armitage had arrived.

'So I see,' she said, noting that the two men were only a few steps behind her elderly servant.

'Forgive our intrusion,' said Seth Armitage, one snowy brow raised above a discerning eye, his other eye half closed as if guarding some secret. 'We bring good tidings. Is it a bad time?'

Her smile was wider than it had been in a long time. 'No. On the contrary, it's a very good time.'

Judging by their reaction, neither man thought her insensitive for appearing so affable so soon after her husband's death. Few people had liked Robert – especially men. As for women – she thought of the way he'd deluded her. Robert was a charmer. She'd fallen. But never again, she promised herself. Never again.

James Birkett, who looked at her more directly now she'd attained a very youthful widowhood, began unravelling the ribbon from a bunch of legal documents. 'Shellard Enterprises have agreed to a beneficial merger with Wolverine Investments. All it needs is your signature. I've gone through it with a fine toothcomb. So has Seth. It's a good deal.'

Catherine returned her attention to the fire, poking the heaped leaves to help circulate the air. A small flame burst into existence. It wasn't much, but enough to get things going.

'Only a small flame, but enough to start a fire,' she said absent-mindedly.

Seth Armitage, a kindly figure of a man, placed his hand on her shoulder. He'd come to much admire this young lady and showed it quite openly – though not in the same way as James, who was smitten beyond control.

'Indeed you have started a small flame,' he said. 'I think you have it in you to start a fire. I'd like to help you do that, if I may. If you wish.'

Catherine smiled at him. 'That's very kind of you.' She switched her gaze to James and saw him blush in response to her smile. 'How about you, James? Would you like to help me start a fire?'

His blush deepened. 'Very much, Catherine. Very much indeed.'

She nodded thoughtfully. In her short life she had finally found men she could count on.

'This is a very fine house,' said Seth, casting his eye over the rear façade. There was a gap in the crumbling cornice at various points on the second floor and cracks half hidden behind a virulent creeper. 'Or could be,' he added. 'But never mind. You should be able to afford better than this in time – with my assistance, of course.'

She nodded. 'I have just the place in mind.'

The Douro Valley, the walls of Castile Villanova and its tinkling fountains were like a vision among the dead leaves and spurting flames.

'If you'd like to go back into the house, gentlemen, I'll be with you shortly. There's something I have to do first.'

Immensely pleased with her response, they did as she suggested.

The smoke from the fire blew into her face and stung her eyes. It failed to distract her from her mission. As the small flames grew into larger ones, she picked up the cotton nightdress lying at her feet. Holding it between finger and thumb she let it fall into the fire. She was no longer the unwanted child locked away in a Portuguese palace. She was a woman and a Shellard and her star was rising.